Ruth Hamilton is the bestselling author of seventeen previous novels set in the North West of England. She was born in Bolton and now lives in Liverpool, and she writes about both places with realistic insight and dramatic imagery.

For more information on Ruth Hamilton and her books, see her website at: www.ruthhamilton.co.uk

D1102839

DOROTHY'S WAR

Ruth Hamilton

CORGI BOOKS

DOROTHY'S WAR
A CORGI BOOK : 0552151688
0780552151689

Originally published in Great Britain by Bantam Press,
a division of Transworld Publishers

PRINTING HISTORY
Bantam Press edition published 2005
Corgi edition published 2006

1 3 5 7 9 10 8 6 4 2

Corgi Books are published by Transworld Publishers,
61–63 Uxbridge Road, London W5 5SA,
a division of The Random House Group Ltd,
in Australia by Random House Australia (Pty) Ltd,
20 Alfred Street, Milsons Point, Sydney, NSW 2061, Australia,
in New Zealand by Random House New Zealand Ltd,
18 Poland Road, Glenfield, Auckland 10, New Zealand
and in South Africa by Random House (Pty) Ltd,
Isle of Houghton, Corner of Boundary Road & Carse O'Gowrie,
Houghton 2198, South Africa.

Printed and bound in Great Britain by
Cox & Wyman Ltd, Reading, Berkshire.

Papers used by Transworld Publishers are natural, recyclable
products made from wood grown in sustainable forests. The
manufacturing processes conform to the environmental
regulations of the country of origin.

I dedicate this book to two women who have given me friendship, support and argument since 1987.

Heartfelt thanks go to Diane Pearson, who discovered me (actually, I discovered her long before I met her – wonderful writer) and Linda Evans, who kicked in when Diane retired.

Diane, you taught me everything I know about this writing game. Linda, no one else on God's earth could have filled Di's shoes. Sometimes, you even *sound* like her. Never mind, it may be curable.

Ruthie xxx

The menagerie

I must say goodbye to Jack and Vera (usually known as Dumb and Dumber). They were much loved cockatiels and they are missed.

So it's hello to Loony Rooney and Charlie Farley (budgies) and . . . erm . . . hello to Oscar. He is a ring-necked parakeet, Wedgwood blue, beautiful and dreadful. Hand-reared by Barbara Kerks of Bolton, he gets involved with coffee, tea, biscuits, chandeliers, my bits of Royal Doulton (not hand-painted periwinkles – Mrs Bucket), visitors, earrings, bracelets and watches. All remote controls and phones are hidden during flight times. He is naughty. I like him.

Sam (black Lab) is now nine and still agile. Fudge (brown Lab) is seven and continues laid back and morose in appearance.

My cat – Lady Geraldine Bundle – Geri for short – has moved on to a more peaceful life with my younger son in Southport. In view of current chaos, I may well join her.

Acknowledgements

Avril Cain, for laughs, for peppered steaks on Saturdays, for accidents with wheelchairs, dogs, cats, post offices, fine red wines, knickers, bathrooms, kettles, bottles of milk, keys, sofas, spectacles, certain items dropped on College Road and all the other day-to-day chaos with which this priceless sufferer from MS regales me. I love you, Avril.

Simon Topliss, for helping me through the death of Queen Victoria. I was not around at the time – Simon *certainly* wasn't – and he found out the exact time, etc., for me. I think I would have liked old Victoria.

The *Bolton Evening News* – especially Angela Kelly – for unswerving support through what begins to feel like a lifetime.

David, Sue, Michael, Lizzie, Sam, Fudge, Jack and Vera – my family (human and animal) – and the expected grandson, who is keeping us all on our toes and his mother awake at night.

ONE

'She's not pulling out of it.' Elsie Shipton shoved a stray steel curler back into place beneath the green scarf she wore turban-fashion round a busy head. That head was seldom still. Emblem Street residents had decided that if they wanted to know the state of the nation, they needed only to look at Elsie Shipton's head. It was now bobbing about like a cork on heavy tidal waters. 'I don't know what to do for the best, I'm sure – it's like talking to the wall. That's a right bloody nosedive she's in, Lois.'

'Not as bad as her poor husband's nosedive, though.'

'That remark were in bad taste.' The head, motionless for a split second, stepped up a gear. 'Battle of Britain the poor lad were in and don't you forget it, Lois Melia. We mustn't make light of our fallen heroes.' Rear gunners never got a chance, she mused. And he'd been a lovely young man, Stephen Dyson – well groomed, polite, a hard worker. They didn't make many of his sort wherever men got minted. That saying about the good dying young had been

11

well illustrated in the Battle of Britain and at Dunkirk. If this carried on, half the young men in the armed forces wouldn't be coming home at all.

'I didn't mean nothing by it.'

'Aye, well, think on before you talk. That mouth of yours has a mind of its own – it wants connecting to your proper brain, if you've got one. I've enough on worrying about her in the middle without mithering over you putting both feet in your gob every time you open it. Her in the middle's not well. I've tried chatting, sitting with her, getting her some pork we'd be best not talking about – I even laid my hands on a couple of extra ounces of Cheddar last week, but she couldn't be bothered. She's not right and she's as thin as a rake. Her'll end up in Tonge Cemetery if she doesn't shape.'

Lois Melia, a large woman in her late forties, dragged a tray of jam tarts out of the fire-side oven. 'I'm sick of plum jam,' she said quietly.

But not quietly enough. Elsie Shipton homed in again. 'Young Steve Dyson'd be glad to be sat here eating plum jam. Give over moaning till you've something proper to moan about.'

Lois bridled. It wasn't often that a person found the temerity to lock horns with Elsie Shipton, but enough was enough. 'Listen, Elsie. I know I'm not the sharpest knife in the drawer, only it's hard enough with Dorothy Dyson to think about every time I speak – God love her. If I have to watch every word while you're around, I might as well join a bloody nunnery and be done with it. I'm tired unto death of treading on eggshells.'

Elsie sniffed, clicked her tongue and lit a treasured Woodbine. Lois Melia was getting above herself, and, at her size, would have been better staying at ground level. Though she did resemble a fully inflated barrage balloon . . . 'I've lived in this street all my married life, I'll have you know.'

'I do know. We all know. You tell us often enough.'

'Aye, well, that's as may be. She needs help. I can't just hang about like boiled ham at four-pence while she's in a decline. Four months is a long time to sit there doing nowt. Losing her baby put the tin hat on her life and I can tell you that for no money. I've seen women go clean off their heads after a miscarriage. She's got nobody except her mam and dad and, well, the least said about them the better, from the sound of things.' According to Dorothy-in-the-middle, her mam, Molly Cornwell, wasn't worth the ink on her birth certificate. 'It's a damned shame, Lois, and I feel one hundred per cent bloody useless.'

'Me and all, Elsie. I feel lost and that's the top and bottom.' Lois sank into a chair. Her feet were killing her and she was getting a headache, too. Elsie Shipton in full sail was enough to give anybody multiple ailments. 'It's hard, Elsie. I can't lay my finger on a single sensible idea for Dorothy. And it's not for want of trying – we've both tried, you and me.'

'I know, love. See, apart from this, that and

13

the other, she's supposed to work. Which is what I came here to talk about. There's going to be the Ministry of Don't Stop at Home on Your Backsides now, isn't there? Even I cook a few dinners at the munitions, and I'm in my sixties. She's nowt more than a spring chicken compared to me. We'll have to shove her into something before she gets parked with the yellow girls. I'm not having her turned into a yellow girl on top of everything else.' The 'yellow girls' made weaponry for the troops, and the chemicals involved were responsible for their apparently jaundiced complexions.

'Where, though?' Lois placed her tarts on a cooling rack. 'Where can she sit doing bugger all for the war effort? Because she never blinking well moves, does she? Oh, blood and stomach pills – here we go again.' The sirens were screaming. The big woman jumped up with all the energy she could muster and closed the blackout curtains. 'See you later,' she called after Elsie's disappearing back.

Before going home, Elsie Shipton entered the house between hers and Lois Melia's. Dorothy Dyson was huddled over a weak fire, a half-eaten sandwich and a cup resting on the fireguard. Without speaking a word, Elsie covered Dorothy's window. She stared at the young woman for a few seconds, then went next door to ensure that her own home was showing no light to the Luftwaffe. It was a crazy world and no mistake. Something wanted doing, and quickly. That bloody Hitler needed shooting for a start, the mad bugger.

Elsie sat by her fire and realized that she was crying. For some inexplicable reason, the woman next door was the embodiment of war and its senselessness. She wondered when Dorothy-in-the-middle had last taken a bath. And how was she managing for money? There had to be a limit to the length of time a person could keep still, keep quiet and keep eating.

Stirring herself, she picked up a pan of broth and set it on the fire. Somebody had to carry on carrying on, she pondered. But her thoughts remained on the other side of the wall as she waited for explosions or the all clear. Perhaps Dorothy Dyson had it right after all, because there seemed precious little point to any of it.

She knew every crack in the wall, every stripe on her tablecloth, each clip of cloth pegged into the rug. She had pegged the rug herself and Steve had helped. Help was, perhaps, an inappropriate word for the mess he had made, a mess she had undone during his absence. *He's absent all the time now.* Time. The clock was noisy and she couldn't understand why she wound it every night. It was probably habit. *I wasn't made to be on my own. Is Mam right? Can I not manage by myself? Am I completely useless and spineless and frail?*

Under the staircase, there was a horsehair sofa that had once belonged to Steve's gran. It accepted only one person as sitting tenant, because the slope of the stairs prevented a second from occupying the bottom end. It was all right for lying on, though. Dorothy didn't go upstairs any more. When her physical mechanism demanded sleep, she spread an old blanket on the prickly couch, placed a pillow at the end nearest the coal-hole door, and slept there under an eiderdown. The marital bed had been cold for months. She couldn't sleep in that great big thing knowing that he would never come back.

The baby had been lost on that sofa. Blood everywhere, a knife twisting in her belly, losing Steve all over again. *Tiny doll, perfect, pale, no bigger than one of my hands.* Why? What had she done wrong? Elsie from next door had been here that night, had been crying when the baby had emerged after just five months in the womb. *I didn't cry.* The blank time had gone on for a while now. It was almost as if Dorothy had died in that moment when the telegram had been opened.

There were bombs quite near. They would be going for munitions or for Barton aerodrome over at Manchester, but they were forever missing their targets by miles. Trinity Street station might well have been on the Germans' list, as might factories. She should have been in a shelter, yet she had never bothered, not since the baby. The neighbours didn't bother, either. There had been the odd stray missile, but no apparent targeting of Bolton. Perhaps tonight would be the night; perhaps she would escape at last.

Her thoughts were breaking up again, were becoming bits and pieces that fluttered about

16

in her head like a cloud of disorientated butter-flies.

Oh, she suddenly remembered the Regent cinema on Deane Road. They had gone there together, she and Steve, had ignored the air raid warning on the screen. A few other people had stayed, too, but she could not remember the name of the film. Then he had gone away and he wasn't coming back. Pots on a shelf rattled – the Germans were up above. She couldn't concentrate. Her mind was all over the place – the Regent cinema, walking on the moors, waving goodbye at the station. *Goodbye, Steve. I love you.*

Dorothy Dyson heard her own, the one with her name on it. It whistled. The whistle became a scream and she remained where she was, in his chair by the fire. There was a cigarette burn on one of the arms. Steve had burnt the hole and had gone down in a burning plane. Soon, she would join him. Why was it taking so long? Was God enjoying her endless wait for death?

The earth shook and the noise was deafening. Air seemed to be sucked out of the room; her chair was thrown back against the window. Glass shattered, landed in her hair. But she wasn't dead. She could feel the warm blood pouring down her face and the air she breathed was full of dust. Her lungs did their job automatically, forcing her to cough up the grit she had in-haled. *I am alive. I am not going to be released from this. God is making me go on and on and I don't want that.*

Rumblings continued outside. It was cold. Someone shouted, 'Gas!' and she rose to her feet, the ground trembling as she walked towards the scullery. There was no scullery; the single-storey room had been sliced off the back of the house like a portion of cake. There was rubble everywhere and it was still moving. *Elsie. Where is Elsie? Elsie, who has done her very best for me, who sat with me and coaxed me into eating, may be dead.* The Germans had not dropped gas, had they? That shouted warning had probably referred to the fuel that lit these houses and served the gas rings in the sculleries. *Where is Elsie?*

Clambering across mobile rubble, Dorothy managed to get into the yard next door. The wall between numbers 32 and 34 no longer existed and the flat slabs from which it had been constructed served as a bridge over which she staggered. There was blood in her eyes. 'Elsie?' The smell of gas was almost overpowering. 'Elsie?'

Elsie Shipton appeared at a hole in the wall, a gap created by another absent window. 'Dorothy?'

'Get out, now,' the younger woman ordered. 'Come on, you've no time, there's gas. Move, move,' she screamed.

Elsie was in shock. 'Lois is on fire,' she managed eventually.

'Gas,' repeated Dorothy. 'The planes might come back. Come on, we'll run up to my mam's house.' There was nowhere else, was there? 'We could have an explosion any minute, Elsie. You have to hurry up.'

Elsie's head began to nod. 'You don't talk to your mam.' Dorothy Dyson never spoke to anyone, but she was talking now, wasn't she? 'God, what a mess.' Acrid smoke mingled with dust to make a soup that threatened near-blindness and the inability to breathe. 'I hope he's all right.' 'He' was her husband, Pete, who was employed to drive medical supplies to hospitals and first-aid points all over the northwest.

'Any port in a storm,' answered Dorothy. And this was some storm.

But Elsie was going nowhere without Lois. She looked towards number 36, saw flames coming from the scullery. The gas main would blow any minute, she felt sure. Holding on to Dorothy's skirt, Elsie made her way towards the gap where the back gate had hung, stumbling on bricks every other step.

Out in the back alley, the pair stood and watched the warden carrying Lois out of her house. She was limp, arms dangling towards the floor, one slipper missing, apron torn. 'She's dead,' whispered Elsie. This wasn't supposed to happen. The war was somewhere else – mostly in London. 'Lois can't be dead.'

Steve couldn't be dead, but he was. 'Elsie, let's go. There's nothing you can do here and—'

'She moved. Her head moved.' Elsie took a step towards her friend. 'Look after her,' she told the warden. 'She's precious. I've known her half my life. Save her, or you'll have me to answer to.'

The warden, in a hurry to escape from the

leaking gas, shouted at Elsie and Dorothy, ordering them to leave the area. 'Now!' he boomed. 'Get out of here before you both end up in bits and in buckets.' He made his way to the bottom of the street, Lois's considerable bulk causing him to call for help. Only when two wardens had disappeared with their human burden did Elsie allow herself to be propelled towards the main road.

They stood on Derby Street and watched the houses burning. Elsie, deeply shocked, found no words while her life went up in flames. She clung to Dorothy, a woman who, until this night, had spoken few words in months. It occurred to her that the bomb had done some good for her neighbour, because this was the first time in ages that Dorothy had shown any sign of life. The gas main blew, causing more damage than any bomb. 'I hope they all got out,' whispered Elsie.

'Come on.' Dorothy led the way up the road and into View Street. From the top of the hill, they saw, via the one flat side of Bolton, a red sky with explosions on the ground below. 'They've got Manchester,' said Elsie. 'God help us, there'll be nobody left.'

Dorothy stared at a door she had not seen in some time. Even in the dark, she knew it: brass knocker, brass letterbox, the number 33 – also in brass – at the top. *I don't want to be here, but there's nowhere else to go.* She knocked.

'They'll be in the shelter,' Elsie muttered, her throat thick with dust.

Mam wouldn't go in a shelter. Mam wouldn't

mix with her neighbours, had never been one for cups of tea, or chats over a wall. Dad wasn't much better, although he didn't share Molly Cornwell's cruel streak.

The door opened and an eye peeped out. 'Who is it?'

'Me,' replied Dorothy, 'and my neighbour. We've been bombed out.'

The gap widened. 'Get in before I start showing light.'

The two women entered a dim hallway and were led through to a rear living room. 'You're hurt.' Molly Cornwell studied her daughter, who had turned her back on her family some four or five years ago. Dorothy wasn't fit to be out in all this noise, had never been fit for much. 'Sit down.' She went to get the first aid box from the sideboard.

Dorothy sat. She made not the slightest sound while her mother picked glass from her hair and cleaned the scalp. *I shouldn't be here. I should be with Steve, but there is no Steve and I can't come back to this.*

Elsie, too shocked to notice much, remarked inwardly that her next door neighbour seemed to be reverting to type: no noise, no movement, no effort. 'All our stuff will be gone,' she said finally. 'I don't mean furniture and the like. It's photos and memories that matter. It's all gone up. The gas did it. Yon bomb must have fractured a main.' She closed her eyes and prayed for Lois. Lois was a big woman, but she wasn't strong. Fat people were sometimes made weak by the weight they carried.

Dorothy trembled, but she controlled the tremors as best she could. A woman for whom she entertained no love was pulling fragments of glass from her head, was applying something that made her skin sting, but she refused to flinch. She wanted to run back down Derby Street to search through the rubble for something – anything – that had belonged to Steve. Her hand strayed to the pocket in her skirt, fingers closing round the silver locket. Like a disobedient child, she felt a thrill of joy. She had him here with her – a photograph and a curl of his hair were in her presence.

'That should do it.' Molly Cornwell stepped away. 'You were lucky – one of them pieces could have gone right through to your brain.'

I have no brain. You wouldn't let me sit for my grammar school scholarship, would you? It wouldn't have done me any good, you said. I couldn't have coped, you said. I was better off at Sts Peter and Paul Seniors, you said.

'I'll get that kettle on.' Molly put away the first aid kit, then went into the kitchen.

'Are you all right?' mumbled Elsie. There was something about Molly Cornwell that forced even the garrulous Elsie Shipton into temporary near-silence. The woman was beyond cold – she was an iceberg, and Dorothy seemed as doomed as the *Titanic* had been. The girl was actually frightened about being here, in her own mother's house.

Dorothy nodded.

'I'm worried about Lois.'

'Yes.'

Elsie's head began to move slightly. 'Nice house they've got here.'

'Yes.'

Elsie wanted more than a yes. 'Have they got a real bath upstairs?'

'Yes.'

'Look, you had plenty to say when you were trying to shift me up yon road. Are you going back to how you were? Because if you are, you'll have to be how you were somewhere else. In case you hadn't noticed, we've no homes. I shudder to think what my Pete will go through at the end of his shift. He'll think I'm dead. And Lois could be, poor soul. I didn't like the look of her at all, Dorothy. She could get pneumonia with that bad chest of hers.'

Molly appeared with tray and cups. 'Our Dorothy'll be stopping here with us. This is where she should be. From what I've heard, she wants looking after.'

Elsie's head stepped up a pace. 'She has been very well looked after, Mrs . . . er . . .' The name slipped Elsie's mind for a moment.

'Cornwell.'

'Mrs Cornwell. Me and Lois Melia have been keeping an eye on her. She's been a bit quiet since her husband died and since she lost the baby, but she's been seen to. Nobody gets neglected in my street.'

Molly Cornwell sniffed. Living just nine streets away from her daughter, she had heard about the two tragedies, but had stayed away. All along, she had known that Dorothy would need her sooner or later. Well, here she was. 'She belongs with her own.'

There was something unsavoury about Molly Cornwell, a glint of triumph in her eye, as if she had just won a battle of some kind. Dorothy Dyson wasn't one for chatting about her past, though she had said a word or two about her parents, about Molly's being the power and about Tom Cornwell's not having the guts to stand up to his wife. 'She's twenty-six,' Elsie said. 'She's used to having her own place.'

'That's as may be.' Molly Cornwell took a sip of tea. 'But she's always been bad with her nerves, has our Dorothy. She were never one for playing out – used to sit reading all the while and writing in her precious diaries. Lived in fairy tales, did our Dorothy.'

Because I had to. Because you told me I was good for nothing else. And worse. Oh, yes, you did a grand job of raising me, you old witch.

Elsie sat back, her cup trembling in its saucer. She had decided that she didn't like Molly Cornwell one bit and that a single night here would be more than sufficient. She glanced at Dorothy. 'We were happy enough in our little street, weren't we?' Elsie wasn't going to give this female grim reaper the satisfaction of knowing just how miserable her daughter had been. 'We minded each other,' she added, her eyes challenging the householder. 'It's a case of loving thy neighbour, isn't it?'

Molly passed round a plate of home-made biscuits. When Dorothy made no attempt to take one, she tutted loudly. 'Keep your strength up. I know you've missed my baking.' She looked at Elsie. 'Although I say it as shouldn't, I'm a very good cook.'

Yes, and you should have a cauldron and a couple of mates to help you stir the spells. I remember your little black book and your herbs. Dorothy unfolded herself from the cramped position into which she had curled. Very slowly, she rose to her feet and turned to her Nemesis. *This creature birthed me. Steve made me promise I wouldn't come back to this house if anything happened to him. It happened. The dead baby happened. The bomb happened. I am here.*

Molly raised an eyebrow. 'Your bedroom's still as it was, except there's a second bed in it. Your friend can have that.'

'Pete will think I'm dead,' said Elsie for the second time. 'I don't know where he is, so I've no way of letting him know I'm all right.'

'If a warden saw you walk away, your husband will be told.' Molly placed the biscuits on their tray. Dorothy continued to stare at her. 'Well?' she asked. 'What's up with you now?'

'There is nothing up with me. There never was anything up with me. Thank you for taking us in, but we'll make our own arrangements as soon as possible. We won't be staying here.'

Elsie watched the two women, her jaw ceasing to chew while tension mounted in the overheated room. The fire burned fiercely and the atmosphere was making a steady approach towards nastiness. There was more to this than met the eye – a lot more.

'Why?' Molly asked. 'There's trouble enough with bombed-out folk needing places to stay. You've got somewhere – you've got here.'

'Have I?'

'Of course. Now, don't talk daft. Just get yourself upstairs and have some sleep. You know what you're like if you go a night without sleep.'

Dorothy's head shook slowly. 'I have gone many nights without sleep. There was no one to strap me into my bed, you see. No one to complain when the bed was wet – wet because I couldn't get out of it. I have lost the best man in the world.' And she was talking to the worst woman she had ever known. 'Now, listen to me. I am here because of Elsie. Elsie is sixty-two years of age and it's cold outside. I would have slept in an ashpit if I'd been on my own. Elsie is my good friend and neighbour – I am here for her sake and only for her sake.'

Elsie Shipton swallowed the last mouthful of tea with an audible gulp. She hadn't heard a speech of such length from Dorothy Dyson since . . . since for ever. Determined to concentrate without being obvious, she leaned back in the chair and closed her eyes.

'You've no gratitude,' snapped Molly.

Dorothy offered no response.

'Years we slaved for you. Your dad near broke his back in the pits – that's where he is now – half a mile underground, slaving like a workhorse. They're having to work extra shifts with the war.' She patted her hair in a self-satisfied fashion.

'Because you want to be a cut above, he had to be a cut underneath,' came the quiet reply. 'He does as he's told. He always did as he was told. If he'd been half the man Steve was, he would have stood up to you.'

'I only wanted things nice for you—'

'Rubbish. You wanted a back boiler, electricity and a plumbed-in bath. You wanted new wardrobes and a Hoover and a sewing machine.' Dorothy turned and tugged Elsie's sleeve. 'Come on. Don't be falling asleep in here.' She led her companion out of the room and up the stairs.

The voice followed them, though its owner remained at the foot of the staircase. 'You don't know what I went through, having you. Then you were delicate and had me worried out of my mind. You are the most ungrateful daughter on earth.'

In the bedroom, Elsie asked, 'What's the matter, love?'

Dorothy smiled sadly. 'Don't ask. Just go to sleep.' She lay down and stared at the familiar ceiling. Mam was still shouting in the hall, but the words were no longer decipherable.

Elsie began to snore. Dorothy continued to listen for her mother, but the grumbling died and peace was restored. Though Elsie's snoring was hardly peaceful, Dorothy mused. When she was sure that the older woman slept, she got off the bed and began to go through drawers and wardrobe. Fashions had changed, but her size had not, and since she had left home with scarcely a rag to her back, most of her old clothes were still here.

She found her dad's Great War kitbag and some pillowcases and stuffed clothes and shoes inside, moving slowly and noiselessly so as not to disturb Elsie or alert Mam. It had always been like this – secrets, retribution, anger. Softly, she moved to one end of the wardrobe and pulled up a loose floorboard. The diaries were still there. She pulled them out and placed them with the rest of her things. She had everything now. Her life, her sufferings, her thoughts and fears, had all been written into cheap exercise books. *I have found me. I can't find Steve and there'll never be another like him, but I have myself. All of me.*

There was no way that she could stay here. When her rudimentary luggage was hidden under her bed, she finally lay down. Mam would come in and look at her, as would Dad once his shift allowed him home. So she turned her face to the wall and covered her head with the sheet. She didn't want them staring at her, making plans for her, interfering in her life.

'You have no life,' she told herself softly. There had to be a place for her somewhere. Steve would not have wanted her to be like this, almost unconscious for much of the time, a non-participant, a waste of space and of oxygen. 'Make a life,' she commanded herself.

Where could she go? What was that bit she had seen in the paper, about that place where mothers and babies would be staying in the relative safety of the countryside? Bromley Cross, that was it. There was a big house – what was its name? She could get herself Red Cross trained and do some good for a change. Her eyelids became heavy and she drifted between sleep and wakefulness. It would be all right.

Tomorrow, she would be out of here.

*   *   *

By 1919, Dorothy Cornwell had become used to having a father. Born soon after the beginning of the Great War, she had known only a mother, and the arrival in her life of a father had been odd, but by the time she started school Dad had become a part of the household. He was a quiet man and he went out to work, so life continued much as it had before, except for Gran. Gran had looked after Dorothy while Mam had been employed in the mill during the war, but Gran was no longer needed, because Molly Cornwell had given up her place in the spinning room.

There had been an argument of some kind, doors had slammed, Mam had been angrier than normal for a day or two, then things had settled down. 'Where's Gran?' Dorothy had asked one day. She had been told to mind her own business and, after that, she had never asked again. But she remembered the quarrel, those two female voices raised, then the silence after Gran had gone away.

There was no point in asking Mam for

explanations. As her fifth birthday drew near, Dorothy, who had spent most of her short time on earth in the company of adults, looked forward to school. She was unsure of the nature of school, but she knew that other children in the area went there every day. She would stand at the window and watch them playing in the street after tea, at weekends and during school holidays, her feet itching for hopscotch and skipping games, but she was not allowed out. Dorothy was a delicate child. Almost every week, she was taken by Mam to see the doctor, and one kitchen cupboard was filled with lotions and potions for Dorothy's various ailments.

Sunning Hill school was on Derby Street, just at the bottom of View Street. It was big, with an ornate Victorian frontage and tall railings to keep the children safe from traffic. The yard nearest to the road was for older children; those under the age of eleven played in a flagged area at the back of the school. Dorothy, both scared and excited, was taken to town for new clothes. She had gymslips with two buttons on each shoulder, white blouses, grey cardigans and black leather boots. 'Can't I have clogs?' she begged. Everybody wore clogs for school – only the better off had shoes for Sundays and special occasions.

But Molly Cornwell did not approve of clogs. Clogs were for common people and Molly Corn-well was a cut above. 'No,' she said, 'and just be grateful for boots. Them that have to wear clogs are poor. We aren't poor.' Molly's great-aunt had left her some money, so she and Tom were buying their house. Folk who owned houses did not wear clogs. 'You're not clattering about in those heavy things – they'd be too much for your legs.'

Even before she started at school, Dorothy knew that she was going to be different. She had never used a skipping rope, had not played throw-and-catch with a ball, was not familiar with the rules of games. The tying of laces had been mastered, and she could dress herself without help, but leapfrog and ring-a-ring-a-roses had never come up on Mam's agenda. All the other children would know how to play, but Dorothy would have to start her school life with a completely blank sheet.

A few days before the great day arrived, Molly bought new pencils, crayons and a reading book. Although unhappy about allowing her offspring into the world, she was determined that the delicate child would be – like herself – a slice above the common herd. 'Sit,' she ordered.

Dorothy sat at the table.

'I showed you how to write your name, didn't I?'

'Yes, Mam.'

'Right – do it.'

Dorothy wrote her name. She wrote it ten times before Molly was satisfied with the result. Then, when offered the reading book, the child read it aloud from cover to cover, with no hesitation.

Molly frowned. 'Who's been teaching you?'

'Gran showed me. We used to read when you

were at the mill.' They had gone to the park, too, but Gran had made Dorothy promise to say nothing about those outings. There had been ducks and swans, trees, flowers and miles of grass. Once, there had been a band, men in a little circular building with no walls, just a roof held up by poles. The men had worn red uniforms with gold braid and one at the front with a short stick had been in charge. He waved it so hard that he nearly fell off his tiny podium a couple of times. Trumpets and drums had played and the music had been magical.

'Children are rough,' Molly said, 'especially the boys. They have irons on their clogs and you have to stay away from them. I've seen legs near flayed after a kicking.'

Dorothy swallowed hard. Why would anyone kick her?

'And you tell nobody about anything in this house – do you understand?'

Dorothy nodded.

'They don't need to know about me having to fasten you into bed, do they? We don't want all the world asking questions about your nerves. Sleepwalking's not something to be talked about. And other things – keep your mouth shut. I want nobody knowing my business.'

Other things? Which other things? Because Dorothy had sparse experience of the world outside, she owned no yardstick against which behaviours might be measured, compared and categorized. Her whole existence had been encapsulated here, at number 33, View Street, a house from which she could see the Town

32

Hall clock down below and, across town, the moors rising in the distance. She knew shops, of course, because she went for groceries with Mam and had to stand still and talk to no one.

'You say nothing about me, right?'

'Yes, Mam.'

'What goes on here is nobody's affair but mine. I have spies, you know. If I find out you've said anything, you'll be for it, young lady.'

The young lady in question was enrolled in the first class at Sunning Hill in September, 1919. She was given a peg on which to hang her coat and the sign above her peg was a little yellow daisy. The girl next to her had a red rose picture and a shaved head, so Mam was up in arms right away. 'Don't you sit next to her,' she said, 'or you'll be catching that filth. Sending a child to school in that state – they should be ashamed.'

No other mothers had come into school, so Dorothy was already different. The clatter of wooden-soled clogs on the stairs had been the first warning, and Mam's presence was the second. Now, she was being marched into the classroom by a very angry Molly Cornwell.

The teacher sat at a high desk. Behind her was a large blackboard and, leaning in the corner, two canes advertised the very business Mam had spoken about – difficult children were always punished. Dorothy was already difficult, but that wasn't her fault. Mam was making the difficulties.

'Yes?' The teacher had a stern face and grey hair pulled tight into a bun. Her clothes were all black and she looked older than Gran.

Mam spoke quietly. 'This is my daughter, Dorothy Cornwell. She's fragile. Will you make sure she sits next to nobody dirty, please? I saw one girl with ringworm in that cloakroom. I don't want Dorothy coming home with some filthy disease.'

The teacher frowned, and frowning seemed to be a strenuous business, because her forehead was made taut by the severe hairstyle. 'The child in question will be wearing a bonnet,' she replied. If ringworm was to be an issue, what would this woman do when scarlet fever broke out?

Molly wasn't satisfied. 'And I don't want her going out at playtimes. She suffers with her chest – and with her nerves. If she plays out, she'll only get poorly again and she won't be able to come to school.'

Beryl Isherwood had been teaching children from the Daubhill end of Bolton for over thirty years. Experience allowed her insight into the characters of children and of their parents. Straight away, she recognized the type. This was a controller, a would-be monarch of all she surveyed. 'Dorothy will grow stronger, Mrs Cornwell. They all have their little coughs and colds for the first few months.'

'It's not a matter of little coughs and colds,' replied the indignant mother. 'She gets the bronchials. We're always on the lookout for pneumonia.'

Dorothy realized that every child in the room was listening to the exchange. She wanted to run away, but there was nowhere to go. If only the floor would open up and swallow her . . .

'Mrs Cornwell.' Patience was etched deeply into the name. 'Children are supervised at all times. When they go into the playground, a teacher is in charge. Other teachers go for a cup of tea and a rest, then we return to our class-rooms. Who will look after Dorothy when she stays in here? Would you have another member of staff go without a rest period in order to mind one child?'

Molly shifted her weight from foot to foot. She could find no answer except the one she offered now. 'I can come and look after her while the others are out playing,' she said.

Dorothy wanted to die. She was five years old, big enough for school, but Mam was turning her into a baby and a whole class was listening. No other mothers were offering to come to school to mind a child, were they?

Miss Isherwood stuck to her guns. 'Collect her at lunchtime and take her home until the afternoon session begins. At playtime, she will mix with the other children. I cannot make provision for her. If she is too frail for normal school, perhaps you should go to town and ask for a place at the open air school – that's where weaker children will be going once the school is passed into the hands of the corpora-tion.'

The Industrial School? Molly bridled. No child of hers would ever go to one of those places. Even if the name did get changed from Industrial to Open Air, it would still be a place for inferior, poorer and often neglected children. 'Dorothy's not going there,' she snapped. 'I'm not having her pointed at in the street.'

The teacher opened the lid of her desk and withdrew the register. 'If you don't mind, Mrs Cornwell, I have a class to run. Dorothy – sit there.' She pointed to an empty seat.

'She's not sitting with a boy,' cried Molly.

Dorothy walked away from her mother and sat next to the boy. She feared the wrath of her mother, but the ridicule she might receive from her peers was equally terrifying. It did not occur to her for one moment that all the other new children were as afraid as she was; that they, too, had no idea of what to expect on their first day at school.

Molly glared at her daughter and left the classroom in a hurry.

Miss Isherwood called the register, instructing the children to reply 'Yes, Miss,' when their names were spoken. Dorothy kept her head down. She dared not look at her classmates, because she was not one of them. Mam had made her stick out like a sore thumb and she was covered in shame.

But all that was forgotten when Miss Isherwood announced her intention to give the children a first day treat. 'Story time is usually at the end of the day, but, since you are brand new, I shall begin with a nice story. You have all been very good and very brave, so you deserve something special. This is your reward.'

Dorothy was enchanted. The teacher did different voices for each character, bringing to life a tale of a prince, a princess and an enchanted forest that grew and grew until it had twisted its way all round the palace in which the princess lived. Like the trumpets in the park and the swans on the water, this was magic. The princess had to wake up, because she had been asleep for many years. She didn't walk in her sleep, so she didn't need strapping in. The prince hacked his way through the forest and kissed the princess and everyone lived happily ever after.

When Miss Isherwood told of an ugly godmother who had placed a curse on the young royal, Dorothy saw her own mother. Mam wasn't really there, yet she was in Dorothy's head and she put poison on the needle. But, in the end, everything turned out well, because the prince found a way through all the twisted trees. It was wonderful. Dorothy wanted to keep the book that held the stories, but it belonged to the school.

After the story, everyone was given a reading book. 'Can anyone read a few of those words?' asked Beryl Isherwood.

Dorothy could read all of them, but she didn't like to say. She was already the odd one out and there was no point in making matters any worse. All she wanted was to blend in, to be part of the class, to be ordinary. If reading would make her stand out, she would be better not to bother.

Playtime arrived. Children lined up to get

coats and make for the playground. Outside, they stood in clusters and watched the old hands taking their leisure – cowboys and Indians, marbles, tig, and general rough and tumble.

Dorothy was mesmerized. She saw no kicking, no fighting, no bad behaviour at all. She also saw her mother at the other side of the railings and the rate of her heartbeat increased. Again, there were no other mothers. Mam was waving and shouting, though the sound of her voice was muffled by playground noise.

With her shoulders rounded in shame, Dorothy went off into the girls' toilets. She closed the door and sat down. If Mam could have seen her, she would have gone mad, because children who were fragile could never sit on a public toilet. The little girl remained there until the bell rang, then she joined her class, eyes averted from the figure on Goldsmith Street. She was not going to be different. No matter how long it took, Dorothy Cornwell would be one of the crowd.

They did sums and Dorothy got them all right. It was easy stuff, but some of the other children had no idea about counting and taking away. The boy next to her, Alan Partington, copied everything from Dorothy's slate, so he, also, got ten out of ten.

A bell rang. Once again, coats were collected and children went off home to eat their mid-day meal. Dorothy had trouble keeping up with Mam, because Mam was in a particularly black mood. She was muttering under her breath about teachers who thought they knew everything even though they had never married and had children.

A dish was slammed down on the table in front of the child and she was ordered to eat its contents. She didn't like tripe or onions and was always sick if forced to have them, but she knew better than to attempt refusal. After two mouthfuls, she vomited into the kitchen sink and was ordered up to her bedroom.

'But we're having painting this afternoon,' she cried. She felt perfectly well now that the tripe and onions were no longer resident in her stomach. 'Painting and drawing.'

'You're not going. You've been sick and you'll stop at home.'

It wasn't fair. Dorothy hovered for a moment in an insane place where running out through the front door seemed to be an option, but that was mere imagination. Molly Cornwell had spoken and Molly Cornwell's word was law. There was no real choice. Dorothy climbed the stairs, entered her bedroom and closed the door.

She didn't weep. Her grief was too deep to be accessible and she was tired. It occurred to her that she had spoken only to Alan Partington on her first day at school, that she had helped him with his sums and that apart from him she had met no one.

It was a long day. At four o'clock, she stood at the window and watched children passing on their way home. They laughed and shouted, pulling and pushing each other. Two boys kicked a can and a few girls skipped along with ropes. Dorothy's eyes were wet as she observed the antics of her peers. She was different; she would probably be different for the rest of her life. Worst of all, there was nothing she could do about it.

TWO

Elsie Shipton opened her eyes and tried to work out where she was. There was no Pete, the bed was too soft and the blankets felt wrong. A sore throat shocked her into recalling yesterday's events and she heaved herself up, discovering that she was fully dressed, though her shoes were missing – ah, there they were, on the floor. She had no home. She didn't know where her husband was and Dorothy Dyson had disappeared. The other bed was so neatly made that it appeared virginal. 'Dorothy?' she stage-whispered in the direction of the door. 'You there, Dorothy?' There was that peculiar woman downstairs and Elsie didn't like the thought of her getting hold of Dorothy. Where the heck had the girl gone?

When her shoes were in their rightful place, Elsie opened the curtains, was shocked to see that the window owned exterior bars. Hadn't all metals been commandeered? Railings from Noble Street had gone to be made into munitions, leaving steep and dangerous steps up to the front doors of houses built above cellars. Perhaps the government had decided not to bother with these few pieces of iron on a first floor rear window, though it didn't seem fair, not when Noble Street kiddies were always falling down and banging their heads, just for the want of a handrail. She could commit murder for a cup of tea, she felt sure. Her throat felt as if someone had given it a thorough going-over with coarse sandpaper.

'Bloody corset,' she grumbled, wishing she'd found the strength to remove the item before getting into bed. It was bad enough having to wear whalebone during the day, but twenty-four hours at a stretch was a bit much. It was a stretch, too, strong elastic with panels stiffened to the point of agony. She tugged and pulled at her undergarments until the bone-ends found new areas of flesh to trap, then she walked back to the window. Why had this room been made into a cage? Were the bars there to keep people out, or to keep someone in? Were any other windows in the house barred? She shivered. Or had Dorothy been shut in like an animal? Surely not?

'Good morning.'

Elsie jumped. 'Good God, you nearly had me out of my skin. Where's Dorothy?' She took the proffered cup of tea from a hostess whose facial expression fell rather short of welcoming. Tea – thank goodness for it. After two scalding swallows, her throat felt better.

'She's downstairs.' Molly Cornwell sniffed, folded her arms and stared at the visitor. 'I've sent Tom down to the wardens' office to tell them you're safe. They'll find a way to let your husband know, save him worrying about you getting blown up with the rest.'

'Thank you.' Elsie took another gulp of tea, was grateful when the hot liquid cleared her vocal cords to the point where words emerged painlessly. 'It's my neighbour I'm really worried about, Mrs Cornwell. Big woman, bad chest and not built for speed, you see. She were on fire, you know. We got out just in time, or we'd have gone up with the gas. Doesn't bear thinking about. God, I hope Lois is all right.'

Molly closed the curtains. 'Nosy neighbours,' she explained. 'No idea of how to mind their own business, some people.'

Elsie, who felt fairly sure that the woman had wanted to hide the bars, said nothing. Her spine tingled slightly, and the feeling could not be blamed on the corset alone. No, this mother of Dorothy's was a queer fish, all right. It was clear that she had been pretty in her youth: good bones, decent skin, a shine on the hair. She was still the sort of stunner who could probably attract men. Looked at properly, she was the spitting image of her own daughter. Yet she was ugly and the ugliness came from the cold, expressionless eyes. There seemed to be no joy in her, and this was not a recent sadness, Elsie felt sure of that. The woman was a professional misery, with nothing good to say about anyone.

'So, what will you do?' Molly was asking now. 'So many people made homeless – it's tragic.' The voice remained unemotional.

Elsie's head began to nod. 'Well, I've a sister married to a farm labourer, but they're a long way out, and since my Pete's in charge of delivering medical supplies we might need to stop down near town. I don't know, I'm sure. Pete will have to work something out, because I wouldn't have the faintest idea where to start looking.'

'Dorothy should move back here.' Molly took a duster from the front pocket of her apron and flicked it over a chest of drawers. 'She'd be all right with us. It's her proper place – it's where she belongs. This house and everything in it is Dorothy's inheritance. She knows she's always welcome here – it's her birthright. No need for her to go wandering about looking for a home, is there?'

Elsie finished her tea. She didn't know what to think about poor Dorothy Dyson. Dorothy wouldn't have come here at all except for Elsie's needing a bed for the night. 'I'll take her with me,' she said. 'She can come and stop with us. The other wardens will find us a couple of rooms somewhere. It'll all come out in the wash, as my old mother used to say.'

Molly closed the door. 'Look,' she said, her voice almost a whisper, 'our Dorothy's nervy. She's always been the same, on edge all the while, jumping at the slightest noise, needing somebody with her when she went out. We worry about her, me and Tom. She was born nervy and she wants watching. She's never been strong – I went to a lot of trouble rearing her. In and out of the doctor's week in and week out

– it was a terrible time. We thought she'd never reach her tenth birthday.'

It was somebody else who needed watching, Elsie decided as the woman left the room. She wouldn't have trusted Molly Cornwell to mind a goldfish, let alone a vulnerable young woman. The creature was too . . . Elsie struggled for words. She was too in charge, that was the answer. It was as if Molly Cornwell imagined that the world had been created just for her and for no one else. No wonder poor Dorothy didn't favour the idea of stopping here.

The corset was murder. Elsie went to the bathroom, sighed longingly when she saw the proper cast-iron bath and an inside toilet with a chain. But as she fidgeted with whalebone and performed her ablutions, she decided that she would have chosen Emblem Street, a tippler lavatory in the back yard and a tin bath hanging on a nail in preference to Molly Cornwell's house any day of the week. It was a sad house, papered with heavy misery over cracks too deep to be mended. 'You're getting fanciful in your old age,' she told the mirror. But she needed to get out of this house and she couldn't understand why. It felt a bit like prison, she mused, especially the room in which she and Dorothy had slept. What would firemen do, she wondered. If they had to break into that bedroom, they'd need cutting gear to save lives.

She went down to the living room and found Dorothy sitting by the fire. Dorothy had been sitting by the fire since her husband's plane had gone down. After the miscarriage, she had changed position for a while and had lingered on the horsehair sofa for a couple of weeks, but Elsie had managed to get her back to the chair. She was in a different chair in a different house, but she was still carrying on like a dead woman. Or was she? The young woman's eyes were quick to catch her neighbour's glance, and she was actually trying to convey a message.

Dorothy whispered, 'My stuff's outside the back gate.'

'Eh? What stuff?'

'Old clothes – shoes and jumpers. I left home with nothing.'

'Oh. Right.'

'We eloped.'

'I see.' She didn't see, not completely, but she wanted to sound encouraging.

'We have to get out. If you hadn't been here, she would have locked me in the bedroom. She's not right. She's never been right. There's something wrong in her head and me being born just seemed to make it a lot worse.'

Molly Cornwell entered with a false smile and a plate of toast. 'There you go. Get that lot down you before you set off, Elsie. You'll need your strength if you're going house-hunting. Don't worry about our Dorothy, because she's had hers earlier on. We'll look after her, me and her dad. We did it for long enough, so we know what's what.'

Dorothy nodded, so Elsie accepted toast and more tea. While the woman of the house pottered about with her duster, Dorothy mouthed her

46

instructions. She was going to make a run for it, pick up her stuff and— And Molly was watching, so the lip-reading session was temporarily suspended.

Elsie chewed, her eyes fixed on her young neighbour.

Dorothy would meet Elsie at half past nine at the wardens' office.

'Am I missing something?' Molly's radar was plainly turned on to the point where even a fruit fly would have registered. She looked from one woman to the other several times. 'Well?'

'I was just telling Elsie she should go to the hospital and ask after Lois. Lois lived at one side of me and Elsie at the other. They've known each other for donkey's years, and Elsie won't rest till she's seen Lois. She might have been badly hurt last night.'

'Right.' The word 'suspicion' was all but printed across Molly Cornwell's forehead. 'You'll be stopping here, then, Dorothy? We'll get you a new ration book and a gas mask. You'll be all right here with your own folk. It'll save you rattling about town looking for digs.'

No reply was offered. Dorothy stared at her mother for several seconds, then suddenly jumped up and ran into the kitchen. The door was locked and the key had been removed. *It's happening again. She's going to keep me here a prisoner and I can't allow it. I have to put a stop to it. I'm twenty-six and she can't do this, because I have rights. Steve said I must never come back here. I am not staying here. I don't care what I have to do, but I am leaving this house.*

Dorothy returned to the living room, an enormous carving knife held tightly in her right hand. She rolled up her sleeve and, without flinching, stroked the knife over her flesh until blood flowed. She made a second cut, then a third, her gaze fastened to her mother's face.

Elsie spat out a mouthful of toast and cast it into the fire. Its sizzling was the only sound in the room. She looked hard at Dorothy's arm and realized why the girl never wore short sleeves, even during summer. Old wounds, white now, stretched all the way up to the elbow of her left arm. Sweet Jesus, the girl had been cutting herself for years.

Dorothy spoke. 'Now, Mam, you will give me that key or the next cut will be yours. I'm sure you bleed like everybody else.' She continued to lock eyes with her mother and waited for a few seconds. 'Key!' she shouted.

Molly Cornwell, reacting like someone in a trance, removed the key from her pocket and placed it on the sideboard. Dorothy, her stare unwavering, picked it up and smiled. 'No more, Mother, dear,' she said. 'It's my turn at last. I am well into my twenties and Steve got me away the first time. Now I am getting myself away. You can't keep me any more. You have no power over me, none at all.'

'You'll never manage,' replied Molly, her voice strangely altered. 'You're useless without me – and you know it. If you'd come here, I would have saved that baby and—'

'And made it your own? Your very own? A thing you could have controlled?' She glanced briefly at Elsie. 'Take this key and get out,' she said, her voice gaining strength with every word. 'Don't worry about these cuts, Elsie. I know what I'm doing. I learned the hard way. This mother of mine sent me almost as mad as she is.'

Elsie stumbled into the back yard and heaved up every mouthful of toast and every drop of tea. Dear God, what had she just witnessed? Which one of them was crazy? Was it Molly, was it Dorothy, was it both of them? Her knees weakened and she travelled to the gate by steadying herself against a wall. What she had watched was more sickening than last night had been, because there had been something so personal about it. Bombs dropped by enemies were one thing, but hatred such as this was another matter altogether.

Dorothy joined her in the back alley. She passed Elsie a scarf and asked her to tie it round the wound. 'It isn't deep,' she said. 'Just enough to frighten her into letting me go. Forget about all that in there, please.'

Elsie tied up the arm. 'Would you have knifed her, love?'

Dorothy shook her head. 'Somebody should, but it can't be me, because I am her daughter. No matter what she has done and said, she's still my mother. I know how to handle her now, that's the only difference. I'm not a child any more.'

She sounded old and tired, Elsie decided, but

49

Dorothy Dyson was not mentally ill. Something or somebody had driven the girl to the edge and that somebody was probably carrying on with her dusting and cleaning as if nothing worth mentioning had occurred. 'Come on, love, we've got to find somewhere else to lay our heads tonight. Pass me that pillowcase and let's get a move on. It's too cold to be hanging about waiting for Christmas.'

The tingling in Dorothy's arm reminded her that she was alive. She didn't know whether she wanted to be alive, but she was sure of one thing – if she had to remain in the world, she would not be living at 33, View Street.

'Have you stopped bleeding?' Elsie asked when they reached the main road. Her legs weren't doing too well – it was probably the shock of last night and the inexplicable scene she had just witnessed.

'Probably. I only just broke through the skin, so it wasn't as bad as it looked. I've seen a lot worse, so don't you worry.'

Elsie swallowed hard, as her throat was sore again after the bout of sickness. 'You've done it before and you've gone deeper, haven't you? I saw the marks.'

'I don't talk about it, Elsie. It was another life in another place and I thought it was all over. I thought she'd be different after a few years, but she isn't. She'll never alter. There's something in her and . . . oh, never mind.'

Elsie stopped and placed a hand on her friend's shoulder. 'What did she do to you?'

Dorothy shook her head. 'Look, as I just said

– I don't talk about it. If I did, people would think I was crazy, because some of it's so far-fetched that it's just not believable. I'm tired and you're tired. I've lost my husband for good and you've lost yours for the moment. We've no-where to live and we don't know where we'll be sleeping tonight. There are enough nightmares without thinking about my mother and—' She broke off abruptly. 'Oh, bloody hell.'

Elsie blinked. 'What?' Her head twisted this way and that in search of whatever had shocked her companion. She had never before known her to swear – had never heard her saying much, really.

'It's my dad.'

He was a short, thickset man, with coal written all over him. Like many miners, he had developed a stoop and the skin round his eyes seemed dark, as if coal dust had soaked into the tissues. 'You're off, then,' was his greeting.

'Yes.'

'What's in the bags?'

'My clothes. Everything in Emblem Street's burnt. These are the ones from years ago. I'll have to shorten them, I suppose.'

He sniffed. 'Your mam'll be upset. You know how badly she takes these things, Dorothy.'

Elsie noticed that he didn't quite manage to look at his daughter when he spoke to her. He seemed embarrassed almost to the point of pain, weight shifting from foot to foot, hands pushed into his pockets as if he didn't quite know what to do with them. 'Is this your neighbour?' he asked.

'Yes.'

'Her husband knows she's all right.' He made no attempt to achieve eye contact with Elsie, either. 'Well,' he said, 'I'd best be getting back before your mam starts worrying. I'm on lates this week.' Without so much as a ta-ra, he walked on, head down, hands buried, feet slurring against the pavement.

Dorothy looked at Elsie. 'Don't ask,' she said. 'He was her first victim. If he ever had a spine, it's been turned into jelly.'

Elsie was at a complete loss. She should have been worrying about finding somewhere to live, but her head was filled by pictures of a barred window, a furious woman with a knife, an older woman with eyes as cold as steel, a man who seemed to be as much use as an ice cream fireguard. What the hell had gone on in Dorothy Dyson's life? How could a mother be so cold, so empty?

Dorothy was staring at her feet. 'I wanted clogs like everybody else,' she said softly.

'What?'

The younger woman inhaled and made a brave attempt to smile. 'Take no notice. I start talking daft every time my house gets blown up. Anyway, I know where I'm going.'

'Do you?'

Dorothy nodded. 'Yes. It's called Burbank Hall – I just remembered. It's up Bromley Cross and it's recently been taken over – a safe place for mothers and babies, likely some evacuees, with a nursing home round the back some-where. They're looking for general staff. I may not be a general, but I don't mind working my way up. I'll have to kick off as a private, the same as everybody else.'

Elsie was immobilized. The girl was cracking jokes – she seemed almost happy. What the heck had happened? How could a bomb and the loss of her home make a person cheerful?

Dorothy, a few steps ahead, stopped again and turned. 'What's up now, Elsie?'

'You're different.'

'From what?'

'From how you were, how you are.'

Dorothy offered no reply. She had sat there, had waited for the bomb to claim her miserable soul, had survived. She had faced her mother and her father, had thought about tomorrow for the first time since . . . since the baby. She could walk, she could talk and she would work. Perhaps people who survived a bombing saw things with new eyes. It was time to move on, because the sitting-down place wasn't there any more.

Elsie caught up with her. 'My sister lives up Bromley Cross – her husband works the farms. Happen I'll see you up there some time when we get the chance to pay a visit.'

They called in at the wardens' station, found that Pete had checked in and would be back in an hour after he had found a billet. Elsie was parked in a chair and given a cup of tea, while Dorothy, who was penniless, received a sum sufficient to pay her fare to Bromley Cross. She threw her arms round Elsie and whispered in her ear, 'Thanks for being a mother to me,' then she disappeared quickly so as to avoid weeping.

With her Great War kitbag and her pillow-cases, she waited at Moor Lane bus station for her transport to arrive. The air, which remained sticky from last night's raid and the resulting fires, was further thickened by grey effluent born of cotton manufacture. They were making shrouds, she thought as she stepped onto the bus that would take her out of a town she had always managed to love. Steve hadn't needed a shroud, because he had had no grave, no burial service. Like many in the air force, he had disappeared without trace.

Dorothy would be just like everybody else. The sadness wasn't going to shift until it was ready, and gallons of tears remained in her system, but there now existed a mould into which she might pour herself. She would throw her soul into a reserved occupation, would claim her place in this crippled society. With husband and child lost to her, she had to do her bit – she owed that much to them and to her beleaguered country.

There was no choice; Dorothy's war had to be fought until victory could be achieved.

Burbank Hall was a long way from the bus stop. But the fates were on Dorothy's side and she hitched a lift on a flat cart that was taking supplies of vegetables to the mansion. The scent of wet earth on newly dug potatoes and carrots accompanied driver and passenger through lanes and along dirt tracks. Their horse, a shire of massive proportions, did not believe in hurrying, so Dorothy enjoyed her first view of countryside in years at a pace that was pleasingly leisured. It was magnificent.

She had come up here with Steve, had rolled about in fields, had paddled in streams, had been young, happy, in love. Stepping stones, small waterfalls, sheep and cows out to graze – all had figured in those heady, carefree days of courtship. She remembered being alive here in the woods and fields, tumbling about in hay, feeding horses, running from an angry bull. It was a good, healthy place. Last night's bomb had done so much for her – it had awoken her soul and had sent her here, to a place that she had always imagined to be just like heaven.

Apart from a few wisps emerging from farm-houses, there was no smoke. Crystal clear autumn air stabbed her lungs, clearing her throat of yesterday's disaster and sharpening her brain until she felt almost cheerful. But cheerfulness came at a price, and she closed her fingers round the locket, apologizing inwardly to a man who had died and to a child who had never lived. She could accept that she was alive, but happiness was something she expected not to experience for some time.

The house came into view, its breathtaking beauty compelling her to drink in every crazy, ancient window, every door, each course of criss-crossed Tudor black-and-white frontage. 'How old is it?' she asked the driver.

He removed his cap, scratching a balding

head with the same hand, as his other was occupied by reins. 'First records is 1483,' he told her, 'but I think there was a house here before that. A man name of Chadwick had what they called a fulling mill – something to do with finishing the cloth by using water. Chadwick was spelt differently back then, with an e on the end. There's a Chadwicke House in the grounds. Then, later on, some landed chap bought Chadwick out, lived here and got his income from farms and fulling rents. That new lot's been here since the seventeenth century.' He pointed to the house. 'The house has had new wings built on a couple of times at least. You can't see them from here, the extensions built by the new lot. They make a square at the back – a square with one end missing, that is.'

'Which new lot?' It occurred to Dorothy that she was actually asking questions and taking a real interest for the first time since . . . since Steve and the baby.

The man smiled, his grizzled face wrinkling until it imitated a pickled walnut. 'When I say new, I mean not fifteenth century – but the new family's been here three hundred years. I'm a bit of an amateur local historian in my spare time – I've had stuff published in the *Bolton Evening News*, you know. Right. They are the Burbanks – that's why it's called Burbank Hall. They didn't build the original place – their ancestors, I mean – but they've owned it for a long time and built a wing on a couple of hundred years ago.'

'And the War Office borrowed it?'

'Nay.' The old chap shook his head. 'It got volunteered and it were snatched up. That way, the family gets to keep some of it instead of getting cleared out altogether by the government. Massive place, it is. Takes some heating, mind. The Great Hall still has real chandeliers on chains – they're worth a fortune on their own, and I believe they hold a good few hundred candles between them. Then four fireplaces in that one big room – it's like trying to keep a blinking barn warm.'

It was magic. It was like Sleeping Beauty all over again with Miss Isherwood reading from a storybook, her eyes peering over steel-rimmed spectacles each time she got to a particularly good bit. 'It's enormous,' Dorothy ventured.

'It is that, girl. Tell me, are you here for work?'

She nodded. 'Yes – I got bombed out last night. My husband's dead and I . . . I have no children, so I am here to do my bit.'

The old man patted her hand. 'Eh, it's not easy, is it, lass? I've two grandsons God alone knows where, one on the sea and the other driving a tank. I heard about the bombs and the gas blowing down in the town. You were lucky. More than a few lost their lives last night. See, I'll put in a word for you. You seem a smart enough young lady, so let's hear what Mrs Crumpsall has to say.'

They stopped at a side entrance and the driver jumped down. He entered the house and returned very quickly with a round, rosy-cheeked woman of indeterminate age and pleasant

57

features, who walked to the cart and spoke to Dorothy. 'Hello, love. I'm Jill-of-all-trades, don't know whether I'm coming or going. Will you step inside? Only I've that much to do, I'm in a tizz. I think I'm supposed to be housekeeper, but with a house this size, *they* can keep it and welcome.' She carried on grumbling happily while Dorothy followed her inside.

'Take no notice,' whispered the driver. 'She's got a heart of gold, has Ivy Crumpsall. She's like an overseer, Red Cross trained, certificates in cooking, talking and putting the world right. And she's a beautiful knitter.' He collected Dorothy's things and passed them to her. 'I'm Amos Foster,' he said, 'and I hope I see you again, because you're a sight for sore old eyes.'

The kitchen was the size of Dorothy's whole ground floor in Emblem Street – a ground floor that no longer existed. She accepted a cup of tea and sat at a table that must have been twelve feet in length.

Ivy Crumpsall chattered on about the family's having its own kitchen put into the bit they had kept for themselves, beds for mothers and babies, a nursing home in the grounds, the price of sheets . . . and could Dorothy iron?

There was no space into which Dorothy might insert an answer, because Ivy went on at the speed of an express train with no brakes. At last, she slowed down. 'Right, what's happened to you, then?' She picked up a list, wrote something down, then stuck the pencil behind her ear.

'We got bombed last night. I think the next street took the worst of it, but I lost my scullery, my neighbour was on fire and the gas mains blew, so—'

'Where was it?'

'Emblem Street.'

All colour drained from Ivy Crumpsall's face. 'Did you say Emblem Street?'

Dorothy nodded.

Temporarily speechless, the woman leaned on the table for support. 'That's our Elsie's street – Shipton, she's called. Good God.' She jumped up.

'Elsie's all right, Mrs Crumpsall. She stayed with me at my parents' house last night and I left her not much more than an hour ago, waiting for her husband. He was on duty when the bombs dropped.'

Ivy Crumpsall sat down abruptly. 'Right, that's it,' she said. 'They can move up to Bromley Cross and live in our cottage. My Sam stops here with me and does odd jobs round the farms. Our Elsie said she'd never leave Bolton, but we'll have to see about that. Look.' She grabbed Dorothy's hand. 'This place isn't up and running yet – we're still getting it ready. Will you stay? I'll catch old Amos and he can run me to the bus stop. I'll drag our Elsie up here by her hair if needs be.' Ivy's head, which possessed the same mobility as her sister's, was bobbing wildly as she spoke.

'I'll be happy to stay.'

'All you have to do is answer the doors. There's some pea and ham soup – warm it up

59

for your dinner – or lunch as the posh folk call it. Just hold the fort, flower. I'll be as quick as I can.' She ran to the door, ran back again straight away. 'Them there bells.' She pointed to a row of marked bells on a board. 'There's only one connected now. Madam still carries on like the Queen of bloody Sheba, so if she rings, go through to the front of the house – out of that door, turn left, keep going till you can go no further. Double doors, their living room's got. Tell them I won't be long. They've got their own girl, but Madam still likes to throw her weight about.' She grabbed coat and bag and disappeared in the twinkling of an eye.

Silence reigned. Dorothy poured herself another cup of tea, heard the clopping of Amos's horse as it pulled the cart towards the distant bus stop. 'I feel as if I've been wrung out and hung out to dry,' she told a large ginger tom that dropped in to lap milk from a saucer. The cat flicked its tail a couple of times, mewed at her, then got on with the business of feeding itself.

In spite of the frantic speed at which she had been introduced to country life, and despite the fact that she owned nothing at all beyond a few old clothes, two pairs of shoes and a handbag, Dorothy was in danger of experiencing a degree of contentment she had not expected. Fifteen hours earlier, her dying soul had been sitting by a dying fire and nothing had mattered. Then the bomb, the saving of Elsie, the time spent in the company of Mam – all these factors had come together to serve as catalyst.

She walked to the kitchen door, looked out on a world whose war seemed to be over. It wasn't over, of course. But life was almost bearable and Elsie could well be on her way up to the village of Bromley Cross.

*   *   *

Beryl Isherwood was firm, but fair. She was not a mother, yet she regarded herself as parent to all who had passed through her life in a career that spanned well over three decades. She had encountered silly children, naughty children, poor children, dull children, plus two or three geniuses born to parents who could scarcely read or write. There was no accounting for Mother Nature's quirks.

Dorothy Cornwell fell into no particular category. Certainly quicker to learn and brighter than most of her companions, Dorothy was an oddity. She was the first pupil in thirty-odd years who had needed to learn to play. Whilst control over smaller movements was more than adequate, her body seemed not to know itself, so that skipping, rounders, gymnastics and even plain running were difficult. She wrote well, read like a child three or four years her senior, could paint, draw and produce acres of tidy, accurate arithmetic, but when it came to throwing and catching, she was as awkward as a two-year-old. Beryl couldn't work her out.

'I think it's something to do with the mother,' she told the headmaster one afternoon at tea break.

Bernard Moss studied the attendance register. 'She certainly has a lot of time off.' He calculated the days. 'She's been here almost exactly half-time. There's something approaching a pattern – as if she does just mornings – then the pattern breaks and it's three days off, two days in, a week off, a fortnight in . . . is she ill?'

Beryl put down her cup and saucer. 'She's ill, all right. She's one hundred per cent crackers.'

'You mean the mother.' This, from Mr Moss, was not a question. 'Yet so persuasive and convincing. Are there any siblings?'

'None. One nest, one fledgling, one rod of iron. Dorothy won't talk about her home life. The others?' She shrugged. 'I know whose dad keeps getting drunk, whose mother's having a baby, whose grandmother's very poorly. They tell me what they eat and where they've been at the weekends. Dorothy? Nothing. When they do their journals – those who can write a bit – it's all princesses and castles with Dorothy. When I ask her about home, she shuts up like a rabbit trap – it's a reaction and it's automatic. She's been told to say nothing.'

He closed the register. 'Nothing about what?'

Beryl nodded. 'That's the burning question. Everything about Dorothy is different – the boots, the perpetually clean clothes, the anxiety about getting the slightest mark on a blouse, her neat work. I believe she's a victim of obsession, but I'll never prove it, because Dorothy is terrified.'

'Of her mother.'

'Yes.'

Bernard Moss knew Beryl Isherwood very well. She was head of infants, an excellent teacher and a good judge of character. If she expressed concern about a pupil, she was right nine times out of every ten. 'I'll do the letter, then.' Standard procedure was a letter from the head teacher, followed, if deemed necessary, by a written warning from the School Board. In the event of that's producing no result, School Board representatives would visit the home until the matter was resolved. 'Consider it done,' he said.

Beryl went back to her class. There was something in little Dorothy Cornwell's eyes, a silent pleading, a need to be loved and valued. For that very reason, the child was a frequent recipient of praise from her teacher, was often wreathed in damped-down smiles and radiant blushes, her inner pleasure shining forth despite all efforts at concealment.

While many of the others were still messing about, Dorothy was ready and waiting at her desk, spine straight, eyes bright, soul clearly demanding information. The child was a sponge that soaked up anything and everything. She loved school – that was obvious. Not for the first time, the thwarted mother in Beryl Isherwood was wakening.

If the teacher could have achieved her own way in the matter, the child would have been removed from her mother and taken to 114, Willows Lane for tea, toast and maternal attention in a decent home. She was beautiful, too; a child in whom any parent should take pride.

Flaxen hair, clear blue eyes and a loneliness that cut through years of self-control to hack away at the emotions of Miss Beryl Isherwood.

'Quiet,' she shouted. 'Spelling test time.'

Dorothy Cornwell smiled. She was good at spelling.

The doctor was here again. Dorothy knew all about 'doctor' days. On these occasions, she was not required, and she was expected to remain upstairs in her room until Dr Clarke had gone away. This arrangement seemed perfectly in order, as the child knew no differently. When Mam took her to the doctor, it was for Dorothy to be examined; when the doctor came to the house, he talked to Mam about how to make Dorothy better.

While they talked, Dorothy glued herself to her parents' front bedroom window and watched the games. The house was situated on the highest part of a hill, so the street at each side fell away, allowing for adventures and accidents galore. Children used home-made go-carts, old prams and decrepit, rusting bikes from which the brakes had been removed. By these means, they propelled themselves at considerable speed in all directions, their behaviour involving bleeding, lost skin and a great deal of noise. It was thrilling to watch, so Dorothy looked forward to doctor days, because she could sneak into her parents' room and observe the fun.

A couple of boys rattled by on squeaky scooters. One lost a wheel, his balance and all dignity just outside number 33. Dorothy raised the window a few inches – nails knocked in by Dad under Mam's watchful eye prevented a full opening. 'Are you all right?' she shouted to the lad. She recognized him from school.

He grinned ruefully. 'Aye, there's nowt broke except me scooter. My mate's got a better one. Would you like a go on it? It gets up some speed, you know.'

'I can't.'

'Why not?' He picked up himself, the wheel and the remains of his mangled vehicle.

'I'm not allowed.'

He screwed up his face and stared at her uncomprehendingly. 'You what? Can you never play out?'

Dorothy shook her head. 'Never. I'm supposed to be fragile.'

'What's that?'

'I get ill,' she replied. 'Mam won't let me out. She says I'll be hurt.'

The boy shook his head – she looked right enough to him and she had the prettiest hair he had ever seen. Not that he cared about girls with pretty hair, of course. 'So what do you do all the time if you can't play out?'

'I read stories, I write and I do sums. Oh, and I've got a dolls' house.'

He scratched his head, glad that he wasn't fragile. 'What's your name?' he asked.

'Dorothy Cornwell.'

'Oh. Right. I'm Stephen Dyson. My friends call me Steve. See you again.' He ran off in pursuit of his escaping companion.

Dorothy closed the window quietly. That had been an adventure and she felt excited by it. She had never before opened a window to talk to somebody. It had made her feel just partially contained and the boy, in allowing her to know his nickname, had suggested that she might become his friend. He was older, in the junior school, and he didn't mind falling down and getting hurt. That was a brave lad and he was placed immediately in the category of prince. A bold prince would get her out of here one day, and Steve Dyson was definitely bold.

She sneaked back to her own room to mull over her secret. In her imagination, she became an exquisite and delicate princess locked in a tower and Steve Dyson was a handsome young rescuer who was destined to come to her aid. He would arrive not on a one-wheeled, rusty and disgraceful scooter, but on a white charger draped in purple with coats of arms embroidered in golden thread. The prince would wear armour and, in a gauntlet, would be holding a red rose just for her. Awakened by a kiss, Dorothy would ride away with him on his purple-draped horse.

Placing herself on her bed, Dorothy spread out her hair until it seemed to match pictures she had seen at school. Then she folded her hands on her chest and made her face calm and beautiful. Her imagined dress was of silk so fine that it would float like gossamer when he picked her up. The colour of the gown was a silvery white and she would be pale after sleeping for one hundred whole years. There were pearls in her hair, and a diamond-encrusted tiara sat on the small table next to her bed.

Her eyes opened. Who had made her sleep for a century? Who had taken that sleep-poison and wiped it on the needle she would use? The face loomed over her, an older version of her own features, eyes slightly darker, much colder, some hard lines appearing around the mouth. It was a disappointed face, it belonged to her mother and it was no longer in her waking dream – it had become real.

'Doctor's gone.' Molly Cornwell studied her daughter. 'What have you done to your hair?' The child looked pretty, far too pretty for Molly's comfort. Should the hair be cut short, perhaps? Did this child – young though she was – realize her own beauty?

'It came undone,' replied Dorothy. 'I'm sorry.'

'Well, you'd better come down. The doctor says you've to drink plenty of milk and eat your greens.'

Dorothy followed her mother down the stairs. Everything was extra-shiny and extra-tidy, because the doctor had been. Mam was very respectful towards Dr Clarke and hung on his every word. He had been present at Dorothy's birth, though Mam always stressed that a midwife had done the 'real business', because she didn't like the idea of a man messing about 'down at that end of things with a baby coming'.

'Drink that.' A glass of milk was placed in

front of the child. 'Then you can go and play with your dolls' house.'

Dorothy sipped her milk obediently. 'Can I play with my dolls' house on the front steps?'

'No. You'll catch cold. And you've not to sit on steps – you'd get piles.'

When the glass was half empty, Dorothy tried another tack. 'If I stand up and put my dolls' house on the top step?'

'No. I've told you before – you're not hanging about the streets like that rubbishy lot out there. They've got nits, worms, scabs and all sorts. Bad enough that you have to go to school with them. No use spending time out there playing with infection. That would be asking for trouble and a hospital bed, mark my words.'

Dorothy watched Mam. She was at the mirror making herself look ordinary for when Dad came home. For Dr Clarke, she had shiny hair, shiny shoes, pink cheeks and pink lips; for Dad, she had scraped-back hair, slippers and no adornments. Perhaps Dr Clarke was Mam's prince in armour, but Mam didn't need a prince in armour, did she?

'What are you staring at?'

'I was thinking how nice your hair was for Dr Clarke.'

Molly arrived at the table in a split second. 'Keep your mouth shut,' she ordered. 'You know nothing about anything. You're too young for complicated grown-up things, so mind your own business. Go and dress your dolls – your food will be ready in an hour.'

Dorothy drained her glass and trudged off

upstairs. Every day was the same. She settled down to await her prince and this time her dress was of pale gold with beads sewn onto the bodice.

He would come. One day, he really would come.

THREE

She sat alone for almost half an hour, elbows on the long table, chin resting in her hands. Instructed to answer doors and the family's bell, she was reluctant to leave the kitchen, yet she felt drawn to the outside and, finally, she placed a chair in the open doorway so that she might see the yard, at least. It was a mild day and she found herself nodding off in the gentle sunshine. Sleep in her mother's house had eluded her for several hours, and even after she had managed to lose consciousness, she had heard them coming in to look at her, had managed, just about, not to flinch when the sheet had been drawn back so that they might examine her face.

Mam had whispered about 'her' girl coming back to her rightful home and about Elsie leaving tomorrow. She had been half right, of course, because Elsie had gone, but so had 'her' girl. Molly Cornwell's daughter was sitting in a doorway waiting for life to start again, and there wasn't a damned thing Molly could do about it. She had escaped. For a second time, Dorothy had achieved freedom.

A storm brought Dorothy back to wakefulness, though its creator was not meteorological by nature. The personification of greased lightning was suddenly bouncing round the old kitchen, opening and slamming cupboard doors and drawers, rattling pots, pans and cutlery. 'I'll bloody swing for her,' cursed the clatterer. 'Anybody'd think I'd pinched her flaming cake slice. Who the hell wants a cake slice? If I took a cake slice home, my mam wouldn't know it from a bloody coal shovel.'

'Hello,' said Dorothy.

'Hang on a minute, I'm looking for solid family silver here. Not that the family's solid, but their blessed cake slice is. That woman will drive me to physical violence any day now.'

'Can I help?' Dorothy asked.

The lightning paused for a moment. 'Have you got a gun?'

'No. I think I must have dropped it during the bank robbery.'

The small, red-haired girl stood in the middle of the kitchen, hands on hips, cheeks bright with temper. 'There's only me left,' she said. 'And it's more than one person can bear, is this. She needs a full battalion waiting on her hand and foot all the while. Selfish? She invented the word.'

'Who?'

'Little Lady blinking Fauntleroy – queen of Burbank Hall, mistress of all she surveys and two bloody Pekingese dogs. She wants her cake slice. She's not having cake, but she wants the cake slice. Everybody else has gone to the war and I'm left with Dunkirk on me own. There's folk dodging bullets a few hundred miles away and I'm running round after a piece of silver.'

'And two Pekingese dogs?'

'You're catching on. She's got a mood on her. Ever since Mr Andrew gave the house away – she thinks he gave it away – she's had a gob on her like three wet Sundays. How am I supposed to manage, eh? This is my time off, but I have to find her missing cake slice.'

'I'll help.' Within seconds, both girls were rummaging through every container in the kitchen. The short, plump, curly-haired maid gave a running commentary. She was nearly seventeen and thinking of joining the Land Army. She didn't want Red Cross, because she was no good with blood and folk with bits missing. She couldn't join the Wrens because the Wrens were choosy and anyway, she'd been seasick on the boating lake at Barrow Bridge. She wasn't cut out for domestic work and she'd rather be outside digging up spuds. And she didn't like Pekingese dogs.

'Lizzie?'

The girls froze momentarily, then turned to the inner doorway.

Dorothy studied the picture of elegance in a plain frame created by the door jamb. The mistress of Burbank Hall was short, slender, beautifully dressed and annoyed. She had perfectly coiffed dark hair, brown eyes, good skin and two sniffling, salivating dogs at her heels.

Her penetrating gaze was fixed on Dorothy. 'And who might you be?'

Some devil in Dorothy yearned to supply a frivolous answer, but she was homeless and afraid. 'I'm Dorothy Dyson,' she replied.

'With Mrs Crumpsall?'

'I think so, yes. She asked me to wait until she comes back. Her sister's house was bombed last night – so was mine.'

Brown eyes travelled downward, as if scanning Dorothy and filing her in some compartment marked *pending*. The slow gaze moved upward and, with mockery scarcely concealed, she spoke. 'That must be the result of living in a town. We have seen no bombs, of course. One has very little trouble in the countryside.'

It occurred to Dorothy that it would take a very brave man to tackle Mrs Burbank – with or without weaponry. Eyes like these seemed to have the power to return any missile to its place of origin within seconds. She was like Molly Cornwell, but probably without that special craziness.

The woman redirected her attention and spoke to Lizzie. 'I found it after all. It was at the back of a kitchen drawer. Silver should keep company with no other metal. You will clean it and return it to its rightful place in the dining room.' She gazed round the room. 'Such a sad thing, being forced to give up one's own home.' She sighed. 'I suppose we must all make our sacrifices.' On this note, she left the arena, both Pekingese snuffling in her wake. The two girls listened intently until her footsteps had died in the distance.

Lizzie threw herself into a chair while Dorothy tidied the mess created by their search. 'She's a witch,' moaned the seated girl. 'She was a witch when I started here, but I didn't care, because I never saw much of her. Now there's only me – I can't miss her, can I? If I had that bloody gun, I'd make sure I didn't miss her.'

'Bang, bang, you're dead?' Dorothy closed the last drawer.

'Too true. And what's your excuse for being alive?'

Dorothy told the tale of the bomb, omitting to mention her mother and the night spent in View Street. 'So here I am,' she concluded.

'Well, Dorothy, welcome to hell – though Mrs Crumpsall's all right. I'm the one in real hell. My name's Lizzie Murphy; I look after her and her son. Her other two sons are away fighting or being officers and I'm stuck with her. She's called Isobel and she's nasty.'

'I see.'

'You will see. She's supposed to have nearly nowt to do with whatever they're making here – convalescent home, evacuees, mothers and babies. But that nose of hers gets everywhere. And poor Mr Andrew – well, it's a shame.' She went on to inform Dorothy that poor Mr Andrew had suffered polio as a child, had a limp and one shoulder slightly higher than the other. 'So he can't fight. Madam has his suits made specially,' she said, 'so he'll look like a gent. She thinks him being a bit crippled is something to be ashamed of – common, like.'

It took more than level shoulders to make a gentleman, thought Dorothy. 'Does he work?'

'Oh, aye – he's a trained head doctor. Psychiatrist or psychologist, I think they're called. Says he's into trauma. That's the effects of shock. Not that he says much to me, like, but I overhear stuff when I'm in there. They had to make a new kitchen and I can't find anything. She's taken all their treasures – she thinks they're treasures – into the front part of the house.'

'The oldest bit?'

Lizzie nodded. 'There's not an inch of wall without a picture on it – ugly bloody things and very dusty. Ornaments everywhere – you can't move without worrying about the Ming Dynasty. Her dogs are Shang and Ming – she's mad about Chinese stuff.' There was a short pause. 'No, she's just mad altogether.'

It occurred to Dorothy that she had ex-changed one house of lunacy for another, yet in this instance she preferred to stick with the devil she didn't know. She listened while the house was explained to her. The wing in which she currently sat was the Burbank Wing, as it had been added by that family. Across from it was the New Wing. The New Wing was older than the Burbank Wing and yes, it was all a bit much to take in.

The kitchen had windows on both sides. Facing the door through which Dorothy had entered was the stable block; windows on the opposite side of the room overlooked a formal garden set in three sides of a square, the front being the original manor, the two added wings being New – which was older – and Burbank, which was the latest addition.

'Then there's Chadwicke House,' Lizzie explained. 'Hang on, I'll pop the kettle on – I'm parched.' While she rattled tea things, she explained about the older and smaller manor, which was also Tudor and very crooked. 'They'll have to nail the beds to the floors if they're using it as a convalescent home.' She stirred the tea. 'Otherwise, they'll have recovering patients flying out of the windows. You can't put anything down in there – it moves. Residents won't need to be in the RAF – they'll be airborne anyway.'

A smile tugged at Dorothy's lips. How could a life change so dramatically within a single day? This time yesterday, she had been trying to force herself to eat a cheese sandwich; now, she could have tackled a whole cow with potatoes and gravy thrown in. It was probably the country air, she concluded.

When they had drained their cups, Lizzie settled down by the fire in Mrs Crumpsall's rocker. 'You go for a walk,' she said. 'I'm off duty for another hour or so and I'll stop here and keep my ears open. Well, nearly open.'

Dorothy thanked her companion and left the house. The stables were occupied and she made her way along the block, talking to inquisitive creatures who had come to look at the latest arrival in their lives. She had never feared animals and was happy to stroke noses and allow thick, drawn-back lips to investigate her hands. These beasts of burden were beautiful, she decided.

Avoiding the front of the house – the very oldest part, in which she felt most interest – she studied sandstone additions with turrets and finials, saw a summer house, fountains, beds of dying flowers. All around, farmland rose and fell, rose yet again in its determination to form the Pennine chain. There was no war here, not yet, not until its victims would arrive for treatment at the planned convalescent home. But there did seem to be a virago already in the family part, the section Dorothy avoided in order not to attract the attention of the woman. That female could probably start a world war on her own. She reminded Dorothy of Mam, but she wasn't Mam, wasn't related to Dorothy, was therefore less of a threat.

She walked a few hundred yards, and found Chadwicke House in a dip well away from the Hall. It was a showstopper: completely Tudor, no additions, just string courses in many patterns, and windows of glass so old that it probably deformed anything spied through those many uneven eyes.

'Might I help you?'

She swung round to find a man just a couple of yards behind her. 'No, thank you. I am here for work, but Mrs Crumpsall needed to go out.' He owned a shock of tousled, dark hair, brown eyes and what Dorothy termed an educated face. She could not understand why his face seemed educated, but it clearly did.

'I am Andrew Burbank.'

She swallowed nervously. That woman was his mother, then. 'Dorothy Dyson. My house has gone, I have nowhere to live, so I need work with accommodation provided. Mrs Crumpsall seemed to like me well enough, and I am waiting for her to come back.'

'Very well. I shan't detain you.' Yet he lingered. 'You like old buildings?'

She had spent her life in old buildings, castles built in her mind, created, furnished and decorated by an imagination that had saved her sanity right through childhood. 'Yes,' she answered, 'and I love Tudor best of all, the half-timbered type. It's a reminder of Shakespeare, isn't it? These houses were here when he was.'

'You are fond of Shakespeare?'

Dorothy shrugged. 'The sonnets, mainly. I have read some of the plays, but I never saw one. I'd like to, one day.'

'Which ones?'

Oh, heck. He was dragging her into a field in which her knowledge was severely limited. '*The Merchant of Venice*, I think.'

'Ah, human values, caskets, pound of flesh and poor old Shylock.'

She didn't know what to say, so she pulled something from the recesses of a self-informed mind. 'If you prick us, do we not bleed? If you tickle us, do we not laugh? If you poison us, do we not die?' Her education, which had been achieved in the isolation of her bedroom and in the reading rooms of the Central Library, had been her saviour. Only in books and in her own imagination had she ever claimed a degree of freedom.

'That's the chap.'

He possessed, she decided, a voice from which expression had been almost completely stripped, yet he was not as cold as his mother. There was an awkwardness in his stance, as if his weight depended on one side of his body rather than the other. Then she remembered the polio and remarked inwardly that his shoulders seemed level enough to her. It was very sad that such a handsome man should have been attacked by that dreadful disease. She remembered something else, too. 'You're a psychiatrist,' she blurted before thinking.

'I am – for my sins. Psychologist, too. The psychologist studies the disease and the psychiatrist finds the drugs. I prefer to manage without medicines, but needs must when the devil drives.'

He should take a look at Molly Cornwell, she thought. His own mother, too, seemed rather less than steady in the head. Who would worry about a cake slice while a war raged? 'For your sins?'

'It's just a saying. I had no chance of becoming anything involving strenuous movement, so I became a doctor.'

'Ah.' She considered that for a moment. 'You'd have to move fast if a mad patient took a dislike to you.'

His eyes were laughing, though his mouth remained unmoved. 'In circumstances where rapid movement is required, I manage.' He nodded quite deeply, producing what almost amounted to a bow, then turned and walked back towards the Hall.

She watched him and tried very hard to feel no pity – the limp was noticeable. Then it occurred to her that she should feel pity, should welcome any emotion that concentrated on a being other than herself. Dorothy Dyson had sat long enough in a pool of tears, had wept for her own tragedy and for nothing else. She would weep again, would miss Steve, would mourn that lifeless child, but other people mattered, too. And he really should be using a walking stick.

Dorothy returned to chaos. Elsie Shipton had taken the fireside rocker and had also taken to weeping. The shock of the previous night had finally exacted its toll and she was reduced to a sobbing wreck in a borrowed coat. 'Oh, Dorothy,' she wailed. 'Poor Lois. She's bandaged up like one of them there Egyptian mummies what got shoved in pyramids. She were trying to talk to me, but I couldn't understand nothing what she said. Poor, childless widow since her husband fell off that chimney.'

Pete Shipton winked at Dorothy. He was not making mock of his wife's distress – Pete often greeted people with a wink. 'She'll be all right in a minute,' he said.

Elsie continued to wail. 'She should never have married a steeplejack in the first place – that's a terrible, dangerous job, is that. And he were a daft bugger, always taking chances. At least me and Pete have our Eddie and our Stanley and the grandkiddies.'

'Aye,' said Pete.

'She's got nothing and nobody and no home.'

Deciding that Elsie had worked herself into enough of a state, Pete put his foot down hard. 'Else!' His voice had an edge to it. 'Shut up, for goodness' sake. I don't know whether I'm coming or going as it is. Dorothy's in the same pickle – we none of us know where we're sleeping tonight.'

Ivy came in from the pantry. 'Oh, yes, we do. Pete, you and our Elsie can stop in the cottage. Me and Sam'll stay here – we often do. Dorothy will be sleeping here, too – plenty of rooms and plenty to do. And don't kick off about your job and your medical supplies – we'll find a way to get you there. Elsie, stop moaning – you're the same size as me and you can wear my clothes.'

Dorothy noticed that both sisters nodded when they spoke. So, as well as the already esteemed Lizzie Murphy, there promised to be some synchronized head-bobbing to provide amusement at Burbank Hall.

Elsie, indignant now, was suddenly dry-eyed. 'I'm not living up here,' she announced. 'It's the back of bloody beyond and I wouldn't know what to do with myself. Stuck in a flaming cottage all day while he's at work? Who do I talk to? Myself? A cow?'

Ivy slammed a milk jug onto the table. 'Listen, you old misery. You can come up to the Hall and fettle while this place gets done up. Then you can take a bus to town and see

81

your friend in the infirmary. It's healthy up here.'

'It's boring.'

Ivy glared at her beloved sister. 'Boring people get bored,' she said. 'Find something to do and stop whining. I've enough on without you acting like a two-year-old whose doll got broke. I'm being inspected every other day. Ministry of This, That and the Other, Ministry of Nosy bloody Parkers, how many beds to a room, how many bathrooms? Now, give over. I'm getting a headache.'

Dorothy dragged a chair across the floor and placed herself next to Elsie. 'You'll be all right.'

'What about poor Lois? She's a big woman and she'll get bedsores.'

'The hospital will look after her. Elsie, it's beautiful here – it's like living in a poem.'

Elsie stared hard at her erstwhile next door neighbour. The bomb had actually done some good. Leaving aside the events in View Street, Dorothy Dyson had improved no end in the past few hours. 'You've roses in your cheeks, girl.'

Dorothy patted Elsie's hand.

'Living in a poem?' The words had only just filtered through the older woman's clouded mind. 'What the bloody hell does that mean?'

Dorothy smiled. 'It's "Nicholas Nye" – Walter de la Mare. It's Wordsworth's daffodils. It's what they wrote about.'

Elsie shook her head. 'Are you on tablets?'

'No.'

'Well, happen you should be. Where's that

flaming tea, Ivy? My stomach thinks my throat's been cut.'

Mother was in petulant mode again. Andrew Burbank, who had survived polio, medical school, smug specialists who considered house-men to be dirt, two brothers who had treated him badly, plus the relatively early death of his father, was at a loss when it came to his mother. She was neurotic and she refused all medical help. She was selfish, childish, and domineering and he was all she had left in the world for the time being.

'If anything happens to Richard or to Charles, I don't know what I shall do,' she moaned. 'Even my home has been invaded. God alone knows what will be done to it.'

Andrew stirred his coffee and glanced through the window. That flaxen-haired girl was walking away from the house with Mrs Crumpsall and a couple who were unknown to him. Was Dorothy Dyson leaving? Why did it matter? He wasn't interested in her, while no woman worth her salt would be inclined to look benignly on a cripple, whether he were a doctor or a dustbin man.

'Andrew?'

'Yes. Mother?'

'Listen to me. I shall need more wardrobes. Get those dreadful workmen to bring across some more from New Wing.'

'Yes, Mother.'

Sometimes, she felt as if Andrew were laugh-ing at her. He was not given to outward demonstrations of emotion, yet she was sure that he found her silly. She wasn't silly – she was merely unhappy. Her husband was dead, her two younger sons were absent, while this oldest boy was running about psychiatric wards in Bolton and was talking about treating shell-shocked and damaged servicemen here, at Burbank Hall.

'We are confined to a handful of rooms,' she moaned, 'and this part of the house is so damp in the winter.'

'We have twelve rooms between two of us, Mother.'

'Eleven – there's the maid. Lizzie Murphy knows nothing of silver and how to treat it. There were creases in the cloth on my breakfast tray this morning, and there is no more home-made marmalade.'

Andrew sighed. There were men being blown to pieces all over Europe. Hitler was dropping bombs just about everywhere, and Mother was offended by poor ironing. Sometimes, he wished he were an ordinary, middle-class man with an ordinary, middle-class family. She was so trying.

'You treat me with patience, Andrew, but never with love.'

He turned and looked at her. She was a spoilt product of parents who had over-indulged her and of a husband who, to compensate for his womanizing, had given in to her every whim. Her two younger and fitter sons were not here to amuse her and she had been abandoned to the mercies of her oldest, a man who had learned long ago to hide his feelings. Taunted at school by sportsmen, Andrew had taken refuge in books, which had made him into a swot. A swot who had been unable to field a cricket ball or enter a rugby scrum had been no favourite among his peers. 'Mother, I am myself and I can be no one else.'

She picked up her cup and took a sip of Earl Grey. There was not much left, and soon she might be reduced to drinking inferior teas. It was all too terrible for words. 'There was a new girl in our kitchen. Our old kitchen, that is.'

'Yes, I saw her.'

'Oh?'

'Yes, she was walking in the grounds and I met her near Chadwicke House. Pleasant enough young woman; knows a bit about Shakespeare.'

'She had a Bolton accent,' said Isobel.

'That is no crime, Mother.'

'Did I say it was a crime? I was merely remarking that she speaks with a Lancashire accent and that Shakespeare is not usually on the agenda in such households.'

Andrew placed his cup in its saucer. 'What do you know of *The Merchant of Venice*?' he asked.

Isobel picked an imaginary hair from her blouse. 'Lizzie will need to bring in some more coals,' she said. 'See if she is in the kitchen, Andrew. And ask her to bring my silk shawl.'

Smiling slightly to himself, Andrew Burbank left the room. Like many of her generation, Mother was an uneducated snob with few interests beyond her immediate environment

85

and its petty distractions. She occasionally did embroidery or knitting, but she read only glossy magazines and was as empty-headed as he imagined the average London debutante to be. The world was crazy, he was a psychiatrist and he was unsure of just about everything. Charity began at home? How could he cure a woman whose ignorance allowed her to feel absolutely perfect?

Lizzie smiled at him. 'Hello, Mr Andrew.'

He sat at the table in the new kitchen. 'She wants coal and her silk shawl,' he said.

Lizzie, who would have liked to strangle the mistress with said shawl, went off to do her bidding. She would get into the Land Army as soon as possible, but she worried about Mr Andrew. Who would look after him? In the coal store, she paused and thought about that. She was one of the few who knew how to help him. Sometimes, his bad leg ached so severely that it showed in his face. She would give him a certain footstool, would bring the most comfortable slippers, had even been known to help him off with his shoes. Few understood Mr Andrew, because he was quiet and always placed himself last. People thought he was stand-offish, but he wasn't. It had taken Lizzie only six months to learn that Andrew Burbank was a damaged soul and that the one who had done the damage was the wearer of silk shawls. Bloody woman. She needed a good hiding, and that was an indisputable fact.

After filling the scuttle, Lizzie brought the shawl and handed it to her mistress. This woman was disappointed in her oldest son. Yet Andrew was worth ten of either of his brothers. They couldn't be trusted to treat a horse well, couldn't be trusted near drink or with women. Lizzie could not leave him. The Land Army would remain a dream, because she was required here. Where else might he run for companionship? Who else would sit in a silent kitchen with that brooding young man who had little to say for himself?

'There's a draught,' complained Isobel.

'All the windows are closed, ma'am.'

'The cold air whistles straight past those old panes. But Andrew will not hear of replacements – he says they are in character with the house.' She pinned the shawl into place. 'They are certainly not in character with my rheumatism.'

Lizzie left and closed the door. Rheumatism? Let her try polio and its lifetime legacy of pain. She re-entered the kitchen. 'Do you fancy a piece of apple pie, Mr Andrew?'

'Yes, that would be appreciated.' He sat and ate pie with a servant, fully aware that she did not mind the fact that he preferred not to speak. Lizzie Murphy was a chatterbox, a joker and a hard worker. She had taken the trouble to know him and, for that, he would always be grateful.

*　　*　　*

The fire had probably been started by somebody in the senior school upstairs. A furtive cigarette taken by a teenager into a stock cupboard, its burning end thrown to the floor at the sound of a teacher's footsteps – it didn't take much to start a fire in a store full of papers and books.

The whole building was evacuated, registers were called, children accounted for. Juniors and infants lined up in the rear yard of Sunning Hill, coats abandoned inside, most personal possessions left to face the wrath of the smoke. The fire brigade was in the front yard, but officers instructed both head teachers to close the school for the day in case a second seat of fire might be discovered. Arson could not be ruled out at this stage, and the safety of several hundred children took priority.

Each class was broken down into units of ten; some parents were fetched by teachers, several mothers taking home their own children plus the offspring of those whose parents worked and whose homes were nearby. But when it came to young Dorothy Cornwell, Beryl Isherwood declared her intention to take full responsibility for her safe return to View Street. 'I want to get in there,' she told Bernard Moss quietly. 'There is something very wrong in that house – the child lives in her imagination only, and there has to be a reason for that.'

'You'd remove her if you could, wouldn't you, Beryl?'

'I would. I'd take her in a flash and give her the sort of home she deserves. She doesn't want much, poor little thing – just safety, warmth, love and a bit of freedom.' She thought for a moment. 'Here we are, all qualified, can't get near a classroom without proof of our own education, yet any fool can breed. There are some parents who don't know or deserve what they have.'

He agreed. 'Is she ill treated? Physically, I mean?'

'It's psychological damage, Bernard. Doesn't show except to people like us, though you'd think the family doctor would have picked up on something. Dorothy's a prisoner. She sees life only at school or through glass.'

'Through a glass darkly? Corinthians, isn't it?'

'Yes, it is. For some reason I shall probably never work out, Dorothy is the victim of her mother's need for control. Why, though?'

He shook his head. 'Because at some stage Molly Cornwell lost control of her own life? Because she's the embodiment of evil? Because she cannot bear to watch another human enjoying herself? It's a mystery. But yes, take Dorothy home. I shall see you tomorrow.'

Beryl Isherwood led the child across the main road and up the hill to number 33. Dorothy was tense; the closer they came to their goal, the more agitated the little girl became. 'I'll go in by myself,' she said. 'It's a doctor day.'

'A doctor day?'

'Yes. Dr Clarke comes to our house and they talk about getting me better. If the living room door's closed, I have to go upstairs until Mam and the doctor have finished talking about me.'

Beryl would not be dissuaded. It was her duty to inform all available parents about the fire in the school. Also, a seed of suspicion had just been planted in her mind, and no matter what she might be forced to endure, Beryl Isherwood required some answers.

They reached the house. Dorothy took a key from behind a loose brick and let herself in, the teacher hot on her heels.

Beryl found that she was scarcely breathing. She exhaled, concentrated on the pretty vestibule door with its colourful lights, red, blue, yellow and green glass in a beautiful leaded arrangement. The hall was neat, with a mirrored oak stand, a shoe rack, a container for umbrellas. A girlish giggle drifted under a door.

Dorothy, torn between the desire to comply with her mother's expressed wishes and the need to warn her about Miss Isherwood, broke away and threw open the door to the living room. She blinked slowly, because something very strange was happening. Mam was on the table, her feet resting high on the doctor's shoulders. The noises coming from her were strange; moans, groans and little squeals. Dr Clarke's trousers were a puddle of grey cloth round his ankles and he was moving very quickly back and forth. Mam was ill. She had to be very ill for the doctor to be acting in so strange a fashion.

The man turned, saw the child in the doorway, pulled away from the woman on the table. Dorothy saw the look of pure horror on her mother's face, watched her as she scrambled gracelessly into a sitting position. 'What have I told you?' she screamed. 'Get upstairs now.'

Beryl Isherwood entered the picture. She waited until the doctor had covered himself, her eyes fastened all the time on the woman on the table. When the man had pushed his way past Beryl and out of the house, she finally spoke. 'Dorothy, go upstairs, dear. Bring all the clothes you can carry, then go back for more. I am sure your mother will find us some bags and a suit-case.'

'Stay where you are,' screamed Molly.

Dorothy, torn between two female figures of authority, was frozen. Mam was standing up now, was straightening her skirt. 'You are not taking my child away,' she said.

Beryl nodded. 'I understand your concern perfectly, Mrs Cornwell. So, if you would kindly hear me out, I shall clarify the situation for you. You have a choice. You may choose between your daughter and your reputation. The reputation of your gentleman caller will enter the equation, of course. Dorothy will be taking a holiday and I shall be bringing her work up to scratch. This you will agree to on a voluntary basis once you have considered the alternative. Come, Dorothy. Show me where your bedroom is.'

Dorothy led her teacher upstairs. Together, they emptied wardrobe and drawers, placing all the child's garments on the bed.

'Are there any bags?' Beryl asked.

Without speaking, Dorothy went to her parents' room and returned with two battered suitcases. Beryl Isherwood filled them, then passed Dorothy a coat. 'Put that on, dear. It's quite a walk up to Willows Lane.'

91

The suitcases were placed near the front door, then Dorothy went back into the living room. Mam was sitting very still and staring into the fire. 'Go,' she said. 'Go on, get out of my sight.'

Dorothy left her home in the company of Miss Isherwood. Although she could not work out the reason, she now knew that Mam and the teacher did not like each other. Panic fluttered in her five-year-old chest, because she understood life with Mam and could not imagine living anywhere else. Did Miss Isherwood have a cane at home, would there be lessons all the time, would playing outside be forbidden? The final question she aired, and was told that she would be allowed to play as long as she did not wander too far.

'I've left my dolls' house,' she ventured.

'You may play with mine. It's one I had many, many years ago and it's precious, but you are a careful child and I know you will keep it safe.'

With that, Dorothy had to be content. She was at the mercy of adult decisions and there was no alternative – she would go where she was taken and would stay where she was put.

So began the happiest time of little Dorothy Cornwell's life. She played in the street, learned the rules of rounders, was shown how to bowl, how to hit a ball and how to catch it. She mastered double-unders, the skipping rope turning twice under her feet each time she jumped. Queenie-oh, who's got the ball was another favourite, along with hide-and-seek, hopscotch and French cricket.

She was no longer strapped into her bed. If she needed the bathroom or a glass of water, she could get up and walk about, then go back to bed when she had finished. The sleepwalking stopped. Not once did she find herself waking in another room or halfway down the stairs. When she spoke about the sleepwalking and the straps, Miss Isherwood seemed upset for a while, so Dorothy dropped the subject and did not mention it again.

Beryl Isherwood, delighted with the progress of her charge, took the child to visit her mother once every week, while Molly was issued an open invitation to call at 114 Willows Lane any weekday after school, but she never came. This disappointed Beryl, who wanted Molly Cornwell to see how a child needed to play and socialize with her peers. Dorothy blossomed, became noisy, though not disobedient, continued an avid reader and writer of stories. But now she had a day-to-day life about which she could write in her journal at school. She survived her first heavy fall, a couple of fights and a tree-climbing experiment that went horribly wrong when a bough parted company with the trunk. She was, at last, a child.

One evening in November, Dr Ian Clarke arrived. His noisy motor car rattled its way over cobbles and parked itself outside number 114. From the parlour window, Beryl watched as he plucked up courage to leave his vehicle. He had been sent, of that she felt certain, by Mrs

Cornwell. Beryl lifted the dolls' house from the best table and placed it in a corner by Mother's chair. Then she thought better of her action and put it back on the table – let him, too, see that he had entered the home of a child. She spread Dorothy's books and papers across the same table – this was a place of learning and of happiness. It was certainly not an address at which a married woman fornicating with a doctor might be found.

Dorothy was next door with two children from the local Catholic school. The little girl had been muttering darkly about making Christmas presents, because she was allowed secrets and she no longer viewed life through a glass, darkly. Briefly, Beryl smiled – she knew only too well the damage that could be achieved by three infants armed with glue and paint.

She answered the door. 'Come in.'

Round-shouldered and looking distinctly sheepish, the general practitioner of medicine entered the house. 'Where is she?' he asked without preamble.

'Next door.' He looked better in clothes, Beryl decided. There was nothing quite so ridiculous as the sight of a man with his trousers down, socks pulled up to the knees and creased shirt flap dangling. 'Come into the parlour,' she said.

He sat on the sofa, while Beryl placed herself in the chair that had once been the favourite of her beloved and now deceased mother.

'I'm here about Dorothy,' he began.

'I had gathered that.' She was determined not to help. This man was morally bankrupt and a

94

disgrace to his profession. Perfectly composed, she placed folded hands on her lap and waited.

'Her mother misses her.'

Beryl nodded.

'She wants her back home. You have no right to keep her here.'

Again, no reply was offered.

'This is tantamount to kidnap,' he pronounced.

Beryl waited for more.

'Have you nothing to say?' he blurted, his face darkening.

He would probably have given an arm and a leg for a double Scotch and soda, she mused. Did she have anything to say? Of course she did. Yet she merely waited and watched while the fool in the hole continued to dig.

'You cannot remove a child from its mother without good cause,' he blustered. 'You are going against all laws of nature, against basic moral law, against—'

'Moral law?' Her voice was dangerously quiet. 'You have the audacity to come to my house, to sit in my home and preach morality? The last time I saw you, Dr Clarke, you were engaged in an act of indecency with one of your patients. A second patient – an impressionable child – was witness to your debauchery. Disabuse yourself of the mistaken concept that a spinster knows nothing of the world. I am fully conversant with most aspects of life – and with the rules of your profession. Mr Cornwell would be interested in his wife's behaviour, I am sure.'

His teeth were bared. 'Blackmail now, is it?'

Beryl settled back in her chair.

'He knows,' he whispered. 'Tom Cornwell is impotent. He cannot father a child, because he is incapable of union with a woman. He is already fully aware that he could not possibly be Dorothy's father.'

She hid the shock very well. 'Then who is Dorothy's father?' she asked after a few seconds.

'I don't know.'

'Does Mrs Cornwell know?'

'I cannot answer that. The only information made available to me is that Molly married a man who is incapable. And, as his doctor—'

'As his doctor, you should keep quiet.'

'Yes, I should. But I can verify her statement. He is not, in the true sense of the word, a man.'

'And you are?' She stood up. Now she knew why Dorothy's father stayed in the background, why he never took her anywhere. Dorothy had but one 'owner' and that was Molly Cornwell. 'He is still her daddy,' she said. 'He remains the man who has raised her, fed her and clothed her.'

The doctor rose to his feet. 'So, you refuse to return the child to her mother?'

'I do. Now, I suggest you go back to your wife and children and become the man you pretend to be.'

'Or?'

'Or I shall drag your name and Molly Cornwell's through mud so thick that you will never be clean again.'

'That would affect the child. You have no thought for her?'

She shook her head. 'Trying to throw the ball back into my court will not be effective, believe me. I should rather see that ball in a court of law, or caught by your patients – they would leave your surgery in droves. Dorothy is already damaged by you and by her wicked, controlling viper of a so-called mother. Fornication does not qualify a person to be a parent, Dr Clarke. The act of giving birth does not make a woman into a mother. Molly Cornwell knows nothing of love. Her nature is the least generous I have ever encountered during a long career in teaching. Dorothy deserves better.'

He walked to the door, paused and turned. 'You cannot keep her for ever, you know.'

'Nothing is for ever, Dr Clarke. Now, I should be grateful if you would leave my house. Go. Right away. It is almost seven o'clock and Dorothy will be returning for her bath.'

The front door slammed behind him and she heard the coughing of his engine. With her head in her hands, she tried to compose herself, because Dorothy had to be protected. She shook from head to foot with shock, with anger and with the screams she was deliberately containing. The need to smash something – anything – was almost overwhelming.

But the teacher in her won the battle and she found herself preparing the child's bath. An innocent little girl had been enjoying herself this evening. She had begged some little 1920 calendars from Beryl and had probably been making a gift for her mother and for the man she called Daddy. There would be paint in her hair, glue on her clothes and a big smile on her face.

Dorothy entered. 'Miss Isherwood, I made a calendar for Mam and Dad. I shall make one for you tomorrow.'

'I see you've been using purple. It's on the end of your nose.'

The little girl grinned. 'It's all over Marie next door. Her mam says she looks very royal, but she has to get her hair washed. Are you all right, Miss Isherwood?'

'Of course I am. Come along, madam, off with the clothes and into the bath. Let's get you un-purpled.'

Beryl sat on a stool and watched her precious child as she played battleships with loofah and sponge. Frightened and still shaky, Beryl Isherwood recalled her own words to the doctor. Nothing lasted for ever.

FOUR

The place was coming together at a fair pace. The Burbank Wing would house staff and several equipment stores, while New Wing – which had suddenly been renamed Clarence Wing after some distant ancestor – was to be a refuge for pregnant mothers and their babies until homes were found for these bombed-out or otherwise displaced persons. A matron and deputy were still to be appointed, along with midwives and all ranks of nursing staff. Doctors would not be resident, but would come as requested to attend difficult births. A small operating theatre for surgical deliveries was nearing completion, as was a nursery for new-borns.

Chadwicke House, which was to be Andrew Burbank's pet project, would be off-limits for all in the main Hall. A wall had been erected and the house was reachable only by those with keys. Lizzie had asked her master to explain the purpose of Chadwicke House and she was now passing on his reply to Dorothy, Ivy and Elsie in the Burbank Wing kitchen.

'It's for people who are sick in the head,' she said.

Elsie was glad that she was not staying at Burbank Hall and she said as much. 'Bad enough sleeping down there in all that dark and quiet,' she said, 'without worrying about lunatics getting to us.' She and Pete were staying in Ivy's cottage. Elsie's only escape into what she termed normality was here, in her sister's domain.

'They're not lunatics,' answered Lizzie Murphy crossly. 'They're people made ill by the war.'

'Lois is ill,' said Elsie. 'But she's not daft in the head. Her burns are healing nicely, they say, so she can come and stop with me when she gets out of hospital. That'll save me talking to trees.' She nodded all the way through this speech and her sister, who was coming and going with cooking pots, joined in with the head movements.

Dorothy grinned. Elsie often held forth at length about the tedium of country life, how much she missed buses, trams, even mill chimneys. She had been heard to declare that she had been buried alive, especially after a night alone without Pete. He often roomed in town when his shifts were awkward and Elsie, never one to hide her light under a bushel, made sure that all around her knew that countryside was not for normal people. Everybody who lived up here was a few currants short of an Eccles cake, she was often heard to declare.

'Some of them are burnt – pilots and other RAF men,' Lizzie said. 'When everything has been done for the burns and there's no chance of them getting any better, the ones who can see

look in mirrors. And they don't recognize themselves. That's when they go a bit mentally ill.
Wives leave them, kiddies cry when they see this
mess and get told it's their dad, so Mr Andrew
wants to help them get back to life.'

Dorothy sat quietly. Steve had gone down in a
plane, at the back end where the gun was kept.
She had read about survivors of RAF missions
who had been burnt and, with their faces
changed beyond retrieval, perhaps they did go
mad. 'It must be a terrible thing to lose your
face,' she said after mulling it over. 'If you think
about it, your face is who you are. It's not
arms or legs, it's eyes and mouth – that's where
feelings show. It's very worthwhile work, Lizzie.
I wouldn't mind sitting with them, reading and
talking to them.'

'Neither would I,' Lizzie said. 'Better than
hanging about with the Queen of Sheba over
there.' She nodded her head in the direction
of the original part of Burbank Hall. 'This
morning, she wanted to know why we had no
oranges. I tried explaining to her that it wasn't
worth risking a fleet of merchant ships just for a
few oranges, so she said she'd have a banana
instead. I couldn't be bothered telling her that
bananas were the same amount of trouble, so I
just left her there, orangeless and bananaless.
I'd be better off trying to explain stuff to a
three-year-old. She's stupid. How can somebody
so rich be so thick?'

Quite easily, thought Andrew Burbank who
was setting up a drugs safe out in the corridor.
Money and education did not necessarily go

hand in hand. Dorothy Dyson knew some Shakespeare and appreciated the work he was undertaking. She had probably known minimal education and few privileges, but her intelligence was inbuilt. He would make use of her, he decided. Dorothy, who had experienced suffering and loss, would be able to help his patients.

Lizzie drifted out into the corridor. It was almost time for her to be summoned by her mistress's bell and she wanted to be ahead of the old dragon. 'Mr Andrew?'

He grinned at her. 'Dangerous drugs in here, Lizzie. Don't be slipping them into the Queen of Sheba's Earl Grey, because I'll probably get the blame.'

She blushed to the roots of her bright red hair. 'I'm sorry,' she mumbled.

'Don't be. You merely put into words what others think. Mother will settle down when my brothers come back. She can be a sore trial, but we have to understand that her life has been narrow and barren. Yes, she has three sons, but she knows nothing of the world out there.'

'Yes, sir.'

'Don't "sir" me, Miss Lizzie. And ask Dorothy Dyson to report to the front office in Chadwicke House today. Her function here is not yet clearly defined and I may have a post for her. Tell her two o'clock – unless she has something else planned.' He locked the safe, winked cheekily at his servant and limped away, thanking God for people like Lizzie. The Lizzie Murphys of this world made life bearable.

Lizzie ran back into the kitchen. 'I have to be quick – she'll be looking for me and a bloody banana. Dorothy – Dr Burbank wants to see you at Chadwicke House, two o'clock. I think he's got a job for you.' She dashed off to explain the lack of bananas to a woman who would probably demand grapes or peaches in their place.

Elsie and Ivy were staring at Dorothy. 'Eh,' said the former. 'She's been chosen, Ivy. If he'd seen her a few weeks back, he would have been treating her, not giving her a job. Are you blushing, Dorothy Dyson?'

'No.'

Ivy punched her sister on the arm. 'Leave her alone – she's had it rough and well you know it. You've been miserable ever since you came up here, Elsie Shipton.'

'As well I might be. It's as lively as an undertaker's parlour down yon.'

'Be glad you've got a roof,' said her sister. 'And shut up.'

Elsie shut up. It was good to see Dorothy with a bit of colour in her cheeks, grand to see her helping in the kitchen, washing dishes, doing a bit of ironing. And it looked as if that nice young doctor might have taken a shine to her – enough to give her a job in Chadwicke House. She wondered whether his interest went a bit further than the purely professional, but Dorothy wasn't ready for any of that carrying-on, not yet.

Still, there was a bob or two round here, that was for sure. And it wasn't much of a limp, really. He was a handsome fellow, good face, could do with a haircut, but nobody was perfect.

'What are you cooking up now, Elsie?'

Elsie sighed. The trouble with sisters who were close in age was that they often read each other's minds. 'Nowt,' she snapped. 'I'm just waiting for Christmas, that's all.'

*   *   *

Martha Cornwell clung to the railings outside Sunning Hill school. She hadn't caught sight of her granddaughter in a long time, and this was probably her best chance of meeting the little girl again. Martha's health, never robust, had plummeted to new depths since she had lost Dorothy.

Martha didn't like her daughter-in-law and never had. The woman had acted as if she had been doing their Tom a big favour by marrying him and Tom, who had always been a quiet lad, had just allowed himself to drift along on the tide of life. 'She needed me once,' muttered Martha under her breath, 'when she wanted to work during the war. Now look at me. Stuck here, trying to catch sight of me own grand-child.'

She remembered days in the park, a ride up to Barrow Bridge, an afternoon at Bolton Children's Library, walks along Moss Bank Way – all in the company of Dorothy, a delightful child. A delightful and oppressed child. Rumours abounded. When it came to gossip, Bolton wasn't a town, it was a big village, because chatter seemed to have wings. Dorothy had been removed. Dorothy was living up Willows Lane with her teacher. Aye, well, perhaps the teacher had realized that Molly was a bad bugger – it was time somebody noticed, that was for sure.

A bell sounded. After a couple of minutes, children whooped their way out of school, lads sparking clogs against flags, girls singing and dancing about, all happy to be free for fifteen minutes. Martha found herself smiling. Dorothy, hands on hips, was giving some other girl the rounds of the kitchen. One hand came up and a finger wagged. This was a very normal child, one who had found herself at last, one who clearly needed to be away from her mother.

'What are you doing here?'

A slight pain in Martha's chest reminded her that she was no longer a well woman. She glanced sideways and caught sight of her daughter-in-law. 'I came to see my grandchild,' she replied. 'What about you?'

Molly shrugged. 'Just passing.'

'And Dorothy doesn't live with you any more, does she?'

'None of your business.' Molly patted her belly. 'Anyway, I'm expecting.'

Martha nodded, but offered no congratulations. Molly Cornwell had lost one item and was replacing it with another – much as she might have done had a household appliance broken. A second little creature was expected and would, no doubt, be shaped to fill the void created by Dorothy's absence. Why couldn't the bloody woman make do with a dog or a cat? 'Why is Dorothy living with her teacher?' The question

105

was out and Martha, unable to retrieve it, would make no apology for its existence.

'She needed extra lessons,' was the lame response. 'Not that it's anything to do with you, of course. Time you minded your own business. You've gone a very funny colour – you want to watch that heart of yours. The doctors have told you to go carefully with your heart.'

'At least I've got one. And there's more to our Dorothy than a kid who wants extra lessons – it's love she needs.' The tiny old woman's face was grim and grey. 'You kept her under. You keep our Tom under. There's something wrong with you – you should be locked up and the key should be thrown away. You're not normal, Molly Bishop-as-was, and you never will be normal.'

Molly smiled, but her eyes remained as cold as ever. 'It's your son that's abnormal, Martha. Me? I've had to fight for everything I've got – and don't you forget it.' She marched away, leaving her mother-in-law to look at life through railings. Martha was a spectator, always would be.

When the children had gone back to class, Dorothy's grandmother gathered her courage before entering the building and forcing herself up to the headmaster's office. She was treated with politeness, given a cup of tea, then Bernard Moss went off to relieve the infant class teacher. 'I'll send her up for a few minutes, Mrs Cornwell. You hang on there – I'll sit with the class while you and Miss Isherwood take some time together.'

Beryl was pleased to see the visitor and invited her to come and have tea with Dorothy whenever she liked. 'You must come,' she insisted.

'Is she happy?' Martha asked.

'I think so.'

'We used to go out, me and Dorothy. Even then, when she were too young for school, that child had to learn to keep her secrets. I don't know what's wrong with Molly, but she's got to be in charge of everything and everybody. Did you know she tied that poor child into bed, then clouted her for wetting it? Supposed to be a sleepwalker, young Dorothy. I'd walk in my sleep if I had to live with Molly Bishop-as-was.'

Beryl sighed. 'Yes, Dorothy told me about the straps.'

Martha continued. 'My poor son doesn't get a look-in. And she's expecting again. She has to have some poor kid to boss around and lock in. Dorothy's not there any more, so she's getting a new one. Like a toy.'

Beryl managed not to shiver. If a new baby was really on the way, then it probably shared no blood with this poor old woman. According to Dr Clarke, Tom Cornwell was impotent; according to Beryl, Dr Ian Clarke might well be the father of the expected baby. 'The arrangement cannot go on for ever,' she told the grandmother.

Martha pondered a question that had haunted her for weeks. 'How did you get Dorothy away from Molly? Was it just to bring her up to scratch with her work? Because that seems a bit drastic to me.'

The dread of such questions had haunted Beryl Isherwood for weeks. The truth could not be aired, so Beryl clung to a lie that matched Molly Cornwell's. 'Dorothy was not reaching her full potential and, because she is a clever girl, I suggested this as a temporary solution. Mrs Cornwell is probably not feeling very well. Pregnancy can be hard for some women. She will need her rest.'

Martha knew that there was more to it – a lot more. The subtle cruelties of Molly would bear bad fruit and such fruit would be harvested by a teacher. The old woman decided to speak up, but to use general terms. 'Dorothy's mother is a rotten lot, Miss Isherwood. Now, I don't know the truth about what has gone on – and perhaps I am best off not knowing – but she won't have parted easily with my granddaughter.'

Beryl nodded.

'The only thing I can think of is that you know something I don't know.'

Again, the teacher inclined her head.

'So you have blackmailed her in a way, have you?'

'It might be viewed in such a light, I suppose.'

Martha's eyes filled with tears. 'I taught Dorothy all her colours, her numbers, how to read. She's clever. She needs no extra lessons. I took her out all over the place – even when she was under three years of age, she knew how to keep her mouth shut. Molly never let her out.'

'I know.'

'You let her out, don't you?'

'As long as she stays in the street, yes. She has a little friend next door – Marie – they are about the same age. I am pleased to say that Dorothy is capable of mischief – she is very much a normal, if rather intelligent child.'

'And she'll have to go back home eventually, won't she?' Martha's eyes remained damp. 'Back to prison.'

'Nothing lasts for ever, Mrs Cornwell.' She waited for a moment before asking, 'Your son – does he try to alter Dorothy's mother's behaviour?'

Martha sniffed, glanced away for a second. This was a sore subject, but it had to be faced. 'He's frightened of her. That may sound daft – a man scared of a woman – but the mad bitch – sorry – is terrifying. She has a power of some sort. You get the feeling that she's capable of anything, up to and including murder. Don't ask me why I said all that, because I haven't the slightest idea of an answer. She's powerful.'

'Insane?'

Martha inhaled audibly. 'I think so, but you'd have a heck of a job trying to prove it. She's pally with the doctor for a start – he'll say she's all right in the mental department. She's never away from the doctor's door. If she'd pushed it any further, Dorothy would have been down for the Industrial School – you know – the one at Lostock? They're talking about turning it into an open air school for delicate kiddies.' She leaned forward, lowered her tone. 'Can you understand why she has to keep Dorothy with her all the time? Why she won't let her go anywhere?'

Beryl understood why the father could not be any more forceful, but that was territory on which she dared not walk. 'Dorothy is Molly Cornwell's property – a part of her. The second child will probably be the same – an extension of herself. It is a huge flaw in the woman. I wonder sometimes why she made Dorothy suffer so badly, why she could not allow the child out of her sight.'

'Do you think it's possible, Miss Isherwood, for a person to be born bad?'

'I don't know, and that is the honest truth. I used to believe that we nurture children into shape, but this sort of behaviour is completely unknown to me. Or it was. If Molly Cornwell is insane or simply bad, I don't know what can be done about it. Dorothy wasn't beaten, wasn't bruised – this is psychological cruelty. I am at a loss, Mrs Cornwell. All I can do is keep the child away from her home for as long as possible. It's a case of one day at a time, I'm afraid.'

Martha Cornwell was afraid all the way home. She sat on the tram, hardly seeing, hardly hearing when the bell clanged. Back inside her own house, all her movements were automatic while she boiled the kettle, made tea, fed herself. There was, as she already knew, absolutely no point in trying to discuss matters with her son. When it came to the subject of Molly Bishop-as-was, he closed himself more tightly than the proverbial clam.

The poached egg and toast bypassed all taste

buds before dropping into an uninterested stomach. Martha knew that she had nowhere else to turn. Seeing the teacher had been hard enough, had caused more than its fair share of chest pains. What made Molly tick? And why did Molly's mechanism turn differently from everyone else's?

It was a mystery and Martha Cornwell died without finding an answer. With her second cup of tea spilling down her best blouse, she suffered that final heart attack and took to the grave all the unanswered questions she had nursed throughout the last five years of her life.

Beryl Isherwood read the announcement in the newspaper and was sad. She did not take little Dorothy to the funeral, though she had to break the news to the child. The only other person who knew the extent of Molly Cornwell's appalling behaviour had left the scene, and Beryl Isherwood was very much alone. Perhaps a sibling might give Dorothy a little more time and space, but, eventually, she would have to be returned to her mother and to her supposed father. As for the new baby – what chance had he or she of surviving Molly Cornwell's particular version of cruelty?

Watching Dorothy playing with her little friend one afternoon in late November, Beryl recognized the extent of her affection for the child. What would happen? Could she really expose a little girl to being branded illegitimate? Panic paid a visit to Beryl's chest and she searched her head for a possible solution. Run away? Change identities? Confuse Dorothy even further? And how might a teacher earn a living when her qualification and character references belonged to a person with another name?

It would not take long for Molly and her doctor friend to realize that Beryl would not spread the word about their behaviour. The stigma would attach to the child and she would grow up knowing that her real father was just a question mark and no more. Time was ticking away, but Beryl would make sure of one thing. This Christmas would be a special one and Dorothy would never forget it.

*　　*　　*

'Sit down, please.'

Dorothy sat. Burbank Hall was impressive, but Chadwicke House, though much smaller, was wholly Tudor and absolutely wonderful. The room in which they sat was panelled, the ceiling moulded; the table on which Andrew Burbank placed his papers had obviously been hewn from a single tree trunk – some of the axe marks remained in the timber. A one-handed clock displayed quarter-hours, and there were ornate chests, curved cupboards and, in the window, a monk's table-chair gleaming with beeswax and careful cleaning. 'Lovely,' she said.

'Most of it will have to be stored. We shall keep some things here and put them all together in locked rooms, but a great deal will go to homes where people have promised to look after special pieces for the duration. We need to take care of history.'

'Yes,' she replied, 'because a country with no history is like a man with no memory. And don't ask me who said that, because I have no idea.'

Andrew smiled. 'I understand that your husband died in the Battle of Britain.' He watched her face, saw grief passing over it, noticed that her right hand flew to a locket at her throat.

'Yes, he died, but I am not sure it was the Battle of Britain. He was a rear gunner and he got shot down.'

'So your husband is now a part of the history I guard so jealously. No one will alter Chadwicke House while I live. But, for the moment, we have people who need this space, people who suffered a similar fate to your husband's, yet survived.'

'Burnt,' she said.

'Yes.' He tapped a pencil on the blotter. 'May I call you Dorothy?'

'Please do.'

'Thank you. Dorothy. They need medical help – doctors, nurses, surgery from time to time. For that they will go into hospitals. But I shall be here to look after their minds. Their lives will never be the same as they were. These were ordinary young men with ordinary young faces and bodies, and the war has turned them into gargoyles. They did not die, but many wish they had. They lost the use of hands, some cannot see, ears have gone, hair is gone and will not grow back. In short, they are not pleasant to behold.'

She nodded.

'I want them to see pretty faces. Not all the time, but a pretty woman here and there never did any harm. I want them to enjoy the company of a nice-looking female who will not run away from them, but will stay and take the trouble to get to know them.'

Dorothy bowed her head. She hadn't thought of herself as pretty in a long time. Steve had declared her beautiful, but he had been biased. These few weeks in the country had gone some way towards restoring her looks, but she would never be the same as she once was. 'I'm ugly inside,' she surprised herself by saying. Was she opening up because he was a head doctor? 'I hate my mother.'

'I am not terribly fond of mine,' he replied. 'Oh, I would protect her against all comers to the best of my limited ability, but she is an unpleasant woman and very disappointed with my deformities.'

Dorothy lifted her head. 'You are not deformed. You've got a limp – so what?'

He raised an eyebrow. 'Then never go swimming with me, because one of my legs is withered.'

She wouldn't care about that, she told herself. He was a wonderful man who was volunteering for a very hard job. 'If you can do it, I can. No, I don't mean swimming. I mean looking at these poor men without flinching.'

He reached across the table and took both of her hands in his. 'Dorothy, it's their souls as well.'

'I understand that,' she said.

'They need help and they are all different, so there is no formula. One will respond to humour, another to feigned anger and impatience. A third may need to cry and others could well want to kick seven shades out of anything resembling a rainbow. They are individuals. There is no single solution.'

'Just the pain,' she said. 'Physical and mental.'

'And you know about the latter.' This was not a question.

'Yes.'

He released her hands and opened a folder. 'I shall leave you now for a few minutes to look at these photographs. They are not things of beauty. If you decide to help, stay here. If, when I return in ten minutes, you are gone, I shall understand perfectly, because you, too, are an individual with limits. Be kind to yourself, Dorothy.'

He closed the door and leaned against it. Oh, he had guarded himself so very well in the past. There had been gold-diggers, of course, daughters of landed families whose ambition had been to ensnare an eldest son of a moneyed line, but Andrew had been impervious to their advances. He had attended few balls, few dinners, few parties. Mother had become cross with him, had indulged in some matchmaking, had been disappointed.

Somewhere, a couple of silly gigglers were ready and waiting for Richard and Charles to return from the war, and Mother would get the grandchildren she craved. But her oldest son was unreachable. Or was he? He closed his eyes and saw Dorothy in his head, printed on his eyelids. She was a thing of beauty, was food, drink and balm for his soul. 'I could look at her for ever,' he mouthed. Even the smudges of worry beneath her eyes were lovely, human, were shadowy echoes of a wounded soul. She wasn't ready. He wasn't ready. The world wasn't ready – it was at war.

She was weeping. He turned and pressed his head against a fifteenth-century door, solid, warm and comforting. Even through this, he could hear her sobs. He remembered having trouble himself when he had first viewed those pictures. Some of them came with 'before' photographs of proud young fliers in their air force uniforms. He knew that she would remain in that room; he was one hundred per cent sure that she would take the job.

The sobbing subsided and he knew that she was awaiting his return. He liked that, would like her to be waiting only for him. But no. She was ready to do her war work and he was preparing to train her. The relationship would be professional, no more. Yet all he wanted in this moment was to dry those tears.

He looked at the hand-carved banisters, the oak panelling, an ornate linen chest just inside the door. Dorothy Dyson belonged in a place like Chadwicke House. She would not fear the nightly sounds made by a structure of such age, would not be a ghost-hunter, a damsel in distress. No. This house was a setting that might have displayed her very well had he been in a position to court her.

There was work to do. He turned the door-knob and went to face once more the most charming and beautiful woman of his acquaintance. As he walked in, she was smiling at him and he knew in that moment that he was lost. Andrew Burbank was in love and he would need all his strength to fight the urges born of such sudden and overpowering passion.

*   *   *

Stephen Dyson was a junior and Dorothy a mere infant when he came to her rescue. She had fallen in the playground and a boy in heavy clogs had tripped over her. While righting himself, the lad had clipped her ear with his clog, and mortification spread across his homely features as he watched the five-year-old's ear bleeding.

Stephen crouched beside her. 'You're all right,' he said. 'Ears bleed something awful when they get cut.' He pressed a none too clean handkerchief onto the gash. 'It'll stop when it's ready. David Thompson, you should look where you're going.' There was an unwritten rule at Sunning Hill – juniors made way for infants. Many large families passed through this school and the minding of younger siblings was taken for granted.

David Thompson said it had been an accident and was sent off to fetch help. Dorothy found herself in the arms of Stephen Dyson, whose friends were allowed to call him Steve. She

117

was placed under a canopy on a bench, handkerchief still pressed against the ear.

'You've no brothers and sisters here, have you?' he asked.

'No, there's just me.'

'You the one from View Street? Dolls' house and not allowed to play out?'

She nodded.

'Keep still, or your ear'll start off again. I once cut mine with my dad's razor – I was pretending to have a shave. I was only four at the time and there was blood everywhere – thought I was going to die. Mam says there's a lot of blood in an ear lobe. She was in a right state when she got hers pierced, I can tell you.'

Dorothy decided that she liked Steve Dyson. If she could have had a brother, she would have chosen someone just like him. He was sensible and he stopped her feeling afraid. 'He didn't mean it. That David boy. I tripped and he fell over me – it wasn't his fault.'

'I know. They've been talking about having two different playtimes – one for infants and one for us. That would be safer.'

She felt safe with him, but she didn't know how to say so. Miss Isherwood arrived. 'In the wars, Dorothy? Thank you for looking after her, Stephen. You are a good boy.'

The good boy went away and left Dorothy to the mercies of the woman who had become her mother. She walked into school, her ear was bathed and her bloody blouse was changed for one out of lost property. 'There,' said Miss

118

Isherwood. 'No harm done. I don't think you'll have a scar.'

But Dorothy wasn't listening. She was looking through the window at her saviour. He was leaping about, chasing other lads and he was very quick and strong.

'Ah.' Beryl Isherwood placed a hand on her charge's shoulder. 'Is that your hero now, Dorothy?'

'Yes,' came the prompt reply. 'I like him.'

'Good choice, Dorothy. Grammar school material, that one. Now, come and help me with the sum books. You'll see him again later.'

Molly Cornwell walked into the surgery. Her lover, who had been expecting her, leaned back in his seat and admired her as she settled in the chair at the other side of his desk. She was unbelievably beautiful, unbelievably calculating and, he suspected, pregnant again. 'Molly.'

She cast a look of near-disdain in his direction. 'I want her back,' she said baldly. 'This one can't take her place. She's our first and she'll always be our first. Get her.'

'I tried. You know I did.' It was the coldness that fascinated him. That such a frigid temperament could be heated to the point of no return in a relatively short time was a source of great pleasure to him. His wife, a sickly creature of placid nature, was a pale shadow compared to Molly. But two children? Neither belonging to her husband, a decent though impotent man who knew exactly where he stood in the eyes of his mischievous wife? Would a second baby

119

finally rupture the membrane behind which Tom Cornwell lived? 'So. You are pregnant, then?'

'Yes. It is due in June, I think.'

He stared hard at her. 'This is foolishness, Molly.'

She lifted her shoulders. It might have been foolish in his opinion, but in hers, it meant at least another thirty shillings each week. The money for Dorothy continued to be paid even though the child now lived elsewhere. 'I want her back,' she repeated.

Ian Clarke sighed. 'The teacher saw us. Dorothy saw us. A scandal of such a nature could lose me my position. Molly, I am not wealthy. This is a poor area and my patients cannot always pay my bills. How am I to keep two children as well as my own?'

'These are your own.'

'I am married.'

Molly smiled. 'You were married the first time you ravished me across this desk. You were married every time you came to my house. Nothing has changed.'

Nothing had changed. As soon as this woman walked into a room, Ian Clarke's senses were alert. She was fire and ice intermingled, she was exquisite pleasure, she was sin personified. Even now, while he worried about the future, he longed to have her again. She was an adventuress and nothing was taboo with her. 'You drive me to the brink of insanity,' he told her. There would never be another like her – and for that, the world ought to show some gratitude . . .

'How is your wife?' she asked, her tone expressionless.

'She is unwell again.'

'Will she die?'

Ian raised an eyebrow. Florence was fading slowly. She had never been particularly strong, and repeated pregnancies – not all of which had borne fruit – had rendered her weaker. But did Molly think that he would marry her in the event of Florence's death? He shivered involuntarily. He could never place Edward, Sarah and Daniel in the care of a woman such as this one. She was a raging nymphomaniac who had married a shy and incapable man. Dorothy had been born seven months later, had been 'premature', had been a good eight pounds in weight.

'Will she die?' she asked again.

'We all die. It is the only certainty.'

'Then when she does, I shall get an annulment, as my marriage was never consummated.'

He shook his head in disbelief. 'Then how will you explain Dorothy? And the one you carry now? Immaculate conceptions?'

'We shall marry,' she said. 'Then I can be in your bed every night. Divorce is no longer uncommon. Unfortunately, Tom's mother died recently, so he will need lodgings. But whatever needs to be done we shall find a way to be together, Ian.'

A dart of pure fear shot through Ian Clarke. Molly was his addiction. Some men gambled or drank. His frailty was this woman and the pleasure she gave him. She was a habit he

121

was incapable of breaking; she was sacrilege. He would get specialists to look at Florence, would find some way of keeping her alive. The thought of Molly trying to control his children in the way she had always controlled Dorothy was a terrifying one.

'This will be a son.' There was absolute certainty in her tone.

'And you will keep him shut in the house?'

Molly glanced at the ceiling, then at him. 'Dorothy is my child. When you declare your responsibility for her by marrying me, then you will have a say in her rearing. I do not want her to be led astray. I do not want her mixing with the riff-raff of Daubhill.'

He wondered anew where Molly Cornwell had acquired her idea of self. All he knew was that she had been raised by Margaret and Stuart Bishop – both now deceased – with a rod of iron. The sad fact remained that she was treating her own child in the same way and this he could not understand. 'It is almost time for me to go,' he said.

She grinned. 'Back to the better end of town, eh? Back to your private school children and your sad, grey little wife? Look what you are leaving behind.' She rose to her feet, unbuttoned her coat and revealed a stark naked and exquisite body.

He groaned. This was her power over him and she used it well. Her steely control of Dorothy was obvious and the sword she dangled over the man she had married was his impotence. She knew everyone's weaknesses and her own strengths.

There were to be no more patients tonight. She threw her coat to the floor, announced that the outer door was bolted, walked round the desk and began to undress him. He could not fight her. Molly Cornwell was a spider whose webs were so strong that no one could get out alive. She possessed an uncanny knowledge that told her how to prolong lovemaking, how to hold him back until he reached a zenith where the pleasure was almost pain. She was morphine, was the deadly poppy, the ultimate drug. He did not love her, yet he could not imagine life without her.

And, while he rolled about his surgery with a ravenously hungry mistress, his sick wife was waiting at home.

*   *   *

Dorothy's room was in the Burbank Wing next door to Ivy Crumpsall's. It was panelled, with a fancy ceiling and a four-poster bed from which the hangings had been removed. There were a few paintings left on the wall, but in one of the emptied spaces Dorothy found a hook. On this she placed her newly framed Red Cross certificate. 'I am a war worker,' she told her reflection in an old and distorted mirror. She owned a uniform with a cape and a red cross on the apron. She knew bandaging, splinting, tourniquets and slings.

'I am somebody,' she said. Mam hadn't wanted Dorothy to be anything at all. Had Mam achieved her way, Dorothy would have remained at the house in View Street, eventually becoming nurse to ageing parents. Well, she was a nurse now. She hadn't done the state examinations, but she could care for wounded at a Red Cross post, could clean and dress wounds, had been taught how to treat most conceivable trauma.

Dr Burbank wanted her to address him as Andrew. Not Dr Burbank, but Andrew. The patients would need to feel at home, he had said. Furthermore, he wanted her not to wear the uniform when the time came, so she tried it on now just to get the feel of it. It looked great. She twirled round in the cape, placed the cap on her head and had a good giggle at the vision in the mirror. She was Red Cross and, therefore, a somebody at last.

There remained just the problem of her clothes – those she had removed from View Street. They would need to be shortened, as rationing had dictated that less cloth should be used in the making of clothes, and fashion had followed the rising hemlines. She picked out two skirts and carried them down to the sewing room. Ivy had left the Singer ready for her, and Dorothy pedalled away until the garments seemed to be more or less the right length.

'Hello.'

She turned and looked at him. 'I'm going modern,' she said happily. 'What are you doing?'

He waved some papers. 'Reading notes. Our first two patients will arrive soon. We are, on the face of it, a convalescent home for servicemen. I have asked for the more troublesome cases, of course. It will be very hard toil. Let's hope we come up to scratch.'

She picked up her shortened skirts and made for the door. 'We'll do our best,' she told him. 'Miss Isherwood said that as long as we did our best, that was good enough.'

'Miss Isherwood?'

Teacakes toasted at the fire, long fork, giggles when the bread caught fire. A Victorian dolls' house, Marie next door, purple paint and glue, the best ever Christmas. 'She was once my teacher.' *She was once my teacher and she tried to save me, but my mother won. Mam always won.*

'You look sad,' he said, 'and a moment ago, you were laughing.'

'I'm not sad,' she replied. She had purpose, a reason for being alive. She was herself and he had helped to find her. 'Some of my memories are sad,' she said carefully. 'But it's the same for everyone.'

'One day, you will tell me all of it.'

Dorothy found herself grinning again. 'How can you be so sure?'

'I'm a doctor, so I know everything.'

'That must be nice,' she said as she left the room.

The skirts fitted well and, as they barely covered her knees, she would not look out of place in them. She would be just like everybody else, yet she would be somebody, would be herself.

Andrew Burbank had given her this chance and, for that, she would be in his debt for ever. He knew that she had potential, that she would be able to communicate, that she would care about the people who came here. He was a good man.

Dorothy washed herself and prepared for sleep. As ever, the last thing she removed was the locket. She kissed it and placed it on a small table next to her bed. When she woke in the morning, it would be the first thing she would see and touch. Every day began and ended with Steve, the lad who had picked her up in the playground when her ear had bled so copiously. For his sake, she would care for the men who had not died. Every one of them would be a part of Steve.

FIVE

Florence Clarke lived a tired life in a large, semi-detached house on a tree-lined avenue at the better end of town. With adequate care from her husband, she existed in an area all her own, untroubled, untouched and, for the most part of each day, ignored. A medical man, Ian did his best for her, but their physical relationship had petered out some years ago. This suited her, since his attentions had resulted in six pregnancies, only three of which had reached full term.

Yet she was becoming troubled. Because she had few interests and little of moment to occupy time and mind, she was aware of the slightest nuance in the atmosphere. A sick woman, she was easily affected by the small unhappinesses that visit households from time to time. Whenever her children were discontented, she knew it right away, could sense disquiet from the moment they entered the house. But this time, the troubled one was Ian, her husband of fourteen years. He was not a demonstrative man, had never been a victim of mood swings, was not given to ill-temper, so Florence's concern was increasing, as he was scarcely eating and had little time for their three children.

They sat now at the dining room table, she toying with her food, he not even pretending to make the effort. She had to say something and she was not gifted in the art of instigating conversation. Her husband, a busy doctor in an area of some deprivation, looked exhausted and for the first time Florence worried about his health rather than her own frailty. If Edward, Sarah and Daniel were to lose both parents, that would indeed be unthinkable.

He poured himself a third hefty measure of burgundy.

'You're not eating,' she said.

'Dyspepsia,' he replied. 'I have taken something for it – it should pass soon enough.'

His gastric difficulty had lasted several days, she thought. If he had cancer, or an ulcer on the verge of perforation, how would she manage? The children were all at the noisy stage, though Sarah was slightly quieter than the two boys. Fortunately, Ian had been exempt from war service and had continued to practise medicine on the home front, so she had not been abandoned during the four years of the Great War, but was this to be her punishment? Her own anaemia was trouble enough, but was Ian ill? He looked dreadful and more troubled than normal.

'You mustn't worry,' he said now. 'I am well enough. There has been a lot of this trouble among my patients and I must have caught it from one of them. It will be a bacterium, and goodness knows I must have fought off several of those in recent years. Were I a weakling, I would have succumbed to pulmonary tuberculosis by now.'

Florence chewed on a wafer-thin slice of ham. He was pale. His skin, never dark, had taken on a pallor that put her in mind of her own deceased father, who had been an alcoholic. 'Perhaps you are drinking too much, dear? Please – I am not accusing you of over-indulgence – God forbid – but three glasses of wine on an unlined stomach?' She shook her head.

So she was still able to count, he mused as he rose from the table. But he kept the comment inside, as he owed her enough already. Since his first meeting with Molly Bishop – now Cornwell – he had been guilty of adultery. There had been no physical contact on that initial occasion, but he had wanted the woman right from the start. Hating himself, he stood with one foot on the rug, the other on the fender. Florence would drop dead from shock if she ever learned the truth. A part of him wanted her to die, but not to be rid of her – he simply wished her not to suffer a long and lingering journey towards the edge of existence.

The doctor's wife dabbed a napkin against lips that needed no such attention, as she had eaten too little to warrant it. She rose from her seat and announced her intention to lie down for a while. The dizziness hit her as soon as she stood and she swayed slightly.

He turned. 'Show me your tongue.'

Florence obeyed. She knew it was still bright red and shiny, knew that no matter what she ate, the anaemia would remain pernicious.

'This is not good, Florence.'

'But I try. I promise you, I eat as much liver as I can, I drink milk, I have an egg every morning, vegetables—'

'This is something we cannot understand yet,' he said. 'For some, the diet works, for others . . .' He raised his shoulders. 'It has to be an element in the digestive tract. Whatever it is that attaches iron to red cells must be missing.' She was dying. She was dying and he was in trouble. He had seen a great many anaemic patients in his time, including some who had starved so that their men, who fought for jobs, could eat and continue to be strong enough to work, but this was different. The Clarkes were not poor people. Whatever ailed Florence was a part of her essence and, had he been aware of that earlier, he would not have put her through half a dozen pregnancies.

'I am sorry, Ian.'

'I know. This is not your fault.' He loved her. He loved her as he might have loved a sister and he hated himself for betraying her. 'You are a good wife and mother, my dear. It is difficult and painful for me to stand by and—'

'And watch me dying.' It had never been said before. The words seemed to hang in the air between them, because she could not reclaim them and he was not able to deny fully the fact

130

contained within those few syllables. 'You may have years yet, Florence.'

'No. I am losing sensation in my arms and legs and, sometimes, my brain goes so slowly that I scarcely remember my own name. I feel like a very old woman, my dear.'

It was oxygen starvation. A cure would come – he felt sure of that – but not quickly enough for the mother of his children. 'None of that means that death is imminent.' He tried to look at her, but could not quite manage to meet her eyes. She knew. Many of his patients knew when the end was near. He had been confronted on more than one occasion by an individual who had seemed robust, who had declared himself to be dying and who had passed on within months. Some people had that knowledge and Florence was one of them. Scarcely strong enough to bear her own weight, she was disappearing before his eyes.

'I must lie down,' she repeated before leaving the room.

Ian sat in front of a blazing fire, decanter and brandy globe by his side. The help came in, looked at her ill-received cooking, carried the remains out to the kitchen. She and her husband would dine well tonight, thought Ian. He stared at the flames, almost mesmerized by their movements. It would not be long. Florence was beginning to display the greenish hue he had seen among poor, starving women, a sure harbinger of death if the diet could not be adjusted. Her diet had been tailored to address the problem, yet she remained unable to absorb vital constituents, so the deficiency was an integral part of the poor woman. Whatever she ate, the monster would kill her sooner rather than later.

He swirled brandy around crystal, allowed the firelight to reflect in warm, amber fluid. 'I am drinking too much,' he mumbled. And he knew why. His reason wore a winter coat and nothing else. His reason lay before him across a desk, cold eyes blazing, burning his very soul. She was his disease, his Nemesis, the nadir and the zenith of his existence.

Dear God, what might be done? A second child on the way, her husband owning the knowledge that yet another bastard would take up space under his roof. 'My roof.' Ian drained the glass. He had put down the deposit, he paid half of the mortgage, while some long-dead great-aunt of the Bishop family was awarded the credit. Molly wanted him. She wanted his house, his money and his lifestyle. And Florence, that poor innocent, was making way for the predator. He tried to imagine Molly residing here among the genteel residents of tree-lined suburbia, failed completely. Molly didn't belong anywhere – she was a thing to be avoided.

What was to be done? Over and over the question played; time and again, he hit the same brick wall. He had to stop seeing her. Yet he knew that she had awarded herself so much power that she would make that impossible. She was his patient. She was eminently capable of rendering his life unbearable – would not be beyond exposing her own misdeeds if such behaviour would bring him down. He was trapped by her dedication to the achievement of her own ends, also by his own addiction. She was mercury – solid, yet fluid; she was molten lava, she was ice, she was insatiable.

He drained the glass and poured another measure. Was there anyone else in her net? Could one man alone satisfy the ravenous hunger of such a carnivore? Perhaps he was not the father of the unborn – perhaps Dorothy was not his daughter. Yet, in the absence of proof to the contrary, he had to accept responsibility for both children. To blame someone else would be heinous. Also, in her own eccentric way, Molly was a woman of rather odd principle – were she seeing anyone else, she would probably admit it, even crow about it.

Florence. Poor, ignorant Florence. She had insufficient strength to remain in an upright position for more than half an hour. Even eating took too much energy, while walking more than a few steps was becoming impossible. Specialists? How little was known about the factor, the intrinsic chemical essential to the absorption of certain nutrients. Because his wife suffered, Ian had kept up with research published by endocrinologists all over the world. As yet, the answer remained elusive.

He was drunk. The woman who now clattered dishes would see to the children when they came in from music and dance lessons. They had been denied a mother's touch for several months, while their father, too busy with his work, had recently spent his brief hours at home worrying about Molly Cornwell and the mess she had helped him create. But it was his fault. His own weakness and stupidity had led him here and he had simply drifted along like seaweed on a spring tide. His own lack of willpower sickened him; he was a drunken philanderer with a dying wife and there were no excuses for his behaviour.

Soon, Florence would make her last journey out of this house. He had hidden long enough behind the skirts of a sick wife; when she had gone, the man-eater would try to claim him for her own. He was very drunk. The brandy globe slipped from his fingers to the floor and he slept the fractured sleep of the undeniably guilty.

*   *   *

Dorothy awarded herself the title General Help. She won no pips, no stars and no medals, but she was certainly a general. She laundered, ironed, mopped, swept, dusted, groomed horses, cooked, shopped, made curtains, took notes, typed with two fingers, washed dishes and polished brasses. When Ivy complimented her on the perfection of the last item, she gave the answer that she *was* top brass, was no less than a general and that all involved should be grateful to her.

Ivy smiled down at the bread dough she was kneading. This neighbour of Elsie's had bucked up no end since coming out of the town to Bromley Cross. Dark shadows had disappeared from beneath eyes that had begun to sparkle; there was colour in her cheeks and a spring in her step. 'Have you ever ridden one before?' Ivy asked.

'No.'

'Then why do you want to go clarting about on one of them great big things? It's a long way to fall.'

'Andrew does it.' Dorothy caught the glance. 'He says I have to call him Andrew so that the convalescents will feel at home.'

'At home? In Chadwicke House? There's not one straight chimney flue in that blinking barn. Every bloody fire comes back to you – smoke, smoke and more smoke. Make sure they all have gas masks. But horse-riding? What's got into you at all?'

'It's something I've always wanted to do.'

'Oh aye? Well, I wanted to marry Rudolph Valentino, but he stood me up at the altar. Three weeks, I waited. We don't always get what we want.'

'Oh, Ivy, you sound like my mother.'

'You're not fond of her.'

'True. She's straight from hell.'

'That's a terrible thing to say.'

'It's a terrible mother to have.'

Ivy waited, but no further information was on offer. This girl was deeply hurt, had been disturbed long before the deaths of husband and child. Underneath the newborn levity and humour was a layer of sadness, and that sadness was her very foundation, the stone on which she had been built. Nothing could be done; she

would open up when she was good and ready –
if she ever became ready. Had Dorothy Dyson
put her anguish into words, the tears might
have flooded the kitchen. A change of topic was
required. 'You know what, Dorothy? I swear to
God I'll swing for that sister of mine.'

'What's she done now?'

'Yes and well you might ask. She's got a
wireless. Old Amos gets her accumulator
charged up and she has the bloody thing on at
full blast. My cottage will be rubble. It's all
Glenn Miller and some other bloke with a lot of
trumpets. She says she misses the noise, so she
has to make her own noise. She needs to get
back to town sharpish before she damages the
community. She's broken my best vase, the lock
on the back door and Sam's favourite pipe – his
Sunday one. Said she was cleaning. I think she
should have gone into demolition work. There'll
be nowt left for me to go back to once this war's
over. All there'll be is her bloody wireless.'

Andrew poked his head into the kitchen.
'General Help?'

'Yes?'

Ivy noticed the blush. Dorothy probably
didn't know she was blushing, probably didn't
realize that she was being courted, but the
elemental knowledge was there all the same.
She reacted to him, but never questioned her
reactions. It was an ill wind that brought no
good with it, Ivy thought. The war had hurt this
girl and pain had shocked her back to life.
Dorothy Dyson had been put on the road to
salvation by bombardment.

In the corridor, Dorothy awaited further instructions. She was everybody's right arm and she liked it.

'Are you any good with babies?' he asked.

'I don't know. I never had much to do with them – I'm an only child.'

'They're a bit stuck in New Wing – I mean Clarence Wing. Could you sit in the nursery for half an hour?' He paused. 'Or would that be too painful?'

She bit her lip before replying with a question of her own. 'Who told you?'

'Ivy.'

'Ah. Well, what's done can't be undone.' She touched the locket at her throat. 'Perhaps I'm not meant to be a mother. I've never had a proper mother myself, so I'd have to learn the rudiments.'

'She's still alive, I understand.'

'Yes, very much so.'

He glanced away from her. 'If you ever want to talk about things – about your life and how you feel – I shall be only too willing to help. I manage to reach the root of most people's problems. Not all people, of course. My job's a grey area. But I use hypnosis – which makes me a quack in the opinion of some people. All I can say is that it sometimes works. Think about it.'

He was living life in short sentences again. Dorothy smiled inwardly, because this new friend spoke either in tomes or in brief bursts – no middle ground. He was a prisoner. There were no bars on his window and no straps on his bed, but his mother held all his emotional

137

keys. With two younger brothers abroad, Andrew was his mother's sole support. He carried the role with apparent ease, yet she sensed that it bothered him.

'I'm not ready yet,' she said, 'but I'll give you my diaries from when I was a child.' God – why had she said that? 'Only I don't want to talk about any of it till – till some other time.' She trusted him; she scarcely knew him, yet she was offering him her childhood in writing. 'It may take me a while to actually talk about things.'

'That I understand. But I am here, General, so make use of me when you are ready. Or allow me to prepare you.' When he was with her, his leg ached with a vengeance, as if trying to remind him that he was not whole, that he should not place himself in the vicinity of so perfect a creature. The shell was beautiful, he reminded himself, but inside, Dorothy was damaged. The crippling of this young woman had been mental, not physical. He could and would mend her.

'How much do you know already?' she asked.

'Not a great deal. That you were unhappy. That your mother was the primary factor. That you suffered. That your husband was shot down and the child was lost.'

'Yes.'

'So I should not ask you to help in New Wing?'

'Clarence Wing,' she reminded him. 'I'm here to do my bit of war work. If my bit of war work involves babies, then so be it.' She left him and crossed the garden. The only way to reach Clarence Wing was via this route, as the original part of the house remained the domain of Andrew and Isobel, which fact left Clarence and Burbank as two separate buildings.

Dorothy was completely unprepared for what she found. He was six weeks old and an orphan. His mother, hit by falling masonry, had lived long enough only to allow this child to be taken from her by surgical means. He was tiny, premature, unhappy about feeding and had a tube up his nose. Into this, Dorothy passed small amounts of milk. Then she sat with him, sang to him and rocked him to sleep. He wasn't much bigger than her own dead baby had been. This child might have fitted into a shoebox with room to spare, she mused.

The matron, who was busy with more pressing matters, popped in from time to time and was satisfied that Dorothy was sensible enough to keep an eye on little Matthew Taylor.

From the garden, a wise young doctor, too, was watching. She had lost a baby and was holding a baby. It was no cure, but it was a remedial step in the right direction. Andrew Burbank intended to do all he could to help with the mending of Dorothy Dyson – also known as General Help. Encouragement had not been on her parents' menu, and he intended to provide her with a feast of it.

*   *   *

The fair was in town. Dorothy rolled pennies, threw darts at playing cards, tried hoop-la and

139

shying hard wooden balls at coconuts. She won sixpence, a small teddy bear and a coconut. It was all magic. Beryl led the child past a large, hot brazier and into a tent where black peas were served with vinegar in thick, white cups. For afters, a toffee apple – her first – was consumed.

At the highest point of the big wheel, she sat with her teacher and looked at the fairground below. It was a special moment, a top of the world instant, and Dorothy pulled it into her memory for future reference. This could not last; nothing as good as this could possibly endure. Mam was close by and would pounce sooner or later.

'Dorothy?'

'Yes, Miss Isherwood?'

'Why are you crying?'

'I didn't know I was.'

'Perhaps it's the cold air?'

'Yes.'

It wasn't the cold air at all – Beryl knew that. The child was testing her wings for the first time in her life, was being entertained, was having fun. The word 'fun' seemed not to be in any dictionary owned by the Cornwell household. Everything was new for Dorothy – the children next door, street games, the fair – she was seeing life at last. Beryl didn't know what to do about Christmas, though. A child should be with her parents, yet it was going to be difficult, because Molly Cornwell would lock Dorothy in.

As if reading the thoughts of her guardian, the little girl spoke. 'Don't send me back. She'll keep me. I'll get strapped into bed to stop me sleepwalking and I won't be able to play out in the street.'

Beryl found herself wishing that Molly Cornwell would walk into the path of a tram. The father, who was about as powerful as a small glass of water, did not enter Beryl's mind. The evildoer was Molly Cornwell and the thought of sending Dorothy back to her turned the teacher's stomach. Perhaps it was the black peas, she thought as she helped Dorothy out of the big wheel seat. 'Let's go home,' she said.

But Dorothy had her eye on just one more fair attraction. 'Mam says they're all gypsies and not to be trusted because they wander about and steal. But please, Miss Isherwood. Only this one last thing. I want to know if dreams really do come true.'

Beryl gave in. But she went in with the child, because this was the almost exclusively adult domain of fortune telling. A grubby woman in a dirty turban sat at a table whose surface was covered by a bright red cloth and the tricks of the trade – tarot cards, a crystal ball and ordinary playing cards. 'I don't get much call to do kiddies,' she said. Dark eyes fixed themselves on Dorothy. 'Cross my palm with silver,' she ordered. Dorothy took a florin from Beryl and gave it to the woman.

'Sit.'

Dorothy sat.

The woman took Dorothy's hands and studied them. 'Riches,' she declared. 'Riches and a good, long life. Don't be held back. Children. Two, at

141

least – and one other unclear. That's a child you will look after, but it may not be your own.' She looked hard into the girl's eyes. 'Don't be held back,' she repeated. 'It's all here. Three loves. You'll have the love of three men. She'll try to stop you.'

Beryl shivered – the night was turning very cold.

The gypsy looked up at the woman. 'It's not you holding her back. You're trying to move her on, but she has to come into her own.' She smiled at Dorothy, displaying gaps between darkened teeth. 'The love of three good men,' she repeated. 'Three men, two or three children and another child will come to you, Sleeping Beauty.'

Dorothy gasped audibly. That was her favourite among all the stories she had read and heard. 'Does the wicked witch win?' she whispered.

'No, she will taste her own bitterness. Heed me, child. There is money here and it will find you. Use it well.'

Beryl Isherwood forced herself not to sigh. A five-year-old girl having her fortune told? This was nonsense. But Dorothy was hanging on to every word, just as she had always swallowed each fairy tale recounted at school. 'Come along,' Beryl said.

'Wait.' The gypsy held up her hand. 'There are lies on paper.' She was addressing Beryl now. 'Documents. Lies.'

A chill travelled the length of Beryl's spine. It was foolishness, it had to be foolishness, but how

142

had this crone come to imply that Dorothy's birth certificate was not the whole truth?

'This little girl is not related to you, but you are her minder for now, I take it?'

'Yes.'

'She has a long, hard road. It will divide and she will have choices. But that will all come when she is older.'

This truth was applicable to every human, thought the teacher. No young person made decisions – the whole world was organized so that mothers, fathers and educators were in charge until children came of age.

'Even then, she will try to stop her. You know who I mean? A woman? Even when this little one is grown, there will be traps waiting.'

Beryl decided that enough was enough. 'Now, Dorothy, come along. It is late and we should be going home.'

Dorothy stared at the old woman. 'Will I be happy?'

Again, the terrible teeth displayed themselves. 'Yes, you will. In the end, you will be very happy.'

But Dorothy, who was only five, knew that 'happily ever after' was for grown-ups and that she had a long road to go. She boarded a tram with the only woman who had ever shown her love. It was a fair way up the brew to Willows Lane. It was a million miles to 'happily ever after'.

Molly Cornwell lingered outside the house, a scrap of paper clutched in her left hand. It was

143

an item she had torn from the *Bolton Evening News* and, small though it was, it represented the largest weapon she had ever owned – except for her beauty, she supposed. What use was beauty if a woman could not employ it to her own advantage? What use was a newspaper clipping? It was beyond price. She smiled. She was about to enter his abode while he was at surgery and, with any luck, she would be an established part of the household before he even knew about it. Perhaps he should know; perhaps she should find a way of making sure that he knew she was applying for the position.

She walked up the path and knocked at the door. A woman answered. She had brown hair, a brown skirt, brown shoes and a beige apron. 'Yes?'

'Is Mrs Clarke in, please? I've come about the position of home help.'

The retiring domestic servant swept her eyes over Molly. She looked like someone prepared for a tea-dance, not for tending a sick woman, three children, a busy doctor and a house too big for its own good.

Molly repaid the compliment. What a frump the servant was – enough to make any ailing patient worse. 'Is it all right if I come in?' She was admitted, then led through to a very nice parlour where Florence Clarke lay on a day bed.

'This woman wants the job.' There was a decided edge to the incumbent's tone. She sniffed and left the arena. She could not bring herself to imagine the invader performing the more intimate tasks required by Florence Clarke.

Molly dragged a chair and placed it next to Florence's couch. 'Now,' she began, 'what can I do for you, Mrs Clarke? General housework, a bit of nursing, some cooking?' Molly could see that the woman was extremely ill. Any prettiness she might have enjoyed had been eradicated by grey-green pallor and the atrophy of muscle. She was almost skeletal, too, and could not possibly linger on earth for more than a few months. So, this was his wife. No wonder he had looked elsewhere for a bit of pleasure.

Florence, further wearied by the imminent exit of her long-term employee, merely nodded. All she needed was someone capable, willing and available. 'Mrs Morris is leaving me,' she sighed. 'After two years.' She focused on the applicant. 'You do own suitable clothing? Of course, there is an allowance made for necessities—'

'That is no problem,' said Molly. 'I have plenty of work clothes at home. Tell me – what are your particular needs?'

While Florence droned and gasped her way through diet, personal hygiene and the needs of her children, Molly investigated the room, her eyes lighting on pictures, ornaments, rugs and a very valuable clock. He lived well, it seemed. There was nothing reminiscent of the back streets of Bolton in this house. She sniffed quietly. Unless she was very much mistaken, the rug was silk and the glassware cabinet contained a great deal of high-grade lead crystal. 'Pardon?' She sensed a question hanging in the air.

'I asked whether you have children.'

'Just the one girl.' Molly placed a hand on her flat belly. Nothing showed, not yet. And this unborn baby shared blood with the offspring of the woman on the couch. 'She is at school and I can get her minded if need be. I am clean, quick and I can cook.'

Florence could not afford to be choosy. Mrs Morris, whose elderly husband had suffered a stroke, would be leaving almost immediately and the gap needed to be bridged. 'Shall we say a month's trial? What is your name?'

Molly picked up a pencil and a piece of paper from a small table near the head of the day bed. 'Here, I shall write it down for you with my address. I already know your husband, because I am one of his patients.' Oh, yes. Let him explode when he saw the name, let him fight against her month's trial. He dared say nothing and would do nothing. She placed the paper within reach of the sick woman, then rested a gentle hand on her arm. 'I am very sorry that you are so ill, Mrs Clarke. If you give me the job after a month's trial, I'll make sure you don't regret it.'

Florence picked up her porcelain bell.

'No, no,' insisted Molly. 'Don't disturb Mrs Morris. I can find my way to the door without any help.'

'Thank you.'

'When shall I start?'

'Monday, please. Mrs Morris will show you your duties.'

Molly left the room. Her duties? Her duties, indeed? Florence Clarke had a marriage certificate and three children of his, but Molly had two. Well – one and a half. The hallway had a floor of polished parquet with a blue runner marking the length of it. There were some good paintings on the walls with fancy, gilded frames. A grandfather clock sang the hour. It was a nice house and she wanted it.

'They'll need help Christmas Day, you know.'

Molly swivelled and looked at Mrs Morris. 'I can see that for myself, thank you. Mrs Clarke is clearly a very sick woman.'

Patience Morris, a good Methodist with a no-nonsense approach to life, was not keen on the new woman. She had listened from the hall and knew full well that a month's trial had been offered. 'I'll see you on Monday, then. Start at a quarter to eight with breakfasts and we'll take it from there.'

She closed the door when Molly had left, then returned to her baking. 'I wish I could stay,' she muttered as she pounded dough. But her husband needed her and she knew where her duty lay. That madam who would be starting next week probably owned no sense of duty to anyone. Patience feared for Mrs Clarke, but the situation could not be remedied. She covered her bread mixture with a cloth of boiled muslin, set the kettle on the stove and wondered how she could tempt the lady of the house to eat.

She decided to talk to Dr Clarke at the earliest

opportunity. There was something about the woman who had been interviewed today, a coldness, an absence of expression, a lack of humanity in the eyes. Mrs Clarke needed kindness and the very virtue after which Patience had been named. The children, too, required a mother figure, as their own female parent was becoming too exhausted to fill the role.

Florence was trying to cough again. Patience rushed into the parlour and helped her mistress sit up. The poor lady was fast becoming too weak to clear her own airways and pneumonia was probably threatening to sign the death certificate. The sputum mug remained as dry as a bone and Florence fell back onto her pillows.

'I wish I could cough for you,' said Patience. The trollop who had visited today would not care a jot, might even leave Mrs Clarke to drown in her own fluids. But Patience's daughter could not continue to look after the disabled man at home – and home was where charity began. There were no choices for Patience. She returned to the kitchen and carried on with her duties, all the time praying that she might be wrong about the new woman. Appearances could be deceptive, she told herself repeatedly. Perhaps the new woman would settle down and do a good job. And perhaps pigs would fly . . .

*   *   *

Isobel Burbank was far from happy. She had even taken to walking outside, fur coat wrapped tightly against the weather, gloved hands clutching each other for comfort while she kept an eye on Andrew. He was teaching that girl to ride. At the beginning, Isobel had tried to ignore the situation. It would pass, she had told herself. Andrew was a doctor, and his interest in the girl was purely professional. But there was little of purity or of professionalism in his expression when he was in the company of Dorothy Dyson. This had to be stopped.

When the two riders had returned to the stables, Isobel went back into the house. Lizzie Murphy had disappeared to take lunch in the Burbank Wing kitchen, and the Tudor part of Burbank Hall was empty except for the mistress of the house. Quickly, she doffed her outer garments and went into her son's small study. He had let slip the odd comment about Dorothy's mother and Isobel intended to find out about the woman. She would feign concern for Dorothy and would try to make an ally of her mother.

It was a long list – nurses, midwives, orderlies, welfare officer, on-call doctors, burns units from which recovering airmen would soon arrive. Her eyes raked through the pages until she found the name and address of Dorothy Dyson's next of kin. Andrew was not a fan of Dorothy Dyson's mother, who had done all in her power, it seemed, to hold on to her daughter. Isobel committed the information to memory, then left the office exactly as she had found it, with everything back in its rightful place and— She stopped in the doorway. Something had registered almost unbidden and she turned, went back to the desk, picked up a sheet of paper.

Sleepwalking probably due to anxiety caused by forced containment.

Nightmares? Are these still occurring?

Patient has an above average IQ and is perceptive.

Mother obsessive and controlling.

Mother beautiful in her time – jealous of Dorothy's looks?

Father non-communicative.

Dorothy may respond to hypnosis and regression.

She has bonded with baby in Clarence Wing.

She enjoys riding.

Physical health much improved.

Isobel read the notes twice, her ears straining for the slightest warning of her son's return. This was his private domain and she was reading notes whose contents were meant to remain confidential. At the bottom of the page was a small doodle. It was plain that he had sat here with the list, had been thinking about Dorothy Dyson. He had drawn a heart with an arrow through it. She shook her head in near disbelief. Surely a doctor should know better than to display his feelings in such a way?

She opened a drawer, found a small pile of exercise books, opened one and saw the name *Dorothy Cornwell* printed at the top. Greedy eyes scanned several pages penned by the hand of a child. It was enough for Isobel. The girl had been oppressed by her mother and probably wanted to stay well away from her even now. The mother was the answer; the mother would get the girl away from Andrew. How? Isobel had no idea, but she was armed, at least.

A door slammed. She replaced the exercise book, walked out of the study and went to meet her son. He was warming his hands at the drawing room fire.

'Rather cold for riding, isn't it?' she asked.

'Invigorating,' came the reply. She was leading up to something and he knew exactly what it was. He waited.

'And how is Mrs Dyson progressing?'

'Well enough,' he said. 'She has no fear of animals, which is always a bonus.' His mother was deficient in the area of formal education, but her antennae worked well enough when it came to the social arrangements of her three sons. Now, she feared Dorothy. Dorothy was not of the correct calibre, because she wore no pearls and spoke without an edge of cut glass in her words. She was not of the right class; was not a suitable candidate for entry into the Burbank family.

'You spend a lot of time in her company.' The tone was accusatory.

'Mother, there is nothing going on.' He decided to address the problem head-on, because he was becoming sick and tired of the constant hints and queries. 'She is not interested in me.' He looked into his mother's eyes. 'Why should she be? She is a beautiful young woman who could have her pick of men from just about anywhere. I am a cripple.'

She shivered. 'I wish you would not use that word.'

'Why? Mother, I am sorry that I was careless enough to contract poliomyelitis, but here is what I am. I am a man with a frozen shoulder and a shrivelled leg.'

'You are also a man of some standing.'

He nodded. 'Indeed I am – as long as I depend on the good leg.'

'You are being deliberately obtuse. You know what I mean. We are an old family with a faultless pedigree and you are a doctor. Your papers on the treatment of trauma were extremely well received.'

He smiled. She had noticed him only because his two younger and fitter brothers were not around to amuse her. Now, she feared that her firstborn would fasten himself to a female from the lower orders. 'If Dorothy Dyson would have me, I would marry her tomorrow,' he said quietly. 'It is time for some new blood. Remember, Mother dear, that the best horse is one of mixed parentage – a little bit of the Arab, a pint or two of Irish blood. The women from my so-called level of society do not hold my interest. I have no wish to spend my life with someone who knows all about fashion and nothing about anything else.'

He was describing her; he was criticizing his own mother.

He continued. 'She is well read, decent and worthy. She comes not with an empty silver spoon, but with a cartload of common sense. I have never enjoyed myself as much as I do now when teaching her to ride. She is hungry not for riches, but for learning.'

Isobel stared hard at him. He was head over heels in love with a servant he scarcely knew. The source of the strength he had suddenly acquired was a blond-haired girl with an affection for horses and little else to recommend her. Or was it? Had the very disease that had almost claimed his life given him time and space in which to think? All three boys had enjoyed a university education, though the other two, solicitors with decent firms that were attached to reputable chambers, lived as near-gentlemen. This son alone had the ambition, the tenacity and the brains to get right to the top of his profession. 'You are a very handsome man,' she told him. He was. He was blessed with a well-defined face, wonderful eyes and luxuriant hair that always seemed in need of cutting.

'Eye of the beholder, Mother. You are prejudiced.'

'She is wrong for you, Andrew.'

'She would not look at me, Mother.' After declaring his intention to change, he left the room.

Isobel, frustrated almost to the point of anger, snatched up an embroidery frame with the intention of attacking work she had scarcely started. She threaded the needle, but her fingers, suddenly unbiddable, were in no mood for dexterity. After throwing down the piece, she rose to her feet and stared out at a landscape that seemed bleak. He had to be stopped. He was not a man to be easily stopped. She needed to be clever.

The mother. Isobel needed to see the mother,

would bring her here, would do all in her power to separate her son from Dorothy Dyson. The girl's maiden name – according to the list – had been Cornwell. So Isobel needed a Mrs Cornwell of 33, View Street, Bolton. That mother had locked a child in a room, had tied her to a bed. She might prove useful.

Two robins clashed mid-air, twin bundles of anger whose tempers were echoed in their vibrant display of chest plumage. Fierce little creatures, they were. Could she be fierce? Could she find the energy required? Could she face the wrath of Dr Andrew Burbank, a man whose very profession allowed him glimpses of people's inner mechanisms? One of the robins flew off, while the other, clearly routed, fluttered into a nearby low-hanging branch. It was a cruel world.

There had to be a way. She recalled conversations she had heard between her two younger sons, snatches referring to the recovery of evidence and the exploration of circumstances described as mitigating. There were little men employed by chambers, people who went about digging and rooting about in the seamier details of life. She needed one of those nameless little men; she needed to get to chambers. She needed a fierce yet anonymous little fighter with no scarlet feathers on display.

Manchester. Andrew received extra petrol, as he was employed by several hospitals in the northwest. Wool. Yes, wool was the answer. She would go with him to Manchester on the premise that she had heard a rumour about cheap wool, would declare her intention to begin a knitting circle in nearby villages. Why not? The acreage was swamped by Land Army girls, so why not donate more than vegetables to the war effort? The prospect of knitting socks for soldiers was not an attractive one, yet the instigation of such activity could well empower her in this very important arena. All was fair in love and war, and Isobel would attack both simultaneously.

Lizzie Murphy returned. 'Do you want your dinner now, Mrs Burbank?'

'Lunch,' sighed Isobel.

'Lunch,' repeated the maid.

'Yes, please. My son will be back shortly – he is changing.'

Lizzie closed the door and made off in the direction of the newly installed kitchen. He was changing, all right. Mr Andrew had taken quite a fancy to Dorothy Dyson. As she prepared the meal, Lizzie hummed to herself. Unless she was very much mistaken, the old bat would be getting her comeuppance in the not too distant future.

'Lizzie?'

She turned and grinned at him.

'I shall take lunch in my study.' He left.

Lizzie, still humming, prepared two trays. Madam was not going to be pleased, but Lizzie Murphy was absolutely delighted.

SIX

He was livid. He paced up and down the living room until even Molly began to experience a few brief stabs of fear. She had expected him to be angry; she had not envisaged a scene such as this one. It was plain that he failed to see the sense in what she was doing. It was simple enough – she would get to know his sons and his daughter so that the passage from mistress to wife might prove smooth. Why couldn't he listen? Why wouldn't he accept that she was taking the job? Clearly, his wife was at death's door and someone would have to step into the breach, but the man seemed beyond reason.

'Your own little girl had to be taken away from you,' he yelled. 'You squashed her every thought and deed, ridiculed her, locked her in, left her lonely and unable to meet her peers. You have absolutely no right to walk into my house. As for my children – they need better care than you are capable of giving.'

She glanced at the party wall and hoped that the woman next door had gone out to do her usual Thursday stint of shopping at Bolton market. He was making enough noise to warrant a reading of the Riot Act.

'You are not normal,' he said, his tone quieter now. His face was no more than a few inches from hers. 'You controlled poor Dorothy until the child had no sense of her own self-worth. You made her less than an animal. Why fasten her into bed then complain when the poor child wets the mattress?'

'Training,' she snapped. 'It helped her to develop bladder control. And she is a sleep-walker, as you well know.'

'Bladder control? She could also have developed kidney trouble,' he answered smartly. 'You wouldn't allow her to play in the street, wouldn't take her anywhere further than the local shops – what sort of life is that for a small child? And now you have the temerity to arrive at my door, to speak to my dying wife and expect to be allowed to interfere in the raising of my children? No! It will not be possible. You are completely unsuited to the task and we both know it. You do one thing well, Molly. One thing and one thing only. Beyond that, you are useless. And I am sure that you can't cater for Florence's needs.'

Molly sat at the table and poured tea, the only outward sign of discomfort showing in a slight tremor as she picked up the teapot. He needed her. He loved her. She would win this battle, no matter what weapons she might be forced to employ. It would be best if she stopped listening to him, as he was making no sense and no progress towards sense. Like a two-year-old in a tantrum, he needed to be ignored until the over-played storm had passed.

'I shall tell Florence how you have inflicted pain and misery on your own child. When she hears about you, she will change her mind instantly. You will not cross my threshold again. Do you hear me? Molly? Are you listening?'

She bit into a biscuit and hoped it would not choke her. Had she gone too far? 'I want to help you,' she said, honey dripping from the words. 'Mrs Morris is leaving and you need someone. Your wife can't carry on without help, as well you know. She's very weak.'

'You want to be there when Florence dies so that you can move in and take her place. You will never take her place. Molly, you are a whore with just one client. I have paid for this house, for Dorothy's living expenses, for some of the furniture. Above all, I have paid for my sins.'

Molly finished her biscuit before speaking again. 'And I have one child of yours—'

'You do not. Her teacher has her.'

In spite of the interruption, she glided on seamlessly. 'And another child of yours in my womb. I did not make this child by myself, Ian Clarke. I did not make Dorothy by myself, either. And I saw no star and was visited by no shepherds and no kings when I pushed her out into the world. You have responsibilities. I shall care for your wife and for your legitimate children well enough. If you forbid me to take the job, I may be forced to reconsider my options. Just settle down and stop making such a fool of yourself – you are beginning to look and sound ridiculous. If you were a child, you'd be having your legs slapped.'

Weary after a hard morning's work, he sank into the chair opposite hers. Self-loathing debilitated him even further and he wondered, not for the first time, how and why this creature always held the highest trump cards. He was the one with the education, yet she bested him repeatedly. Hating her was becoming easy. Yet he wanted her even now. 'Your options?' he asked. 'Which options are those?'

Molly raised her shoulders. 'Perhaps your children should be told that they have a half-sister already and that we expect another little stranger in a few months.'

'It would kill Florence.'

'Yes,' she said, 'it probably would.'

'You are evil.'

Again, she shrugged. 'I am taking care of my own interests. And Dorothy's, too. When your wife is dead, you will have no reason not to marry me. You could adopt Dorothy and no more would need to be said about the matter.'

'And your husband?'

'Is impotent. That can be proved.' Her hands curled into fists. She wanted the better end of society, the pretty rugs, the car and the fur coats. She wanted a big garden, the fancy clocks, the pictures in gilded frames. She wanted decency, money, a chance to meet a better class of neighbour. It didn't matter what needed to be done – she would achieve her goals through this man, because he was in debt to her.

'So you would declare Tom to be less than a man. How would you explain Dorothy?'

She half smiled. 'We shall leave Bolton and start again somewhere else. My marriage will be annulled quietly, then we can get on with our life together.' Her fingers were working to undo the buttons of her blouse and she was licking her lips as if in anticipation of a feast.

Ian jumped up. 'No,' he said. 'Don't start that business now.' She knew how to manage him and he loathed her for it.

She continued to undress. He could not resist her and she knew it. Like many highly intelligent men, he was victim of his own desires and nothing on earth would change him. 'Come here,' she whispered.

'Molly, this has to stop.'

'You would starve without me and well you know it. I am the only person who allows you to be yourself. Imagine.' She rose and threw away her garments. 'Imagine coming home to me every night, Ian. Imagine me in your bed.' She knew why his need had become more urgent of late, had inhaled the scent of impending death that surrounded his wife. He wanted life, love, excitement. With the pins removed from her hair, she shook her head and allowed flaxen waves to tumble to her shoulders. She was beautiful and she knew it. Her chin raised itself and she tapped an impatient foot on the ground.

Ian groaned. What the hell was he going to do? Florence, a good, honest wife and mother, was losing her fight for life. No matter what was done for her now, the poor woman would be dead within months. And here stood perfection and evil all in the one glorious, baleful package, body supple and toned, teeth even, eyes . . . The eyes carried no expression, yet they sparkled with vitality. 'I don't want you to hurt her or to damage my children,' he mumbled, his voice thickened by desire.

'I will be good,' she promised.

'You don't know how to be good.'

'Then come here and allow me to be bad.'

So it happened again and he knew that he was powerless in her company. She was inventive, uninhibited and an expert in her chosen field. There were no taboos. Molly knew every inch of him and allowed him the same freedom with her body. The sensations she inflicted upon him were almost painful and he gave himself up to them, lived only for the perfect moments in which he revelled. She had won. She would always win until he found the backbone to place himself and his family beyond her reach. But she was right – he could not imagine life without the pleasure she brought to him. For over six years, this female had owned him. He could not deny her, could not stop the inevitable.

When it was over, she lay on the rug and allowed firelight to play on her curves. Hating himself, he dressed and looked down at her. She had turned him into something less than decent and he did not know how to escape, because she had been made for this. Marry her? Never.

'Do you love me?' she asked.

'No,' he replied immediately. 'You are my tobacco, my alcohol and my cocaine. You are bad for me, but I am addicted. It is impossible to love you, because you display no affection for anyone. There is a space in you where the soul should be. You are not human.'

Molly blinked. 'Of course I am human.'

'Physically, yes. But inside, in your mind and heart, you are completely alien. You don't love Tom, you don't love Dorothy and you certainly don't love me. You love you, Molly. Just you. You have neither sympathy nor empathy in your constitution. There is just self and that self will do anything to achieve its ends. You want a larger house, a car, nice furniture. You want to be married to a doctor, because you consider a doctor to be worthy of you. We have nothing in common.'

She stood up. 'We have what we just did together.'

'Yes.'

'Is that not enough?'

'No.' He fastened his waistcoat. 'No, Molly. Sexual activity without love turns us into dogs. We feel the urge, we join, we separate. Humanity demands a meeting of minds between two people. When did we last have a conversation? With a marriage partner, there are things to discuss – there's a social life, the running of a household—'

'You have servants for all that.'

Ian picked up his hat. 'I cannot discuss with a servant my daughter's progress in school, my son's chances of a place at Oxford. Children come first, you see. That is how mankind is designed – to protect and improve its young. You are the exception. Molly, you are singing from a hymn sheet all your own. I need only look at your daughter, at how you have used and abused that child, to know that you are not right in your head. You are an over-sexed psychopath.'

She studied him. 'What happens now?' she asked.

Ian shook his head, planted hands deep inside pockets. 'What happens now is that I go home to my family, while yours is kept away from you for safety's sake. As for the rest of it, I shall leave that entirely up to you. I cannot stop you, cannot tie your wicked tongue, cannot make you normal. If there is a single shred of decency in you, you will fail to arrive for work on Monday morning.' He turned on his heel, left the room and marched out of the house.

When the front door slammed, Molly shivered. The room was warm to the point of stuffiness, yet her bones felt icy. 'He will never resist me,' she told the beauty in the overmantel mirror. From childhood, she had been perfect. While still in her early teens, she had used her sexuality for her own ends, had reduced grown men to tears after seducing them. With the help of those older men, she had studied her craft, had investigated all possibilities, had conquered males in their dozens. But now, there was just this one, this man – and she wanted him, would go to the ends of the earth to claim him, should that necessity arise.

Tom Cornwell? She smiled. From him, she had expected and received everything else – a steady income, silent adoration, obedience. Tom was her eunuch, her servant and her bread-winner. But he was no longer enough; he had never been enough. He knew she went else-where for the comforts he was unable to provide. Yet there was one thing he did not know. In so far as she was capable of committing herself to anyone, Molly Cornwell was the prop-erty of Dr Ian Clarke. He pleased her as no one else had ever done; he made life liveable, even pleasurable. There would never be another like him. She was convinced that she loved him and could not survive without him. As for him – she could twist him round her little finger.

So, what should she do now? The job at the house was hers for the taking, but she wished not to anger him further. 'I shall go,' she said aloud. 'I shall go and make myself indispensable to Florence Clarke. She will believe that an angel has come down to help her through her final weeks on earth.' The job would be done to a standard approaching perfection. Molly would show her lover that she was good for more than one thing.

What would an angel wear? A domestic angel wore brown and beige, it seemed, and she was not prepared to travel down that road. She was blonde, she was beautiful and she would wear black and white. If she hurried, the market would still be in full swing and there would be pretty aprons in pristine white – she could sew on a little bit of lace, perhaps. With her hair scraped back into a sensible pleat, she would look the part.

Molly snatched up handbag and coat. Just as she had learned to use her sexuality, she now intended to work on her domestic skills. New cookery books. She needed to find tempting morsels and to learn how to present them well. The children might enjoy a few treats – home-made biscuits, cakes and pies. Yes, she needed some more books.

Closing the front door, she strode off towards her next adventure. It was just a case of playing a part and allowing him to see her in a different light. She was going to be a good companion, a perfect housekeeper and an excellent nurse. His excuses would run dry and he would marry her.

*   *   *

Isobel Burbank lingered in the doorway of Greenhalgh's butchers. Her handbag contained, among other things, a photograph of the woman she sought. In the same envelope rested an account of Molly Cornwell's movements over a two-week period. The little man had done his job very well; Molly Cornwell had her hair washed and set in Deirdre's Salon at two o'clock every Thursday afternoon.

At precisely a quarter to three, Deirdre's doorbell jangled and Isobel stepped out from her hiding place next door. She turned her ankle, staggered, lost a shoe and dropped half a dozen packages. Moaning as convincingly as she could, she sought support from the nearest lamp post and lifted the stockinged foot out of a puddle.

Molly watched the scene with interest. As Deirdre's door closed behind her, she eyed the woman who had just stumbled out of the butcher's shop. Unless Molly was very much mistaken, the shoes were hand-made and the coat was wild mink. This was an elegant woman, a person of substance, so Molly ran to her aid. She retrieved the shoe first. It was made of the softest kid in a shade that almost matched the mink. 'Is your foot all right?' she asked. 'Shall I put the shoe back on?'

Isobel nodded. 'Thank you, dear. It's my ankle. I'm sure I shall be able to walk shortly. The shock, you see. I cannot think what happened, because the pavement here is quite level. I am not given to accidents.'

Molly picked up the packages and placed them in her own empty shopping basket.

'I believe I left my basket in the library,' said Isobel. 'I am having a very silly day. May I borrow yours? I shall bring it back as soon as possible, be assured of that.'

'Keep it,' replied Molly. 'I've a couple more at home. But you need to sit down for a few minutes.'

'I think you are right.' The plan was working splendidly. She allowed Molly to help her into a nearby café. 'Stay and have some tea with me,' she said. A waitress took their order for tea and scones, then Isobel studied her companion. She was extraordinarily beautiful and the likeness to her daughter was even more evident now than it had been in the snapshots taken by the private detective. Had it not been for a few lines around the eyes, this might have been Dorothy Dyson's older sister. 'I hope they have some butter,' she said to open the conversation. 'The war, you know. Such a nuisance. There are no decent teas to be had for any price.'

Molly nodded. 'Yes. I shall be starting work soon in an engineering factory. Not on the floor, you understand, but as a clerical assistant. We must all do our part. Soon, there will be a law stating that all women must go to work while the men are away.'

Isobel sighed. 'My part is supposedly to supervise two dozen or so land girls. When one owns acreage, one must hand it over to the ministry. We are bound to account for every beast and every inch of earth. I go round sometimes, but the tenant farmers have most things in hand. Then we have mothers and babies in one wing of the house and I am nominally in charge of all that, too, simply because I am the householder. There is a housekeeper of sorts – a rough and ready type – so I have to keep watch over all of it. I am quite worn out.'

Molly pricked up her ears. This was, indeed, a wealthy woman. 'Where do you live?' she asked casually.

'Outside Bromley Cross. It's healthy, at least, and we have seen no bombs, though we have watched a few fires in Bolton. Do you live in the town?'

'View Street.'

The scones and tea arrived. Isobel looked at the dark brown liquid and tried not to shudder. Strong tea was a prerequisite in most Lancashire households, so she must grin and bear it. The scones looked dry and boasted very few raisins. A bright yellow blob perched on each plate was definitely margarine, but she would not complain. 'Do you have children?' she enquired, knowing the answer well enough.

'A daughter. She's away doing her war work somewhere or other. She married, but her husband was killed and she lost the baby.'

'Very sad.' Isobel worked hard not to frown as the foul liquid attacked taste buds unused to such assaults. 'I have three sons. Two are in the army, but the oldest of the three – Andrew – is at home with me. He's a doctor.'

Molly's mind shot backwards twenty-odd years and found the face of the medic who had betrayed her, the man she had loved with all her heart, who had declared her to be without heart. 'Do they not have doctors in the forces?' she asked.

'Of course they do. But Andrew was damaged by polio when he was a child, so he is unfit for service. He has taken Chadwicke House – a building separated from our main property. He will be nursing airmen who have been burnt.'

'Is he a burns expert?'

'No. He studied psychology and psychiatry.

Andrew will be dealing with mental wounds. The damage does not end with a scarred face. It goes a great deal deeper than that for most of those poor souls.'

'I suppose it must.' Molly took a bite of scone. She would have given just about anything to work up there in the fresh air away from town. Occupations in the countryside were reserved, so this woman might provide an ideal opportunity for her to escape the engineering works. 'I love the countryside,' she said. 'Open spaces, fresh air.' She sighed. 'My idea of heaven. I'd love to live there.'

'Would you?' Isobel took another mouthful of tea. Bringing Dorothy's mother up to Bromley Cross might not prove sensible. She chewed on a crumb of scone. But it could be an accident. After all, this woman's surname was not the same as Dorothy's . . . Oh, it all needed a great deal of thought. She leaned forward. 'My dear, I thank you for your help.' She had intended to delve further, but she needed to wear her thinking cap for a few days.

'You're welcome, I'm sure.'

The idea had been to chatter away about the house, the residents and all who worked at Burbank Hall. She had intended to mention Dorothy by name, thereby arming this woman with the knowledge of her daughter's whereabouts. But another possibility loomed: the chance to bring Molly Cornwell up to the hall and install her nearby. All decisions needed to be carefully weighed. 'Please meet me here at the same time next week,' Isobel suggested.

'I shall return your basket filled with fresh vegetables – a taste of the countryside you love – and we shall share another plate of dreadful scones.'

Molly employed the most dazzling among her repertoire of smiles. 'That would be lovely. I don't start work until after Christmas, so I can be here.' She would definitely be here . . .

'Splendid.' Isobel stood up. 'You see? No great damage done – I can walk perfectly. I must go now, because my son will be waiting to drive me home. You have been most kind. My name, by the way, is Isobel Burbank.'

'I'm Molly Cornwell.'

'I shall see you next week, then.' Isobel left the café.

Molly ploughed her way through the rest of her scone. It was not particularly tasty, but food was food and rationing was a fact of life. Isobel Burbank. Even the name sounded wealthy and important. One wing of the house held mothers and babies? One wing? The woman must live in a mansion. She would find out exactly where Isobel Burbank lived, would try to find an excuse to travel up to her house, because engineering was not Molly's idea of fun. Factories were full of women and old men these days, so the potential for diversion would be limited. Yes, she would grab her chance and use it. Fate might just be on her side for once.

The man who had met the king of England lay in a corner bed, face turned to the wall. An arm, still bandaged, lay on top of the quilt, its more comfortable twin tucked into the bed with its owner. Dorothy placed a carafe of fresh water on the bedside locker, then sat down and waited. Captain Stuart Beddows had spoken scarcely a word since arriving at Chadwicke House.

'You must drink,' she whispered. 'Unless you want that tube back.'

He remained motionless.

'Please, Stuart. Just a mouthful, then I shall read to you.'

He moved slightly and she reached across with the glass tumbler, a drinking straw bent into an L-shape touching his lips until he took a drink.

Dorothy's eyes were filled with tears. He probably had no hair under the bandages and God alone knew what was left of his face. Well, the doctors who had tried to stick him back together would have some concept, she supposed. Even taking a sip of water exhausted him. Proper food was not yet on the agenda, but he had accepted small amounts of soup and soft vegetables whenever she could persuade him. This was his fourth day and he was, so far, the only occupant of Chadwicke House.

'Read,' he said.

'What shall I read?'

'Ten out of ten. God bless the Senior Service.'

He surely knew the story off by heart by now, but Dorothy found the *Daily Express* and went through the same paragraphs all over again. The story of the David and Goliath encounter had dominated the presses earlier in the month, and she relayed it all over again.

'Two Italian convoys of ten ships each,' he said.

'Yes. And Captain Agnew is one of our youngest naval officers,' she read. 'A tiny flotilla of British ships sank the lot.'

'Amen. Of course, our own RAF boys have sent some of them down to Davy Jones's locker. We've been bombing ships for weeks. Ten out of ten twice over, though. That is quite something. And Russia? Is that Nazi dog still making progress?'

She found the *Sunday Dispatch*. 'The Germans have taken Rostov and are on their way to Moscow.'

He groaned. 'I would smile if it didn't hurt. Only a fool takes on Russia. Hitler has no chance now, just as Napoleon had no chance in 1812. The Germans will be bogged down in two feet of snow. They'll be losing fingers and toes and God knows what they'll eat. They may have to eat the fingers and toes.'

Dorothy did the smiling for both of them. He was talking. Apart from the odd word, Stuart Beddows had remained silent since his arrival. This was partly due to physical pain, but most of his unwillingness to communicate was the result of abandonment by a fiancée who had been unable to cope with his probable disfigurement.

'How's Libya?' he asked now.

'Our tanks are ploughing through.'

'And the bombardment of Germany continues?'

'Yes. They can't win, Stuart.'

He turned his head slightly. Bandaged eyes meant that he could not see her and no one knew how well he would see when the bandages had been removed. 'Tell me about you,' he said. 'Describe yourself.'

'I'm blonde and I have blue eyes.'

'Are you pretty?'

'Yes.'

In spite of great discomfort, he laughed. 'A real northern lass, then. Tell the truth and shame the devil.'

'Exactly. Now, Stuart, I must go to feed Matthew. I told you about him, didn't I? He is coming along nicely, taking his feeds. I wish I could say the same about you.'

'It hurts,' he said.

'I know. You were badly burnt.'

'Not that,' he answered. 'Julia hurt me. I don't blame her for not wanting to live with a monster, yet it was still painful. You know that I may be blind?'

'Yes.'

'And you are wearing Chanel.'

He was missing nothing, she decided. Andrew had given her the perfume, had told her to use her voice, scents and touch to communicate with this poor young man. Now, the poor young man was asking the inevitable question.

'He died,' she answered when the dreaded words had been spoken. 'He was RAF – a rear gunner.'

'I am sorry. Sometimes, I wish . . .' He allowed the words to perish before birth, because he

173

realized that he might pain this young woman all over again. 'Forget I said anything,' he said.

'Don't wish yourself dead,' she said softly. 'My wish is that I could nurse Steve. He nursed me once when I was five years old and my ear was cut. It wouldn't matter what he looked like after a fire, he would still have been my Steve.'

'Are you sure?'

'Absolutely positive.'

'Then Julia did not love me.'

Dorothy closed her eyes and worked hard not to hate a woman she had never met. 'I can't speak for Julia,' she said. 'We are all different and she probably has her own strengths and weaknesses. She may get over it. She may come back to you when she has thought it all through.'

'No,' he replied. 'Without all this – before the plane went down – we were growing apart. People change. War certainly alters perspective. She may well have met someone else in London. She's Red Cross.'

'So am I.' Julia would have seen burns, surely? If she was anywhere near the East End . . . Perhaps Julia knew that the scars cut right through to the soul and that it took an Andrew Burbank to start the mending process. Even Andrew expected no miracles.

'Go to your baby,' he ordered. 'Leave me some peace, woman.'

She left him. The man who had been visited in hospital by King George VI and Queen Elizabeth could not be mended by royalty, by

174

medicine, by words from a person who had not been trained for this. All he truly needed was the love of a woman who had walked away. As Dorothy Dyson walked away, she kept a little piece of him with her, because she knew abandonment and had never quite coped with it herself.

Matthew Taylor was making his presence known very loudly. She lifted him, changed his nappy, washed her hands, picked up the bottle and fed him. He fed best when Dorothy held him, so this was becoming a part of her routine. *Please, God, let this be the last war. Let all the Hitlers die out, because this baby is the future and I don't want to see him covered in bandages twenty-five years from now. Amen.*

As the child fed, she sang 'Run, Rabbit, Run' very softly. He liked that one and 'Pack up Your Troubles'. What would happen to Matthew at the end of all this? His father – if he owned an acknowledged father – might be away or dead. The mother's parents had died in the bombing and no other family had been traced thus far. 'I wish they'd let me keep you,' she whispered. 'I lost my baby and you lost your mother, but they'll make it complicated. Just because I'm a widow, eh? If my baby had lived, they would have let me keep him. But they won't let me keep you. If Steve hadn't died, I could have adopted you. Shall we run away, you and I? Shall we go and live in a cave near the sea?'

Andrew Burbank flattened himself against the wall just outside the door. From the information he had gleaned about her mother, he would have expected Dorothy to encounter difficulty in attaching herself to a child. When it came to arguments about nature versus nurture, he came down on the side of the latter, because relationships were copied behaviour patterns. All the love Dorothy had known had come from an old teacher who had managed to rescue her for a while. Yet she loved this baby boy and handled him well. And he should not be eavesdropping – it was becoming a disgusting habit and was probably a symptom of some sort of psychological misbehaviour. He entered the nursery. 'That young man is coming along in leaps and bounds.' He pointed to the baby.

'He is. And he's never still.' She paused. 'Andrew?'

'What?'

'They won't let me adopt him, will they?'

He felt as if his heart would shatter into a million pieces. She was a golden-haired Madonna with a 24 carat heart. Sometimes, when he looked into her eyes, he experienced a strange desire to drown in their depths. He smiled inwardly. The wish to die a pleasurable death was perfectly normal – he had studied it. 'They will probably seek a married couple for him.'

'I thought that.' The child was edging towards sleep, so she removed the teat from his mouth and raised him onto her shoulder, rubbing his back gently in order to aid digestion. 'Four fluid ounces,' she said proudly.

'You have done well with him. I hear he was a reluctant feeder.'

'He wanted a mother,' she said. 'That was all he really needed.'

'Yes, we all need a mother.' Perhaps she would say more, but they were in a roomful of newborns, so this was hardly the place for detailed discussion. 'Will you let me help you?' he asked. 'I've read most of your diaries. Let me find a way to—'

'Perhaps one day, yes.'

A crazy idea was shifting through his head with the speed of an express train. If she would marry him, the baby could be theirs – he knew which strings to pull. Madness, he told himself. But it was a lunacy in which he could indulge privately – there was no harm in dreaming. 'Regression might be the answer,' he said. 'Think about it.'

'I am all right as long as I am away from her,' she replied. 'I've accepted the fact that she doesn't love me and can't love anybody. It's just the way it is, the way it always was. My mother isn't a whole person and she never has been whole.' She placed the sleeping baby in his cot. 'I had to manage her.'

'How did you do that?' Andrew asked.

She rolled up her left sleeve. 'My mother was and is terrified by the sight of blood.'

In spite of all his training, Dr Andrew Burbank shivered.

Dorothy smiled at him. 'You see? Stuart's state of mind is caused by the state of his body – the burns and so on. My state of body was

177

caused by the state of my mind. So Stuart and I are vice versa – two sides of the one coin. It cuts both ways.' She smiled wryly at her feeble pun. He knew what she meant. He seemed to know almost everything about the business of existing as a human being.

'Self-harm is a weapon used by many young women,' he said.

She nodded and fastened her cuff button. 'It is a cry of desperation. It's the work of a person so unnoticed that she begins to feel invisible. Blood is bright and very dramatic. Blood made me real and made her terrified. It got me away in the end. It got me here a few weeks ago.'

'Yes – I noticed that some of the marks are recent.'

'Surface wounds,' she answered. 'I am now an expert and should train to be a surgeon.'

'You have too great a soul for that. A surgeon is a butcher whose meat walks away . . . well, most of it does. It never appealed to me. I have always been fascinated by the psyche, by Freud and Jung – both of whom were as mad as hatters, by the way. How is Stuart progressing?' He led her out of the nursery.

She told him about repeating his favourite piece from the paper, about his questions and comments.

'You broke through, then.'

'Your mother's Chanel broke through. He talked about Julia.'

'Good sign. Someone will come to remove the bandages soon and to assess him for further reconstruction. He has been through hell – only just got his plane over England before coming down in flames.'

They crossed the courtyard from Clarence Wing to Burbank Wing, each engrossed in the conversation about Stuart Beddows. They did not notice the figure at a window of the original building, did not see the tightening brow and the balled fists of Isobel Burbank.

Isobel studied her son and his companion. Women as beautiful as Dorothy Dyson should be locked away somewhere for the good of the nation. The way the girl walked showed a degree of confidence in self that would not normally be available to someone who had been kept down by a domineering mother. At the same time, there was little of real vanity about her. Isobel had spoken to her twice only, yet in spite of herself had been struck by the girl's poise and good manners.

According to more notes discovered in Andrew's office, Dorothy's mother was virtually insane. She had what Andrew had described as an overwhelming need to be in total control of her immediate environment and all who occupied it. Much of the jargon had been beyond Isobel's limited comprehension, but there could be little doubt that Molly was what Ivy Crumpsall might have termed 'crackers'.

Isobel knew nothing of Freud and Jung, but she was an expert on her own oldest son and could have written papers on the subject. Illness over a period of months had welded him first to hospital, then to home, where he had been

179

forced to relearn the arts of walking and of co-ordinating smaller movements involving his hands. She remembered reading to him, playing cards and dominoes with a child made so clumsy by polio that he could scarcely hold the pieces. Even so, he had routed his father at chess on many occasions.

She recalled the pain he had endured and the humiliation caused by his physical difference from the norm. There had been no outdoor sports for Andrew, though he swam like a fish and rode well. Team games had been beyond him and, in his teens, he had married himself to books and studies.

And now? She turned from the window and picked up her knitting. Now, he was in love. Isobel was frightened. Richard and Charles had been through their fair share of young women, but Andrew had carried on with his research into the subject that held him both fascinated and confused. Head over heels, she mused as she worked on a sock for some anonymous serving soldier. Andrew had never walked out with a young woman, was not one for social gatherings, would prefer to be wrapped in reading, so the first fall was always going to be a heavy one, she supposed.

She chided Shang, one of her Pekingese. 'Don't chew the wool,' she said absently. The thought of losing Andrew to that girl was not palatable. He was a man of means, well respected in his profession and as a landed gentleman. Dorothy Dyson had baited her trap with honey and Andrew was a starving man.

It had to be stopped. The thought of Burbank blood being diluted and contaminated by the daughter of an insane woman was unbearable. Perhaps if Andrew were to come into contact with Dorothy's mother, he might change his mind – surely the daughter could not be whole if her background was not impeccable, if her genes were suspect?

A thought pushed its way to the forefront of Isobel's consciousness and she did not welcome it. Andrew had become her companion over the years, while his two brothers, men of the world, had not been close to her for at least a decade. They came and went, but Andrew was a fixture. No, she told herself determinedly. No, it was just this particular girl. Someone of a higher calibre would have been welcomed with open arms.

The knitting went awry almost of its own accord, and she spent several minutes picking up lost stitches. It had to be done; the pattern must be maintained. And she was not referring to her stocking stitch.

*   *   *

Molly arrived at work as arranged on the Monday morning. Mrs Morris's husband had taken a turn for the worse, so it was straight in at the deep end with eggs, bacon, toast and tea. With no one to show her the ropes, Molly simply had to get on with it. She noticed him at the table, brow furrowed from the moment he clapped eyes on her, while three children of various ages were dotted around the same board.

They ate their food politely, though Molly knew that it was probably well below standard. With her hair and clothes dampened by sweat, she carried on blindly until the young had left for school and only Ian remained. She was washing dishes when he entered the kitchen. 'I suppose you have attended to my wife?'

Molly clapped a hand to her brow, causing further dampness from the washing-up water. 'Oh, Lord. How could I forget her?'

'Quite easily,' he snapped. 'Carry on with the dishes – I shall see to Florence.'

They both clattered, he arranging a breakfast tray, she making her way through a seemingly endless pile of crockery and cutlery.

He returned. 'You will give my wife a bed bath, then you will dress her. After that, she will rest on the upstairs chaise until she is recovered. At eleven precisely, she will take milky coffee and two plain biscuits. Lunch is at one. There is a list of her dietary requirements pinned to the inside of the pantry door. On the top shelf in there, you will find a small box containing housekeeping money. Buy what you need. After lunch, Florence will remain on the day bed. Cleaning and so forth you fit in as best you can. My wife comes first, my children a close second.'

She stepped towards him. 'Ian?' she said softly.

'Here, I am Dr Clarke. Here is where you should definitely not be. But I have quite made

182

up my mind that nothing can be done about you and your atrocious behaviour. You will mind Florence and do as she asks. Hurt her and I shall kill you. I know how to do that without leaving the slightest scrap of evidence. Dinner will be at six. You will do the dishes and leave. It is a long day, but the pay is good. At weekends, a young girl comes in. She and my daughter manage between them.'

A thrill of terror that verged on excitement touched her spine when he spoke of murder. She noticed how implacable his tone was, how he glided from murder threat to timetable without the tiniest change in his expression. She should not have come.

'You should not have come.'

Was he reading her mind? 'I have to be near you,' she said.

'And I have to be near my patients. Good morning.' He picked up bag and coat and left the house in three or four long strides.

Molly sat down. Her first ninety minutes in this house had been exhausting – and the immediate future promised not to be too cheerful. She had an invalid to wash and feed, a large house to clean, shopping, washing and ironing to do – and there was to be a family meal at six o'clock. She was tempted to run, yet she dared not. He needed working on, must be seduced by her nearness.

Weary already, she climbed the stairs. It was time to face her real rival and she might as well make the best she could of it. She filled a bowl with warm, soapy water and made her way

towards the master bedroom. When she passed
the children's rooms, she glimpsed a level of
untidiness that verged on the chaotic, but she
would cope. With her teeth gritted, she walked
towards the wife of the man she wanted. 'One
thing at a time, Molly,' she mouthed silently.
'One thing at a time.'

SEVEN

Molly borrowed books from the Central Library and pored over them for several days. She learned about pressure points, bedsores, diets and blanket baths. 'I'll show him,' she mumbled to herself. 'Thinks I'm good for just the one thing, does he? Well, he's got a shock coming his way.' Determined to shine, Molly threw her not inconsiderable intellect into the arena. If she could read about it, she could do it; from books, she had learned her recipes and from books she would learn how to be an irreplaceable nurse. Wearing black, white and an expression of cheerful encouragement, Molly Cornwell threw her whole self into her unaccustomed work.

Florence was delighted with her new carer. She expounded Molly's virtues whenever she found the energy to speak and, after just a couple of weeks, it became plain to Florence that she had found a treasure. 'I feel blessed,' she told her husband. 'Patience Morris was good to me, but this new girl is an angel. She studies, you know. She reads all kinds of literature just to learn how to keep me comfortable. And it's

185

lovely to have someone so pretty and full of life. I can't begin to imagine life without her.'

Ian continued to eat his steak and kidney pie. It was difficult to live without Molly – that fact had been hammered home to him on many occasions. But an angel? The angel had a second child of his in her belly – he was already father to one who was currently staying with a teacher in order to be beyond the reach of Florence's angel. Lucifer had been an angel, he thought as he enjoyed his food. Lucifer had become Satan; now, a female Satan was attempting a return to favour. And yes, she was pretty. She was beyond pretty. Molly Cornwell would not have looked out of place in a Hollywood film. As for acting, she could probably have managed that with very little effort.

Edward, Sarah and Daniel were equally enthusiastic about the new member of staff. Mrs Morris had been a stickler for correctness, but Mrs Cornwell was brilliant. She sang, told jokes and had even done a bit of clog-dancing one afternoon. She owned no clogs, but she had made a fair job of it, laughing away at Edward's attempt to accompany her on the spoons. Determined to master the art of spoon-playing, he was currently having another stab at it with his own and his sister's dessert implements.

Ian slipped into the kitchen where Molly was preparing a jam pudding. 'I know what you're up to,' he whispered. She wasn't fooling him for a moment. The nape of her neck, from which a curtain of hair had been swept, was decorated by small tendrils determined on escape from sensible imprisonment.

'So do I,' she answered. 'I'm very good at custard.'

'Don't be obtuse. You may convince my poor wife and the children, but I am not in the least way impressed. You are the consummate actress.'

Molly stirred her custard and poured it into a jug. 'Your children are Dorothy's brothers and sister,' she said quietly, 'and your wife deserves some spoiling. I am doing a good job and you cannot deny it.'

'You have no feelings for any of them. You are just trying to make yourself indispensable.'

'And I am never at home when you need me, am I? How are you managing without me?' He was definitely tense and, Molly thought, the longer she kept him waiting, the better. Starvation would do him good, she mused as she went about her tasks. He would come to her soon; he would find a way.

'I don't need you.' After delivering the lie, he left the kitchen.

Molly followed him, pudding in one hand, custard in the other. She noticed that Florence had already withdrawn from the table – presumably to the day bed in the front room. Her meal, almost untouched, remained where Molly had placed it fifteen minutes earlier. She poured some custard into a dish, picked up a teaspoon and declared her intention to feed Mrs Clarke by force, if necessary.

Edward watched his new friend as she disappeared with his mother's dish. 'She makes things happen,' he said.

'She certainly does,' agreed Ian. 'Now, come along and eat your food before I steal it from you.' He could hear her in the next room. She was trying to coax Florence to eat a little of the custard. Angrily, he began to attack his portion of jam pudding. She had been right – he did miss her. He could scarcely bear to look at her, because his body, definitely beyond the reach of his brain, was screaming for her. He would never find another partner like her, yet he had to put the children first. Sexual athletics were all very well in their place, but that place was not in the home of three innocents. When would he get her on her own? When could he enjoy her again? She was so near, yet so out of reach that he was almost in pain.

'You're not eating,' said his daughter.

His hunger was not for food. Ian Clarke's appetite could be appeased only by the ministrations of his wife's self-appointed, self-educated nurse. He finished his pudding, excused himself and left the table in a rush. Sometimes, he could scarcely bear to look at his own sons and daughter.

She was washing dishes. 'Did Florence eat?'

'A little.' She turned and deliberately brushed past him as she carried some crockery to a cupboard. Smiling to herself, she marked his sharp intake of breath when their bodies met for that instant. The power remained. He might try to escape, but he would never manage without her.

'When do you leave?' he asked.

'In about ten minutes. I've put Mrs Clarke's clean nightdress on her pillow. Will you cope?'

'Yes. After I have driven you home.'

She stood very still, hands on hips, head thrown back so that he could see a pulse beating in her long, slender neck. 'So we progress from kitchen table to a car, do we? Forget it. I shall take a bus. I have things to do at home as well. You don't own me, Ian.'

'Don't make me beg,' he said.

She half smiled. 'We are too noisy for a car. I have often wondered what my neighbour makes of all the shouting we do. No. You must get a room for me nearby. Tom won't mind – he is quite capable and he knows I am working for a sick woman. I won't be missed.'

'Does he know that you are pregnant?'

'No.' As always, she offered no comment about the opinions of her spouse. He was a man in name only, so he occupied few pages in the book of Molly Cornwell's life. 'Get me a room,' she repeated. 'I could do without travelling to and fro – I am here almost eleven hours a day, you know. It's hard work for one woman.'

Even his fingertips tingled as she studied him. He wondered anew about the physical embodiment of Satan, wondered whether some people were born bad. Were that the case, the opposite would be true and he knew of no one who might fill the description of God on earth. Florence believed this to be an angel, but Molly

Cornwell was a devil in an exquisitely beautiful container. He wished that he had never met her.

'Tongue-tied?' she asked.

His children were in the next room. Another of his seeds had taken root inside Molly Cornwell, another Dorothy to be mistreated and controlled by a creature who should not share space with people too young to fend for themselves. 'Molly?'

'Yes?'

He swallowed hard. 'Let me abort that baby.'

She grinned. 'What? A slight slip of your hand and he and I are both gone? Not likely, Ian.'

'I would not do that.'

'Really? In your position, I certainly would.'

He knew that already. He knew that she was clinical, unfeeling and merciless and that he continued to want her. There was plainly a dark side to his own nature, because every sensible and sensitive cell in his body screamed to be free of her. Molly wasn't right in the head. Ian's exposure to psychology, minimal though it had been during training, was sufficient to make him master of that undeniable truth. 'You are evil personified,' he muttered. 'You are the side of Eve that found the apple and persuaded her partner to lose Paradise.'

'Then I have my uses,' she replied. 'Without Eve, none of us would have been here. Two perfect people, thousands of years old, would be the only humans on earth.'

She had an answer for everything, was probably endowed with an intelligence quotient higher than his own. Had she been educated, she would have been lethal. 'I'll find you a room,' he said. It would have to be something above an office, a place unoccupied at night, because she was right: their lovemaking – if such it could be termed – had never been a quiet business. Everything the woman did, she did well. Sometimes, she did things rather too well.

'You don't love me,' she said.

'No, I don't.'

'You could get prostitutes.'

'I already have one.' He swung round abruptly and left the kitchen.

Molly finished clearing away the debris, found her coat and went to say goodbye to her employer. She stared down at the wasted body of her lover's legal partner. The skin was grey and the breathing shallow. Florence Clarke could not last much longer. Molly needed to work harder on his children, as they would provide the greatest of her weapons. Well, the second greatest, she supposed. Florence was asleep, so Molly bade the children farewell and left the house.

From an upstairs window, Dr Ian Clarke watched his torment as it sashayed its way towards Chorley New Road. In his mind's eye, she stood naked before a fire, body gleaming from recent exertion, hair tumbling down her shoulders, hands on hips, triumph lighting those wonderful yet almost empty eyes. The violence of his lust both appalled and enthralled him. He could never marry her.

But was Molly Cornwell as clever as he had

been led to imagine? Was she lacking the sense to realize how powerful a doctor really was? A building empty at night except for the two of them, an unconscious woman, a capable man standing over her . . . Exasperated by himself, he moved away from the window as soon as she had disappeared onto the main road. He wasn't planning anything, he told himself firmly. Yes, he could render her unconscious and yes, he could abort that poor child. He could, but he wouldn't, because he did not believe in murder.

Then he went downstairs to find the local newspaper. Poring over *Accommodation to Let*, he failed to find exactly what he sought. But there would be another paper tomorrow, yet another the day after that. He would find a place eventually. Meanwhile, he must continue to live the life of the truly tormented.

*   *   *

Dorothy, who had sworn that she would be there, sat on a chair at the end of Stuart Beddows's bed. A newly arrived surgeon was peeling layers of bandages from the young man's face and neck. Stuart was to be assessed for further surgical intervention. More important, this was the moment when he would find out whether his eyes worked. Discovering that she had almost stopped breathing, Dorothy inhaled a huge draught of oxygen.

'You're more nervous than I am,' said Stuart, who was acutely conscious of sounds, scents and changes in the small space around him. In a moment, she would see him; in a moment, he would lose her. Lose her? He had never owned her . . .

Dorothy chided herself inwardly; she needed to work on her failings. There were now four residents in Chadwicke House and she wanted to help, not to hinder, the recovery of her patients. Controlling her breathing carefully, she watched the surgeon at work.

Andrew came to stand beside her, placing a hand on her shoulder. He had shown her the photographs and she had accepted those images, but he was aware that she was yet to come to terms with living, breathing disfigurement in a person she knew. He squeezed musculature that was strong, yet not over-developed, wondering how she would react if she were ever to return the favour. His left shoulder, diminished by polio, was almost flaccid. As for his leg – well, that was not a thing of beauty, either.

Stuart flinched while the last layer was carefully removed. Then, when a thick, soft pad was lifted from the orb, his left eye opened and he saw her. At first, she was a figure in a mist, a creature apparently lost in fog. The cloud slowly lifted and he gasped. 'I can see you, Dorothy. And I am happy that my first vision is such a delightful one.'

She studied him. The left side of his face was absolutely perfect and untouched. His skull, not too badly affected, owned areas where hair was attempting to re-establish itself. But the right side was not good. Strips of dead and blackened flesh hung from the temple and the eye was sealed closed. The cheek resembled a relief map of uneven territory, and the rises and falls continued down the neck. There was no ear. A shrivelled mass occupied the area where that organ had once sat.

'Lovely,' declared the visiting burns specialist. 'We have a perfect template from which to work, because one side of your face is virtually untouched. This will all need to settle, of course, but we shall certainly be able to restore some of your former glory, Captain Beddows.'

Stuart continued to stare at Dorothy. A woman such as this was surely a reason to want to stay alive. 'Dorothy?'

'Yes?'

'Bring me a mirror.'

Without hesitation, she went to fulfil his request.

'Is that a good idea?' asked the surgeon.

'Yes,' replied Andrew. 'For Stuart, at least. He has prepared himself for today – haven't you, old boy?'

But Stuart's gaze was fixed on the returning figure of Dorothy. How he looked suddenly mattered, because she was the very embodiment of perfection. He thought of the many hours she had sat with him, sometimes just holding his hand while he went through the nightmare all over again, often reading to him from newspapers and from books. She delivered Shakespeare's sonnets very well, yet she insisted that she had received minimal education – something to do with a mother who had lacked ambition.

'There you are.' She placed the mirror in his good hand.

Stuart looked at the damage and swallowed hard. Children would run away from him, he decided. Wherever he went, people would stare because the vision in the mirror was scarcely human. 'Bloody mess,' he said. 'Do we uncover the arm yet?'

'We'll have a look, yes.' The surgeon set about the business of unwrapping Stuart's right arm. 'Good thing I am left-handed,' said the patient.

The arm was badly burnt, but he was able to move his fingers, though the effort caused considerable pain. 'It's so tight,' he said. 'I have clearly been cooked in a very hot oven. Bloody Germans, eh?'

'I'll send a nurse to dress it.' The doctor stood back and smiled. 'We shall leave your face to the elements for a while, I think. The dead tags I shall trim now – you won't feel a thing. Then, when Mother Nature has done her best, we'll ship you off and have a go at mending some of the damage. I suspect that the eye is beyond repair, but we can give you a glass one eventually, just to make the face more even. Yes. Well done. We shall do our very best for you – I can promise that.'

Dorothy excused herself, offering as reason the lie that she was needed elsewhere. In the staff toilets, she shut herself inside a cubicle and found that she was shaking. Had Steve burned to death? Had he died with merciful swiftness or had he suffered the pain of fire? Steve – Stuart – even the names began with the same two letters . . . No. This was not Steve come back to her. But perhaps Stuart had been sent so that Dorothy could do for him all she had been unable to do for her husband.

The outer door opened. 'Dorothy?' It was Andrew.

'What?'

'Are you all right?'

'Yes.'

'Are you sure?'

'Yes.' She had told more than one lie today. 'Andrew?'

'Well?'

'Is it all right if I go to my room until Matthew's next feed? I am feeling very tired.'

'Of course it is.'

Andrew walked back to Stuart Beddows's room and entered just after a nurse had finished bandaging the arm.

'Where's Dorothy?' Stuart asked.

'Having an hour off,' replied Andrew.

The man in the bed sighed. 'I take it that I am the first mess she has seen in the flesh – she told me about the photographs.'

'Yes, you are the first.'

Stuart fixed his eye on the other man's face. 'You are fond of her,' he said. 'I have noticed that your voice changes whenever you address her. As you told me a while ago, the blind depend on other senses and I have sensed your interest in Dorothy. If I were whole, I'd

196

give you a run for your money, doc. She is a stunner.'

Andrew smiled ruefully. 'I am not whole.'

'I have listened to your limp and now I have seen it with my own one eye. But you have your face, Andrew. I have half a face, which is, I suppose, better than none. You're a handsome man and you don't realize it. I probably wouldn't have noticed it myself had I not become afflicted. I was a handsome devil, you know.' He lifted up the hand mirror. 'Has she run away from the sight of me?'

'She's tired and she has to attend to the baby.'

Stuart glanced through the window. 'Quite a place you have here. And this isn't the main house, I am told. My family is well to do, but not on as grand a scale as this. Oh, you might phone my parents, by the way, and tell them not to come for a while. Mother coped with the bandages, just about, but the sight of this will break her heart.'

'Very well.'

The patient brought his gaze back to his psychiatrist again. 'Have you asked her?'

'Asked whom what?'

'Have you asked Dorothy to marry you?'

There was, Andrew decided, no point in attempting to delude a man as honest as Stuart Beddows. Also, since Andrew expected complete frankness from his patient, he should heed his own rules and offer the same in return – up to a point. 'No, I haven't. I don't know her well yet and she is still recovering from miscarriage and sudden widowhood.'

'And not in that order.'

'No. Her husband's death was probably a contributory factor in the early labour.'

'But you like her.'

'Yes.'

Stuart smiled with the side of his mouth that permitted mobility. 'Then go to it. Not to proposal, not yet, but courtship could be the medicine she needs. There is a loneliness in her.'

Andrew simply shook his head. The man in the bed was using as early therapy the transference of thoughts and worries to other people – to Dorothy, anyway. If he thought and talked about her, he would not be looking in that mirror and facing the devastating truth. He was dreadfully scarred and that would never be completely concealed, whatever cosmetic surgery might be tried.

'You've never had a girlfriend, have you?' was the next question.

'No.'

'Because of the limp?'

'Probably.'

'Then what chance is there for me? At best, I can expect pity. Is that how you have felt? Have you dreaded rejection, or, worse still, charity?'

Andrew sighed. This was hardly the therapy he had envisaged, patient questioning doctor and trying to help. 'Are you saying, "Physician, heal thyself"? Is that your game? Because the next weeks and months are not going to be about me, Stuart. You may make some enquiries, but the healing of me is not on the agenda.'

'So a cripple will mend a cripple?'

'I hope so. Since I was eight years old, I have been an outsider. I played for no team, ran no races and fought no wars. Oh – I am not asking for pity, by the way.'

'You won't get it – not from a chap with a face like this one. Continue, Doc Burbank.'

'My exclusion became my strength, because I developed into a watcher. I am not completely of the Carl Jung persuasion – he was a mad book-burner – but I agree with him in so far as to say that psychology is learned not from reading, but from watching and absorbing one's fellow man. Also, I do have a little insight into the area of physical disability. So, I researched and wrote papers on the effects of physical trauma and lasting disfigurement. Now, I am here to practise what I preach.'

'I'm the guinea pig.'

'One of them, yes.'

Stuart glanced at the mirror once more. What were his chances of coming to terms with this? Julia had taken one look at the bandages before dashing off – how would she have felt had she seen the true horror? 'So, you are to mend my mind.'

'It isn't broken, Stuart.'

'Just bent slightly?'

'You need to adjust and I believe you can.' The truth was that the shock had not yet hit home. Since the removal of his dressings, Stuart Beddows had not been alone, had not really

199

confronted himself. As long as he could find a distraction, he would focus on it, because that helped him to avoid the main issue. Only when alone would he begin a process that would inevitably include depression, anger, even the desire for permanent release via death.

'It's going to be hard.'

'Yes, it is.'

'Perhaps I should not keep repeating this, but I was a good-looking chap, Andrew. I joined the RAF to kick the hell out of Germany and to be a hero. All I achieved was the ruination of my own life.'

'And the flattening of several vital factories along the Rhine – or so I have been told.'

Into this scene of high drama, Ivy Crumpsall arrived unannounced. She started first on Andrew. 'Don't be looking at me like that – I've known you since you were young enough to have your bum tanned. And if you want to know where I got the key to get in here – no bloody comment.' She approached the bed.

Stuart found himself face to face with a virago. He noticed that she didn't flinch when she caught sight of his face and decided that nothing on earth could terrify this woman.

'It's you I want to talk to,' she said. 'I'm Ivy Crumpsall. Who the bloody hell do you think you are?'

'Erm . . . what?'

'All right then, what. What the bloody hell do you think you are?'

Andrew stepped forward. 'Mrs Crumpsall—'

'Mrs Crumpsall my ear hole. It's between me

and him, so don't be pushing your psychiatric nose into this, or I'll flatten it.'

Andrew, who knew Ivy of old, had heard enough of ear holes and noses, so he did what he always did in the face of Ivy's pseudo-fury – nothing at all. She was a tank with no brakes and little could be done to stop or divert a vehicle of such weight. He thanked God for Ivy. She had a way of getting to people that was not very subtle, but she was positive, bossy and full of love. He became a near-silent witness for the next few minutes.

'I don't know why I bother.' Her tone was injured to the point of grief.

Stuart waited. He had never seen the woman before and he couldn't think why she had turned up so suddenly out of the blue. But the situation had provided a little light relief and he decided to err on the side of submission.

'My fingers are near down to the bone,' she said. 'Nigh on twelve hours a day I am at it. Twelve hours.'

'Remarkable,' replied the patient. 'Whatever it is, it must be addictive.'

'Don't you be getting clever with me – I've had that from him all his life.' She jerked a thumb in Andrew's direction. 'Some people – just because they've been to school – think they're better than what I am. Well, I'm one that fights back. Tell him, Mr Andrew.'

'She's one that fights back,' repeated the doctor obediently.

Ivy folded her arms. Her voice became a travesty of what she might have termed 'poshness'. 'Could the gentleman please tell me what he requires in the area of menu? Will I fetch a gun and kill a couple of pheasants? Or happen I should run to the corner shop with my ration book and get some caviar. Because I am telling you now, Mr Royal blinking Air Force – any more full trays coming back to my kitchen will be returned to you and the contents will be poured into your slippers. All right?'

'Ah, you're the cook.'

'No, I'm Winston Churchill in a frock. Now, what have you got to say for yourself?'

'Sorry, Mr Churchill.'

Ivy bit back a smile. His poor face was a mess and no mistake, but she had seen this sort before – and the mess she had seen would soon be arriving at this very place. Yes, Lois would keep an eye on him. In fact, Lois would keep two eyes on him, because Lois's fire had never reached her eyes, thank God. 'Also,' she threatened, 'I have a spy coming here any minute now. She's my sister's neighbour, God help her, and she got hit by a bomb dropped by the other team, so think on.'

'Think on what?'

'Just think on, that's all. From what our Elsie says, Lois Melia's on the bossy side. Mind, coming from our Elsie, that's a bit rich, because she's bossier than a bloody RAF pilot who doesn't know what's good for him. Oh, yes, your Waterloo is on its way. I've only met Lois a couple of times, but she's a gradely lass and she'll mark your card for you.'

'I can hardly wait,' said Stuart.

'So that's sarcasm, is it? I'd sooner have black pudding any day of the week.' She turned to Andrew. 'Lizzie Murphy says your mother says she needs the vet.'

'Wouldn't a doctor be better?' asked Stuart.

'Shut up,' was his reward for the contribution. 'Now, I can't remember which of her Pekes is badly and neither could Lizzie, but your mam wants the vet to have a look at its backside. Mind, if it wasn't for all the huffing and puffing, you wouldn't know north from south with them bloody dogs.'

'Which end huffs and puffs?' enquired Stuart just before being told yet again to shut up.

Andrew walked to the door. 'Come on, Ivy Crumpsall. I can't leave my patient to your tender mercies.'

Out in the corridor, Andrew put his arms round the weeping woman. 'Thanks for what you did in there.'

'What's his future?' she sobbed quietly. 'He's only a lad.'

'With people like you around, he'll be all right. You did more for him then than I can ever do, more than a surgeon might achieve. You made him human. You brought everything down to brass tacks, just as you always do. I am proud of you.'

'And I'm proud of him,' she replied before blowing her nose. 'I've made a nice chicken soup for tonight – happen he'll eat a bit of that. Why do we have to have bloody war, eh? And your collar's creased and you could do with a shave.'

'Ivy?'

'What?'

'Shut up.'

They walked on, he to his mother, Ivy to her kitchen and the organization of meals. At the cooker, she stirred her soup and threw in a handful of barley. Barley would stick to his ribs and keep him warm right through the winter – or so her old mother had always said. His face stayed in her mind and, for Ivy, he would remain a living, breathing reminder of the travesty named war. There would be German lads just the same, faces burnt off, limbs missing, lives altered almost to the edge of reason.

Lizzie poked her head round the door. 'Her Majesty says it's food poisoning.'

'Good,' snapped Ivy. 'Pass me the blinking arsenic and I'll do the other one for her. They're not dogs – they're bloody floor polishers with the handles missing.'

'Are you all right?' Lizzie asked.

'Course I am.' She had a whole face and two working arms. She was getting on in years, but she was in one piece. 'Is the vet coming?'

'I think so.'

'Then send him to Room One in Chadwicke – there's a pilot wants force-feeding and a distemper injection.'

Lizzie withdrew. Sometimes, there was neither rhyme nor reason to old folk, so she would go back to the dogs.

*　　*　　*

The Christmas of 1919 would remain an island of almost pure happiness that would be for ever preserved in the heart of Dorothy Corn-well. She had many presents and was allowed next door to enjoy the day with Marie Templeton and her family. After the visit, she was taken back to Miss Isherwood's house where, in the tiny dining room, she shared with her teacher and best friend a feast of roast capon and vegetables, followed by a Christmas pudding that flamed merrily when a match lit the brandy.

'We never had this at home,' she said. 'Mam doesn't like Christmas much and Dad's always tired. He works hard, you see.'

'Yes.' Beryl did not want to drag information from the child, but she would not prevent her from opening up whenever the mood took her. 'My mother didn't like Christmas, because her own mother died on Christmas Eve. But we still had a tree and all the trimmings. Queen Victoria was the first monarch to send cards. She and Prince Albert got an artist to draw them and their children standing under a tree inside the palace. That's how it all began.'

'Really?'

Beryl smiled. 'No, not really – people in Europe were bringing trees into the house centuries ago. I think a monk went across and decided that a fir tree was like a triangle – Father, Son and Holy Spirit – so that was when Christians started to notice the tree. Martin Luther – you will hear about him when you are older – lit tree candles to show his children how stars shone in the night. I have one because it's pretty.'

'Yes, it is,' agreed Dorothy, leaning back in her chair. 'I've eaten too much and my dress is tight.'

Someone knocked at the front door. Beryl, who was expecting her sister and brother-in-law for supper, wondered why they had come so early. But, when she reached the door, she found a letter on the mat and heard a car chugging its way down the street.

Her name was on the envelope, so she opened it and discovered a Bolton Savings Bank book. She looked inside and found that five hundred pounds had been paid into an account in the name of Dorothy Cornwell. Five hundred pounds? How many years might Beryl have had to work to acquire such a sum of money? Dr Clarke had left it – of that, Beryl was absolutely certain. In spite of his behaviour with Dorothy's wayward mother, this was surely a man of some principle.

'Who was it?' Dorothy asked.

'Just a message from a friend, dear. Now, you read your books while I clear away the dishes, and then, when my family arrives later on, we shall play charades.'

While she washed dishes, Beryl thought about the bank book. She was no longer young and this nest egg needed to be kept safe for the child. She would take it to the very bank in which the book had been issued and they could take care of it. Then, after New Year, she would write and tell Dr Clarke of her decision – if he wanted to give more money to his illegitimate daughter, he could go to the bank and do just that. He was her father. He had to be Dorothy's father.

The doorbell sounded again.

'I'll go,' shouted Dorothy.

Beryl dried her hands and emerged from the kitchen. Molly Cornwell had entered the house. She handed a package to Dorothy, then spoke to Beryl. 'Thank you for looking after her,' she said. 'I couldn't possibly care for Dr Clarke's wife and my daughter at the same time.'

A cold finger ran the full length of Beryl Isherwood's spine. Molly Cornwell had plainly blanked from her mind the real reason for Dorothy's residence in Willows Lane; she was also in charge of the health of her lover's wife. Not for one moment did Beryl doubt the power of the beautiful visitor. In her bones, she knew that Molly would commit any crime in order to achieve her goal. She was blinkered and never looked to the sides of her life; was bent on pursuing her own happiness, whatever the cost to others. 'Would you like a glass of sherry?' she asked.

'Thank you, but no,' came the reply. 'I did most of the dinner for the family last night – Dr Clarke needed just to warm some of it. But I am needed now to clear things away. Poor Florence is beyond all that, I'm afraid. She eats little and lies down for most of the time.'

'Your husband? What is he doing today?'

'Gone to a friend's house – he knew I had to work.' Molly glanced at her daughter. 'Aren't you going to open it?'

Dorothy unwrapped the doll. It was well dressed, with coat, hat and a pretty frock underneath. 'Thank you,' she said.

'You'll have to think of a name for her,' said Molly. 'Well, I must go. Duty calls, as they say.' She left, bequeathing to the room a scent that was flowery and expensive.

Beryl shook herself. She had not shown her visitor out and that was unforgivably rude. But the front door slammed closed and the woman was gone.

Dorothy was staring at her doll. She had removed its hat to reveal blond hair flowing down to its shoulders. Dolls with hair were a rarity and Dorothy knew that she should have felt grateful, but she didn't.

'Have you thought of a name?' Beryl asked.

'No.'

'What about Goldilocks?'

The child placed the doll on a chair and picked up her book. Beryl watched from the doorway while the little girl tried to concentrate on the written word. She was clearly having difficulty until she stood up and turned the doll to face the back of the chair.

'Why did you do that, Dorothy?'

'It looks like her.'

Beryl, who needed to ask for no further information, returned to the sink, rolled up her sleeves and carried on with the job. Sooner or later, Dorothy Cornwell would be returned to the shapely but cold bosom of her mother. As the girl grew older, her peers would begin to pass remarks about her living with a teacher, would accuse her of being a recipient of favouritism. All the same, every time Beryl considered returning Dorothy to View Street, that finger of ice played with her bones. Yet it had to be faced. One day, Dorothy must go back to her mother.

Molly admitted herself to the house. She heard children playing in the dining room, found Florence in her usual place on the day bed in the drawing room. 'How are you now?' she asked.

'My head is spinning, Molly. I love my children dearly, but they do make such noise. Please don't chide them – this is Christmas Day and Christmas is for children. Ian is upstairs – I think the noise is too much for him, also. He went out for a drive to clear his head.'

Molly washed her mistress, applied surgical spirit to pressure points, combed her hair and went off to attack dirty dishes. The kitchen was a war zone and she began on it immediately. 'Men,' she muttered as she piled up the many items, 'they couldn't organize a riot in Moscow.' She confiscated some meat to take home for herself, filled the sink and began on the mountain of glassware and cutlery.

So engrossed was she in the mammoth task that she did not hear him entering the kitchen. Nor did she flinch when his hands cupped her breasts, when his hot breath caressed her neck while he pressed his body against her buttocks. 'Go away,' she said softly. 'Your children are three strides from here, no more.'

'Molly,' he groaned. 'God, I hate you and I want you.'

She clouted him with the dishcloth, not even bothering to turn as she flicked it over her shoulder. 'Go away,' she repeated. 'I'm not losing my job just because you have no self-control.'

'I've found a place.' He reached round her again and placed a key in her apron pocket. 'The address is on the label,' he said. 'Bottom of Chorley New Road above a firm of accountants. It's furnished and it has a double bed.'

'We've always had a double bed, though you refused to use it.'

'Because you share it with Tom.'

'It isn't a marital bed. You know he's still like a little boy in the downstairs department. Now, be off with you and let me get on here.'

'You are torturing me.'

'Good. Now go away before I find an interesting use for this carving knife.'

He left her to it. She was to prepare sandwiches before leaving and the pudding, a sherry trifle, she had made the day before. If he did not find some release soon, he would go crazy. Even in dark, sensible work clothes and a white apron, she was the very embodiment of sensuality. He lay on the bed and tried not to think of her, but she was tattooed indelibly onto every thought in his head.

His eyes flew open. He knew her well enough to realize one thing – she would not go home without examining her rooms on Chorley New Road. He could lie in wait for her. Quickly and quietly, he descended the stairs and gave his wife the excuse that a terminally ill man needed him for pain relief. Outside in his car, he considered the lie he had just told – it was the need for his own relief that forced him away from his family on Christmas Day.

He hid the car on a side road and let himself into the flat. It was of a decent size, with its own bathroom, a dining kitchen and a large bed-sitting room. She had to come. An hour ticked its slow way across the face of his watch. He lit a fire and placed himself on a chair nearby. A lamp flickered on a side table, its wick in sore need of trimming, but he stayed where he was. She would be here soon and he wanted no more light to betray his presence. In his mind's eye, he could see her now, firelight playing over the curves, head thrown back, breasts thrust forward, that challenge in her huge, ice-blue eyes. It was she who dictated the pace, she who gave the commands, he who obeyed in order to achieve the pleasure she was so capable of giving him. Where was she?

A rueful smile played on his lips. She knew. Florence would have relayed the lie about a sick patient and Molly, so certain of her own role in this relationship, would realize that he was waiting for her. A part of their ritual was the waiting she imposed on him before and during their mating. She could lead him almost all the way up the path, then, without warning, she would stop everything in order to prolong the business. It was the same with everything she did, he supposed. From bedsores to fornication, she studied each aspect until she reached perfection. Had she gone home in order to prolong his agony? She was clever, she was dangerous and she was standing in the doorway.

'Hello,' he said, his voice pitched considerably higher than normal.

She stared hard at him. 'You are waiting for me, I take it.'

'Yes.' He moved to rise from the chair, but she ordered him to sit and he sat, an obedient dog taking orders from a cruel owner.

She threw down her shopping bag, then, with excruciating slowness, undid the buttons of her coat. 'I prepared myself,' she said.

Ian could scarcely breathe. When the coat had been peeled away, she stood, legs wide, stockings held up by lace garters, her body scarcely covered by a tiny, lace-trimmed white apron. 'Stay,' she said again. Her hands moved to her hair and she made the release of her crowning glory last at least a whole minute, one pin at a time, one lock released, waves finally cascading down to alabaster shoulders.

He was in pain and she knew it. She wanted him as much as he wanted her, but she had learned that the greatest pleasure arrived only after denial and long postponement. 'Don't touch me,' she said as she moved to the bed. 'You may undress and lie next to me if you wish, but you must not touch until I say so.'

So the flat was declared open for business and she did her work well that afternoon. When she finally allowed him access, they both screamed uncaringly, because no one could hear in the office below or in the empty house next door. When he was finally spent, he collapsed onto a pillow and wept. He wept for Florence, who was dying, for his children, who deserved a better father, for himself, who needed this evil woman to a point where he no longer managed his own spirit.

'That was nice,' she purred.

Nice? It had been shattering, magical, perfect and terrible. It had been a sin large enough to swallow many souls, and he felt the same regret that always visited him after contact with Molly.

'Why are you crying?' she asked.

'Florence,' he answered.

'Was she ever like me? Did she scream?'

'No. She was never in the least way like you.'

She leaned on an elbow and turned, one perfect breast resting heavily on his chest. 'It must be terrible for you,' she said. 'You hate me enough to want me dead, yet you can't resist me.'

'It is confusing, yes.'

She covered his mouth with hers, but continued to talk. 'Do you want to go home?' Her tongue played with his lower lip. 'Do you?'

He realized that she was offering him a turn of his own, the upper hand for once. Almost savagely, he claimed her again, his pulses racing when her eyes gleamed with a mixture of pain and pleasure. Like him, she needed the pain, because pleasure would never be enough for either of them.

EIGHT

There had been a magical Christmas many years ago, when Beryl Isherwood, now long dead, had given Dorothy a wonderfully happy day marred only by the arrival of Molly Cornwell with that terrible doll. The doll had stayed behind in Willows Lane, had never been loved or played with. It had reminded Dorothy of Mam, so she had ignored it completely. During her childhood, every doll bought by Mam had been blonde and beautiful and all had remained unloved and pristine in their containers.

Now an experienced woman, Dorothy knew perfectly well what her mother had been doing with the doctor that day – the day on which Miss Isherwood had taken her away. She had never told her father, because Tom Cornwell did not invite confidences and did not deserve pain. But Mam was what might be termed 'loose' and this unattractive quality was tied up with the other flawed components that had come together to form the creature known as Molly Cornwell, née Bishop.

'You dreaming again?' Ivy Crumpsall thumped

214

Dorothy playfully. 'Them there sprouts won't peel themselves. Get fettling with that knife, lady, or there'll be no Christmas dinner till New Year.'

Elsie Shipton was seated at the table with what she had described as a ton of potatoes. 'How many more of these bloody spuds do you want, Ivy?' she asked her sister, head nodding furiously. 'I feel as if I've been sat here since last Preston Guild. My bum's gone numb.'

'It'll match your head, then. And give over moaning,' said the cook, also nodding. 'We had weeks of you didn't like the countryside, three days of the cottage was haunted—'

'Well, I didn't know you had a fox, did I? All that scratching about at midnight – what was I supposed to think it was?'

'Then there was your feet. I've never heard anybody going on about feet like you did. You must have been the first woman in living memory to go on about her feet for two hours solid. Fallen arches?'

'Dropped metatarsals,' snapped Elsie, 'and don't you forget it. That nurse said I must be a martyr, because it isn't often you get two dropped in two separate feet at the same time. I bet you I made medical history in Bolton Royal Infirmary.'

'Aye, well, belt up before I start the post-mortem. Dorothy?'

'Yes?'

'Are you having your dinner in here with us, or are you going to sit with your young man?' Both heads were suddenly motionless while their owners awaited an answer.

Dorothy felt the heat in her cheeks. 'I don't know who you mean.'

'Hear that?' Elsie waved her potato peeler. 'Her's got more than one from the sound of it. Looks as if she can pick and choose between them.'

Dorothy kept her head down and continued marking crosses in the bases of her peeled sprouts. They meant Stuart Beddows, of course, but they were yapping up the wrong tree as usual. Or were they? Still, their teasing wouldn't spoil her fun, she decided. There was to be a feast at the big kitchen table. It would have to be in relays, because the skeleton staff needed to take turns, but it would surely be fun.

'Stuart Beddows is having his dinner at the table with the others in Chadwicke,' declared Ivy. 'They're all walking about, so they can sit down and behave themselves for a change.' She mopped her fevered brow. 'Thank goodness for two big ovens,' she muttered. 'I'm cooking a full flock of geese here. It's hot work, too – I'm wringing wet through. Elsie?'

'What?'

'How's Lois doing?'

Elsie shook her head sadly. 'She can bear to put a scarf round her neck now and hide some of it. But her chin's a mess, and all round her mouth's still sore. She's fed up, but they say she can move into the cottage with me soon, because her psycho-wotsit's not damaged. I think that means she's right in the head, so there's something to think on. Only a woman can take that sort of thing on the chin, and her chin's where

216

she took most of it, poor soul. She's lost a lot of weight – she couldn't eat for ages. But she's not as down in the dumps as some of them there blokes.'

Dorothy thought about the man who had been the first to arrive. She liked him. She liked him a lot – liked him more than was good for either of them, she supposed. He was educated and gentle, and would soon be leaving Chadwicke House to go for the first of many operations. She would miss him. She missed a sprout, too, and nicked the end of her thumb.

'Come here,' chided Ivy. 'We don't want blood in our sprouts, missus. Let me see to it.'

The bandaged digit allowed Dorothy the opportunity to leave the overheated kitchen and its argumentative occupants. Much as she loved the happy bickering and synchronized nodding between Ivy and Elsie, there was seldom any peace when the two of them came together, and Dorothy had thinking to do. She walked round the garden that was bordered by the original Burbank Hall at the front and a wing at each side. At the open end of the uncompleted square lay the beginning of a long driveway at the top of which sat Chadwicke House.

From a window of the original Tudor build-ing, Isobel Burbank watched, as usual, two Pckingese dogs wedged one at each side of her in the oversized armchair. Had she gone too far? The decision had been swift, because Molly Cornwell had been due to begin working in an engineering factory within a few days of the start of 1942. All that had changed now, and

Molly would begin her war work here, in the village of Bromley Cross. She was to oversee the Land Army girls, keep them in order at their various lodgings and make sure that they stayed out of trouble. They were, on the whole, a crass and loudly spoken bunch of young women, far too much for Isobel. Molly Cornwell would be infinitely better at keeping them under control.

'Would you like coffee, Mother?'

'No, thank you.' What would Andrew say when he discovered the identity of the new overseer? 'We shall take Christmas lunch in the breakfast room,' she said. With Charles and Richard away at war, there was no point in opening up the larger dining room. 'Where are you going now?' she asked him. 'I thought you were staying to have coffee?'

'I thought I'd see how Ivy is getting on.' Poor Ivy was cooking for everyone – for staff and patients, as well as for Andrew and his mother. 'I won't be long.'

She watched him as he disappeared into Burbank Wing, was not in the least surprised when, after a few minutes, he walked into the garden and met the girl. 'I did the right thing,' she said aloud. 'Anything that gets her away from here is worthy.' It was, she supposed, rather a coincidence that the supervisor's post should go to Dorothy's mother, but who could prove that Molly Cornwell had been chosen deliberately? As far as Andrew knew, Isobel had no idea of Dorothy's next of kin, so he could have nothing to say in the matter, surely?

In the garden, Andrew caught up with Dorothy. She was a fast walker, but she adjusted her rhythm when he drew level with her. 'Happy Christmas,' she said. 'I have escaped from the battle zone.' She showed him the bandage. 'Drastic action, but well worth the effort.'

'Cutting yourself again?' he asked, one eyebrow raised.

'This was an accident, I promise. If I ever cut myself deliberately, you will be the first to know, because Ivy is terrible at bandages. How she passed the Red Cross exam I shall never know. So, when I need another bandage, I shall ask a trained doctor.' Such time would never come, of that she felt sure. Self-mutilation was a teenager's game and she had used it recently only as a way to get out of View Street. 'My mother is terrified of blood,' she reminded him. 'That's how I used to manage her – by showing her some blood. I became so desperate, I had to use whatever worked. There's no need for me to do that sort of thing any more.'

They walked in companionable silence all the way to Chadwicke House. He unlocked the gate and stood back while she passed through into the grounds. 'Going to see Stuart?' he asked casually.

'And Lois. She was my neighbour from the other side.'

'You were wedged between Elsie and Lois?'

'Yes.'

'Enough to make anyone cut both wrists,' he said. 'Between the devil and the deep blue sea? Frying pan and fire?'

She giggled. 'They called me Dorothy-in-the-middle. That was my title. Sometimes, when they were cross with me, I was just her-in-the-middle. I was very well cared for. Without Elsie and Lois, I would probably have starved.'

'Tell me more about your mother,' he urged.

Dorothy shrugged. 'Remember the whited sepulchre in the Bible?'

'Yes.'

'That's my mother. Flawless beauty on the outside, dust and rotted flesh indoors. She was – and still is – very attractive. I've seen grown men falling off bicycles or walking into lamp posts when she passed by. There'd be a glint in her eye when that sort of thing happened – like triumph. Forty-eight, she is now, but she looks about thirty-five. She's evil.'

'What made her evil?' he asked.

Again, Dorothy lifted her shoulders. 'God knows. From what I can gather, she had a normal childhood, no big shocks or tragedies. She seems to have been born the way she is.'

'Nature over nurture?'

'Yes.'

That, mused Andrew, would be termed psychosis. He had seen little enough of that, most of it in mental hospitals, but a psychotic walking about unchecked in the community could be a danger to many, as well as to herself. 'Has her doctor noticed nothing?'

She smiled wryly. 'Our first doctor – when I was a child – noticed everything. He was her lover, you see. That was how Miss Isherwood got me away for a while, because she brought me home from school and Mam was – well – in a compromising position with Dr Clarke. I don't know what the next doctor thought of her, because I didn't see much of him. I saw a lot of Dr Clarke, though. Mam told me I had to be polite and well behaved – now, I know why. Dr Clarke might have known she was crackers, but he looked at her as if he adored her and hated her all at the same time. Even though I was young, I noticed that.'

'She held sexual sway over him, then.'

'Yes. Once Mam gets hold of you, it's nearly impossible to get away. Unless there's blood.'

'Rather drastic, Dorothy.'

'Living with Mam was even more drastic. I was a virtual prisoner.'

'You were a rival.'

She stopped dead in her tracks. 'What? From birth? At eighteen months of age, at five?'

'You were her all over again. She was locking you in to save her second self, because somewhere inside perhaps a grain of decency told her that her life was wrong. She wanted to protect you from harm and she went too far.' He nodded. 'On the other hand, I could be completely wrong. But one thing is certain. She's ill, Dorothy.'

'Oh. Will I inherit it?'

'You would have seen it by now. I would have seen it. Your nervousness is a reaction to the way you were raised, to your husband's death and the loss of your child. You're normal.'

'I'm glad.'

They separated at the door to Chadwicke

House and Andrew watched sadly as she made off in the direction of Stuart Beddows's room. She was becoming extremely fond of the occupant of Room One. Dr Andrew Burbank was pleased for his patient, but Andrew the man had met the woman of his own dreams, and she had just walked away in the direction of someone else.

She was both unaffected and unimpressed by physical shortcomings. Had Stuart Beddows been out of the picture, Andrew might have stood a chance, albeit a chance whose standing favoured one of his lower limbs over the other. Mother was on the warpath, of course. He was thirty years old and was wandering about like a lovelorn loon, thereby sending his mother into a frenzy that was almost – but not quite – silent. Even Stuart, blinded as he had been by dressings, had noticed alterations in the tone of Andrew's voice when he had spoken to Dorothy.

'Physician, heal thyself is right,' he muttered just before he entered Room Two. He had lost her. Not that he had ever got close, but Dorothy Dyson was well out of reach, which fact would, no doubt, please Isobel Burbank very well. Mothers? They were a blessing and a trial. His was more of a trial, as was Dorothy's, but someone would be happy, at least. He got on with work for a few minutes, because work was the only antidote.

*   *   *

Molly Cornwell took the stairs two at a time. Without knocking, she threw open the door to Ian Clarke's bedroom. He had one leg only inside his trousers and he staggered when the door flew inward. Had she finally gone completely mad? 'What?' he shouted. 'You shouldn't be in here.'

'I can't wake her. She slumped off the day bed and I lifted her back onto it, but I can't make her wake up. I tried shouting and tapping her face, but nothing worked—'

'The children? Where are they?'

'They've gone down to the park with their friends – they've all had new bikes for Christmas. Hurry up! She could be dead as far as I know.'

He fastened his clothes and pushed his way past her onto the landing. Florence had been quite talkative when they had taken coffee together at eleven; he had even managed to hope that she might be rallying slightly.

She was alive. He massaged her hands. 'Florence?'

The eyelids flickered. 'Oh, my goodness,' she said breathlessly. 'That was quite a dream. I was walking in the air – not flying – walking. It was beautiful, so clear and fresh.'

Ian, who had heard many tales of near-death experiences, was not surprised. She was weaker than a newborn kitten, could no longer raise a cup to her lips, was becoming almost completely dependent on him and Molly Cornwell. It would be soon. No woman should endure such suffering, he told himself. Had his poor wife been a dog, a vet would have put her out of her misery months ago.

'Where were you?' she asked.

'I was changing. I have to go to visit a patient.' This time, he was telling the truth.

'Ian?'

'Yes?'

'Look after them. The children, I mean. They are more important than your patients. It won't be long now. I have to know that my children will be cared for.' Two fat tears gathered in the reddened corners of her eyes.

He bit hard on his lower lip. This damned disease had no respect for position in life, for diet, for medicine. One day, some clever clogs would find the cure, would isolate the factor that helped vitamins and minerals to attach to red blood cells, but the answer would not come in time for Florence. He held her hand while she drifted off to sleep again.

Out in the hall, he sobbed until his very core felt drained and dry. Then he picked up the telephone and requested a connection to a fellow doctor. After establishing that his patient would be attended by someone else, he turned back towards the drawing room. He didn't know how long Florence had left, but he wanted to be here for her today.

Molly closed the kitchen door quietly, then leaned against it, hands behind her back. That was the difference, she told herself. The weak and weary female in the drawing room had earned his tears. 'Who would weep for me?' she whispered into the empty room. No one loved her. No one had ever loved her. She was not lovable. Although she possessed the power to overwhelm almost any man, her make-up was not real; she was a house built on a flat-bed foundation, with no underpinning to the structure. Panic paid a visit to her breast and she caught her breath sharply. Ian was her scaffolding; without him, she would be unable to exist. Was that love, she wondered.

She rolled short crust pastry so quickly that it threatened to tear. Dorothy didn't love her and neither did Tom. As for her parents – well, they were long forgotten. She stilled her hands for an instant. Her mother had done the right thing once, she suspected. But had it been right? And why would no details come to the forefront of Molly's mind? Why was there a gap, a long pause where childhood should have been?

Ian? He wanted the body, rejected the soul and the mind of his mistress, believed that she lacked heart and feelings. How he had sobbed just now for a woman whose charms had not been remarkable, whose personality, diminished by chronic illness, had probably never been robust or even interesting. 'I am bad,' she whispered before continuing with her tasks.

Molly, who revelled in adventurous sexual contact, seemed unable to meet anyone at all on an emotional level. It was almost as if she had parts missing, but she didn't even know what she lacked. Looking at the behaviour of others was all very well, but nothing could teach her to be what she wasn't. Normal. She wasn't normal. The hard part was the knowing. How much easier life might have been had she not understood her own separation from the main herd. And no one could give her what she lacked, so she had to travel as before – on instinct, blinkered almost to the point of blindness.

He came into the kitchen. 'She won't last the week,' he said quietly.

'I'm sorry.' And she was sorry, but mostly because Florence's death might spoil the pattern of her own life. Had she grieved at her own mother's deathbed? No. As for her father – well, the less frequently he was considered, the better. He had seldom cared for anything beyond his next drinking session in the local hostelry.

'Molly?'

'Yes?'

'Thanks for helping my wife. You know I didn't trust you when you first arrived here, but you have done an exceptional job – quite remarkable, in fact. And the way you have kept Florence so clean – I bless you for that. It isn't easy and you have been an absolute brick – I am grateful.'

Molly's eyes pricked. Someone was praising her, and she had not heard praise since . . . she couldn't remember. 'She's welcome,' she said. 'That's a very ill woman.' She carried on making her apple pie. If only she could feel something for Florence. If only she could feel something real for the man who stood beside her. Love? Was that what she had for him? Or was it just another simple need, a hunger, a thirst requiring intermittent appeasement?

'I'll always look after Dorothy,' he told her, 'and the other one, also.'

She raised her head, eyes narrowing as she looked straight at him. 'What about me?' she asked.

Her? She was a bridge to be crossed when it was reached and not before. And she was not a steady bridge, not one to offer safe passage across raging waters. Didn't a woman think first and foremost about her offspring, about the welfare of her young? 'You'll be comfortable,' he said before leaving the room.

Molly dropped her rolling pin and stared ahead into an empty future. She would be comfortable. She would not be married to him, would not be stepmother to children whose welfare and amusement had become her responsibility in recent weeks. The thought of endless years in View Street with Tom was almost unbearable. She had known what she was marrying, had told him that she would go elsewhere for pleasures of the flesh, but what would happen when her looks began to fade, when no one wanted her? She was twenty-six and most women in these parts were well finished and on the scrap heap by forty.

In the drawing room, Ian was perched on a footstool at the side of his dying wife. Molly stood in the doorway, watched his lips moving, failed to catch the contents of his whisperings. To incur such devotion, a woman had to be truly adored. This skeletal figure with thinning hair, transparent hands and grey-yellow skin was the love of Ian Clarke's life. It was nothing to do with sexuality, with imagination and inventiveness. Real people met at a level that was non-existent in Molly Cornwell. She was a hobby, no more. Some men collected stamps, some played with trains, others impaled beautiful butterflies and moths on pins. Some kept a woman on the side.

The woman on the side returned to the kitchen to peel potatoes. Soon, this would all be over and she would face a long, lonely future in a large, lonely world.

*   *   *

The proposal arrived on the first day of 1942. Dorothy shocked him and herself by accepting it. She held on to Stuart's good hand and pledged herself there and then, no time to think, to reason with herself, to question her motives. He had to believe in his future, had to know that he remained personable enough to attract the love of a normal, pretty woman.

But she found herself quite unprepared for the reaction of her employer. He glared at her across his desk, bewilderment plain in face and voice. 'What the hell do you think you are doing, Dorothy? Have you never heard of the fine divide between pity and love? You feel for him – of course you do – we all do, but marriage? That is the commitment of a lifetime and well you know it. He is Steve again – can't you see that? You are planning to do for Stuart what you never had the chance to do for your husband.'

She folded her arms.

He pointed at her. 'And that's a gesture of defiance and of defence. You can't get rid of me by folding your arms, madam. You are doing what you consider to be the decent thing, but a loveless marriage? How can you contemplate such an action?'

This was going to be the unedited version, thought Dorothy. Andrew had two modes – staccato and lengthy – and she was receiving the latter. His colour was rising and his hair, seldom tidy, seemed to have taken on a life of its own. 'If I am making a mistake,' she said carefully, 'then it is just that – it is my mistake, my own, my property. You should concern yourself with your patients, not with me. If you believe my marrying him will affect his health and make him ill, I shall listen to your arguments. Otherwise, stay out of it, Andrew. This is none of your business.'

'Do you love him?' He watched her closely, noted that her eyes closed and that when she opened them, her gaze had moved away from him. But she looked at him again almost immediately. 'Well?' he asked, though he already knew the answer – had read her doubts just seconds earlier.

'Yes, I love him.'

'As a husband? As you loved Steve?' Again, he noted that her eyes betrayed her.

'No two loves are the same, I'm sure.'

Andrew shook his head. 'I know that you are an intelligent woman. I understand your grief, your isolation, your need to establish yourself as

229

part of a family unit. But he is marked – and not just on his face. Have you any idea of the number of men who killed themselves after the last war? They came back, worked, had children, made homes. But somewhere deep inside, there was an emptiness, a terrible void that grew bigger as time passed. It was their stolen youth, Dorothy. Wilfred Owen wrote the "Anthem for Doomed Youth". Have you read it? "And each slow dusk, a drawing-down of blinds"? Read it. Thousands died in their souls. Those who survived the battlefield did not survive its remembered horrors.'

She sat down and bowed her head. 'If you want the truth, I am not completely sure – but who is? I need to be needed. He needs to be wanted. We are the same. His face is marked because of what happened to his body in that aeroplane. Now, he suffers in his mind. I understand that. I suffered in my mind until I escaped my mother – and my body is marked because of her. Yes, I made the scars; yes, she held the knife against my soul. To be hated by a mother is a terrible thing. I shall marry him. He will be well cared for and so will I. He loves me.'

'I know he does.' Andrew stood up and walked to the window. 'In five years' time, when you are tied down by a couple of children and a man who feels different from everyone else, where will you turn?'

She made no reply.

'When he wakes in the night screaming and beating out imagined flames—'

'I'll be there. I will be there, Andrew. Now,

230

have you quite finished? We are to be married as soon as some of the surgery is done and he is ready to leave here. Oh, and I wondered whether you might help us adopt little Matthew Taylor.'

He nodded. 'I shall do all in my power. Leave that with me.'

She thanked him and walked out of the office.

Andrew, suddenly tired, lowered himself into an easy chair by the window. Mother was watching again, was hard against the flawed glass in their temporary drawing room. From this distance, she seemed small, yet she made herself large just by her way of life. All around her, grim chinoiserie would be adding to the air of gloom she carried with her in the absence of her younger and more robust sons. She, at least, would be pleased by the news. As he looked, Isobel shrank back into the shadows where, no doubt, she would amuse herself with embroidery, knitting, or the company of those two dreadful dogs.

Dorothy. Oh, Dorothy. He had no doubt about her motives. She wanted to devote herself to the improvement of Stuart Beddows, was convinced that she could bring joy into his life, that she could make him whole again. But Andrew, who knew how deep the damage went with Stuart, realized that Dorothy was a lifeline, a comfort and a base to which he could return when life became cruel. And it would be cruel. Stuart needed not external girders, but inner strength that would harden his core and make his ego robust. Dorothy could never be his skeleton, his framework, his inner stability. That could be developed only through time and with the help of a trained counsellor.

'You want her for yourself,' he told the mirror as he attempted to flatten his wayward curls. He loved her. He loved her, needed her and could not have her. Heartbroken, he went about his duties, because the job was the only thing that made sense.

* * *

Molly sat as still as stone, no sound emerging from her lips, no sobs, not the slightest whimper. But down her cheeks poured a water-fall, a sheet of tears left running unheeded to her chin, from which the collected wetness dropped rhythmically onto her clothes.

Ian didn't need to approach the bed; his wife was dead and he must send at once for her own practitioner. A huge swell of relief filled his chest, because the last few days had been terri-ble. Florence had sunk into coma and Molly had not left her side in over forty-eight hours. It was a release, a blessing for an excellent mother and a wife who had always been true, supportive and calm. He walked past his mistress only to close properly eyes that had opened slightly after death. 'Goodbye, Florence,' he said, bend-ing to kiss a forehead already visited by the chill of death.

'It wasn't me,' said Molly. 'It wasn't me, honestly.'

Even through his grief, the doctor could not

help noticing the terrible state of Molly Cornwell. She didn't move. Saline continued to pour from eyes that scarcely blinked, yet she was absolutely motionless. 'Did you say something, Molly?'

'Wasn't me,' she repeated. 'It was him. He can't get Dorothy, can he?'

'No, he can't.'

At last, she looked at him, though her eyes remained vacant, as if staring into a different dimension. 'Dorothy is me,' she said clearly. Then she turned away from him and continued as before, body rigid, tears flowing fast down the beautiful face.

Ian left to fetch the family doctor who lived just a minute's walk away. When he returned, Molly was performing her usual duties in the kitchen. Before following his colleague upstairs, he glanced through the door and saw that Molly was perfectly calm and that her tears had dried in that very short time. But there was protocol to be observed, a death certificate to obtain, an undertaker to find. There were children to be fetched from friends' houses where they had been placed during their mother's final days. They had to be told, and Ian needed to be the one to tell them.

It was ten o'clock before he got the chance to see Molly again. She had persuaded the children to eat, had listened to their grief, had packed the three of them off to their rooms where all were now sleeping. He found her lying on Florence's day bed. Clearly exhausted, she had fallen asleep fully dressed, one shoe still on a foot, the other on the rug. He poured himself a brandy and sat by the fire. His wife had been dead for approximately four hours and would remain in that state for the remainder of time.

'She didn't know, Ian.'

'Ah, you're awake.'

'Yes.' She sat up and swung her feet to the floor. 'Florence just stopped breathing. She didn't know about us. I never said a word and I am sure you didn't. We didn't hurt her, so don't worry on that score.'

He studied her. 'When you were crying, what did you say?'

Molly yawned. 'I never cry. I haven't cried for as long as I can remember. Crying and wailing are against the rules of my religion.'

He tapped fingernails against the crystal globe, then swilled the last of the brandy around before swallowing it. 'You said something about it not being you, about some man getting Dorothy. Then you said that Dorothy was you.'

She shook her head. 'Nonsense. You must have been hearing things.'

'Molly, I heard you. And you wept – your blouse was wet through – look how wrinkled it is.'

'Of course it's wrinkled. I fell asleep on here, didn't I? And I haven't taken a bath in two days, haven't changed my clothes except for the absolute essentials. You must be in shock.'

He realized then that they were both telling the truth, and that she had no memory of the episode. But the death of Florence had triggered some long-buried memory in this woman's mind, something she had tucked away and hidden from herself, possibly since childhood.

She rose to her feet. 'I shall sleep in the spare bed in Sarah's room, if that's all right. You need to rest and start the grieving process. If the children wake, I'll see to them.'

'Good night,' he said as she disappeared into the hall.

He stayed where he was all through that night, making of the vigil a punishment for himself, a requiem for his dead wife and a prayer for children who must now grow without the protection and guidance of a mother. Even while ill, the poor woman had loved her children, had taken an interest in his work, had never tried to hold him back whenever a patient had needed him, whenever he had needed Molly. All those lies. All this brandy. He had better make coffee, because he had two sons and a daughter to care for tomorrow, which was now today.

After copious amounts of caffeine, he began to make the list of things to be done before Florence's funeral. He wrote down names of friends and colleagues to be informed, made notes about policies to be cashed and bank accounts that needed to be altered. Florence was with the undertaker, but she would be brought back home and her final journey would be made from this very room, the place in which she had rested until coma had kept her upstairs.

At the end of it all, the burning question remained. What was he going to do about Molly?

*   *   *

Isobel Burbank was in a state of confusion. She had allocated a cottage to Molly Cornwell, and now her actions seemed not to have been necessary.

'Mother?'

'Ah, yes. I am sorry, Andrew, but my mind was elsewhere. You must be very relieved to know that one of your patients, at least, will be looked after when he leaves here. Such a handsome chap, too, or so I am told. I am sure that Dorothy will take good care of him.'

'I asked if you would like another sandwich.'

'No, thank you. We seem to have done nothing but eat since Christmas.' The woman would be in the cottage now. It was minimally furnished, but the accommodation was certainly adequate for a woman on her own. Molly Cornwell's husband, who was a miner, would be remaining at their house in town.

Andrew could see that Isobel was distracted. 'Mother, is there something on your mind?'

'Well, of course there is,' she almost snapped. 'I have two sons fighting in this ghastly war and all mothers worry in such circumstances. Everyone is worried. London is taking a battering, as are Coventry and Liverpool. It's all very well for Mr Churchill to deliver his speeches, but a mother still worries.'

'The Americans are with us now. We can't lose.'

'We may win the war and I may lose your brothers. Pass me the knitting, please.'

Andrew gave up. He wandered off to nurse his own distress at the loss of Dorothy. She was doing the wrong thing and she knew it, but he could do no more to dissuade her.

Isobel threw down needles and khaki wool, dragged on her hat and coat, ordered her dogs to remain where they were, then left the house by the front door. If only she had been less hasty. Dorothy, engaged to that other young man, should stay here and become thoroughly engrossed in him. She was no longer a danger, so all the plans and machinations regarding Molly Cornwell had been unnecessary. What could be done? Should Isobel send her back to town with the excuse that someone else had been taken on to deal with the welfare of the Land Army girls? Oh, what a mess.

She reached Bromley Cross and approached the first row of weavers' cottages. Elsie Shipton, sister of Ivy Crumpsall, lived here now with the burnt woman, the one who had been injured in the most recent bombardment of Bolton. Ivy and her husband were temporarily billeted at Burbank Hall. The cottage allocated to Molly Cornwell was next door to Ivy's. Isobel knocked at the door.

Molly opened it. 'How lovely to see you, Mrs Burbank. See – I have the place pretty already – the rag-and-bone man cleared his cart for me and brought me up with some of my own furniture.' Proudly, she showed Isobel her treasures.

'My husband has enough in View Street – I didn't bring anything he needed.'

Isobel sat down while Molly went off to make tea. There were pictures on the walls, books on a shelf, items of glassware in a cabinet. A new rug stretched itself in front of a roaring fire and Isobel didn't know what to say or do. She accepted a cup of tea. There was no hope of moving this woman out of here. In a matter of hours, she had embedded herself and she would surely make a terrible fuss if asked to leave. This needed to be handled with delicacy.

Molly sat bolt upright like a dog awaiting an order from its master.

'The main thing you must remember is not to come up to the house unless invited. This rule applies to all nonresidents at Burbank, because most of the building is now the temporary property of the government. I think it's something to do with careless talk costing lives – you will have seen the posters. We do have high-ranking air force staff in residence, so we all tread softly.'

Molly hid her disappointment very well. 'Of course,' she replied.

Isobel drew a sheet of paper from her handbag. 'Now, this is a list of land girls and the farms.' She pulled out a second sheet. 'Here's the map. Some of the girls live here in the village. Most stay at the farms where they are employed. Watch for pregnancies, pilfering and idleness. Talk to the farmers. Make duty rotas and be on call as often as possible. Your hours will be long and varied, but a sum of money is allocated for you – it is supposed to be my job, but I have enough to do – and you will be paid by me. I shall visit you twice a week to discuss any problems. Be prepared for farmers knocking at your door very early or very late. This is an important job. You are now a personnel officer and you will write reports.'

Personnel officer. Molly almost glowed when she heard the impressive title, but she hid her feelings as carefully as ever. 'Thank you,' was all she said by way of response.

'So.' Isobel rose to her feet. 'We understand each other. I must go now and attend to other duties.'

Alone, Molly stretched out in front of the fire. This was the chance of a lifetime. She would make herself indispensable, would be here at the end of the war and, with any luck, would be taken on by the Burbank family to work on the estate. Because Isobel Burbank had lost her footing in town, Molly Cornwell had fallen on her own feet fair and square.

It was a lovely little house and the view from the kitchen of the moors was gorgeous. She had a home in the country and one in town. Like a posh Londoner, she would one day be able to travel between the two and enjoy the best of both worlds.

The little room, overheated by an enthusiastic log fire, was cosy. She looked at the beamed ceiling, imagined how the place would be in summer, then drifted off to sleep. In her dreams, she visited another house in another time, a large, well-appointed property in an avenue off Chorley New Road. A dead woman was stretched out on the bed, face devoid of colour, hands cooling, husband planting a farewell kiss on the white forehead.

Within minutes, Molly woke. Her face was wet. It was sweat, she decided before opening the window slightly. It had to be sweat, because Molly Cornwell never wept.

NINE

'Well, what do you think?' Dorothy handed the
letter back to Stuart. 'We can still be married at
Easter, not long after the date we chose. You
will be back here within three or four weeks.'

'If all goes well.'

'Why shouldn't it go well? You've heard what
the man has managed to do for other people –
why should you be the exception? If he can
straighten out some of your burns, let him.'

He smiled with the side of his face that
allowed movement. 'I shall never be handsome
again, sweetheart. He could work on me for the
next five years and I'd still be a wreck. I'm not
sure. Sometimes, hope is a destructive thing. I
am promised more pain – and for what? To own
a face that looks just slightly less like a clay
model of the Himalayas? I'll think about it. Go
for your refs while I chew things over.'

She agreed that he should consider his
options, then went off in the direction of the
main house. In the Burbank Wing kitchen,
Ivy would be waiting with tea, coffee, words of
wisdom and Elsie-next-door who was no longer

Elsie-next-door but Elsie-from-Ivy's-cottage-in-the-village. Lois, too, was seated at the large central table, and when Dorothy entered the room conversation stopped dead, as if in accordance with the baton of some invisible conductor of this chattering orchestra. They had been talking about her, Dorothy presumed. This had happened before, when she had lived in Emblem Street. Women talked. These women talked enough to be Members of Parliament.

She poured her coffee and joined the three women at the table. 'Well? Has the cat eaten everyone's tongue?' She stood and looked at their faces, noticing that all three women appeared rather out of sorts. Neither Ivy nor Elsie showed the slightest sign of nodding – this was serious stuff, indeed. Everyone was suddenly studying a plate, a saucer or a loose button on a cardigan. No one moved while Dorothy prepared to settle herself. 'Well?' she asked, an edge to her voice. 'What's the matter this time? Has there been a national disaster? Do I have to pull out your fingernails to get an answer? Or shall I try some more subtle form of torture?'

Elsie Shipton was staring down into her cup. She seemed lost for words, which symptom was unusual enough to make Dorothy even more certain that something was gravely amiss. Elsie was never at a loss except at times of death or destruction. What on earth had happened?

Ivy got up and clattered a couple of pans. Lois, with a scarf hiding some of the damage to her face and neck, looked straight at Dorothy.

'Me and Elsie have got a new neighbour. I suppose it's Ivy's neighbour, really, but it's ours for the time being, what with her living up here and us stopping at her house, like. So we're the one's what's stuck with it. With her, I mean.'

'Sit down, love,' said Elsie.

Dorothy sat. 'Whatever's the matter with everybody? Has Adolf Hitler moved in? Have we been invaded?'

Elsie sighed. 'Not quite, Dorothy. It's your mother.'

Dorothy's jaw dropped and she closed her mouth with a determined clash of incisors. 'My mother? In Bromley Cross? It can't be. Is Dad with her? She'd never come up here – she wouldn't leave her house for anybody – it's not in her nature. She's got a proper bathroom and electricity and a Hoover . . .' Her words died.

Lois grabbed one of Dorothy's hands. 'We've not seen your dad, but she's there, all right, and Elsie recognized her straight away, remembered her from that night you both slept at View Street. She come up this morning with John Hodgkinson – you know, the rag-and-bone chap, beard, flat cap, never has a wash. Brought some bits of furniture with her, then we heard her rattling about, lighting a fire, shifting stuff round.'

'But why?' asked Dorothy. 'Who told her I was here? How the hell did she manage to find me? Who did this?'

A glance passed between Elsie and Lois. 'Not us,' they chorused.

'What makes you think she's come to Bromley

Cross to find you?' asked Lois. 'Mrs Burbank was there with her – the mistress of this house. She must have given her a job or something. We don't know. If we knew, we'd say, wouldn't we?'

'She'll spoil everything.' Dorothy stood up. 'She will. Somebody must have brought her here – she's after me. Why won't she leave me alone?' Before anyone could speak again, Dorothy left the kitchen and ran all the way back to Chadwicke House. Without even pausing for breath, she threw inward the door of Andrew's office and placed herself in front of his desk. 'Was it you?' she said.

'Was what me?'

She blew a stray strand of hair out of her eyes. 'My mother. Was it you who brought her? She'd never come right up here of her own accord. There's something going on and I want to know who started it, what's the reason for it and how I can get rid of her.'

'You've been running.'

'It's all right,' she remarked smartly, 'I've got a licence to run. Well?'

He saw that she was angry to the point of fury, but, more disturbingly, Dorothy Dyson was afraid. 'Sit down.'

'I don't need to sit down. I don't want to sit down. I don't like being told what to do. The chair's visible – if I want it, I shall use it.' She blew at the same lock of tumbled hair. 'Who brought her?'

'I have absolutely no idea.'

If Dorothy knew one thing about Andrew Burbank, that one thing was that he was no liar.

Deflated, she gave in and sank into the chair. She could not believe what she had just heard in the Burbank Wing kitchen. Yet it had to be true. Nobody would make up a lie of such a size – Elsie would never harm Dorothy, no matter what.

'Perhaps it's someone who looks like her,' Andrew suggested.

'Nobody looks like her. Except for me. We're identical twins, though one of us is twenty-odd years older than the other. She is the spitting image of me and vice versa. The life she gave me . . .' Dorothy's words died. She bit hard on her lower lip, then closed her eyes. 'You've read the diaries. God help me,' she muttered.

'I know your life was bad. From the little you have told me and from the stuff you wrote as a child, I know already that you were unhappy. But, Dorothy, you are a grown woman now and she cannot hurt you. You are old enough to make your own decisions and there isn't a thing she can do about it.'

'You don't know her. She could make the devil himself cower in a corner.' Something occurred to her. 'Andrew, whatever happens, please don't tell Stuart any of this. He is supposed to go into Chester Oakfields soon for his first operation – I don't want anything to hold him back. He knows I don't get on with my mother – I had to tell him a little when we were discussing the wedding – but he mustn't know the truth.'

'I don't know the full truth,' Andrew said.

Dorothy sat very still for a few moments. 'I

sometimes wonder whether even I know all of it – whether I remember things properly. But anyway, she's in the cottage next door to Ivy's.'

'Ah – the one currently inhabited by your neighbours from Bolton.'

'Yes. Elsie met my mother the night the bomb fell. She saw her trying to lock me in again the next morning. Ask her. Elsie will tell you what my mother is.'

He stood up and took his jacket from the back of his chair. 'The mountain will travel to Muhammad,' he said. 'Let me go and meet your mother.'

'On what pretext?'

He thought for a moment. 'Well, we own the house she occupies. Perhaps the plumbing is in need of attention – whatever – I shall think of something. Do you want to come along?'

'I'd rather eat snails.'

'The French eat snails.'

'I always thought there was something wrong with the French. What's she up to, Andrew? Why here? She's lived in View Street since I was a baby – over a quarter of a century. That house is her pride and joy.' She remembered an important point. 'Lois says your mother visited my mother when she moved into the cottage. So that's something to do with it.'

Andrew pondered that point for a moment. 'I'll get back to you.' On his way to the door, he stopped and placed a hand on her shoulder. All he wanted was to take away her pain. No matter what the cost to himself, he had to save her.

Because . . . He didn't want to think about the reasons.

He took the car, partly because his leg sometimes didn't feel like walking that stretch to the village, mostly because a vehicle would make his visit seem more professional. Plumbing. Why would a son of Burbank Hall be concerned about the plumbing? Ah, yes. He could use as excuse the fact that most capable tradesmen were abroad fighting Nazis. All the same, he drove slowly in order to give himself some thinking time. And how on earth had his mother managed to become embroiled with Dorothy's? Perhaps he should have spoken to her first, but he didn't want to turn back now – Dorothy would be waiting.

When she opened her door, he knew immediately who she was. This was no matchless beauty; the match was currently pacing up and down in Chadwicke House or back at the hall. This was how Dorothy Dyson would look when she approached fifty, although few other women would reach their half-century with their looks still near-perfect. 'Hello,' he said. 'My name is Andrew Burbank and I heard that you had recently moved into one of our cottages. I am here to welcome you and to make sure that you are comfortable. There is a shortage of skilled men just now, so I decided to make sure that everything is in good order for you.'

She opened the door and stepped to one side. 'Come in.'

Feeling like a fly coming too close to a spider's

web, Andrew entered the cottage. It was as clean as a new pin, cheerful and warm. Were he to judge a psyche by décor, this woman would probably come up smelling of roses. 'Has Mother visited you already?'

'She has, yes.'

'How's the plumbing?'

She wrinkled her nose. 'Noisy – as if the water has a bad cough. If no one's run the taps for a while, there'll be air in the system. The kitchen copper works, anyway, so I can boil. It'll take me a while to get used to the zinc bath again, but there is a war on and I have a job to do.' She waved a hand towards a chair, her eyes inviting him to sit.

'Yes.' He sat. 'We all have a job to do.'

'Better than the engineering works,' she said. 'Mrs Burbank saved me from that by offering me this job. I've never felt luckier.'

He cleared his throat. 'Which job was it? We have several, you see – the mother and baby unit, the convalescent home, kitchen duties—'

'I'm personnel,' she said. 'I've to make sure that the farmers are all right with the Land Army girls, check on everything, keep their work on track and keep the girls out of trouble and make sure the crops are all on time – with some help from the weather, of course.'

'Ah. So you are to liaise between Civvy Street and the Land Army. A peacekeeper in a time of war. Good luck with it.'

'Thank you.' He was nice-looking, she decided. The limp lent him an air of mystery that reminded her of some character out of a spy film. She judged his age to be around the thirty mark and his clothes as made-to-measure. 'I'm good with people,' she said. 'I don't let them get under my skin, you see.'

That he believed. No one would ever get too close for Molly Cornwell's comfort. The eyes were the strangest he had ever encountered – stunningly beautiful, but absolutely devoid of expression. Any similarities between herself and Dorothy were on the surface; Dorothy's face possessed the ability and willingness to change in accordance with inner mood and with external atmosphere, because Dorothy was normal. This woman was . . . was almost two-dimensional, a lovely painting and no more.

'Can I get you a sherry?' she asked. 'We had a drop over from Christmas and I brought it with me.'

'No, thanks,' he replied. Then, as casually as he could manage, he threw the question into the ring. 'In which newspaper did you find our advertisement? I believe Mother tried two or three of the local publications.'

She regaled him with the story of the chance meeting in town. 'Where was that?' he asked. After receiving her reply, he knew that something didn't gel. Mother's ration books were with local traders and she would not buy meat in town. Mother never shopped except for clothes and those terrible almost-Chinese figurines and pictures she collected. He tried to imagine Isobel Burbank carrying a pound of pork sausages and a couple of kidneys, failed completely. Two manipulative mothers were behind this plan. How silly his own female parent must be feeling now, with Dorothy engaged to Stuart Beddows and her precious son safe without any intervention on her part.

'So your mother was my life-saver,' concluded Molly. 'I get fresh air, a nice little house and the chance to stay away from engineering and bombs.'

'Your husband?'

'He works at Westhoughton in the pits. It would be too far from here, so he's staying on in View Street.'

Andrew stood up. He was angrier than he had been in years. Although he wanted to get back to Dorothy as quickly as possible, the need to see another scheming woman overtook the desire to put Dorothy's mind at rest. He said goodbye and left Molly Cornwell to get on with her preparations for the new job. She had made no mention of Dorothy, and neither had he. But the second woman at the centre of this mess had to be dealt with immediately.

He burst into the drawing room so abruptly that he knocked a gilded Buddha from a stand.

'Andrew!' Isobel cried. 'That is one of my favourites.'

He picked it up. 'Nothing broken,' he said, 'with the distinctly possible exception of Dorothy Dyson's heart.' When Buddha had been reseated in his usual place of residence, Andrew turned on his mother the full force of his anger. A man of iron self-control, he was best avoided on those rare occasions when he lent his temper free rein. 'How dare you?' he shouted.

Isobel assumed an expression of confusion.

'How did you find out about Dorothy's mother?'

She touched her hair. 'I beg your pardon?'

Andrew was now certain of his ground – Mother always patted her hair when giving birth to a lie. 'Buying meat at a butcher's shop in town? While she happened to be getting her hair done next door, where you managed to slip and turn your ankle on the pavement outside, after which you shared tea in that terrible café? You have never carried meat in your life, would never take tea in such a dirty place.'

'I have no idea what you are trying to imply—'

'I am not trying, Mother. I am not even implying. I am telling you that because I had let something slip about Dorothy's past, you took it upon yourself to locate her mother and bring her here. You were afraid that I might fall in love with Dorothy. So you have brought Molly Cornwell into the picture in order to get rid of Dorothy. You are utterly despicable. How dare you interfere? How dare you put that young woman through further torment? You planned this, right down to the last detail.'

Trembling, she picked up Ming and sat down with him in her lap. 'Where are you going?' she asked when her son turned away.

'To pack,' he said. 'I shall move into Burbank Wing with the rest of the staff. I'll visit you to make sure that you are in good health, but I think you are best left alone to enjoy all the hideous stuff you collect. This room is depressing, as is your company.' He slammed the door behind him.

Stilled by shock, Isobel clung to the Pekingese. She knew full well that there was no point in attempting to deny his accusations. As ever, he was several steps ahead of her and could spot a lie from thirty yards through dense fog. Polio had taken away some of his physical abilities, but lying in bed all those months had forced him to hone his mind to the point where he had outstripped brothers and classmates with apparent ease. He was too clever for her, had always been too clever.

With a packed suitcase in one hand, Andrew entered the kitchen of Burbank Wing. He begged Ivy to prepare a room for him, announced that he would be taking his meals with them in the future, then asked after Dorothy.

'We've not seen hide nor hair since she dashed off earlier,' said Ivy. 'Lois and Elsie told her about her mam moving in next door to my house and Dorothy took off as if she had a mad tiger on her tail. From what our Elsie said, that Molly's not right in the head department. Happen you should take a look at her.'

But Andrew was anxious to take a look at someone else. He drove as quickly as he could to Chadwicke House and found Dorothy in his office. It was plain that she had not left the room in over an hour.

'Well?' she asked.

It needed to be the truth, the whole truth and nothing else. In matter-of-fact terms, he relayed exactly what had occurred.

She stared hard at him. 'But why?' she asked. 'Why would your mother do such a terrible thing?'

'My fault,' he answered. 'I mentioned your difficulty with your mother and off went my mother to find her. She must have gone to some trouble to discover your next of kin.' He remembered the list, the diaries in a drawer, and was disgusted anew by Isobel's behaviour.

'But why?' she asked again.

He maintained eye contact with her as he spoke the final and biggest truth. 'Because I love you. Mother, who is endowed with the usual female instincts, realized my feelings for you and took the steps she deemed necessary to separate me from you. Molly is a weapon. I don't know whether Molly knows that you are working here. I gave her no information. I stuck to the landlord act – asked was she comfortable, voiced concerns about the plumbing – that sort of thing. So there you have it – your mother is my mother's weapon. In view of the fact that you are now engaged to someone else, it would appear that all this plotting and planning was unnecessary.'

Dorothy closed her eyes. She saw the straps on her bed, the bars at the window, the knife she had used to get her own way in the end. 'We both have a problem,' she said. 'Your mother's need to control you may be more subtle, but it's there.'

'Yes. Just as I have always been there. Polio kept me close to home, and apart from my time in medical school I have been a permanent landmark in her life. She thinks I'll always be here. My brothers are practically engaged to marry, but I am expected to remain single and at her beck and call for the rest of time.'

Dorothy raised her eyelids. 'Stuart is a place for me to be,' she said. 'More than that, he is a place where I can be myself. We are both marked, and some of the marks are invisible. They're the worst.'

'I know.'

'We belong together.'

A quote from *Hamlet* entered Andrew's mind – 'The lady doth protest too much, methinks'. Hadn't that been spoken by Gertrude, yet another mother? He noticed that Dorothy was becoming restless, was tugging at her hair – and that mannerism, in her case, was a symptom of agitation. 'Dorothy?'

'I'm confused,' she admitted. 'And the arrival of Mam isn't helping.'

'Would you like me to get rid of her?' he asked. 'Because I can.'

She thought about that. 'I'm not sure. She can be vengeful, you see. And, if she already knows I am living here, she will be back. At least we know where she is. Elsie and Lois will keep an eye on her. Oh, I've no idea what to suggest. I wouldn't put anything past Mam – up to and including murder.'

He shook his head sadly. 'I must apologize for opening my mouth in the privacy of my home. If I had said nothing to Mother, if I had acted in a professional manner, none of this would have come about. It's my fault.'

Dorothy smiled wryly. 'My mother is nobody's fault. She simply *is*. She exists, like Cape Horn and Niagara Falls. No one understands her. I doubt very much whether she understands herself. She's an element.'

'An accident of nature?'

'Possibly. Andrew?'

'What?'

'Don't love me. I can't bear it.'

'All right. I shall pull the switch and turn myself off.' He stood up. 'I have patients to see. Two of them get on well with each other, so I shall try a session with both together.' He left the office.

Dorothy looked at the empty chair and realized that she felt lonely – almost bereft. He was her best friend in the whole world. She leaned her elbows on the desk and put her head in her hands. Stuart needed her. Stuart needed a woman who could see past scars and look at the soul. Stuart would return to depression if she left him. Mam was a mile or two away. Andrew was doing his job. Andrew. She loved Andrew.

She loved two men. She couldn't love two men, because nobody did that. Stuart was vulnerable, but so was Andrew. Mam would find her soon, would discover her engagement, would do all in her power to separate Dorothy from the man she loved. She loved . . . She loved Stuart and she loved Andrew and perhaps Mam should be allowed to run amok. She had tried with Steve, had told him that Dorothy was not meant for marriage, that she was too nervy and delicate. But Steve had known Dorothy since childhood and he had not listened to Molly Cornwell.

It was time for little Matthew's feed. As a married woman, she would have a chance of adopting the orphan with whom she had developed a strong bond. He would have a good home, a good father, a mother who would not try to control his every move. She was marrying Stuart. No matter what the cost, she refused absolutely to break his heart.

*   *   *

Life in Mansfield Avenue settled into a routine of sorts after Florence's funeral. Ian, who was working long hours to cover for a sick colleague at another surgery, came home each evening to a hot meal with his children, while Molly, in an effort to make herself almost invisible, remained in the kitchen for much of the time. She prepared breakfasts, packed lunches on schooldays, and provided an evening meal every day of the week. This drudgery she accepted with cold equanimity, as there was always a price to pay in life. Perhaps he would change his mind; perhaps he would realize how much he depended on her and would marry her – after her divorce, of course.

At the beginning of February, he followed her into the kitchen. The children were at dance and music lessons, so the two adults had the house to themselves. He noticed the slight swell of Molly's belly, was reminded of a fifth child on the way. Molly was glorious at any time, but, when pregnant, she positively shone. Her breasts, always full, were now causing stress to the buttons on her blouse. 'Stay tonight,' he said.

'What?'

She had hair like spun silk and he longed to unpin it, to run his fingers through it, to spread it on a pillow. 'Tonight. Stay. When the children are asleep, come to my room.'

Molly put down the dish she had been intending to wash. 'Have you lost your mind? Or shall we wear gags? I am sure that we could do the business quietly if we concentrated, but there is always the chance that we might be heard.'

'We'll be quiet,' he said. 'Please, Molly.'

'No.'

He sighed, exasperation plain in the weight of the sound he made. 'I can't live like this,' he said.

'And I cannot lie on a bed where the only woman I ever respected died. It's Florence's bed.' Florence had meant something after all.

Scruples? She had scruples? His eyebrows shot upward. 'Then I shall buy a new one. If I buy a new one, will you stay?'

'No. I am not sleeping in a room filled with her things, her treasures. And her children would be just feet away. I liked your wife, Ian. She was a decent woman who was good to me in her way. She gave me pearls. She said I was a treasure and she gave me a string of real pearls.' Molly knew that she could never sleep in Florence's room.

'Molly, I need you.'

'You need to lie down with a woman. There are plenty to be had if you look carefully enough – try Manchester Road and Bridgeman Street.'

'I want you. It has to be you.'

She turned away and carried on doing the dishes. He was breathing rapidly and was getting nearer to her. How should she cope this time? Her body wanted him, was screaming for him, but this was not right. It was Florence's house. It could only be Molly's house if she became Mrs Clarke. She turned and gave him a long, open-mouthed kiss. He seemed to have more than two hands and she felt them all over her body. Smiling, she ended the caress. 'If I have ever loved anyone in my life, it has been you. But the answer is still no, because, strange as this may seem, I had feelings for your wife, too. In my opinion, she was an excellent woman.'

'All right. I shall get someone to sit in here and we shall go to the flat.' He undid her blouse and plunged a hand against a breast. She was hot, fertile, pregnant and alive. 'You are a danger to my sanity,' he said before bending to kiss her flesh.

She was in danger of giving herself up to the moment, so she pushed him away. 'Naughty,' she chided. 'Get your babysitter, go to the flat and wait for me. I won't leave here until the sitter arrives.'

He left her. Ten minutes later, he returned, announced that a neighbour was on her way, then went off to the flat.

258

Molly dried her dishes and put them away. From the bread bin, she took a piece of white paper in which a loaf had been wrapped, found a pen, wrote *NO* in capital letters, then took it up to his room. She placed it on his pillow, did not even look at the side of the bed that had been occupied by his dead wife. This was one of the most difficult moments of Molly Cornwell's adult life, as she had never before curbed her needs. She owned but one lover, father to Dorothy and to the unborn, but she would take the reins once more. 'Let him wait,' she said as she descended the stairs.

When her bus passed the bottom of Chorley New Road, she looked up at the windows of the flat, saw a dim light through the curtains, knew that he would be lighting a fire and warming the bed. Her feet itched to leave the bus when it stopped, but she stayed where she was. Ian Clarke would have to learn the hard way.

The next morning, he was waiting for her. She stepped into the house, walked past the open doors to drawing and dining rooms, entered the kitchen and began to make breakfast. He would not come near her until his three children had left for school, but she could almost taste his anger in the air. She served the children, put a plate of food in his place, walked back to the kitchen.

'Your breakfast is here, Pa,' shouted Sarah.

Molly heard him as he clattered his chair in the dining room. There would be fireworks once the children had left, but she had no fear of him. Ian Clarke was an adventurer when it came to lovemaking, but he was not a cruel man. She avoided his eye while clearing the table, listened as he bade his children farewell until this evening. Molly waited. With her back against the sink, she stared at the closed door until it flew inward and crashed against the wall, dislodging a calendar. She walked across the room, picked up the item and hung it back on its nail. 'Are we having a tantrum?' she asked.

'Why?' he asked.

'I got a headache, so I went straight home.'

Headaches were not the province of Molly Cornwell. Headaches belonged with gentler creatures like Florence, who did not over-indulge in fleshly activities and who even went out of their way to avoid them. 'I don't believe you. This is the game again, isn't it? The don't-touch-me game, the payment I have to make before claiming my prize.'

She awarded him a half-smile. 'Oh, no – you are the prey, Ian. I am the hunter. Remember that.' She began to walk back to the sink, but he grabbed her arm. 'Let go,' she said quietly. 'Don't pretend to be in charge of me, Dr Clarke. You don't own me. Now, why don't you go to work? The sick people of Daubhill will be in need of you. You have to cover for an absent doctor, while I have a hard day ahead of me.' She pulled away from him. 'Whatever you do, never threaten me. No one threatens me.'

He released her arm. No matter what he did, she would win. She was in total control of everything she did and of everyone around her. His children didn't mind, because they were at an age when orders from adults were acceptable – and she had never shown to them the qualities that had diminished her own child. Edward, Sarah and Daniel missed their mother and Molly had stepped into the breach, keeping an eye on homework, making sure they were kitted out for school. They liked her.

She was clever and very, very dangerous, he thought as he watched her slow, fluid movements. The woman brought sensuality to the performance of even the most mundane of tasks. She wanted him to beg. Exasperated beyond measure, he swung round, left the kitchen, left the house, the slamming of the front door causing ornaments to clatter in his wake.

Molly went about her business: cleaned windows, washed clothes, prepared the evening meal. Then, when everything was completed to her satisfaction, she crossed the avenue and asked the spinster in the opposite house to sit and wait for the children. 'My husband needs me,' she lied. 'I have to get home. Could you come over in about half an hour? Dinner's in the oven and the table is set.'

Just before leaving the house, Molly went into his bedroom and left the word *YES* on his pillow. Then she left and walked down to the flat, her heart keeping its usual steady rhythm as she prepared to defeat him yet again. He was putty in her hands and she would mould him into a shape that pleased her.

She lit fire and lamps, sat in an armchair and

dozed. The job was exhausting and she needed her rest. After an hour, some inner mechanism brought her to instant wakefulness and she prepared herself for his arrival. This was a battle she had to win and she intended to use every weapon at her disposal. Perfumed and clad in the sheerest silk negligee, she waited for her lover to arrive.

He came. As soon as he was in the room, she wound herself round him like a climbing plant. Starved, he dragged her to the bed and trapped her against the wall. 'My turn,' he said. With a glint in his eye, he did what she usually did to him, playing her body until she screamed for release. Under such delectable punishment, Molly thrived and gave as good as she got, pulling away from him until he had to chase her round the room.

Afterwards, they lay in total silence for a while. Molly dozed until she judged him to be recovered, then she began all over again, slowly this time, treating him with gentleness and many kisses. All the time, her mind repeated the same mantra: *I have to win.*

There was no Florence to consider and Ian wondered, after the longer, slower mating, why he felt so guilty. It was because Molly wasn't right, he told himself. He was using the term 'not right' in the northern sense, because Lancastrians employed those words to label people who were disturbed or backward in the brain department. This one wasn't backward, but she was definitely disturbed.

He stretched beside her afterwards, remembered the day of Florence's death, Molly's noiseless weeping, her statement about 'him' not being able to 'get' Dorothy, the words *Dorothy is me*. She had recalled nothing of the episode later and the incident had not repeated itself.

Later that night, Ian Clarke was to wonder whether he had tempted fate during those moments of contemplation. What happened next was a nightmare he would live with for the rest of his time on earth. It would render him ashamed, afraid and uncertain; it would prove him to be the sort of man he had always derided – a coward, a fool, a rake.

Molly stood up and stretched. Her lover, asleep on the bed, needed to return to his children. The woman from the opposite house had an elderly mother who required help in getting about, so Molly had to wake him right away. She shook him. 'Ian. Ian, come on. You must go home – Miss Smythe's mother goes to bed early.'

'What?' He opened his eyes and looked at her. She was the most beautiful thing on two legs, but he had to leave her right away. 'Molly,' he groaned. He wanted to sleep with her, wake with her, keep her beside him. Was he weakening? Did he imagine that he could turn this devil-goddess into something that might slot into Mansfield Avenue with the rest of the middle-class mice?

'You have to go,' she said.

He sat up and swung his legs over the edge of the bed. As he bent to retrieve items of clothing, she screamed. It was a long, drawn-out sound, high-pitched, filled with terror. Before he raised his eyes to look at her, he saw the pool of scarlet on the floor. She was miscarrying.

Quickly, he jumped up, placed her on the bed and propped her legs on pillows. The doctor took over. Ian the man would perhaps have wanted the baby not to be born – hadn't he toyed weeks ago with the idea of rendering her unconscious and terminating the pregnancy? But the doctor's instinct dictated that he save life, and to that end he fought.

It was useless. He had no equipment, no ice, no hope. He wrapped a bloody bundle in a pillow case and removed it. When he returned from the bathroom, he noted the expression on her face. The tears were there again, but there was no sobbing. Her eyes were different – they were . . . He swallowed. They were the eyes of an innocent child. 'Molly?'

'It wasn't me. I wasn't there. Blood. Take the blood away.'

'Molly?'

'Save Dorothy. Lock it. Save her.'

'She's safe. She's with her teacher in Willows Lane.'

'It wasn't me.'

'No, no. We know it wasn't you.'

'Did you ask?'

'Yes,' he said. 'I asked.'

'Did they say it wasn't me?'

'Yes. They all know it wasn't you.' He turned away from her, pressed a hand against his forehead. The edge of what she was had shown itself again. It had arrived with the death of Florence and now with the bleeding away of the endometrial sac that had contained her child. He was no expert in the field of psychology, but he knew that Molly was irretrievably damaged and that lunacy lived not too far beneath that perfectly formed surface.

'Blood,' she said. 'A lot of blood.'

Quickly, he dressed himself and tore out of the building. Like a man possessed, he dashed round the corner into the Bolton Royal Infirmary. He wrote down her name and the address where she was at present, told a nurse about the miscarriage and about the lunacy. 'She's alone in the flat,' he said. 'Her real address is 33, View Street. I have to get back – my children are alone.' He ran back to the road, collected his car and drove home.

As he sped towards Mansfield Avenue, he heard the clanging of the bell. The ambulance did not have far to go and she would live, he hoped. But, when he sat in his lonely bedroom, he wondered whether life was right for Molly Cornwell. Twice, he had caught sight of a vulnerability he would never have looked for in a woman so unfeeling. Did she suffer somewhere inside? Was there a memory she had wrapped up and placed in a dark recess, an area in her brain of which she was almost unaware? What had shaped her? Would she ever be sane? Would she be better dead? Would the nurse from tonight recognize and remember him as one of the town's practising medics?

The next day, he telephoned the infirmary to enquire after his patient. She was ill, but comfortable, and she had been sedated. He got through the day, scarcely listening as the sick described their ailments, his mind all over the place while he tried hard to concentrate on the next move for himself, for the children, for Molly. What could he do for Molly? Nothing. He had to think about the children. Just the children.

In the end, the decision made itself. He was in need of a new world, a fresh beginning for everyone in the household. America required doctors and his qualifications would be recognized and welcomed in that far off land. He wanted a chance, an escape route. She could mention his name, and even if her sanity were in question his reputation would be damaged beyond repair.

With a swiftness that alarmed colleagues and neighbours alike, he placed his property in the hands of an agent, packed all his personal possessions, locked his door for the last time and led three confused children out of the north and onto a train for London. He could not have helped her, anyway. Even marriage would not have reversed the deep-rooted damage he had glimpsed on those two occasions. She could deteriorate with age, might become unsteady to the point of total insanity. Above all, he owed Edward, Sarah and Daniel the stability Florence would have wished for them.

But for the rest of his life, Dr Ian Clarke would be tormented by the memory of his last sight of Molly Cornwell, and by the dreadful knowledge of his own shortcomings. He had deserted her when her need had been greatest, and his actions had been less than honourable.

Paler and thinner, Molly emerged from the hospital on the first day of March. Once the bleeding had stopped, she had become steadier and the doctors had ceased to worry about her mental well-being. They sent word to Tom, who became her only visitor. He accepted the condolences of staff, many of whom expressed regret about the loss of his child. As ever, he shouldered the burden, because he loved Molly and would always be her obedient supporter, but he could not share her grief.

When she was sufficiently recovered, Molly decided to return to her job in Mansfield Avenue. She caught the bus, went past the infirmary, saw the flat in which the bad thing had happened. At the bus stop, she stepped down and turned first left, as always. Gardens in Mansfield Avenue were bright with crocus and some early daffodils, while a skittish breeze stirred foliage and lengthening grass. It was a nice day, a day when washing would dry well, a day for spring cleaning and plenty of spit and polish. She was about to turn in at the gate when Miss Smythe came across. 'Didn't he tell you?' she asked.

Molly stared uncomprehendingly at the little woman. 'What? I've been in hospital.'

'Oh, I am sorry to hear that. I do hope you are

better. We were all very sad when he decided to leave. But they've been gone a week or more, you see.'

Molly shook her head. 'Gone? Gone where?'

'America.'

Molly staggered back as if she had been hit in the face.

'Would you like to come inside for a cup of tea? I've just made some for Mother.'

'No. No, thank you. I must get back to my . . .' Back to her what? To a husband who wasn't a husband, to a daughter who lived elsewhere? 'I must get back.'

She turned and retraced her steps towards the main road, occasionally using a hand to steady herself against garden walls. He had gone. He had left her, had abandoned her, had taken away Florence's children.

Betrayed and chilled to the bone, she sat on a bench in the park. A few hundred yards away was the flat they had shared; a little further on stood an empty house in which she had cared for him, his children and his dying wife. Florence had been a good woman, had appreciated Molly, had called her a treasure. All Molly had left was a strand of pearls, creamy, smooth and graded in size. She watched mothers with prams and excited toddlers who threw bread to ducks, looked at a life she had never known, at love, at caring, at family.

She was different. She had come out wrong and with bits missing, had deliberately married a man who was incapable, had not wanted that permanent and cloying closeness. Until

Ian. Had she loved him? Was that love? She didn't know. What she did know was that her life had been torn apart and she was lonely.

But she didn't cry, because Molly Cornwell never cried. Weeping was not in her nature.

TEN

No one told Stuart about the upset in Dorothy's life. Elsie, Lois and Ivy, who had no keys to Chadwicke House, did not see him, while Andrew, who had promised to keep quiet about the situation, was true to his word. Dorothy wanted Stuart to be strong and in good spirits when he went off to Chester Oakfields for the first of what was likely to be a series of surgeries.

As the day of his departure drew near, he became pensive, almost withdrawn, and the staff spent time reading to him, found him a wireless and a gramophone, and took him for short walks in the grounds. Outside, without the protection of familiar whitewashed walls and green curtains, he felt exposed and vulnerable; he could not imagine walking through a town, into a shop or even along one of the nearby country lanes.

Andrew spoke to Dorothy about it. 'He's dreading the hospital. I think he has come to terms with the idea of surgery, but he fears meeting people of normal appearance.'

'He won't be the only burns patient, surely?'

'No, he won't. But new nurses and doctors, patients with no burns to their faces – he feels he won't fit in. He is safe here. This is the trouble with convalescence – we can improve people's attitude here, within a familiar framework, but the steps taken out of Chadwicke are the real test. Which is why I have bought the van. We can start taking them out into the world again as soon as I manage to get a petrol allowance for the thing.'

'And if they don't want to go?'

'We wait until they do.' He tapped his fingers on the desk. 'When did you last leave here? When did you last go out into town?'

Dorothy shrugged. 'Can't remember.'

'You mean you refuse to remember. Let me remind you. You have stayed put since your mother arrived in the village – no riding, no walks in the woods, no shopping. She doesn't know you're here. Elsie and Lois won't tell her, and I established that Mother has said nothing. So. When are you going to take a trip outside?'

'I don't know. Don't bully me.'

'You don't like being told what to do.'

'No, I don't.'

He grinned at her. 'In that area, I think you have taken after your mother.'

'Don't say that.'

His smile faded. 'Right. Then I strongly suggest we grab the bull by the horns and plan an invasion. You can't go on like this, Dorothy. Stuart is already afraid of the outside world and he needs to face his fear. As do you. We should visit your mother.' He watched the various emotions passing over her face – shock, disbelief, fear, some anger. 'Well?'

She raised both hands in a gesture of confusion. 'Walk into the lion's den if you wish, Daniel. I shall catch the two fifteen for Bedlam – don't you think you should come with me and see a good psychiatrist? What would Freud say about this death wish of yours?'

He shrugged. 'It would have sexual implications, I suspect. Now, Jung would ask me to go forward and see what happens.'

'Did he die Jung?' she quipped. 'Andrew, stop messing about. I know what you're trying to do – face the demons, all that rubbish. But what you fail to understand is that Mam is very clever and devious. She doesn't want me out and about in the world, and that has always been the problem. How many mothers do you know who have deliberately fed a daughter bad meat and other poisoned stuff? Oh, not enough to kill me, but enough to keep me in the house. How many have denied their children an education? What sort of mother locks a child in, puts bars at her window, ties her into bed with leather straps?'

He had read it all. After going through the diaries, he felt as if he had known this girl for twenty years. 'She can't do any of that now,' he answered.

'The method will have changed, but the madness remains. She'll be exactly the same as she always was.'

'Then she has won. She deserves a medal in her chosen sport, because here you are, locked in, choices decimated, life spoilt simply because she lives a mile or two away. Face her. Tackle her, Dorothy. My mother is furious with me, angry enough to tell your mother the truth. The last time I went to see Mother, she had Lizzie tell me that she was in the bath. She wasn't. I'd seen her at the window just seconds earlier, doing her job as invigilator of anything that moves and breathes.'

'Do you love her?'

'Yes, I do,' he replied promptly.

'Then there's the difference. I have not the slightest affection for Mam. I couldn't raise a hand to her, but I can't stand her.'

'Think about it, Dorothy. It has to be faced. If you and Stuart are both averse to setting foot outside, you will make each other worse.'

He left her to ponder. She sat in his office until the hour to help in the baby unit arrived. Then she went off to fulfil her duties, all the time wondering whether Andrew had been right. He was usually right. Sometimes, his rightness could be quite annoying. She found herself engaged in a one-way conversation with little Matthew Taylor, who, she hoped, would become Matthew Beddows in the not too distant future. Apart from a few gurgles and a hiccup that brought back milk, Matthew appeared to have no opinion in the matter.

The fact remained that Andrew's advice had been sound. An enemy unseen was an enemy twice feared. Dorothy was living a diminished life that would do nothing to improve the state of the man she planned to marry. With half a face, he had to get out there and deal with the big, wide world. With half a heart, Dorothy had to do the same. She had to face the woman who had broken her spirit. Yes, it needed to be done.

Molly was in her element. She had a document case, a smart suit and a degree of authority she had not enjoyed before. But the problems began to arise at the end of her second day, when, exhausted by walking, she came face to face with a fact of life – she needed transport or sensible shoes, and probably both. The farms, spread across the east Lancashire moors in many directions, were not easy to reach. So, with the matter-of-factness that was a part of her natural make-up, she acquired a bicycle and trousers. Many working women wore trousers, and hers were smart, at least.

On her fourth day, she met Michael Cooper, a tenant farmer in his mid-thirties. His wife, confined to a wheelchair by multiple sclerosis, was clearly in no state to attend to his more intimate needs, and by the end of her first week Molly had acquired a lover and the promise of black market meat. Having killed two birds with one stone, she judged life to be satisfactory and settled down to make the most of it.

In front of the overmantel mirror, she practised her vowel sounds, attempting to narrow their delivery to a point where she might be mistaken for an educated person. As she stood there mee-mawing at herself, she caught sight of someone passing by and she turned quickly. She knew that face. Where had she seen her before? Good grief, it was that woman – the one who had come up to View Street with Dorothy after the bomb – what was her name? Elsie something or other. Shipton, that was it. And the next morning, Dorothy had got away by . . . by doing the bad thing. *Blood. Dry mouth. On the floor. Spreading. Big, so big. Don't think about it.*

Molly juggled with her thoughts and eliminated the unsavoury ones. Elsie Shipton had entered the cottage next door. It was best, she decided after a few minutes, to have a fresh start, so she took a tin of pink salmon from a shelf, tidied her hair and followed in Elsie's footsteps.

Elsie opened the door. 'Oh,' she cried with feigned surprise. 'It's Molly, isn't it?' She shouted over her shoulder. 'It's Dorothy-in-the-middle's mother, Lois. Remember how she took me in that night?' The door widened. 'Come in. I never expected to see you out here in the wilds. I thought I'd never settle in these parts, but I managed. Lois keeps me out of mischief.'

Molly entered the house and had her first sight of Lois Melia's scarred face. 'Oh, dear,' she said, 'you did get caught by that bomb, didn't you? What a shame. I hope you're not in a lot of pain.'

Lois nodded. She didn't like being stared at by somebody of low calibre, and this woman's calibre, according to Dorothy, was knee-high

275

to a cockroach. Lois could tell that this one thought a lot of herself, probably considered herself to be a silver spoon above ordinary folk.

'I'm living next door and I've brought you a small tin of salmon.' She placed the offering on the little dresser. 'Cosy, these petite houses, aren't they?' In response to a gesture from Elsie, she sat opposite the scarred woman. 'Does it hurt?' she asked.

'I have to keep my face turned from the fire,' said Lois. 'It needs to be cool. As time goes on, it's getting a bit better. But I'm scarred for life and I don't fancy that there plastic surgery.'

'Shame,' said Molly. 'You hear about these things, but you never think they'll happen to you, do you? Well, you're alive, so that's something to be grateful for.'

'I am,' agreed Lois. 'Didn't Elsie say you lived in View Street?'

'Oh, yes,' replied Molly. 'I'm here for the duration, though. Working for Mrs Burbank. I have to make sure the farmers and the land girls are up to scratch and coping. So, what brings you two up here?'

Elsie answered that one. 'We got bombed out – well, you knew that already. My sister works for the Burbanks and she's cook and bottle washer in Burbank Wing at present. She and Sam have a room there, so she lent us the cottage. I'm getting used to it. Took me a while, but we're all right, aren't we, Lois? We're good company for one another, me and her.'

Lois nodded again. Her face and neck seemed

to tingle more in the presence of this invader. She was the spitting image of her daughter, was this Molly Cornwell, very beautiful and sure of herself. Dorothy was a nicer person altogether, Lois decided. This Molly one looked as if nothing would ever bother her.

Elsie went to put the kettle on. Lois, who couldn't think of a single thing to say, stared out of the window and wished with all her heart that Molly Cornwell would bugger off.

'It's a shame when your face gets marked,' said Molly. 'Will it heal up at all if you don't have an operation?'

'I'm not as bad as some,' replied Lois. 'Dorothy's intended lost the sight of one eye and—'

'Do you take sugar?' Elsie, who had dashed in from the kitchen, had gone so red in the face that she, too, looked as if she might have been exposed to fierce heat. 'And milk? Will you be wanting milk in your tea?'

'Milk, no sugar.' Molly folded her arms. 'You were saying?' She was studying Lois. 'About Dorothy? About some chap?'

'It's a different Dorothy,' gabbled Lois. 'Not Dorothy-in-the-middle. Isn't it, Elsie? A different Dorothy?'

Elsie knew that it was too late. The unaffected part of Lois's poor face now almost matched the neck and chin for colour, and Elsie knew that her own expression had given the game away. 'Go and finish that brew, Lois,' she said. When Lois had fled from the room, Elsie took her place. 'Look, Molly. I don't know what's wrong between you and your daughter, but she's best left to get on with her own life. She's got herself Red Cross trained and a gradely job up at the big house. All I know is she wants to keep herself to herself and that's the top and bottom.'

Molly seemed to stare right through her companion. 'I have to be on my way,' she said. 'Thanks for the offer of tea, but I've a few girls to see tonight. They've been messing about with farmers and they need a talking to.' She walked to the door, opened it, turned. 'Thank your friend for telling me where my daughter is. I did wonder. I've not seen her in a good while.' She left the house, closing the door softly behind her.

Lois ran in. 'Oh, Elsie, I'm so sorry – it just slipped out. She made me uncomfortable – I'd no idea what to say to her. It's her eyes. They look like they belong to somebody else – somebody dead. And now she knows Dorothy's engaged, and it's all my fault. Me gob ran away with me again.'

Elsie patted her friend's hand. 'When that there fellow dragged you out of the house, I could have sworn you were dead. And all I could think was I wished I could cut my tongue out for some of the things I've said to you over the years. I had no excuse. You've been near death and you've got to go to Chester for operations once that lot settles down. Never mind about not bothering with surgery – it'll help and you're having it.' She pointed to her friend's neck. 'You've an excuse for losing your page in life, girl. Yes, you should have kept your mouth shut and yes, the sun should shine every day. But forgetting where you're up to is no crime. Put it out of your mind now – and that's an order. You've not been well.'

'But Dorothy? What will she think of me when she finds out what I've done? And after we promised her, and all.'

'Dorothy's got a heart of gold, love. Though looking at that fast piece of a mother, I'd say she must have got her decency off her dad. Leave Dorothy to me. Now, stop there, put your feet up and have a doze. I'll take a wander up to the hall and see what's what, make sure young Dorothy's kept up to scratch with developments.'

Elsie trudged the uphill stretch to the big house, saw old bag Burbank at her window, carried on up the side till she reached the door to Burbank Wing's kitchen. She noticed Andrew in the corridor at the drugs cupboard and called out to him. 'We've got problems, son.'

Ivy listened avidly while the story was told. Andrew absorbed every word, then returned to the corridor and buzzed through to Chadwicke for Dorothy. Dorothy had her own buzz-code and, unless she was embroiled in something serious, would be here within a few minutes.

Ivy was speaking when Andrew returned. 'I thought I was going to have a heart attack,' she said. 'Fair took my breath away, she did.'

'What's that?' he asked.

'Middle of the night, young Dorothy were stood on the landing like a ghost, white nightie, white face, eyes wide open, but not seeing me. I

279

fetched Sam and he said not to wake her up and shock her, but to talk gentle, like. So I told her to come on and that she was all right and put her back in her room.'

'She walks because she can,' said Andrew.

'What?' the two women chorused.

'Don't mind me,' he said. 'I talk to myself because no one else wants to listen.' Dorothy was walking in her sleep again. It was written in the diaries, and it looked as if her mother's presence in the village was disturbing her at a deep level. She was not tied into bed; she walked because she could. He felt anger coursing through his veins, white-hot adrenalin charging along to quicken his broken heart. What had that evil woman done to her own child? What had his own mother done by bringing this situation back to boiling point?

Dorothy came in and Andrew took her off to a small room next to the drugs cupboard. It contained a table and two old chairs, and they sat down while he arranged his thoughts. 'Don't blame Lois,' he began, 'but she let slip that you're here. Your mother now knows you have a young man and that he has suffered burns to his face. I am so very sorry.'

Dorothy swallowed. 'I told you before, Andrew, no one is to blame for my mother – unless we want to have a go at God. So. She knows exactly where I am. I suppose it was always going to be just a matter of time.'

'Yes. Now will you go and visit her?'

'No.'

'Dorothy, you are protected here. If all else

280

fails, I'll have her bloody well locked up in an asylum the minute she starts on you. It's well within my power, you know. I have friends who would happily co-sign commitment papers after reading those diaries and talking to her.'

She smiled at him. 'They wouldn't. It's not that kind of crazy, you see. It's not a padded cell and straitjacket job. You can't see it. The only time she gets close to raving is if she sees blood. I wasn't allowed red paint. If I had a box of paints, she used to prise the tablets of red out and throw them away. I bet I was the only kid in our street to paint a Father Christmas in a blue-and-green suit. I used Gibbs Dentifrice toothpaste – it comes in a round tin and they are all different colours. I couldn't have red. She never wears red and there's nothing red in the house except for a bit of glass in the vestibule door.'

'You have a red jacket now.'

She smiled. 'Yes – isn't freedom a wonderful thing? Red is my favourite colour.'

He decided not to tell her that she was sleep-walking. As long as nothing dangerous was in her path, she could walk all she liked. Perhaps he would watch out for her, see if he could reach her in a dream-state and talk to her, get her to open up. 'Well, be prepared,' he said. 'If you don't go to her, she will surely find a way of getting to you. My mother has told her to stay away from the hall, but—'

'But Molly Cornwell is and always was a law unto herself.' She touched his hand. 'You have the others to worry about – forget me.'

'You know I can't.' He grasped her fingers. 'You know full well how I feel about you.'

'Andrew . . .'

'Tried to switch it off, but I am stuck in the on position. Stuart is a lucky man to have won you.'

She attempted to reclaim her hand, but her effort was half-hearted. A part of her wanted to scream and run, but she couldn't, because she liked him. She more than liked him. She needed . . . She was engaged to be married. 'I'm sorry,' she whispered. In Andrew, she saw not just safety, not just affection, but excitement, a roguishness behind the warm eyes. Andrew would have encouraged her to grow and reach her full potential – whatever that might be.

'I love you very much,' he whispered. 'Don't be afraid of anything while I am in the world, because I would go to the ends of the earth for you.'

She snatched back her hand and ran, because she would not weep, would not advertise her confusion. Stuart would be waiting for her; he needed her. They would be very, very happy together. When she arrived at Room One, he was sitting on a chair with a newspaper in his hands. He was fully dressed in smart clothes and, with his face turned as it was in that moment, he was a very handsome man. He was going to be her life. There was no room for Andrew, and that thought made her sad.

* * *

Molly sat very still for over a week after her visit to Mansfield Avenue. He had left her. He had dumped her pain-ravaged body in a hospital bed and had sailed off to the other side of the world with his three children. When she thought hard about it, she felt like chasing him across the Atlantic, but America was on the large side. England could have been dropped unnoticed into a corner of Texas without making the slightest impression.

Then the letter came. She stared at it for several minutes before opening it, because she didn't want to read the inevitable words of rejection, but in the end, she had to read it. It had been posted in London and she knew the handwriting very well.

Dear Molly,

I know that you will be shocked by my behaviour and I do feel guilty when I consider what I have done, but there were few options. It could not have gone on. Twice, I saw you in a state that defied description and I was frightened on both occasions. Perhaps I am a coward, but I am looking to my children and attending to their welfare, as none of this should result in their suffering. We could not have married, anyway. Even had you been single, it would never have worked.

I do not know where we shall end up, and I cannot say whether or when I shall return to England. I thank you from the bottom of my heart for the devotion you showed to my poor, dear Florence during the final weeks of her life, also for the care you took with the children during those dark times and after the loss of their mother. If I never come home, please know that I am grateful to you.

Molly, you were special to me. I never met a woman as beautiful or as exciting as you are and I expect that I shall not meet your like again. But, Molly, please heed me now, because I ask you to go for help. As your doctor, I was remiss in not pointing out to you that certain aspects of your behaviour led me to believe that you are mentally or emotionally unstable. There are triggers, usually shocks, which set off a reaction in you that is not normal. This makes me suspect that some buried childhood trauma has left you injured and that sort of thing needs to be discussed with a psychiatrist. Please, I beg you, get advice in this matter. Also, try to be kinder to Dorothy. She is a sweet child.

I wish you a long and happy life, peace of mind and the strength to deal with whatever comes your way.

Ian.

PS This will be posted from London a week after we have set sail.

Molly folded the letter and placed it back in its envelope. Who the hell did he think he was? There was nothing wrong with her and he had never seen her in a state, because she never got into a state. The worst she had ever been was the way she was now, after the miscarriage, after his betrayal. America? Wasn't it full of Red Indians who killed white men? Even so, those Red Indians had better not hurt Florence's children. Florence had given Molly pearls. Florence had cared about her.

Dorothy. *Be kinder to Dorothy*. Just because he had a medical degree, he thought he knew everything. Dorothy. 114, Willows Lane, Beryl Isherwood, teacher, Sunning Hill school. It was time to take charge of life again, to find another lover, to bring home the child, to put Ian Clarke out of her mind for ever.

She lay in a bath of rose-scented water, realizing with alarming clarity that she would never forget Ian until the day she died. The games they had played together had provided the most pleasurable hours of her life thus far. He was educated, which was why he had had the edge over most other men. The domination of any man was a victory, but owning sway over a doctor had been wonderful. She needed someone successful and clever, because the other kind were ten a penny, were no fun and no challenge.

But first, a different sort of mission needed to be accomplished. It was time to bring Dorothy back to her rightful home. Molly dried herself, dressed soberly and did her hair. Beryl Isherwood's power had been diminished considerably by Ian's exit. The teacher could no longer hold on to the child. Molly picked up coat and handbag, left the house and began the long walk to Willows Lane.

She was fighting fit again, was in the right, was intending to reclaim her own property.

Beryl Isherwood was buying Dorothy a new hat and coat for Sunday best. Dressing such a pretty child was a pleasure, and Beryl enjoyed the fashion show in a children's outfitters on Bradshawgate. The little girl paraded up and down in a series of coats, one hand on a hip and a silly smile on her face as she watched the teacher laughing.

An assistant arrived with yet another coat with a matching hat.

'I can't have that one,' Dorothy said. 'It's red.'

'Nonsense,' cried Miss Isherwood. 'It's burgundy.'

'It's still red,' insisted the child. 'Mam says it's a common, cheap colour even when it's dark red.'

'Don't you like red?' asked the shop assistant.

'Not allowed it. Mam doesn't like it. I can have it at Miss Isherwood's house – I can even have red paint at Miss Isherwood's. But not at home.'

Beryl nodded at the shop girl and the coat was put away. Molly Cornwell was a strange creature indeed if she could not tolerate a burgundy coat. They bought a delightful outfit in blue and left the shop.

'Why doesn't your mother like red?' Beryl asked casually as they sat in a little café just off the Town Hall square. 'I've always thought of it as a happy, cheerful colour.'

Dorothy took a sip of milk. 'I don't know. She just won't have anything red. She likes all the other colours, though. Even purple and that's red mixed with blue.'

Beryl drank her tea and shrugged off the subject as just another peculiarity belonging to the woman who had birthed this wonderful child. She had such plans for Dorothy, though her hope of carrying them out was not very strong. The girl would walk into the County Grammar school without any problems. She would be ready to sit her scholarship exam well before the age of eleven. At five, she had mastered most of her times tables and was already approaching the stage where the battle with long division and multiplication loomed on a near horizon.

Dorothy watched her benefactor's face. 'What are you thinking about?' she asked.

Beryl smiled broadly. 'I am thinking of the day you become a brilliant doctor, or a lawyer, or a teacher. You are a very clever girl.'

Dorothy spoke for both of them. 'She will get me back, you know. She always gets everything she wants.'

'Drink your milk, Dorothy. We need to be catching a tram.'

When they walked from the tram stop and into Willows Lane, Beryl Isherwood's heart seemed to miss several beats. The woman was there in the front garden, peering through windows and tapping on the glass.

'See?' said Dorothy mournfully. 'I told you she'd come for me, Miss Isherwood.'

'Perhaps she's just visiting?'

The little girl shook her head. 'No, that's her very best coat. She wears her very best coat when she goes and gets what she wants. There's her going shopping coat, her nearly best one and her very best.'

Once again, Beryl Isherwood was struck by the perception of this child. She seemed to measure people with an accuracy that displayed a maturity far beyond her years. But the main feeling that gripped Beryl Isherwood in the moments it took to walk to her house was terror. She was afraid for Dorothy and afraid for herself, because living with the little girl had allowed her to be a mother for a while, and the future promised to be lonely.

The two women exchanged terse greetings, then the visitor followed Beryl and Dorothy into the house. Dorothy, fully aware of the nature of the business between these adults, took her new clothes upstairs. She would never get to wear them, of that she felt sure. Mam would not want her to go out in something bought by another woman. The child took the items from their packaging and hung them in the wardrobe. Then she sat and waited for her immediate future to be decided. It was a lovely room. She would miss her room, but she must not cry, because Mam hated people who cried.

Downstairs, Molly, having refused to take a seat, came straight to the point. 'Dorothy will be coming home today,' she said.

'To what?' Beryl Isherwood folded her arms.

'To scenes of you copulating with her father on the kitchen table? Yes, the doctor told me. Your husband cannot father a child. I concluded that Dr Clarke is your daughter's father.'

Molly nodded. 'True. But she won't be seeing Ian Clarke again.'

'And you expect me to believe that?'

'Believe what you like, but, as far as I understand, it takes a long time to cross the Atlantic Ocean.'

Beryl steadied herself against the dresser. 'He has emigrated?'

'Yes. I lost the second child – his child – and he left me in hospital and took his other children to start a new life in a new world. Dorothy won't see him again. He won't be coming back.' Putting it into words was horrible. She missed him, ached for him and needed him, and the words served only to hit her anew with the terrible truth.

'I see.'

'Do you? This means that you can no longer threaten to expose us. As it was before, you could hold the blackmail over him and, if you'd carried it out, you would have hurt Dorothy as well. Perhaps you would have taken that chance just so that you could keep her. But now, who will listen to you? No matter what, you won't get to hang on to her. She is now the only person you could damage by speaking up. So she comes home with me today, because Ian Clarke is beyond your reach.' The cold eyes glinted as she spoke the last few words. She had won.

Beryl's legs continued unsteady as she made her way upstairs. She walked into Dorothy's bedroom and saw that the child had already emptied two of the drawers. 'I'll miss you,' said Beryl.

'I'll miss you. Miss Isherwood, I don't want to go. Is there nothing you can do?'

'No, Dorothy. Your mother has rights.'

'Do I have them? Do I have rights?'

Beryl forbade herself to weep. Of course the child had rights. She had the inherent right to life, to bodily integrity, to choose her religion and the methods by which she, in turn, might raise a family. But no one could cater to those rights until Dorothy reached her majority. 'Yes, you have rights. But she is your mother and she can have you removed from here. The police might come if I tried to keep you. I'll still be your teacher. If you have any worries, you can come to me at school.'

Molly snatched up just one case and told her daughter to carry a smaller one. 'I'll be back for the rest,' she snapped before ushering her daughter out of the house. Outside, she threw the last words over her shoulder. 'This case is a bit heavy. I hope you haven't bought her much. We don't need any charity.'

Beryl Isherwood closed her front door and leaned on it for a while. The house was deadly silent and still. The old clock ticking in the front room got louder and, in the end, Beryl went upstairs. The door to Dorothy's room was open. She went inside, looked in the wardrobe and saw the new hat and coat purchased just an hour or so earlier. Had the cupboard been completely bare, it could not possibly have caused the heartbreak that now burst from Beryl's throat. She attempted to dry streaming eyes, turned, caught sight of a piece of paper on the pillow.

She had to stare at it for a while until her vision cleared. Then she read the message in bright red crayon: *Thank you Miss Isherwood and I love you very much. Dorothy*. The child had chosen red, because red had been available to her.

Life, for a spinster who had nursed two ageing parents, was lonely. Into that life had come a shooting star, a piece of brilliance set against blackness, its beauty, short-lived, bequeathing a memory etched for ever on the mind of the fortunate beholder. But now the world was dark again, and there were lesson plans to be done.

* * *

With a bicycle, there were ways and means of getting just about anywhere. Some of the lanes narrowed down into rutted tracks and the going could be rough on two ill-sprung wheels, but the world of Bromley Cross was Molly Cornwell's oyster.

She borrowed binoculars from her new man and hid them in the basket fastened to her handlebars. By following a circuitous route around the rear of Burbank Hall, she was able to view Chadwicke House and part of the bigger building quite clearly. Every spare half-hour was dedicated to her search; Dorothy was her property and she would find her. So blinkered did she become that even her rampant young farmer was put on hold for a while. Waiting did men good, anyway, in Molly's opinion.

When she finally saw her daughter, Dorothy was in the company of a rather well-constructed young man whose face was handsome on one side, destroyed on the other. So, this was Dorothy's chap. Molly wondered if perhaps he had money. He would need something as an inducement to persuade a woman to look at that sight every day.

Andrew Burbank came out and joined them. Molly adjusted focus on lenses strong enough to spot a fox at a distance of several hundred yards. The uneven gait of Isobel Burbank's son seemed more pronounced than it had at close quarters. According to Isobel, he had suffered polio as a child and he was working with injured and disfigured airmen. Oh, well. It took one disabled person to understand the problems of another, she supposed. He was handsome, in spite of the limp. Not only was he a very attractive man, he was probably as rich as Croesus. Oh, how Molly would have loved to live in such a house with a daughter, a son-in-law and, perhaps, even a grandson.

She noticed that he had stopped walking and that the other two had carried on. He seemed dejected. Molly swung the binoculars round and took in the size of Burbank Hall and its grounds. It was impressive, to say the least; it was also his. He was walking back into the smaller house and, in the doorway, he stopped to look back at Dorothy and her companion. Molly's antennae were doing their duty, as ever. He was Dorothy's. All the girl had to do was reach out and take him, because he wanted her.

Molly lowered the binoculars and returned to her bicycle. Dorothy was a damned fool if she didn't choose the biggest cake in the tin. It had been plain from Andrew Burbank's stance that he was interested in Dorothy – and why shouldn't he be? She was as beautiful as her mother had been and would continue attractive for many years. It was a shame that Dorothy seemed to have attached herself to that burns victim, because the Burbank chap was probably one of the best catches north of London.

She glanced at her watch. Michael would be waiting for her back at the cottage – she had timed his visits to coincide with the predictable movements of the women next door. They went off to Burbank Hall every day and stayed for a couple of hours. Right. She could service her lover and have him out of the house before Lois and Elsie returned.

As she cycled back to the village, she thought about her neighbours and the freedom they enjoyed. They could go up to the big house whenever they chose, whereas she had to sit in and wait for the lady of the manor to call. There were lists of land girls, lists of farms, lists of livestock, crop estimates, tables of farm machinery to be begged, stolen or borrowed. Life was just one long list, she thought as she arrived at the cottage, and the contents of life's list had to be checked and discussed at a distance from the opulence of Burbank Hall. It wasn't fair, but it never had been.

Michael Cooper always admitted himself through the back door. There were walls between Molly's garden and those belonging to adjoining cottages, so, with a bit of luck and good management, he could come and go without fear of detection.

When she walked in, he was already stripped to the waist and he had banked up the fire in preparation for her arrival. He smiled a welcome, bright blue eyes twinkling in the clean-cut, weathered face, scooped her up and kissed her. She was older, yes, but she knew how to play.

Molly tried to give herself up to his embrace, yet could not manage full concentration on the task. She was busy thinking about Dorothy and the opportunity that was so plainly lying in the girl's path, the chance of a lifetime just waiting to be snatched up. The kiss was becoming urgent, almost frenzied. What could be done to choreograph the displacement of her daughter's affections?

He released her abruptly. 'Gone off the boil, have you?'

'Something on my mind. I have a lot of thinking to do.'

The farmer stood back and studied her. 'I've come a long way,' he said. 'A very long way.'

She agreed wholeheartedly with that statement, because Michael Cooper would not normally achieve contact with a woman of her calibre. Out here in the sticks, his choice of companion would be limited to bumpkins and Land Army girls. Yes, he had come a long way and was totally out of his depth. There was fury in his eyes and, before she could stop herself, she was laughing in his face.

The hand that slapped her cheek was strong, the size of a small shovel, and it carried behind it the force of a man who had worked the land and tended animals since childhood. Even as he hit her, a part of her mind was admiring glistening flesh made mobile by rippling muscle.

Minutes later, he was gone. Dazed, Molly lay on the green-and-beige hearthrug, heart pounding in her chest, clothes in tatters all over the place. She dared not examine herself, because she could feel a warm fluid on her inner thighs. It was thick, sticky and she knew its colour.

Her whole body ached from the punches and kicks he had inflicted. Her face, already beginning to swell, was also bleeding, but she forbade her hands to examine the source of that nasty liquid. She had been raped. The attack had been swift, painful and vicious. Someone had taken control of her body and it reminded her . . . it reminded her of nothing. She lay battered and bruised on the floor until merciful unconsciousness claimed her.

'Mrs Cornwell? Mrs Cornwell?'

Molly opened one swollen eye. Through a mist, she saw Isobel Burbank leaning over her. Behind Mrs Burbank, two shadowy figures lingered. 'Yes?' she managed.

Lois Melia stepped forward. 'You're all right, love. It's only me and Elsie – remember? Your Dorothy's neighbours from Emblem Street? We live next door and we knew there were summat up when we saw your bike left out.' She addressed Isobel. 'She looks after yon bike. Never leaves it there where it could get borrowed.'

Isobel was very tender. She helped Molly into a sitting position, propping her with cushions against the wall to the right of the fireplace. 'My son's coming,' she said. 'I know he specialized, but he is a fully trained medic as well. Try not to move too much, Mrs Cornwell.'

She could taste it in her mouth, could smell it. Elsie Shipton was placing a blanket over Molly's nakedness. It hurt. Her whole body was one solid mass of pain, but the worst was down below. He had been a hefty man, bigger in all departments than most other males. There was red. She didn't need to look, because the room was filled by it.

'You've been raped, lovey,' whispered Elsie.

'Yes. Water.'

Isobel perched on the edge of a small sofa. 'Who was it, Molly?' The use of surnames seemed ridiculous at a time like this. 'Who?' she asked again. She placed a hand on Molly's hair. 'You must tell us. The man needs to be caught and charged, you see.'

The brain was still functioning at full speed. This event was going to be useful. As yet unable to imagine how Michael Cooper's crime could be employed to her advantage, she told the lie. 'I don't know. He had a woman's stocking over

296

his face. Tall. I would guess middle-aged. Very angry. Very strong. Vicious.'

Isobel bit her lower lip. 'If you remember anything, tell me and I shall write it down. The police are on their way.'

Ah, so Isobel Burbank wanted yet another list. Molly took a glass of water from Elsie and sipped at it. There was something wrong with her mouth, so most of the water dribbled away down her chin.

The door burst open. 'Mam? Mam?' Dorothy knelt beside the battered woman. 'Oh, my God,' she breathed. 'Who did this?'

Molly closed her eyes. 'Don't know.'

The rest of the evening was taken up by the comings and goings of policemen. Molly adhered to her story, was placed in an ambulance with her daughter and Andrew Burbank, then was driven to the Royal Infirmary in Bolton. It was a different ward this time, one in which babies were not a factor. From her hospital bed, she named Michael Cooper, among others, as a visitor, a farmer who had called for advice concerning his need for more help at the farm. His fingerprints would be in her cottage and she did not want him caught. He was potentially useful, but only if he stayed out of prison.

Dorothy touched her mother for the first time in years, holding her hand while Andrew promised convalescence at Chadwicke House. 'You'll be all right, Mam,' the girl said repeatedly.

Alone, Molly knew full well that she would be all right. She would be better than all right, because she would be where she needed to be – with Dorothy. Taken all round, this had been an exceptionally good day. As long as her looks had not been damaged, Molly Cornwell was as contented as she might ever be.

ELEVEN

They came out of the hospital together, and
Andrew noticed how pale and drawn Dorothy
looked. She needed a rest and a sit down with
a good hot drink, so he dragged her off to a
nearby ice-cream parlour with a little cafeteria
attached. She sat with her head in her hands for
a couple of minutes, then looked at her companion. 'There's more to it than she's saying.
Don't forget, I know the woman almost better
than I know myself – I was locked in with her
for years. She's hiding something.'

'Such as what?'

Dorothy shrugged. 'There was Dr Clarke,
followed by a man I saw a few times over a
period of weeks. Others came and went more
quickly – it was like a conveyor belt in a factory.
Later, she worked for another man and went
away with him sometimes – they were lovers for
years. My father has even bumped into one or
two of them and, as far as I know, never said a
thing.'

'Really? How odd.'

She smiled. 'They didn't have arguments –

my parents, I mean. In fact, if I wrote down the number of times I have heard my father speaking, I'd probably get the lot on one sheet of foolscap. Until she got that long-term man – then I got to know Dad a little better and we talked more. Anyway, I may be wrong, but I believe she knows the identity of her attacker. It's just in me to know these things. Like my mother, I seem to have the ability to analyse people.'

Coffee arrived. Andrew waited until the shop-keeper had walked away from their table. 'She doesn't know anyone in Bromley Cross,' he said. 'She's been there just a short time—'

'And she meets people. She goes around the farms and comes into contact with farmers and labourers. The way she looks at the moment isn't pretty, but that's not her. My mother is very beautiful and she needs attention. Dad isn't enough and he never was.'

He nodded. 'Yes, I have seen her beauty – quite remarkable. Possibly nymphomaniac?'

'Yes, or just very needful. She's cold, calculating, unforgiving and vengeful. Adulation is a requirement. All her life, men have fallen at her feet and I am sure she has always been in charge. Perhaps she's finally met someone who doesn't appreciate her domineering attitude. She has a way of being absolutely charming, yet she can change in a split second if she isn't getting all her own way.'

'You are the expert, I suppose.'

'She knows him, Andrew. She couldn't last five minutes without having some grateful fool in tow. And she's planning something. Those eyes may seem blank and cold to most people, but I can see straight through her.'

'It sounds as if she needs a good doctor.'

Dorothy agreed. 'The trouble is that she acts so normally.'

'Yes, which is why we need someone good. Well, if she returns to Chadwicke House for convalescence, she will have a good man. I am the best. So she is in luck.'

She actually managed to laugh. 'If you were modest, you'd be perfect.'

'True,' he replied. 'Now, drink your coffee and let's get back. I need to question you closely before your mother is discharged. Knowledge is power. Cheers.' He raised his coffee cup and winked at her.

They travelled back by tram, then had to walk the last stretch from the terminus to Burbank Hall. 'Does it hurt?' she asked.

'Throws my hip out. Yes, it's a nuisance.'

'I'm sorry.' She was sorry for more than one reason. The longer she knew him, the better she liked him, and she was engaged to marry a needful man whose journey through life was not going to be easy. She could never betray Stuart. But Andrew had been right — the line between sympathy and love could narrow to a point at which they became inseparable.

They entered the kitchen in Burbank Wing and were accosted immediately by three inquisitive women who had clearly been on tenterhooks during all the excitement.

'Nobody's safe,' was Elsie's opener.

'Don't worry,' said her sister with heavy sarcasm, 'I think you're safe enough.'

Lois wanted to know whether Molly's face would be all right. 'She's very pretty, is your mam,' she advised Dorothy. 'It'd be a shame if that lovely face got spoilt.'

'She won't be marked,' said Andrew with certainty, 'and she will come to Chadwicke House for a rest after she gets out of hospital. We'll look after her, won't we, Dorothy?'

'Oh, yes. She'll be well cared for.'

Only Andrew heard the slight amount of bitterness contained in Dorothy's words. He had watched her with her mother, had seen her genuine concern about Molly's injuries. God, he loved this girl. Not only was she a sight for sore eyes, she was a gentlewoman, a unique creature born into misery, raised in misery, yet without a single bad cell in the marrow of her bones.

Elsie, whose radar might have been useful in Mr Churchill's War Office, broke the code immediately. The way he looked at Dorothy – there was a river of love pouring from his eyes, a waterfall the size of Niagara. As for Dorothy, the girl was split in two. She had promised her heart to a man whose decency was unquestionable, but a thief named Andrew Burbank had come along in the night, had dynamited the safe, and now Dorothy belonged to him. Elsie felt she needed a good cry, so she chose the moment to respond to an earlier comment from her sister. 'Hey, you?'

'Eh?' Ivy stirred her gravy.

'What do you mean, I'll be safe? There's

many a good tune played on an old fiddle, I'll have you know.'

Ivy grinned. 'Aye, but you're no Stradivarius, are you? And you lost your bow years ago.'

Elsie sighed. 'Near ones and dear ones? Ivy, we should get a divorce. Why can't sisters get divorced?'

'You'll not find gravy like mine anywhere else.'

'Oh, shut up and see to your cauldron.'

Thus the moment passed. Andrew went back to his patients while Dorothy sat with her three friends at the kitchen table. The room was colder without him and Dorothy hoped with all her soul that life might soon become simpler.

*   *   *

Dorothy never returned to Sunning Hill school. Her mother, who had suddenly decided that nuns were the best educators, moved the child to the school of Sts Peter and Paul in Pilkington Street. Excluded from all religious education lessons, Dorothy began her long walk through the world of English literature. By the age of ten, she was tackling Dickens's *A Christmas Carol* and the headmistress, Sister Agatha, realized that she had a capable and imaginative child on her hands.

The nun sent for Molly and advised her that in the opinion of all staff, Dorothy would benefit from a place in one of the grammar schools. 'She's talented. Better yet, the child is industrious,' declared the monarch of primary education.

Unimpressed and passive, Molly sat through the short monologue. 'No,' she said when the woman finally stopped talking. 'She gets upset. My daughter is very frail. The first weeks of school, she was hardly there – she was at home with me, because she wasn't fit for the stress of it all. In fact, just to prove that her teacher wasn't a dragon, we let Dorothy stay with her for a few months.' This had now become a truth for Molly. She had told the tale more than once, and as time went by, she had convinced herself that her daughter's placement at 114, Willows Lane had been decided on by herself, her husband and Beryl Isherwood together.

'But Dorothy is older now, Mrs Cornwell. She isn't at all nervous here.'

'It shows in different ways,' replied Molly. 'Sleepwalking, bed-wetting, and she goes very quiet. No. She wouldn't cope.'

'So you don't want her to take the scholarship examinations?'

'It would be best if she didn't.'

Agatha stood in the doorway of her office and watched the walking advertisement for the Roaring Twenties as it made its way down a long corridor towards the exit. In a skirt that was far too short and on heels high enough to warrant the use of an oxygen mask, the crop-haired woman in the cloche hat was the epitome of modernity. Did she not realize that women were fighting for emancipation, that females entered Oxford, Cambridge and other good universities? Dorothy's talent was about to go to waste simply because her mother did not wish the girl to shine.

The headmistress returned to her office. Molly Cornwell's was a special kind of cruelty that left no bruises and no broken skin, because it was completely invisible. It occurred to the nun that perhaps the mother might be jealous of her daughter. But she failed to realize that she was one of the few people ever to have glimpsed the edge of Molly Cornwell's mind. Sister Agatha had a school to run in an area that drew pupils from the poorer end of town and her task was not an easy one. With great sadness, she crossed Dorothy Cornwell's name off the list of scholarship entrants. She could try again next year, but, for the moment, she had to give her attention to other pressing matters.

Molly marched back home, heels pounding the pavement as she ate up the distance between school and house. Dorothy would not be going to any fancy grammar school. Dorothy would not be getting ideas above her station in life, would remain safe, would be watched. Dorothy was going to stay where she belonged – with her mother. Dorothy did not need the trappings of a good education – her mother had managed well enough without any particular advantages.

She opened the door and found her daughter in the hall.

The little girl asked no questions. Conversation with her mother was difficult; with her father, it was practically non-existent. Dorothy could tell from the set of Molly's mouth and from the height at which she held her chin that Sister Agatha had failed.

As always, the child turned and went up to her room. She had shelves filled with books, pens, paper, her diaries. She owned a desk and a chair and spent most of her time reading, writing and drawing. There were bars at the window and straps on the bed. After she had been discovered sitting with her legs dangling outside the house, those bars had gone up. She still waved at Steve Dyson whenever he passed along the back alley, but she was forbidden to talk to him or to anyone else.

The days were long and the nights were terrible, as she could not change her position in the bed. Sometimes, she cried out for her mother to release her. Usually, she was forced to urinate where she lay, so she did not allow herself any fluids after six o'clock, no matter how thirsty she became. Often, Mam would have one of her friends downstairs and Dorothy would listen to the laughing, the talking, the moaning and the screaming. But she survived, since she knew she must.

And, because she was a sleeping princess in a tower, she ceased to be Dorothy Cornwell. Before the straps went on, she could lie on her bed, tiara by her side, hair spread over the pillow, body clad in a gossamer-light dress of shimmering gold or silver. One day, someone would come for her. He would rescue her, and Mam wouldn't be able to get her back. Life without bars and straps was going to be wonderful. She would have the children seen by the fortune teller at the fair and would be rich enough to buy them all they needed.

Until then, Dorothy had to live the life Mam had chosen for her. It was not pleasant, though school was enjoyable, but Dorothy knew she had rights, because Miss Isherwood had said so. Miss Isherwood was now someone who waved from a tram or a trolley bus; had become another person removed by Mam. Yet there was hope. There was always hope. In another few years, Dorothy could start her own journey, and Mam would draw no maps for it.

*   *   *

Molly came back to Bromley Cross after five days in the infirmary. Andrew, who had prepared himself via Dorothy and her diaries, still managed to be amazed by the woman who invaded and pervaded the lives of all the residents in the nursing home. This creature of extraordinary beauty and erratic hormones positioned herself at the centre of attention, shone a solo spotlight on herself and became the cabaret. Molly Cornwell's brand of craziness was rational, calculating and almost radiantly pure.

Some of his patients had no visible burns, while others were badly disfigured. He had two officers from bomb disposal who had watched close colleagues blown to pieces and neither man had said much since being admitted to the unit. Trauma responded to a variety of stimuli and, in some cases, the arrival of Molly brought a twinkle to eyes previously deadened by shock. Molly was not an item to be ignored. She focused first on bomb disposal, detonating a couple of fuses within hours of invasion. Amazed by her cleverness, Andrew watched her on that first day, then returned to his office for a conference with his patient's daughter.

Dorothy listened. 'Yes, that's Mam. As long as they genuflect at her altar, they will be allowed to eat from her hands.'

'More likely from her feet.' Andrew's tone was gloomy. 'She is so damned clever. Had I no knowledge of her past, I would write her down as an intelligent, pleasant and sexually attractive woman with concern for her fellows. She's a one-off.'

'Be grateful for that.' Dorothy played with her hair. 'It's a bit close for my comfort, Andrew. Now she's here, she will find out that I am to be married. When I married Steve, I ran away with nothing except the clothes on my back and some spare knickers. She was livid. His death will have pleased her.'

'That's horrible.'

'She's horrible. In 1929, I left school. I was fifteen and Mam had spent months worrying about what to do with me. By that time, I was reading constantly – just to escape everything. My school days were over and I thought I would find a degree of freedom.'

'But you didn't?'

Dorothy shook her head. 'No. I was put to work in Jenkinson's grocery. Bert Jenkinson had been on Mam's list of friends for a long time. He used to visit her on Wednesdays – half-day closing. So there was all the giggling and the moaning and the shouting. We always had plenty to eat. She got him to take me on and she would pop into the shop sometimes, just to make sure I wasn't talking to any young male customers. He made sure I wasn't talking to anyone. When the shop was empty, he would send me into the store room, follow me in and start mauling me.'

'Did you tell your mother?'

'Of course not. Not then, anyway. Later, I told her. She wouldn't have believed me early on. Why should Bert Jenkinson want to touch me when he had her?'

'Your father?'

'Wouldn't have heard me. I think he developed selective deafness and blindness, because he seemed to ignore all she did and said.'

Dorothy's story was almost unbelievable. Her whole history read like something out of a Charles Dickens novel, hardship, ill-treatment and deprivation all being part and parcel of this poor woman's childhood. 'Jesus,' he said softly.

'It wasn't Jesus who saved me. It was Steve Dyson.'

'Your husband?'

She nodded. 'We found a way to communicate. I would pick up a stone on my way home from work, wrap a note round it and leave it near our ash pit in the back street. He did the same. That was how I told him about Bert Jenkinson.'

'And?'

'And Steve dealt with him. He took his brother and two other lads with him. They were all young and brawny and they put Mr Jenkinson in hospital, in plaster and in a bad mood. He never touched me again.'

'The straps on the bed?'

'Ah, removed when I was about thirteen. The bars were still there last November. I continued to walk in my sleep, but she managed to ignore that. She locked outer doors and hid keys. According to her, that was so that I couldn't leave the house in my sleep.'

'Did you stay at the shop?'

'No. I sold nuts and bolts in Gregory and Porritts. She didn't like it. I started to take my time getting home from work and began to meet Steve. In 1937, we eloped.'

'You waited a long time.'

'Yes. I learned patience the hard way. Steve's mother was ill – that forced us to wait – and I had a little money coming, so that was another reason for holding back. And now she will try to organize me again.' She paused. 'There is something wrong with my father. He won't visit her here, I dare say. They don't talk. There was never any moaning or screaming. I didn't see them kissing. He might as well have been a servant of some kind. There's nothing between them, no love, no hatred. They simply share a house.'

Later that day, Andrew had his first session with Molly Cornwell, who, as expected, refused absolutely to be treated. The woman was not one who would hand over control to anyone.

Within minutes, she had started to court him, and he watched dispassionately as she used her body to entice. He was sure that she had scant idea of what she was doing and that her body 'spoke' of its own accord, because she had trained it decades earlier to act in this way. A manipulator, Molly went into automatic vamp mode when in the presence of a male.

No man was safe, he concluded. And, because there were no locks on doors in Chadwicke House, he began to fear for the well-being of other patients in the unit. She would not discuss the attack and adhered firmly to the tale of a masked man, a beating and unconsciousness. He studied her covertly. She and Dorothy were peas from one pod, the daughter being a very faithful copy of the mother. 'You won't let me help you,' he said. 'Without delving into your memory, I have no chance of getting to the root of what happened. If I were to use my quackery – that's hypnosis – you might even identify him.'

She awarded him a half-smile. 'This is a place for people who have had shocks, isn't it?'

'Yes.'

'I'd like to work here. I think somebody who has had a shock is the best to use.'

She had probably seldom suffered trauma in her adult life. Although she had been quick to remove the reds from Dorothy's paint boxes, hadn't she? Perhaps there was something at the back of all this, a memory so painful and unpalatable that it had been buried. 'I have all the staff I need, and Mother wants you to carry on liaising between farmers, workers and the ministry,' he said. She was a vain woman, he decided. Bruises had been covered in layers of make-up and her dressing gown was of fluid satin. Molly Cornwell was a total egocentric – and possibly something worse than that.

'I'm afraid,' she said, pathos layered into the words.

'Of what?'

'He might be out there. He might be waiting for me. What if he does it again?'

'Then you should go home, back to your husband. I have no work for you in Chadwicke House, and if you cannot work as overseer on the land projects, you should return to Bolton.'

Molly sighed. 'I am afraid of bombs, too.'

She wasn't afraid of anything. To get what she wanted, this unreal creature would step on corpses if necessary. 'What happened to you when you were a child?' He watched her as she straightened her spine, saw fingers curling into fists.

'Nothing.'

'Are you sure?'

'Yes.'

'You remember your childhood?'

'Of course. Except for the very beginning, naturally.'

'You were happy?'

'Yes.'

'Were you ever injured?'

'No.'

'Slapped?'

'Occasionally.'

'Abused?'

'No.'

Andrew paused for a few moments. 'I believe you should return to the cottage. You are clearly a strong woman, and, as you seem perfectly composed, I judge you well enough to leave here. Since Lois Melia moved into the cottage next to yours, I have had no other female patients. Chadwicke is geared towards those whose trauma run deep – RAF personnel, bomb disposal chaps and so forth. You should go today, I think. Don't return to your work right away. I shall visit you at the cottage.'

'I want to stay.' She fixed him with a clear blue gaze. 'Just for a day or so. I feel safer in company.' Molly wanted to meet her daughter's young man, needed to spy out the lie of the land. And land was as good a reason as any for Dorothy to return the affections of this blemished yet disarmingly handsome chap. He owned a great deal of acreage and some valuable properties. Living here would be Molly's idea of heaven.

'I can get someone to stay with you at the cottage,' he said.

In that moment, Molly realized something vital. Dorothy had spoken to Andrew Burbank. Keeping the child quiet had been relatively easy, but the woman had started to talk. Molly decided to test the water. 'Dorothy could stay with me.'

'Not possible,' was his reply. 'She has a room upstairs here and is on call for much of the time.'

'She'll get stressed. My daughter is easily upset.

She spent her whole childhood in a fantasy of her own, a kind of fairy tale world.'

'Unhappy children do that,' he said. 'She was unhappy because she was contained.'

'For her own good.'

'Really?' It was his turn to test the water – or rather, the ink. He reached across his desk as if to pick up some notes, knocking over a bottle of red ink from which he had deliberately removed the cap before Molly's arrival. The liquid, released from its own containment, spread and soaked into a large, pale green blotter. The doctor's eyes were fixed not on the spillage, but on his patient's suddenly altered face.

Molly swallowed noisily. 'A mess,' she said in a voice unlike her own.

Andrew offered no comment.

'It wasn't me,' she said. The stuff was flooding the desk. Soon, the whole room would be red and she could not stay in a red room.

'What do you see, Molly?' he asked.

'Too much. I didn't do it. I wasn't there.'

'No. Of course you weren't. Who did it?'

'Not me. Not Dorothy. We weren't there. I made sure she wasn't there.'

'She probably wasn't born when that happened. When the red came, she wasn't born.'

'It's in her. She is me. She brought it with her. It was everywhere.'

'What was?'

She gulped. 'The red. It came when she came.'

'Most mothers bleed when a child is born.' Human females bled regularly, he mused. 'How do you manage your periods?'

'Never look at it. In the fire. Burn it.'

So, it was not just Dorothy who had inhabited a world of fantasy. Molly lived on an island where there was no blood, nothing red, nothing to remind her of an event whose edge she still remembered, though not in a part of her brain that was readily accessible. 'Where was the first red, Molly? Where was the biggest red?'

She blinked, stared at him, crossed her legs and folded her arms. He glanced down at the desk and saw that the bottle had ceased to bleed. Ink soaked into the blotter was beginning to dry and the colour was changing to a brownish shade. 'Do you remember?' he asked. 'Any of it? Anything at all?'

'He was tall and strong and he wore a silk stocking over his face.'

She was back. His trick with the ink had lasted only until the fluid had lost some of its vivid colour. 'You should leave Chadwicke House,' he told her again. 'You will be too disturbing for my patients.'

'Why?'

Andrew leaned forward. 'You know why. Do not attempt to feign innocence, Mrs Cornwell. You have used men all your life. I have no doubt that you have been sexually active from a relatively young age. Your beauty is both weapon and currency. But you are nearing fifty and nothing lasts for ever. In ten years, time will be marching all over your face and your body. Do not attempt to stay here. You will be an outpatient.'

Molly stood up. 'You don't like me, do you?'

'My personal feelings are not the issue here. I act for the greater good and I judge you to be unsuitable company for the men who have come here to rest and to recover.'

'I wish to see my daughter.'

'She is shopping.'

'Her fiancé?'

'Is awaiting reconstructive surgery which has already been postponed twice.'

She looked down on him, her upper lip curling slightly as she spoke. 'You have strong feelings for my daughter – even a fool could see that, and I am not a fool. You're trapped. She is more like me than you know.'

'She is not like you at all, Mrs Cornwell. Dorothy is open, loving and kind. You are shut down, calculating and cruel.' He rose to his feet, noticed that the bad leg throbbed in her presence. 'However, I begin to believe that you were traumatized before puberty and that you have put away all memory of whatever happened to you. Until you allow retrieval of that incident, you will live no more than half a life.'

Molly paused for a moment. 'Some things are best left to rest in peace.'

'Dead things?'

She nodded just once. 'Unimportant events. I had an untroubled childhood with enough to eat and a decent upbringing. We shall leave it there, shall we?' Molly swept out of the room, leaving in her wake a perfume so expensive as not to be available during a time of war.

Andrew sat down, head in his hands. The witch who had just left had vision enough to recognize his feelings for her daughter. She was clever. Her brain, untapped and untended, had concentrated solely on its owner, had never been used for any particular purpose beyond the achievement of her own chosen destiny.

'You may come out now,' he called.

Dorothy appeared from a small store cupboard in a corner of the office.

'That was seriously unprofessional behaviour on my part,' he said. 'No one should be allowed to listen to a consultation between doctor and patient.'

'You spilled ink,' she said. 'To trigger her madness.'

'Yes.'

'But you didn't get very far.'

'On the contrary,' he replied. 'There are two parts to your mother. The second – the one she displays for much of the time – was created deliberately by the first. She has made herself into a shield and into a selfish woman who serves just her own purpose. The reasons are that she needed a place in which to hide and that she demanded compensation.'

'For what?'

'I don't know.'

Dorothy placed herself in the chair vacated by her mother. 'So something happened to her when she was too young to remember it?'

Andrew shook his head thoughtfully. 'On the contrary – she was old enough to remember, but the nature of the event was so disturbing or brutal that she built a wall. She remembers all of it, but has placed it in a lead-lined container with a complicated combination lock. One of the release factors is the colour red. It takes very little imagination to gather that she saw a great deal of blood.'

'She witnessed a murder?'

Andrew steepled his fingers and rested his chin on the apex of the structure. 'Or she performed it. It is hard to work out. She needs the sort of help I have not the time to give. Meanwhile, if she stayed here, she would probably become embroiled with male patients. Her first target might well have been Stuart.'

'I warned him.'

'Ah.'

'He is out in the grounds with one of the nurses. They went into the summer house with coffee and biscuits.'

'Wise man.'

Dorothy blushed. 'She sees that you and I are fond of each other.'

'She has vision, yes. It's a fine brain that has never been employed constructively. Although she can't sympathize or empathize with her fellow man, she has him worked out – she's like someone who studies insects.'

'And sometimes, she impales one,' said Dorothy, 'a specimen to be viewed and analysed from time to time. So, what now?'

'She goes back to the cottage or back to View Street.'

'Will she be safe?'

Andrew picked up his notes and looked at the mess on his desk. 'I'm not worried about her,' he said, 'but I am slightly concerned for the rest of the world.' Then he went off to do his job.

*   *   *

By the time Dorothy reached the age of sixteen, Molly had to admit to herself that control was slipping out of her grasp. No longer tied to her bed, the girl slept when she liked, moved about the house with a degree of freedom she had taken without permission, and was beginning to interfere with the side of Molly's life that had always been impenetrable.

'I shall be having a visitor this afternoon,' Molly advised her daughter one Wednesday morning.

'Mr Jenkinson?'

Molly shrugged. 'What if it is?'

'Do you know why I left that shop, Mam? Because he was always grabbing me. I couldn't tell you that at the time, because he was your friend, but I am telling you now because I am older and braver. Today is half-day closing in our shop, too, and I shall be home by one o'clock. I'd rather not see him.'

Molly blinked. 'Did you get him beaten up?'

'The beating was not my idea. I told a friend what had happened and she sent her brothers round to the shop. If I see him again, I won't be pleased. He's nasty.' Dorothy left for work.

Molly dressed herself hurriedly and went out. Life had turned slightly red round the edges and she walked through a pale mist until she reached Jenkinson's grocery. Fury made her careless and she did not bother to check on the occupants of the shop before entering.

He was slicing bacon. Beside him, his homely, rounded wife was wrapping tissue over a Hovis loaf. Molly awarded Beatrice Jenkinson a cursory glance, then waded in. Two customers stood back as the full force of her fury hit the shopkeeper. 'You touched my daughter,' she hissed.

Bert Jenkinson took his hand off the bacon slicer. 'You what?'

'My Dorothy. Remember? She worked here for a few months after she left school? Beautiful blonde, nice figure?' She turned to the wife. 'He wasn't beaten up for the contents of his till, Mrs Jenkinson. My daughter's friend sent her brothers round to deal with him. He was touching my girl.' She leaned over the counter. 'I'd kill you if we were alone,' she said to the white-faced man.

'I never touched nobody.'

'You lying, no-good piece of scum.' Molly's voice was very soft. 'Dorothy doesn't lie. Why do you think she left here so suddenly, eh? And it's taken her all this time to work her way up to telling me, because I reared her to respect her elders. But why should she respect a man who kept trying to get his hands up her skirt?'

Beatrice Jenkinson dropped her loaf. With a hand to her mouth, she fled the scene and shut herself in the storeroom.

The two customers crept nearer to the door.

Molly grabbed the grocer's tie. 'Nobody touches her – do you hear me? Nobody. She's

320

just a child . . .' The room was darkening and its colour was crimson. 'And you are a fat, nasty, sweaty, disgusting man. Stick to your ugly wife and her jowls – she's as hideous as you are.'

One of the customers cleared her throat. 'I need that bacon,' she said. 'My Jimmy's on shifts and he'll want his breakfast in half an hour.'

Molly swung round. The room returned to its normal shades of dirty green and brown. She smiled at the customer. 'I wouldn't buy anything off him, love. Every time he sees a pretty girl, he goes and plays with himself in the back yard lav. You don't want to be giving your husband bacon sliced and weighed with those hands. Try Davidson's. He's cheaper, better and he doesn't mess with his private parts half a dozen times a day.'

She walked to the door, turned, and smiled at Bert Jenkinson. 'Sorry your wife had to hear all that. I forgot she helps out some mornings. She helps out because you hire pretty girls, torment them and lose them, so she has to step into the breach. Stick to the missus. No danger there – she looks like the back of a number seventeen tram.'

Molly stormed out and found that she was trembling. Grown men should not touch little girls. Those who did touch little girls ought to be killed. Dorothy was her child and she had been protected from birth, yet that fat slob had managed to get his greasy hands on her. 'No,' she muttered under her breath. There was no way to mend the situation now, but he would not touch Molly's daughter again.

Some force of nature propelled her down Derby Street, through the town centre and up Chorley New Road. She stood outside the building that contained her flat, the love nest created all those years ago by Ian Clarke. He had been the one, the only one. Since him, a series of tradesmen had been her company, and she missed him now as acutely as she had then, on the night she had lost their baby.

Her steps slowed while she passed Bolton School and approached the leafier end of the road. Mansfield Avenue. She stared at a door he had touched, at glass behind which Florence Clarke had breathed her last. *You are a treasure, Molly. I want you to have these pearls.* Florence had valued Molly. Ian had still needed her then, after his wife had died. Then Molly had lost him to America and his baby to a pool on the floor. She mustn't think about the pool. Everything bad was red and everything red was bad.

Why was she here? What had she expected to find in Mansfield Avenue? Ghosts? A woman walked through the door into Ian's house and closed it behind herself. The sound it made was a familiar one and Molly inhaled sharply. Where was he? Was he alive, dead, in America, elsewhere? Where was Dorothy's father?

Suddenly exhausted, Molly retraced her steps until she reached the Wheatsheaf. Her feet ached, her back throbbed and she needed to sit for a while. At the bar, she ordered dry cider, carried the drink to a quiet corner and sat down. She took a sip, then sat and stared into the amber fluid until she felt quite mesmerized by it.

A shadow arrived at the table. 'Mind if I join you?' asked its creator.

She looked round the room, saw at least a dozen vacant tables and was about to say that she wanted to be alone, but she looked up and found a handsome man with a gold albert across his good waistcoat. This was no butcher, baker, or candlestick maker; was certainly no fat grocer from Derby Street. 'If you like,' she replied.

He sat down and introduced himself as David Bradley, a man of parts.

'Parts?' she enquired, one eyebrow raised quizzically.

'Part this, part that and part total nonsense,' was his reply.

She found herself smiling. 'I like the total nonsense best.'

'So do I. For the other parts, I deal in land, property, antiquities and anything else that comes my way. May I buy you another drink?'

'No, thank you. I came in for a rest. I think I walked too far today.'

Thus it began. Within an hour of meeting David, she was in his bed in a rented flat on Deansgate. He kept the flat, he said, because he was often in Bolton and needed a pied-à-terre in which to sleep and to make business plans. The place was furnished beautifully, and Molly found herself between cream silk sheets with a man who was sufficiently enthralled by her appearance to tremble at the first touches, yet controlled to a point where he pleased her.

When the lovemaking ended, he looked at her with near-adoration in his eyes. 'What a woman,' he declared.

'Thank you.'

'Will you come again?'

'In what sense?'

'In total nonsense, of course,' he quipped. 'I meant will you come to the flat again? How may I contact you?'

'I have absolutely no idea.' She raised herself onto an elbow and played with the hair on his chest. 'This needs mowing,' she said. Her hand moved suddenly and he moaned as she brought him back to readiness.

'My turn,' she told him seriously. For the first time in years, Molly played her game and watched as he became her slave. Forbidden to even flinch, he lay as still as he could manage while she said the words designed to inflame, while she caressed him to the point of pain before bestriding him. 'Still my turn,' she told him. 'Not once will you move.'

'You like control.' The three words were extruded between teeth clenched so tightly that his jaw hurt.

'I *am* control,' she answered. 'Always, always, I am the boss.'

'Will my turn ever come again?'

'Only when the boss allows it.'

By the end of that afternoon, he was completely lost. This was not a prostitute; she spoke well, dressed well and was a married woman with a daughter. 'Your husband?' he asked.

'Dead from the waist down.'

He lay, hands clasped behind his head, and watched her as she dressed. The sight of a woman undressing was supposed to be stimulating, but this one had perfected the art of covering her body in a way that might easily drive a man wild. 'When can I see you again?' he begged.

Molly raised her shoulders. 'I'm not sure. My husband makes very little money and I must find work. I had been looking for work when I popped into the Wheatsheaf for a rest.'

'Don't,' he said. 'If you need money, I can help you.'

She finished rolling a stocking along her thigh. 'I am not a whore, David. I don't take money in exchange for favours.'

'You can help with my work. Come with me to auctions when I am selling. We shall devise a system of signals and you can bid when I want to lift the price. Please?'

'And if no one outbids me?'

'I can afford that, too. Be my personal assistant.'

'How personal?'

'Very.'

She pulled on her coat. 'One condition.'

'Name it.'

'Give me a key.'

He tilted his head and studied her for a moment. 'Will you bring lovers here? Will you betray me?'

'Never.'

There was a strange honesty to this woman, he thought. Yet he, far from honest, had much to conceal before allowing her access to his flat. 'I shall need to have one cut. Can you meet me outside here next Wednesday at two o'clock? Then I shall have your key ready.'

'Very well.' Without so much as a goodbye, she left the room and closed the door firmly in her wake. Her excitement must not show. She had found another Ian, a man of substance and education, and she must tickle him like a trout if she wanted to land him.

Inside the flat, Molly Cornwell's conquest began to rearrange and verify the life he had constructed for himself away from wife and children. Anything that revealed his real identity was packed away into a suitcase. His business stationery, which bore the legend *David Bradley Enterprises*, was left very much in evidence on the desk alongside compliment slips and cards.

He thanked himself for having invented his alter ego. At first, the reason had been born of a valid need to conceal his true identity, because although he was not particularly recognizable in a crowd, his family name carried clout in these parts. Never one for party-going, he had lived a quiet, wealthy life until his business acumen had raised its head and dragged him into the arena of speculation. He bought at the right price, inflated that price, sold at a profit. By this method, he had doubled his already consider-able fortune in six years.

Now, into his second life had walked a woman the like of whom he had never expected to encounter. He had met her only a few brief hours ago, yet the very thought of her made his heart quicken. Love? Not likely, not after so brief an acquaintance. But he was fascinated, smitten, enthralled.

He thought of his wife at home, neat, arrogant, all haute couture and pedantry. She had not the imagination of a deceased newt and he had tired of her long ago. Between them, they had produced an heir and a couple of spares, and David's adventures, relatively few in number, had been conducted well away from the family seat. He had no need of this apartment in Bolton, as his home was well within reach, but he had been living life on his own terms for several years and had no intention of altering his ways.

He buried his face in a pillow and breathed in the scent of magic. He needed to bathe, because he was homeward bound tonight and Isobel could sense betrayal even in the absence of perfume. She did not want him in her bed; nor did she want him in anyone else's. It was 1930, he told himself firmly. Victoria had died almost three decades earlier and the Great War had altered many people, himself included. It was time for some fun, some relaxation and some honest, vibrant sex. A man was a long time dead and life was for living.

He bathed, dressed, packed his bags. David Bradley would be back next Wednesday. Donald Burbank prepared himself for yet another gloomy evening in the company of a disappointed wife; in seven days, he would meet Molly again and she would lift him out of misery and into the realms of sheer bliss. He was, indeed, a fortunate man.

* * *

She was not heavy. Andrew lifted her in his arms and, in spite of his weakened leg and shoulder, managed to take her back to her room. He placed her on the bed and re-arranged the covers.

'Andrew?'

'God, you made me jump.'

'Am I doing it again?'

He perched on the edge of her bed. 'You were halfway downstairs. It's all right – I'm not going to strap you in.'

She sat up, dragging the pillows into a more supportive position. Mam had gone back to the cottage, yet the sleepwalking continued. It had happened before Mam had come to Chadwicke House, she reminded herself. As soon as Molly Cornwell had arrived in Bromley Cross, Dorothy had walked in her sleep at least once each week. 'I'm sorry.'

He grinned impishly. 'I could climb in beside you and hold you still.'

'I'd like that. I'm not supposed to say so, but—'

'But it's said and you can't take it back.'

'Something along those lines, yes,' she answered.

'Dorothy?'

'What?'

'Do you love me?'

'Yes.'

It was her frankness that appealed to him most. At every twist and turn in life, Dorothy Dyson told the truth – her truth. Andrew knew with blinding certainty that she would not reject any advances he might make, and it took a great deal of willpower to hold himself back. He could feel her legs beneath the blankets, could see in dim light the shape of her hair, which, released from its daytime snood, flowed freely down to her shoulders. 'I must go before I forget myself,' he said, his voice thickening with emotion.

She longed to beg him to stay, wanted to touch his face, his hair, needed to hold him. 'Andrew?'

'Yes?'

'It would break him if I told him how I feel about you. Julia walked away – if I did the same, it might kill him.' She wanted to speak of the mistake she had made, needed to acknowledge to Andrew and, more importantly, to herself that she had loved him from the very start, but Stuart . . . Oh, what a mess.

'If you marry him and go cold on him, that will bring a lifetime of misery for both of you. The world has walked all over his face and a loveless marriage might kill what's left of his spirit. There is no easy answer. But I love you and want to spend the rest of my days with you.'

She reached for him. 'Can you stay for a while without . . . without?'

'Of course I can.'

It was torture, but he managed it. She drifted away in his arms and was not a witness to his tears. He was here to hold her down, to prevent the sleepwalking, to kill her demons. She was warm and she smelled of spring flowers and youth. The pillow, dampened by his tears, would dry before morning, but his adoration of her would continue to burgeon.

Suddenly, she woke. 'It doesn't make any difference,' she whispered.

'What doesn't?'

'That we haven't done anything. Wanting to do something is the same as doing it.' She had betrayed Stuart. She was like her mother. She didn't want to be like her mother.

'I am a doctor and I am helping you to get some restful sleep.'

Dorothy sighed. 'The pillow is wet. You love me so much that you've been weeping.'

'Yes.'

She touched his damp face. He had been crying because he knew the truth and the truth was that she adored him. She loved his eyes, his troublesome hair, his mouth, those perfect teeth. She loved his compassion, his dedication to the job, his withered leg, his frozen shoulder. 'It's not just you,' she told him. 'It's me as well.'

'I know. The love isn't our property – it is an element that has taken us over. What on earth are we going to do?'

'Pray for a miracle? Wait until he's had some of the operations? Elope?' She withdrew her hand, because touching him was exquisite torture.

Andrew threw another truth into the small arena. 'Stuart knows. He's known from the very beginning that I was falling in love with you. He also realizes that we spend time together in a professional capacity. It might not come as a shock if he were told.'

But Dorothy would not take that chance, would not even contemplate any further betrayal of a man who needed her. They both needed her. 'Go back to your room, darling,' she mumbled.

'Don't send me away.'

'Please go. For both our sakes, go.'

'My mother brought yours here to interfere. I had said a little too much about your history – for which I beg pardon – and Mother used it. I think she read notes in my office, too. She may even have found your diaries before I locked them away.'

'But my mother's agenda will have a very different goal,' she told him. 'She will want to make sure I marry Burbank Hall. It wouldn't matter if you looked like the back of a crashed bus or if you were nasty – she wants this house. I can read her like an open book. Please go. I am confused.'

He kissed her just once, but the embrace lasted. Her response was hungry and feverish and he had to tear himself away from her. 'If I stay, there will be no turning back,' he whispered before leaving the bed. He could hear her breathing, quick and shallow. This was a passionate woman and he needed to protect her not just from himself, but also from her own desire.

'I love you,' she said.

'I know.' He left the room at a pace that was remarkable for a man with a crippled leg.

Alone and chilled, Dorothy pulled the blankets tightly against her body. 'Don't let me be like my mother,' she begged of God. Then she fell asleep and she did not walk again that night.

TWELVE

Andrew burst into Room One. 'We've got you on a better list at last,' he told Stuart. 'And it's going to be the Emperor!' Stuart's surgery had been postponed twice due to a shortage of skilled specialists and an increase in the number of people requiring their expertise, and there was no absolute certainty that it would happen soon. Doctors were busy patching up the newly injured from bombing raids and military accidents, so the walking wounded were repeatedly forced to wait.

The patient looked up from his newspaper. 'The what?'

'The best, that's what. I mean who.' He sat on the edge of the bed. 'I think the name is probably from Roman times, though the emperor then was the patient, not the surgeon. Justinian the Second had his nose mutilated in battle – his enemies thought that disfigurement would keep him out of office. But a surgeon rebuilt his nose, which was quite an achievement when you consider the lack of antiseptics and anaesthesia then.'

Stuart noticed that Andrew had slipped into lecturer mode – a sure sign that he was nervous. This patient did not share his counsellor's hope. At this rate, he would be drawing his old age pension before anyone tried to straighten out his face. 'The Emperor? Who the hell is he, anyway?'

'Trained in America and risked his life to get over here. He came in '39, just after the outbreak of war, travelled with a group of young American airmen who volunteered right away. But the Emperor is too old for battle, and he's had to settle for patching up guys like you. He is magic.'

Stuart threw down his *Daily Express*. 'So, what are the chances of its actually happening this time? Dorothy and I have put off our wedding for long enough.'

Andrew managed not to flinch. Sometimes, this fellow's one good eye seemed to see more than most noticed with two. 'It's scheduled for next Tuesday and Dorothy will go with you. She can stay nearby and visit you every day.' True to his word, Andrew had not slept with Dorothy. But all the same, he was a guilty man.

Stuart Beddows was not stupid. Confined for some months to the area around the Burbank properties, he had noticed the change in Andrew and in Dorothy, and he could guess the reason.

'So, you take that first big step in a couple of weeks – if our luck holds,' said Andrew.

Stuart stood up and walked to the window – he was taking a giant step at this very moment,

334

but it had to be done. 'You and I have always been honest with each other, I think.'

Andrew swallowed. 'I hope so.'

'I mentioned a wedding that will not take place.'

Andrew found no words. Talking to a person's back was not easy at the best of times, and this was not the best of times. He could not lie and he could not speak the truth, so he kept his counsel.

'You love her?' Stuart asked.

'Yes. You already know that.'

'And you conceded defeat. I was surprised when she accepted my proposal, because I knew she was fond of you. But her feelings have now surpassed fondness. Am I right?'

Again, Andrew offered no reply.

The man at the window turned and faced his rival. 'It is my turn to concede. But there is a proviso. You will not tell Dorothy that I know about the two of you. Let her continue as she is, because the thought of my distress will make her ill.' He reclaimed his seat in the armchair. 'She no longer confides in me. The distance between us widens every day, but she is a loyal woman. If anything happens to me in that hospital, I don't want her blaming herself. Wait until the first operation is over.'

Andrew continued to hesitate. The idea of keeping anything from Dorothy was startling. Something the size of this would weigh heavily, yet he had to make the promise, because Stuart was an honourable man who deserved respect and support. 'Very well. I won't say a word.'

The untouched side of the patient's face smiled. 'Also, I do have another iron in the fire.' He picked up a letter. 'This is from Julia, my childhood sweetheart. She wants to visit me when she next has leave. I think Dorothy came to me in pity and I came to her on the rebound. Even so, I insist that we make no waves until I return safely from Chester. Let me end the relationship then, when that first big job is over and after Julia has visited. That way, Dorothy will feel no guilt. She'll know only relief when I go back to the woman of my original choice.'

Andrew realized anew that he was in the company of a man whose bravery was astonishing. He had fought for his country almost to the death, had battled demons and, with the help of doctors and nurses, had come through nightmares the like of which no human should be forced to endure. Now, he awaited the surgeon's knife and a series of procedures whose outcome would always be uncertain, and he was considering another person's feelings before his own.

'Agreed?' asked Stuart.

'Agreed.' Andrew walked to the door.

'Be happy,' shouted Stuart, 'and that, sir, is an order.'

Stuart Beddows sat in Room One, heart pounding as he thought about what was about to happen to him. Given a choice, he would have preferred to fly over Berlin in a Lancaster than to sit and wait for surgery. Did he want it? How much could be done to disguise frazzled skin, melted flesh and rigid muscle? There would be a glass eye, a reconstructed septum in his nose, some pain. What was the point? Nothing on earth could possibly make him normal again.

He picked up Julia's letter. She had been afraid, but she wanted to see him again. *You are still my Stuart,* she had written, *and I am so sorry for my crass behaviour. When I can get away, I shall come up to visit, even if I am forced to walk every mile.* Julia was coming. She wasn't a bit like Dorothy, was louder, funnier and brighter than just about any other woman he had met. And she was returning to him. For her, he must make the effort. He had to do it for Dorothy, too. She belonged to another man, but he owed her this much. Stuart opened his newspaper and continued to read.

*   *   *

Molly Cornwell was having the time of her life. She threw herself wholeheartedly into her relationship with David Bradley and, as payment for her loyalty and hard work, she was dressed like a lady in couturier clothes, hand-made shoes and good jewellery. A part of her continued to hanker after Ian Clarke, but David came a close second to the man she considered to have been the love of her life, so she made the best of things.

Pragmatism, always Molly's strength, enabled her to put up a good show even on days when she felt weary, and she fared well at auctions all over the country. Officially an employee of

David Bradley Enterprises, she came and went as she pleased, with the result that her husband and daughter at last found a degree of freedom well beyond the reach of her vision and temper.

Dorothy finally formed a relationship with Tom Cornwell. She discovered that he liked jigsaw puzzles, crosswords and the wireless. They spent many an evening in the company of invisible actors, a jigsaw scattered across the table. She found him to be genuinely quiet, thoughtful and a great reader. 'So I must have inherited my love of reading from you,' she told him.

Tom had always lived vicariously through books and wireless. Molly had married him in full knowledge of his impotence and he understood why – she needed no permission to go off and do exactly what she was doing right now. Her boss had become her life and her lover, while Tom owned no rights over her. Yet he adored his wife and loved her daughter as if she were his own. He kept quiet, brought home the money and made no waves. As reward for his dog-like obedience, Molly allowed him to share her table and her bed, though she was away a great deal these days.

'Dad?'

'What?' He was trying to fit a piece of sky above an almost completed seascape jigsaw.

'You know what she's doing, don't you?'

'Yes.'

'Does it not bother you?'

Tom shrugged. 'I'm used to it.'

'So it's always been like this?'

'Yes.'

For the past four years, Molly Cornwell had been cavorting all over the country in the company of her employer, David Bradley. She made no secret of the fact that he was her lover; neither did she advertise the situation. Dorothy, now twenty years of age, was tasting the edge of freedom for the first time in her life. But Mam always came home at weekends, and was often in residence for one or two nights midweek, so Dorothy and Tom made their arrangements when they were almost sure that she would be absent. Tom allowed himself the occasional pint and a game of darts at his local, while Dorothy, emboldened by her sudden liberation, allowed Steve to visit when Dad was at the pub, sometimes when Dad was not at the pub.

She was head over heels in love and had been in that state for at least four years. Fortunately, the knowledge that Mam might put in an appearance at any moment forced Dorothy to hold back when it came to lovemaking. Evenings were spent with the back door unlocked in case a swift exit should be required, and with ears straining to catch the slightest noise.

Tom fixed another piece of sky into position. 'She'll catch you and Steve, Dorothy – you mark my words.'

'Yes. I was just thinking about that. We keep the back door on the latch just in case he has to get out quickly.' She passed him two more sections of sky. 'What's the matter with her, Dad? Why did she fasten me into bed? Why bars at my window? Why was I never allowed to mix with other children?'

Tom studied the pieces in his hand. 'I'm not sure.'

'And you never stuck up for me, did you?'

He looked straight at her. 'Dorothy, love, there's no point in trying to stand your ground in a hurricane. Best thing is to keep your head down and wait till it passes.'

She sighed heavily. 'She's no act of nature, Dad. She must be aware that she's not right.'

Tom searched for words. Used to silence in his home and noise underground, the miner had enjoyed few chances to converse. 'She's frightened of something or other.'

'What, though?'

'People, more than likely.'

Dorothy folded her arms. 'People? She's afraid of nobody. She shouts first and thinks last and she always has to win.'

He fitted in a bit of cloud. 'Have you never come across the saying "Attack is the best means of defence"? Because that's what it all comes down to with your mam. She takes control and keeps her eye on everything and everybody. It's the only way for her to feel safe.'

'But why? You're not telling me why.'

Tom stared into the fire. He looked through and past flame and coal, travelling back to a time where suspicion dwelt, when half an answer had been planted in his brain. But half an answer was no answer at all, so he said nothing. 'Leave it, pet,' was all he managed.

Dorothy was uncomfortable. There had

been occasions during the past fifteen or so years when she had seen sudden and radical changes in her mother, changes that had all been triggered by one thing and that thing was blood. Molly could not dress a cut finger, was unable to deal with a wound. 'It's to do with blood, isn't it?' Dorothy had started to cut her arms in desperation when faced with Molly's intransigence.

'It may be.'

'Dad, you've seen it when you've come home from the pit with an injury and blood on your clothes. She can't face it.'

'No, she can't.'

'Why?'

'It's called a phobia. With some folk it's spiders or snakes, with Molly it's blood. There's no reasoning with a phobia – it's just there, that's all.' Whatever he knew or suspected, he would keep it to himself. But he remembered a terrible day, police, newspaper reports, a very quiet child in the house across the way.

Dorothy lapsed into the silence with which Tom was clearly more at ease. She helped him with his sky at sunset, then went into the kitchen to make supper. When the front door slammed, she stiffened, lost her way with the bread knife and almost took the end off her left index finger. Quickly, she grabbed a tea towel and wrapped it round the bleeding digit. Mam was home, so the blood had to be hidden.

'Dorothy?' The voice was strident and angry.

Dorothy entered the living room. Mam, in a smart business suit, had planted herself in front of the fire. 'What was that boy doing hanging about on my doorstep? Well?'

Tom stood up, picked a couple of jigsaw pieces from the floor and placed them with the rest.

Molly, furious and beyond the reach of reason, stepped forward and swept the whole puzzle off the table. 'You are just a bloody great kid,' she advised the man she had married. 'Go and make yourself useful, for a change.'

Tom slunk out of the room like a whipped child.

'Well?' repeated Molly. 'What was that Steve Dyson doing?'

Dorothy's shoulders sagged. She pondered for a moment, then decided that enough was enough. 'I am twenty years old,' she said wearily. 'Steve Dyson is my boyfriend.'

Molly's face twisted until she was almost ugly. 'Boyfriend? Boyfriend? Has he touched you? Because if he has, I'll kill him.'

'No, you won't.'

'What did you say?'

'No, you won't kill him. You come in here and throw your weight about when I know very well that you have been sleeping with your boss. I spent half my childhood up those stairs listening to you screaming like an alley cat while men touched you. One law for you and another for me – is that it?' Dorothy was shaking and her heart was beating so fast that the blood from her finger was pumping out, forced by the weight of the engine behind it.

Molly stepped forward and slapped her

daughter so hard that her head made contact with the wall.

Dazed, the girl righted herself and, with slow deliberation, peeled the towel from her finger. Bright red drops tumbled to the carpet. Dorothy raised her hand and smeared blood across her own face. 'Blood, Mam,' she whispered. 'Lots and lots of blood. Did you know I used to prick my fingers to make red for my paintings? It dried brown, though. At school, the other children got fed up with me, because I always used up all the red. It's my favourite colour.'

Molly shrank, seemed to lose inches in height. Her hands moved of their own accord to seek support from the fireguard. Perspiration coursed down her face and she tasted it on her lips. 'No,' she mumbled.

Protecting herself with the shield formed by her own hand, Dorothy walked out of the house and into the arms of Steve Dyson. 'Hospital,' she said, her voice steady. Steve mounted his bicycle while she climbed up behind him. In a standing position, he rode as fast as he could manage all the way through town and to the infirmary. 'Hang on to me,' he ordered repeatedly.

The finger was stitched and Dorothy was given a cup of hot, sweet tea. Although the bleeding had seemed profuse, she was judged healthy and allowed to leave after an hour. They walked back, Steve steadying his bicycle with one hand, supporting Dorothy with the other. 'We have to get away,' he said. 'You can't carry on living with that mad woman, love. As for your dad – well, I don't understand him at all.'

'He's scared of her, the neighbours are scared of her and she terrifies me. You can never tell which way she'll jump. Mostly, she tells other folk to jump – and they do. That's the amazing thing. Till it comes to blood.'

Dorothy stopped outside the Tivoli cinema for a rest. An evening that had started out well with a jigsaw, the wireless and Dad had been ruined by the melodramatic entrance of the witch, and the witch was Dorothy's mother. 'There's some money,' she told Steve. 'I can have it when I am twenty-three. The person who put it in the bank for me must have believed that no one under that age has sense.' The person was Beryl Isherwood – of that Dorothy felt sure.

'That's three years,' said Steve.

'Yes. In three years, we can get married, rent a place and buy furniture. Until then, I am going to look after Dad. No one has ever taken any notice of him. He's just a servant to her.'

'You should leave now,' said Steve.

'No, I'll leave when I'm twenty-three.'

Forced to be content with that, he took her home.

*   *   *

Michael Cooper's wife, Barbara, was seated, as ever, in a chair by the fire. Limited by multiple sclerosis, she went from attack into occasional remission and was currently enduring an onslaught of considerable severity. 'I don't know where he is,' she told Molly. 'I'm in that much pain, I can hardly think.'

Molly dealt with everything, making tea, ensuring that the patient was as comfortable as possible, washing the woman's hands and face, stoking up the fire. She was reminded of a happier time, when Florence and the Clarke family had needed her, when the three children had liked having her around, when Ian had been unable to function without her.

'You took a beating,' said Barbara, looking at a bruise on Molly's neck.

'I did, but I'm all right now. Which is more than can be said for your land girls. We've one pregnant and throwing up all over the place – she won't say who the father is – and another AWOL after a drinking session last night. The vegetables are behind schedule and you've two cows wandered off into the sunset. I've got to see your husband.'

'Get in the queue,' replied Barbara Cooper. 'I reckon he's the father of Jean Sharp's baby and he'll have sold the cows on the black.'

'Does he do a lot of black market trading?'

Barbara shrugged. By her own reckoning, she hadn't much more to lose and would soon have to return to her parents and sisters in order to be properly cared for. 'I don't know, Molly – and that's the honest truth. There's me, this chair and these four walls – I see nowt at all. I wed a bad bugger and didn't even get a child out of him. All I got was this filthy disease and a stupid husband who doesn't know Christmas from Pancake Tuesday. I've had enough and I'm going home to Rochdale – my dad's coming for me as soon as he can cadge transport. I can do no more and I can't answer your questions, love.'

Molly patted Barbara's hand. 'Put yourself at the front of that queue you mentioned, because nobody else will. Bye for now.' She went off in pursuit of the man who had raped her.

She found him. He had his trousers round his ankles and a young woman stretched in front of him across a few bales of hay. 'Lovely weather,' Molly said, her face remaining expressionless while the girl fled and he pulled himself together. She sauntered into the barn. 'You raped me,' she said clearly. 'I protected you when the police asked questions, so you owe me.'

Fear invaded him. Discovered in a position that denied him any dignity, faced by the woman he had raped, he shivered violently. He wanted to tell her that she had been gagging for sex until that particular night, but he retained sufficient sense to know that he was in thrall to this woman and that she had the ability to send him to jail. Uncharacteristically humbled, he murmured, 'Yes. I know. Er . . . thanks.'

Molly's lips curled. 'You owe me a lot. I might suddenly remember the identity of my attacker if you don't come to heel. What about the carrots? And that fallow field could do with a few King Edwards to prepare it for a cereal crop next year – there's a bloody war on, in case it slipped your notice. I'm not daft – I read stuff from the Ministry of Food and I know what you're supposed to be doing.'

'Well, it's been a bit—'

'You're two cows down and I'll bet a few families round here have a nice joint this weekend. Now, listen to me. I'll keep my mouth shut about the rape, the black market and the cows, but when I say jump, you ask how high. Oh and get that wife of yours in her wheelchair and bring her to my cottage – I'll see she's minded until her dad comes for her. You're as much use as a concrete cushion.'

'But I—'

'No buts. Pack Barbara's bags and bring her to my house.' She turned on her heel and marched away. Men were eminently manageable, she told herself as she mounted her bicycle and rode off homeward. All a woman needed to remember was that men kept their brains in their trousers and were a lot easier to handle than puff pastry.

She rode to the back of Chadwicke House and employed her binoculars. There was no sign of Dorothy, nor of the favoured patient with whom Molly had not achieved conversation. Dorothy needed to get her head straight, because Andrew Burbank could provide her with a good lifestyle. The stupid girl didn't know which side of her bread was buttered. Her head had always been in the clouds, Sleeping Beauty, her little diaries and drawings, all those silly daydreams. What really mattered was security, and property was security. How might Dorothy be separated from her young man, yet kept in the company of Andrew Burbank?

When the binoculars had been returned to their basket, Molly lingered for a while, her thoughts moving towards a possible solution. She owned the book and had used it before. It was an innocuous-looking volume, slim, bound in black and always hidden. The need had arrived for real cleverness to be harnessed. Yes. It was time to get out the little black book. And the Coopers would both be useful if she played her cards in the right order. One way or another, Molly would make sure that the once handsome airman would not marry her daughter.

*   *   *

Dorothy started to vomit one Sunday night and, by Monday morning, could not keep boiled water in her stomach. She sent her dad to Gregory and Porritts, asking him to explain that she would not be available for work. It meant that he had to go to town before his shift, but Dorothy, concerned for her workmates, was keen to let the firm know about her illness. Molly, with an expression of concern plastered across her face, plied her daughter with boiled water until some stayed put, then she went off to meet her lover and employer at the flat in town.

A pattern established itself over the months that followed and Dorothy, in danger of losing her position as seller of nuts and bolts, was appalled by her own stupidity once the penny finally dropped. Mam was poisoning her. The situation came to a head when, one morning before work, the girl secreted herself in the pantry and, through a small gap in the door, watched her mother's latest trick. Herbs grown in small pots near the back yard wash house played a part in Mam's venture, as did a candelabra cactus on the window sill. Into Dorothy's omelette went a pinch of this, a sprinkle of that and a bit of flesh from the cactus. Mam kept referring to her little black book – she was working to a recipe. Steve was right – it was time to escape. He had long completed his apprenticeship and was now established as an engineer, so the time to go would have arrived had his mother not been ill. His family, always close, had devoted their free time to the care of their lovely mother.

When the pantry door squeaked into the open position, Molly turned. 'Oh, there you are,' she said.

Dorothy stepped into the kitchen. 'It's the tripe all over again, isn't it? Remember? You used to make me eat tripe so that I would be sick? But this is worse – you are poisoning me.'

'Rubbish.'

Dorothy was never sick when Mam wasn't around. Why hadn't she worked this out months ago? It was time to get away from the woman once and for all. Until she could find a place to lodge, Dorothy would not eat in this house again. If only she could marry Steve immediately. But Steve's mother, a sweet, gentle woman with a marked fondness for Dorothy, was unwell, and there wasn't room in the Dyson house for another married couple—

'What are you planning now?' asked Molly, her tone shrill.

'Oh, shut up.' Dorothy swung round and left the kitchen. It was the nearest she had come to hitting her mother. Upstairs, Molly Cornwell's victim sat on the edge of her bed and stared at bars that had contained her for long enough. There was only one place for Dorothy and she should have remembered it earlier. Miss Isherwood, now in her seventies and long retired, would be glad of some company.

Molly came in. 'I was following instructions in here.' She waved her small book. 'It's all about aids to digestion. Perhaps I put in too much of one thing or another – but I was only trying to help you.'

Dorothy simply stared at the woman who had given her life. Life? Much of it had been a living death, and now . . . 'You could have killed me,' she said after a long pause. 'Control, control, control. Ever since I started work in town, you have been trying to get me to find a job nearer home. Why? Aren't you busy enough buying Queen Anne chairs and sleeping with David Bradley? This time, you have gone too far.'

Molly eyed her daughter. 'I was trying herbal medicine. Why won't you believe me? And what are you going to do now?'

'None of your business. Aren't you late for work?'

'I come and go as I please. He can manage without me.'

'Why? Does he have a second prostitute?'

Molly strode into the room and raised her hand, but something in Dorothy's expression forbade her to strike. It was hatred. Pure, unadulterated loathing shone vividly from eyes so like her own that she was almost transfixed. In that moment, Molly caught a glimpse of her daughter's inner strength. In Dorothy, there was enough of her mother to equip her to fight back. She was young, physically robust in spite of her recurring illness, and she would and could do battle if she chose.

But Molly did not see the wreckage she had created, because Dorothy made sure the door was closed behind her before breaking down. Stifling sobs with her pillow, the girl wept until she was spent. Then she lay on the bed and waited. Her stomach, groaning for food, felt like a great, empty cavern, but she experienced only relief, as she had not eaten her breakfast omelette.

The doses had clearly been measured to make her ill, no more. But Molly would stop at nothing, it seemed, until she had made it impossible for her daughter to venture beyond the area around View Street. She wanted Dorothy not to meet Steve, not to meet anyone, not to have a life. Meanwhile, the woman was in an adulterous relationship and Dorothy had taken enough.

When Mam had gone, when bags were packed, when she had eaten a piece of uncontaminated toast, Dorothy Cornwell left View Street and began the long walk to Willows Lane. There was nowhere else to go and she would tell Steve later, would meet him after he had left his work. She felt pity for Dad, who would, no doubt, reap the full harvest of Mam's fury later on. But Dad didn't seem to mind, had never raised voice or hand against his wife.

A very old woman opened the door to number 114. She walked with a stick and her face was lined with pain, her hair left to hang in greasy strands down to her shoulders. 'Dorothy?'

The visitor fought hard to hide the shock. 'Yes, it's me.'

'You came back. How long has it been?'

'Fifteen years.' The young woman dropped her bags and helped the old lady back into the house. The place, always neat and clean, was in a terrible state. There were papers, dirty clothes, plates and cups everywhere. 'How long has it been like this, Miss Isherwood?' She managed to get the old woman into a chair.

'Months. I have arthritis. There is nothing they can do for me. Dorothy, don't stay here. Don't give your life to me.'

The younger woman sat down. She looked round the room in which she had once eaten Christmas dinner, this place where she had been so blissfully happy for a few months, and she felt as if her heart might break. 'I shall look after you,' she said. 'When Steve comes home tonight, I'll fetch him and his brother and we'll make this place right.' How many children had the good woman taught? What sort of reward was this for someone who had given so much to others? It was only right that Dorothy, Steve and his brother, all of whom had been given a start in life by Beryl Isherwood, should be here for her now.

'Dorothy, you can't cope with me. The neighbours do what they can for me, and—'

'And you have been sleeping in that chair?'

'Yes. I can't get upstairs. The lady next door empties the commode and does a bit of cooking, but everyone has a family and I hate to impose.'

So began the next stage of Dorothy Cornwell's life. Within a week, she had left the shop in town and had turned Beryl Isherwood's best front room into a bedroom. She scrubbed, polished, swept and mopped until the place positively gleamed. To save the old woman's pride, Dorothy accepted a small wage and once again, she was happy. It was her turn to do the reading aloud and she revelled in it, enjoyed being appreciated and loved by a woman older than herself.

In a bed brought downstairs by the Dyson boys, Beryl listened to Trollope, Dickens, Austen and Goldsmith, all read beautifully by the child she had missed for fifteen long years. 'You grew up,' she said at the end of a chapter of *Great Expectations*. 'In spite of her, you have become a fine young woman. I am sad that your education was neglected and glad to see that you have taught yourself. Your money is still in the bank?'

'Until I am twenty-three, yes. And thank you.'

Beryl kept her lips sealed. The money was not from her. It was from Dr Clarke, who had probably fathered this sweet-natured girl. In a clean bed and in a clean nightdress, the retired teacher was content in spite of her pain. She did not dare to hope that this would last, because Dorothy would marry and move away, or that woman would come along to spoil things. 'Good night, dear,' she whispered as Dorothy left her to sleep.

Upstairs in a room she had reclaimed, Dorothy went once more to the wardrobe. The small blue hat and coat, still bearing price tags, hung inside with her other recently added clothes. Pinned to the collar of the coat was the note she had left, red crayon fading now towards pink. 'I won't leave you this time, Miss Isherwood,' she said quietly. 'Even if Steve and I live here after his mother gets better, I'll look after you till the end.'

*　　*　　*

Molly pushed the wheelchair up the slope. Barbara Cooper, wrapped in several layers, shrank down as they approached Burbank Hall. 'Are you sure?' she asked again. 'They're supposed to look after mothers and babies, aren't they? They won't want to bother with a cripple.'

Molly, grim-faced, continued to push. The woman in the chair was a passport into Burbank Hall and Molly would make the most of that fact. 'Stop worrying,' she ordered. 'I've told you

354

– put yourself at the front of the queue for once, because no bugger else will.'

Feeling as if she deserved a fanfare after the long haul from the village, Molly pulled Barbara into the large kitchen. Ivy Crumpsall and her sister were sitting by the fire, obviously taking a break between chores. After parking the wheel-chair between them, Molly spoke. 'I want to see a doctor or a nurse,' she said. 'This woman needs some help.'

Ivy and Elsie exchanged glances. 'Who is she?' Ivy asked.

'I might be in a chair, but I can speak for myself,' said Barbara Cooper. 'Folk think just because I need pushing and pulling about I'm a few bricks short of a load. Well, I'm not. I'm Barbara, I'm freezing and I could murder a bacon butty.'

Ivy studied the pale, thin creature. She looked as if she'd been denied food for months. 'I'll get the pan on, love,' she said. 'Elsie, pour her a cup of tea, then buzz through for help.'

In response to the bell, Andrew arrived to find Dorothy's mother ensconced with the two older women and a very thin Barbara Cooper. 'Hello, Mrs Cooper. What's the problem?' he asked. There certainly was a problem, because the invalid was disabled not just by illness, she was undernourished to the point of cruelty.

Barbara, glad that someone had the sense to address her, was blunt with her answer. 'I'm clemmed,' she said. 'Starved to the bone. He's a pig.'

Molly spoke up. She needed to be in Michael

355

Cooper's good books, so she shielded him as best she could. 'Mr Cooper's busy,' she said. 'He's a farm to run, he's short on labour and some of those land girls don't know a potato from a five-bar gate. He can't manage a sick wife on top of everything else, so I made him bring her to my house. I've wheeled her here to be looked after, because I have a job to do as well. When her dad can get petrol, he's going to take her home to Rochdale.'

'He's still a pig,' said Barbara.

'She means her husband, not her dad,' said Elsie helpfully.

Andrew stared at Barbara. He remembered her as a fresh-faced bride ten or more years earlier, roses in her cheeks, flesh on her bones and hope in her heart. The problem was more than multiple sclerosis – this was muscle wastage and neglect on a scale he had never witnessed before. 'Do you have meals at home?' he asked.

'Depends.'

'On what?'

'On whether the pig's got a sow to roll around with. Or a drink. He likes his ale. I get bits and pieces, but not a square meal, no.'

Andrew turned his attention to Molly Cornwell and his eyes narrowed slightly. What was her game this time, he wondered. She wasn't here for Barbara Cooper's sake, was she? The woman was probably nosing around after her daughter, a daughter who was about to become unengaged from Stuart Beddows and engaged to Andrew, though nothing could be said until Stuart's first surgery was completed. 'We'll look after Mrs Cooper from here,' he said. 'We'll feed her up as best we can, then I shall take her back to her family in the Chadwicke House van. You may get on with your work now.'

Molly stood up. She smoothed her clothes, patted her hair and spoke to Barbara. 'I'll try to visit you before you go home, love.'

The wheelchair-bound woman smiled. 'You're a godsend, Mrs Cornwell. If it wasn't for you, I could have wasted away before my time. He's a pig. He always was a pig and he always will be a pig.'

'I like pigs,' said Andrew. 'Intelligent creatures.'

'I like pigs and all,' replied Barbara smartly. 'Preferably between two slices of bread or with a bit of apple sauce.' She grabbed Ivy's bacon sandwich and began to devour it ravenously.

Andrew showed Molly to the door. 'I'll look after her.'

'You do that,' ordered Molly. 'Time somebody did. But he can't run a farm and keep an eye on her, Dr Burbank. He's not got time to give Barbara the care she needs. Terrible illness, that. It starts when they're young and she'll take a while to look after every day. She'll be best off with her dad and the rest of her own family.'

Andrew watched Dorothy's mother until she had disappeared from view. She was quite a complex character. There was, he suspected, a small part of her that really did care about doing the right thing by Barbara Cooper, yet she tied everything up in a parcel shaped to suit herself. It was a deep injury she owned. This wasn't nature – it was nurture, shock and a survival mechanism. That might never be proved, but the doctor could sense it and wanted to gain access to it. She had been right when she said she knew about shock, though the rape had not been a factor. This went a lot deeper than any recent event. 'I'd need buckets of red paint,' he mumbled quietly as he re-entered the kitchen.

'Talking to yourself again?' asked Ivy.

'That way, I am sure of an audience,' he replied. 'I always listen to my own advice. Now, Mrs Cooper, I shall keep you here, in Burbank – we can easily prepare a room. Once we have you strong and fed, I'll take you home to your father. It'll take a week or two, but we'll manage. All you need to do is eat and exercise as best you can.'

Barbara closed her eyes and thanked whichever god looked after the wives of selfish pigs. She would be fed, kept clean and taken home. It was as if all her birthdays had arrived simultaneously.

*   *   *

He wasn't there. Molly sat the whole morning and through lunchtime, becoming agitated in spite of firm resolve. She knew full well that Dorothy would not be in when she got home, and she had a fair idea regarding the address to which Dorothy might have moved – 114, Willows Lane. Yes, she would have returned to her geriatric teacher and Molly would be left alone with the silent one.

The hours ground by with monotonous slowness and a level of fear began to skirt the edge of thoughts that were already troubled. David Bradley could not stay away from her. He was bound to her, was a complete slave to her and seemed to be head over heels in love. The man was married and had children, but Molly was the real woman in his life. She had no way of knowing how to contact him, so she went through his papers at the desk, searched bedroom, bathroom and small kitchen. There was no evidence of his other life. She stood at the window and willed him to arrive, but he did not come.

It was happening again. Like Ian Clarke, this newer lover had abandoned her to the fates and the second rejection hurt, though not as deeply as the first. She dozed in a chair, felt Ian's hands as they crept around her body while she washed dishes, ironed clothes, prepared meals for him and his family. Poor Florence. *You are a treasure, Molly, and I want you to have my pearls.*

Edward, Sarah and Daniel were trying to learn to play the spoons. Florence needed a good wash. Ian was at the surgery and soon he would meet her at the flat. Her eyes flew open. The red. A lost baby. A man who abandoned her for a new life at the other side of the globe. Aloneness. Dorothy gone. 'I'll bring her home,' she said.

But she had awoken to a different time and Dorothy was no longer biddable. 'I only tried to save her,' Molly whispered. Dorothy needed to be safe from . . . She needed to be safe.

Boys were different. A son would not have brought with him all the worry and the fear. But Dorothy was not a son.

The clock had stopped. Molly rewound it and placed it on the little mantelpiece. Sometimes, while in bed with David, she had screamed out the name of another man, one she should have forgotten, and David had not been pleased. But that was not the reason for his absence. The clock was unusually noisy and Molly was unusually empty. She owned no sense of David, no instinct to tell her that he was on his way.

At four o'clock in the afternoon, she made her way homeward. The sky, grey, made leaden by emissions from factories, seemed to have been created just for her, as it reflected perfectly her mood. She was alone again. Deep down in a place she seldom chose to access, Molly was certain of her total isolation.

Dorothy had gone, of course. Her room, stripped of clothes, was bare except for books. 'From one empty place to another,' she said aloud as she sat on her daughter's bed. Dorothy, perfectly beautiful and vulnerable, was out there in a cruel world and Molly could not save her from . . . From things. From people. From pain. 'I don't know who I am without her. I don't know who I am without Ian.' David did not enter the equation and Tom had never been a factor.

Downstairs, she made a stab at cooking, leaving Tom's plate on a pan of hot water to stay warm until he returned. That was the deal – he paid her and she fed him, washed and ironed his clothes, slept in his bed. Her own meal, virtually untouched, was scraped away. Life was formless and meaningless and Molly was in no need of nourishment.

The newspaper dropped onto the mat in the hallway, but she left it where it was. Had she opened it, she might have noticed an announcement regarding a Donald Burbank who had passed away peacefully in the night, but it would have meant nothing to her. The ex-magistrate was mourned by a wife and three sons, but not by the woman he had truly loved, as she had no knowledge of his true identity.

Life was bleak. Day became night, night became day, and Molly plodded on with housework, cooking and shopping. She visited the flat just once more, only to discover that the locks had been changed. Rejected twice by men of means, Molly fought the self-pity and took a job in a dress shop in town. Sooner or later, she would meet another companion, but she missed the auctions, the bidding, the games in and out of bed.

It was 1936 and she was getting no younger, but her time wasn't up yet, not by a long chalk.

THIRTEEN

Isobel was lonely and ill-tempered. Her son, a man of supposed education and talent, had spoken few words to her during recent months. She had seldom felt more thoroughly punished, had not been as acutely upset since the death of her husband. Donald, a level-headed man of business, had used his commercial activities as cover for profligate behaviour, and had become involved towards the end of his life with an anonymous woman whose charms had kept him away from the house and from his family for days on end. That had been a betrayal, and now she had been betrayed all over again by Donald's son.

Had Isobel been asked to nominate one individual among her acquaintance as a thoughtless and uncaring person, Andrew would always have been at the bottom of any list. He was a good man, a kind man whose understanding of humanity allowed for forgiveness and fresh starts, but he was intransigent in this particular matter. It was all ridiculous. Dorothy Dyson was engaged to an air force captain and there had been no need for her mother to be relocated to Bromley Cross, no need for Isobel to try to separate Andrew from Dorothy. But the suspicion lingered. Andrew was still interested in Dorothy Dyson and would probably marry her in a flash if Stuart Beddows ever left the scene.

The company of Lizzie Murphy and of Shang and Ming was not enough, so Isobel opened up a little sitting room a few times a week and started a knitting circle. The wives of farmers and tradesmen were not the company Isobel might have chosen, but the knitters allowed Isobel a glimpse of a horizon beyond that cheeky, red-haired servant and two delightful dogs of limited intelligence and variable temperament.

Lizzie Murphy was plumping cushions in the area whose name had been changed to sewing room. Sewing room? It was more like a death trap – ornaments everywhere, occasional tables whose title should have been changed to frequent, because there were at least half a dozen of the damned things. Mrs Burbank was a blinking pest, and since Mr Andrew had moved out of the family quarters, there had been no relief at all for Lizzie. The dusting was continuous, as were the complaints and the monologues about the world's going to the dogs. That was another thing – dogs. Lizzie, a consummate animal lover, could not abide the two ruined and supposedly Chinese monsters belonging to Isobel.

'Lizzie?'

'Yes, Mrs Burbank?'

'Have you polished that fireplace?'

'Yes, Mrs Burbank.'

'Well, do it again. I can see finger marks and a slight bloom on the grate.'

A slight bloom? Would that be a rosebud or a bunch of deadly nightshade? Lizzie began the job all over again.

'Put some effort into it,' sniped Isobel.

The last straw was always a comparatively weightless item. Lizzie, who had been through hell and high water, had taken enough. Sick of making a bed twice, of polishing silver that didn't need polish, of trying to brew tea of exactly the right strength, Lizzie Murphy reached the end of her rope when the bloom appeared on the hearth.

'What are you doing?' asked Isobel when Lizzie downed tools very noisily. 'I asked you to do that fireplace again and—'

'You didn't ask me. You never ask me. You just stand there barking at me. Between you and them two ugly Pekingese buggers, I am sick of being snapped at. I'd rather stop in a bloody mental hospital than here with you and your blinking dogs. Even your son's had enough of you. Now.' Lizzie began to throw all her cleaning equipment into its basket. 'Tell you what, missus – do it yourself. Because I have had e-bloody-nough.' Lizzie was standing now, arms akimbo, facial skin doing battle with red hair in the colour stakes, voice high-pitched and unsteady. 'The way you treat me is . . .' Lizzie trawled through her vocabulary. 'Despicable,' she finally managed with a visible degree of triumph. One of the teachers at school had used the word quite often and Lizzie was glad to borrow it.

Isobel swallowed audibly. Never in her life had she been addressed in such a fashion. A hand flew to her throat and massaged a single strand of perfect black pearls. 'Have you finally taken complete leave of your senses?' she asked.

'No, I've just found my senses. You are a miserable, black-hearted woman and I am going into munitions. So stick that in your embroidery frame and decorate it. You don't know what life's about, Mrs Burbank. Try having eight brothers and sisters and a mam dying of TB in her lungs. Try having a dad who's that drunk he doesn't know Tuesday from breakfast. Try working for a spoilt cow who's never had to worry about not being able to go to school because of a broken clog. Then try finding some other kid to slave for you, because I am sick to the back teeth with you, your dogs and your blooming fireplace. Oh, and all your bloody ugly ornaments, too.'

Isobel sank into a chair when Lizzie had left the room. Shaking from head to foot, she rose again and staggered to the bell pull. Ivy Crumpsall could sort out this small matter. If the girl wanted a reference, she would have to sing for it, because Isobel had no intention of putting pen to paper. Andrew would, though. Oh yes, her son would turn against her and favour the servant every time, because Andrew was always on the side of the supposedly under-privileged.

Ivy entered the arena, head bobbing like a cork on choppy seas. 'Mrs Burbank?'

Isobel sighed heavily. 'That girl turned on me,' she said. 'I asked her to clean the fireplace and the language she used was unbelievable.'

Ivy chewed her lower lip. She knew Isobel Burbank of old and had known Lizzie Murphy from infancy, so she understood the situation well enough. The old days were gone, and Mrs Burbank would not put them to rest. Defunct was the time of the hovering butler and the biddable chambermaid. Two world wars had altered the balance of power, and servants were fewer on the ground and a long way from obsequiousness – was that the word? 'I can't think what to say.' Ivy truly was at a loss.

'Find me someone else.'

'There is no one else. Everybody's farming or doing war work – there isn't the staff to choose from any more, Mrs Burbank.'

'There must be somebody.'

'Not that I can think of.'

'Then what am I to do?'

An apology would be out of the question, Ivy supposed. 'Do you want me to go and talk to Lizzie?'

'Why?'

'See if she'll change her mind and stop.'

'No. Her behaviour was unforgivable. I don't suppose you could spare me some time?'

Ivy's head shook vigorously. 'I'm cooking for the staff, the mothers and Mr Andrew's lot – I even do yours sometimes, as you know. That's

just about all I can manage. I'm into my sixties
and not as quick on my feet as I used to be.
Sorry, Mrs Burbank.'

'Your sister?'

'Much the same. She did a bit of cooking
in town for munitions folk, then the bomb
knocked her sideways in more ways than one. It
took a lot out of her, you see. She peels me a
few spuds and looks after her burnt neighbour,
but that's as far as she goes, I'm afraid.'

Isobel lowered her head and pondered.
'Then we must advertise in town, Mrs
Crumpsall. I cannot manage this place.'

She couldn't manage a bowl of trifle, thought
Ivy, though she said nothing. This madam had
never lifted anything heavier than a powder
puff of perfumed talcum, so she certainly
wouldn't be able to clean twelve rooms in a
house as old as God. 'Well, I don't know what to
suggest, I'm sure.' Ivy had a casserole in the
oven and she didn't want it to dry out.

'What about Molly Cornwell's daughter?'

Ivy blushed in spite of her age. The relationship between Andrew and Dorothy was a topic
for speculation in Ivy's kitchen, but she couldn't
raise the matter here. 'Captain Beddows goes to
Chester soon for his first operation and I think
she'll go with him. Other than that, she has a lot
to do in Chadwicke House. Oh, and she's minding that farmer's wife – her with the multiple
sclerosis. Seems her husband wasn't feeding her,
so Dorothy's seeing to her.'

'Mrs Dyson's well thought of?'

'Oh, yes. She's thinking of being a proper

psychiatric nurse when this war's over. Mr Andrew says she has a bent for it.'

'Good.'

'Erm . . . I've stuff wants seeing to, Mrs Burbank. If you don't mind, I need to be getting back to the kitchen. I'll ask round. If anybody knows of anybody who might want the job, I'll let you know.'

There was but one string left to Isobel's bow. She would not permit Lizzie Murphy to stay for one more night; nor would she allow herself to live in a dirty house. Molly Cornwell might have an answer. She knew which farmhands were good and which were useless and which had wives in need of an occupation. Looking after a house that accommodated wounded men and bombed-out babies would count as war work, surely?

After shunting the two Pekes into the kitchen, she stood awhile and listened to the sounds emerging from Lizzie Murphy's ground floor room. The girl was plainly in a temper even now, because doors and drawers were slamming while the odd swear word was spat from the lips of the tiny, russet-haired virago. 'Let her get on with it,' Isobel whispered as she let herself out of the house. She had a key to Molly's cottage and could sit in wait for her if necessary.

She was in. Straight away, Molly was on her feet and bustling about with kettle, cups and milk while Isobel told her tale of woe. 'The young these days have no manners and no appreciation,' concluded the visitor.

Molly blamed the parents and said as much. 'I

kept Dorothy in check,' she said. 'I was so firm that she held it against me and still does to this day. But I would defy you to find a more polite woman than my Dorothy. It sounds as if your young maid got away with murder at home. But don't you worry, because I'll look after you.' Molly's brain was running at a hundred miles an hour and there was no time for brakes, no time for reasoning.

Isobel accepted a cup of suitably weak tea. 'How? You've all those girls to watch and all those farms to account for.'

Molly motored past the objections. 'One thing I have, Mrs Burbank, is energy – I have always been a hard worker.'

'Even now? After what happened?' The woman had been raped, after all. 'Are you sure you can manage?'

'Of course. I'm not going to let something like that slow me down – why should I? He put me in hospital, but he's not taking away any more of my life.' She would become an acrobat and the item she would juggle would be time. All women did that anyway, she supposed, but they didn't think about it. She was forced to think about it right now – and quickly. She had to look after farmers and Mrs Burbank and a good job needed to be done in both areas. 'Look, give me a minute while I get my head straight. I'm not having you sitting up there with nobody to help you.'

'You're very kind, Mrs Cornwell.'

She wasn't having Isobel Burbank living in that grand house on her own – Isobel Burbank would have a companion, would depend on that companion even after the end of the war. Isobel Burbank needed a treasure and Molly was a treasure, because Florence had said so. The pearls passed to Molly by the hand of a dying woman were far prettier than those dark things round Isobel Burbank's scrawny neck.

After a few moments of thought, Molly spoke up again. 'I've got it,' she said. 'You're on your own and I'm on my own. Your son's living with the staff and so is my daughter. Now, if I give up this cottage and move into Lizzie's room, you can help me with the farm paperwork and I'll do the cleaning, cooking and shopping. I'm not needed full time to supervise land girls – they'll get themselves in trouble no matter what. I can mend, I can iron and I can wash. You won't need to pay me any more than you do now and we'll both have company. And I'll still oversee the farms.'

Isobel found that the idea grew on her. There was a gentility about Molly Cornwell, an elegance not often visible in those from her walk of life. She might not rank high in the opinion of her daughter, but Isobel had come to know the woman as sensible and hardworking. 'Very well,' she said. 'We shall try it for a month, during which period either of us may back out with no need for explanation.' Andrew would not be pleased, but Andrew no longer resided with his mother – he was too busy with those airmen and Molly's daughter, who was, thank goodness, engaged elsewhere to be married.

'Good,' said Molly. 'I shall move tomorrow.

I'll be up with the lark and half the housework will be done before nine. Then, after a few hours out and about, I shall be back to do the rest.'

'Won't you get tired?'

Molly laughed. 'There's a war on – everyone's tired.'

When Isobel had left, Molly considered this latest development. She would be nearer to Dorothy and, should the need arise, she could call upon her little black book plan: a few herbs, a pretty cake, something to slow down Captain Beddows or Dorothy – or both. There would be no wedding. No matter what it took, Molly was determined that she and her daughter would be remaining at Burbank Hall and not just as companion to a rich widow and aide to her son. Dorothy would marry into the family and Dorothy's mother would benefit from the match.

Poisons? Would they be needed? Michael Cooper could visit his wife and, at the same time, could cut down Dorothy's airman with a well-seasoned pasty or a nice, sweet cake from the local bakery. Michael was in her power – he had raped her and she was capable of having him charged. But the lie of the land was changing all the time. For now, Molly would simply go with the flow and enjoy living in the luxury she had always deserved. Dorothy would be useful at last.

*   *   *

Steve Dyson hung on to his beloved Dorothy's hand. 'You have to stop this,' he whispered. 'It's not pneumonia and that's the main thing. He's giving her the medicine now, and after he's finished he'll tell us what's what.'

Dorothy stifled a sob. For months, she had cared for Beryl Isherwood and now it looked as if the end was on its way. That sweet, kind gentlewoman, who had been in constant pain for a very long time, could scarcely breathe.

'Reminds me of Mam,' said Steve. 'I know she's over the TB, but I'll never forget the way she was. We're feeding her up now that she's out of hospital, but she'll never be the same.'

'I know.'

'Ishy was the best teacher I ever had.' The big, brave lad wiped a tear from his face. 'All the years she gave, and she ends up a ball of pain and just us to look after her. Where's her sister gone?'

'They retired to Morecambe. Her husband died and she's got the same as Miss Isherwood. She can't even write a letter – the neighbour does it for her. What I want to know, Steve, is this – why do some people live good, clean lives and finish up so poor and ill? The bad seem to do a lot better.'

'In this life, yes.'

'I'm not sure about God,' Dorothy said.

'As long as God's sure of you, that's all that matters, according to Mam. I'm a bit like you – I've no idea.'

The doctor came in and gave his opinion. Beryl Isherwood had pleurisy and he didn't want to move her. With luck and good management, she would pull through, but she needed turning in her bed every hour. Pressure points wanted rubbing with surgical spirit as long as the skin was intact, and he would leave some cream in case a bedsore should appear.

When the medic had left, Dorothy and Steve drank tea and pondered their immediate future. They were both temporary carers, though Steve also put in eight hours at the engineering factory. Two married sisters covered hours of daylight in the Dyson household, but Steve and his brother had to take over after work. Mam would get better, but Miss Isherwood would remain in pain even after her chest had improved. 'I don't know what to hope for,' he said.

Dorothy understood him completely. Had Beryl Isherwood been a dog or a cat, a vet would have put her down years ago. She could scarcely walk, was unable to hold a pen and needed all her intimate requirements to be dealt with by somebody else. 'I couldn't have clogs, had to stay away from ringworm and wasn't to sit with a boy. Mam showed me up that first day.' Dorothy smiled through unshed tears. 'Miss Isherwood wasn't impressed. She looked so important in those days with her hair scraped back and no smile on her face, and those very dark clothes. Then she read us a story and no one on earth could have done it better. She was strict, but kind. I never saw her use a cane.'

'She used it to point at the alphabet, but I'm sure she never clouted a kid,' said Steve sadly.

'I know. Now look at her. She's just an old

373

woman waiting to die. It's not fair, Steve. My mother, with all her men friends and her cruelty, is walking about like a fashion plate. Why is everything upside down?'

'That's the same question, isn't it? You're asking whether and when Ishy will get her reward. I don't know.'

They held hands until it was time to give medicine and fluids to the old lady. Two children who had stood in line, who had chanted multiplication tables, who had been taught by a gifted teacher to write good English, now attempted to repay their debt.

Breathlessly, she thanked them; determinedly, they held back their tears. This woman had led them through infancy and now it was their turn to do the steering. But Ishy's journey had but one destination and all three of them were aware of that.

Steve kissed Dorothy good night, then went home to help another dependent woman. There had to be a reward at some stage. For Beryl Isherwood, there must be a heaven.

*   *   *

Lizzie Murphy's room was about ten feet by twelve, so things weren't as bad as they might have been. It was beamed, the plaster was uneven and the windows were draughty, but the whole house was beautiful. Hand-hewn planks formed the floor, the axe marks of long-dead artisans still visible beneath several layers of varnish. Molly had a draped bed, an ancient chest with a hinged lid, a tall set of drawers that required determination when it came to opening and closing, and a gigantic wardrobe with huge, flawed mirrors on both doors.

Molly had come home at last. She was in the right setting, Just along a corridor was Burbank Wing, where staff took meals and where all cooking was done. At the opposite end of the main hall was a second wing, once known as New Wing, more recently nominated Clarence. The mothers and babies were in there. According to Isobel, Dorothy had taken quite a fancy to a little orphan and would be applying to adopt him once she was married. But she wouldn't be marrying her brave pilot – no. Dorothy would be allying herself to this great house and all the land that surrounded it. Molly had always belonged in a place such as this, and here was where she intended to stay.

Chadwicke House was a problem. Just about visible from the main buildings, it could be entered only by those who carried keys or by expected visitors. It was locked, because the patients it contained were not pretty to behold and some of them were not yet prepared to be in the company of unmarked people. Molly's intention had been to have Barbara Cooper admitted to Chadwicke House, but legend had it that the woman was in Burbank Wing, so sending Michael to visit his wife was no answer, either. There had to be a way of getting into Chadwicke House. Molly needed to meet Stuart Beddows and to slow him down somewhat.

It was time for a little light supper, so Molly

came out of her room and walked to the stairs, intending to descend to the newly built kitchen. Halfway down, she stopped and realized that her eye had snagged on something or other, rather as a broken fingernail might interfere with threads in a garment. What had taken her subconscious attention? She retraced a few steps, and hung on to the banister when she realized what had disturbed her. It was David.

How many shocks had she received in her life? Why did the air darken when something like this happened? Through a red mist, she saw him, younger than when she had last met him, handsome, clean-cut, extremely prepossessing. David Bradley Enterprises. He had bought all kinds of antiques, but clocks had been his favourite. And the one at the bottom of the stairs, Molly had bought. In a Liverpool auction room, he had closed his eyes just for a few seconds, the signal that he would not bid, but that she must until he stopped her. The clock, a grandfather, was very ornate, with flowers, the sun, the moon and stars sprinkled on its old face. David. David Bradley had been Donald Burbank. Like many who changed their identities, he had clung to his true initials.

She sat on the stairs, remembered going to the flat and waiting for hours. He hadn't come. Nothing would have kept him away – nothing short of death, that was. Molly knew that if she were to question Isobel Burbank, the date of her husband's death would coincide with his failure to arrive at the flat in town. Since him, there had been nobody real, no one who

376

had come anywhere near the man she had desired all those years ago. Even David had been no more than a bandage for the wound; farmers and factory workers came nowhere near the standard set by Molly Cornwell. No. The standard had been set by Dr Ian Clarke, and he was long gone. David Bradley had come closest, and this was his house.

The red faded. Inside Molly's head, a child screamed. It was a drawn-out and high-pitched noise and it wasn't real. It came in the night sometimes, and she would wake bathed in sweat and tears, but with no memory of the nightmare. Except that it was red. The colour of the bad dream was red. The older she grew, the more often the dream came, but it was not real, had never been real.

David. He had been sweet and had loved the game. He had bought gifts of silk and solid gold, had given her the watch she wore to this day. An heirloom? No, it had been new. Isobel would not recognize the timepiece. So, this had been David's real home. Here he had lived with his wife and three sons, here he had died and here his mistress now sat on the stairs, chin on her knees.

'Mrs Cornwell? Are you all right?'

Molly smiled. 'Of course. I was just looking at all these ancestral paintings. I felt as if they were watching me as I came down the stairs.' She stood up. 'I shall make us something to eat, then you can teach me backgammon, just as you promised.'

'Very well.' Isobel watched the woman as she

made her graceful way to the lower floor. She would do. Molly Cornwell would do very well indeed and would be a vast improvement on her predecessor.

'I wouldn't go back if she paid me in solid gold, Mr Andrew. She's mad. And them dogs of hers bite and chew things, including human beings. They want putting out of my misery and everybody else's, too. No. I don't care what I have to do, but I'm not going anywhere near. I know she's your mother and I'm not blaming you, but she can bugger off and that's swearing.' Lizzie dropped into a chair near the fire in the Burbank Wing kitchen.

Ivy kept her head down, while Elsie and Lois peeled vegetables. Nobody liked Isobel Burbank, but this was her son. He could say what he liked about her, but he might well defend Isobel if anyone else tried to shove in a tenpenny-worth.

'You may stay here if you wish, Lizzie,' said Andrew. 'You can work as an orderly over in Chadwicke and help out with the kitchen as well. No need for you to go away to Bolton. Ivy will find you a room and you just put your things away when you've got a billet. Meanwhile . . .' He breathed deeply. 'Meanwhile, I suppose I had better go and visit Mother.'

As he left the kitchen, he heard Lizzie addressing Ivy behind him. 'You'll have to do her meals. Cooking is beneath her and she'd have no idea how to start. But don't ask me to deliver anything down yon. If I never see your Mrs Burbank again, I'll be pleased.'

Sadly, Andrew shared that sentiment on occasion. Mother was a one-off, or so he hoped. She still demanded to be served and the world had changed. According to Isobel, she was the only one marching correctly to the drumbeat; in reality, the woman was so far out of step that she stuck out like a boil on a baby's bottom.

He walked down the corridor and entered Mother's living quarters. She was seated at a card table with the backgammon board between herself and another woman who believed in tight control, and Andrew was not pleased. He cleared his throat. 'What's going on here?' he asked.

'Backgammon,' replied Isobel. 'A game you and I used to share until you took yourself off to live at the other end of the house.'

Molly studied the man. He had an extremely handsome face and he needed a haircut. There was an air of mad professorship about him, as if he had many important things to do and the improvement of his appearance did not feature on the list. He didn't like Molly and he didn't think much of his own mother, either. And he had an unnerving habit of looking straight through a person, as if he could see past skin and flesh and into the inner mechanism of the human mind. Also, looked at in the light of new knowledge, he certainly resembled his father.

'Why are you here?' he asked Molly.

Isobel answered. 'That dreadful girl has left.'

'I know.' He shook his head slightly. 'She had taken enough from you, Mother. She will be working for me.'

Isobel was not in the least surprised.

'Why are you here?' he asked again.

Molly employed one of the more winning of her many smiles. 'Your mother needed me, so I came. I am staying in the maid's room.'

'Whose idea was it?'

'Mine.'

He leaned against the door, as if trying to stay as far away as possible from the women. 'You two deserve each other,' he said. Then he concentrated on Dorothy's mother. 'If you come anywhere near Burbank Wing, Clarence Wing or Chadwicke House, I shall have you out of here faster than a bullet from an automatic weapon. Stay away from me, from my staff, from my patients.'

'And my daughter?'

'Will know where you are. Dorothy has little time. When she is not tending patients, she is with a baby who needs her. When she does have a spare hour, she is studying psychology under my guidance. The girl wants a career and she shall have one. The days when you held her back, tied her to a bed and put bars at her window are long gone.' He looked her up and down. 'You are an interesting woman, Mrs Cornwell. It is my belief that you require psychiatric care and counselling, but you will not heed me, will you?'

The fixed smile remained, but she did not answer him.

He turned his attention to his mother. 'As for you, the straps and window bars were not needed, because polio was my guard. Although you don't share the well-disguised lunacy of this woman, you are still a loveless creature with no care for anyone beyond yourself. Yes. You will do very well together.' He opened the door and turned. 'I hope there's nothing red in the house. We all know about red, don't we, Mrs Cornwell?' He left the room.

Isobel stared at Molly. 'What on earth was all that about?'

Molly raised her shoulders. 'It's Dorothy. She was a sleepwalker and I had to tie her into bed. The bars at the window were there because she managed to climb out.'

'In her sleep?'

'Yes,' Molly lied. 'It was all done for her own good. As for education, perhaps she is ready for it now, but when she was younger any stress sent her into a terrible state of nerves. Mothers always get the blame, Mrs Burbank. If there is anything wrong, it is our fault.'

'But he said you need help.'

'Dorothy has twisted everything.'

'And the colour red?'

'Never liked it. I saw a man die under the wheels of a tram and there was a lot of blood. It became a phobia.' And Dorothy had made good use of it, had made herself bleed whenever she wanted her own way. But Molly would not tell Mrs Burbank about that, because she had plans. Mrs Burbank would be Dorothy's mother-in-law if Molly got her way.

Isobel pondered. Andrew never lied. But had he been too ready and willing to hear Dorothy Dyson's side of the story? Had his

381

obvious affection for the girl led him to believe every word she uttered? Molly Cornwell seemed a sensible enough woman – there were no signs of disturbance now that she had begun to recover from her ordeal at the hands of a rapist. 'My son goes too far,' said Isobel. 'We shall get along well, you and I. And, as we agreed earlier, if either of us wants the arrangement to end within the month, there will be no need for explanations.'

Molly nodded her agreement.

'Let's carry on with your backgammon training. In my experience, sons always come back in the end.' Isobel hoped she wasn't tempting fate with that statement, because she still had two sons abroad. 'Although daughters are supposed to stay closer to home.'

'Except for Dorothy,' sighed Molly. 'But never mind. As you say, we shall manage very well, you and I.'

*　　*　　*

Miss Isherwood lasted a lot longer than anyone, including the doctors, had expected. She survived two heart attacks, single pneumonia and a second bout of pleurisy before succumbing finally to double pneumonia in November 1936. Steve and Dorothy were both with her when she died, and were glad that the end was peaceful. They made all arrangements, as Miss Isherwood's family was depleted to the point where just one sister, also crippled with arthritis, remained alive.

On the day of the funeral, they returned to the house and talked about the future. The house, which was rented, had to be vacated as soon as possible, but the furniture and all Miss Isherwood's other possessions would revert to the surviving sister. Everything would be sold, and the good woman could use the proceeds to help her through what remained of her life.

The couple began the process of going through the dead teacher's things. Steve was of the opinion that he and Dorothy should marry right away, and to this end they worked diligently to find a home. The money banked in Dorothy's name was not yet available, as Dorothy needed to be twenty-three in order to have access to the account. But they would try to manage to be married soon.

They sat by the fire and talked about the funeral. Over one hundred ex-pupils had attended, many at the behest of Steve, who had applied emotional blackmail where necessary. Miss Isherwood had deserved a good send-off and she had received one.

Steve held Dorothy's hand. 'I know you think she was the only one who ever loved you, but you've still got me.'

She knew that. But Beryl had been the only older person who had loved Dorothy. Beryl had believed in her, had tried to persuade her to get on in life. 'Leave me,' she had often said. 'Go and start your life – please. Marriage is a wonderful institution, but an education is a necessity. Educate a woman and you educate a family.'

'She was a mother to me,' wept Dorothy. 'She pushed me and pushed me, but I wouldn't leave her.'

'I'll look after you.'

'I know you will.'

'And I'll never leave you.'

'I know you won't.' But Dorothy, along with the rest of mankind, knew that 'never' did not exist and that all things ended, whether they were good or bad. 'So, now that your mam's all right, where are we going to live?'

'I'll find somewhere.'

'You'd better be quick, because the landlord wants this place back and I am not going home to be poisoned again.' She raised her left arm. 'As for having to make myself bleed just to get away from her – well – that's no fun, either. I don't want to live with her again, ever.'

They decided that even if Dorothy had to sleep on Steve's mother's sofa, she would not go home. As they talked about their future and its immediate difficulties, the doorknocker rattled. Steve got up to answer it and returned with Tom Cornwell in tow.

The visitor twisted his cap in nervous fingers. Never a great talker, Tom had a tendency to stutter his way through life in short, easy sentences. 'Sorry your teacher's dead,' he achieved after a few seconds. This was followed by, 'Come home, love.'

Dorothy bit her lip. 'She's not giving me her herbs and spices again, Dad. No, sorry.'

'She won't,' he said.

Steve spoke up. 'Sorry, Mr Cornwell, but your

wife's too dangerous to be near Dorothy. I know you've had to put up with her all your life, but Dorothy doesn't need to. We'll get married and find a place.'

Tom stared at the floor. 'I've got some of my mam's furniture,' he said. 'Stored in a shed up Deane. Saved it for you. Bed frame, some sheets and blankets. Need airing. Been there a long while. Hope some of it's still all right.' He sighed, as if tired out by so many words.

Dorothy stood up and took hold of her father's hands, removing the cap and placing it on Miss Isherwood's table. 'She'll do anything to stop me from marrying.'

'She won't,' he replied, 'because she's not there.'

'What?'

'Not there,' he repeated. 'Neither sight nor sound in five weeks.'

Dorothy blinked a few times. 'Have you told the police?'

'Nay, no need for that. She's got herself well known in antiques, so she left the frock shop and she's stopping in London for a bit, working for some man that knew the other one she used to work for. They say he's dead.' From Tom, that was another speech of remarkable proportions.

'She'll come back,' said Steve. 'You know what they say about bad pennies, Mr Cornwell. I don't want her near Dorothy.'

'I know, lad. Let our Dorothy stop with me till you find a place.'

So it was decided that Dorothy would return

385

to View Street for the time being and, in the event of Molly's returning for Christmas, Dorothy would spend the festive season at Steve's house in order to avoid her mother's imaginative and dangerous cooking.

Tom walked home, head bent against a chill November wind. He knew – just as he had always known – that he should be doing something about the situation, yet he felt as powerless as ever. Stripped by nature of manhood, he had been grateful for the mantle provided by Molly, the shield she had allowed him to borrow since the day of their wedding. Had he been a man, none of the bad stuff would have happened to the girl he had not fathered, yet who had always been his daughter.

He tightened the woollen scarf about his throat. The Bishop family had lived across the street from the Cornwells. He and Molly had grown up together, had attended school together, had looked after each other. Molly, an only child, had owned hardworking parents and enough clothes to keep her decent in an area of extreme poverty. Other children had been jealous of her and Tom had become her guardian. As payment, she had fed him scraps from the Bishops' table. This reciprocal arrangement had carried on right through childhood and into adolescence.

Tom turned into View Street. She had always been beautiful. He wondered when it had all started, yet scarcely dared think about it. The big event was one he usually chose to forget, but Bolton had never completely forgotten it, while suspicion, whose weight varied between mild and acute, had resided in his brain since 1901. Queen Victoria had taken most people's attention, anyway, because she had died on the same day. But on 22 January 1901, a happening of enormous moment had visited John Street.

As he removed his coat and sat down by his own fireside, Tom Cornwell was transported back in time, was standing at the front window with some of his siblings. There was screaming and shouting, the police came, every adult in the street was questioned. The next day, Molly was too ill to play out. She never played out again after that cold day. Tom still walked with her to school, looked after her in the playground and made sure that the other children did not bully her. For her part, Molly continued to bring food for him, and he outstripped his brothers in size and strength until he left school. But she became uncommunicative almost to the point of silence, remained quiet until her teens.

And it had carried on from there. Tom had gone into mining, Molly into cotton, and both had progressed towards adulthood. He remembered that his feelings for Molly had changed and that his body had remained the same. She had attracted admirers from miles around, yet she had clung fiercely to the safety known as Tom Cornwell.

He poked the fire and threw on some coal. Rumours had abounded. It was a well-known fact that young Molly Bishop enjoyed the company of older men. Some even said that she was paid for her services, while others simply watched the girl any man would have given his pension to acquire. But she had married Tom. In the end, Molly had settled for safety and familiarity. She knew his condition and made it plain that she would seek physical contentment elsewhere, but she would feed him and care for him. Her side of the bargain had been honoured – he had been comfortable. She had used men all her life, while Tom, unable to interfere, had watched in silence as his wife had enjoyed dalliances all over the town.

Molly was approaching middle age. The big love affair with Dr Ian Clarke was a thing of the past and she had never been the same since the man's disappearance. The older she got, the more desperate she became. It was as if she chased some invisible rainbow and a pot of gold that had never existed. And the way she had treated Dorothy defied all decency. From the age of seven years, Molly Bishop had locked herself into her own house on John Street. From infancy, the movements of Dorothy Cornwell had been restricted to the point of cruelty.

Sometimes, when Molly had sat at the other side of this very fireplace, he had watched her covertly, had seen damped-down pain in the eyes of the child she had been. But 22 January 1901 had marked the end of Molly's childhood and the beginning of some contained and unspeakable torment. The terrible agony, papered over by the passage of time and by sheer, dogged determination, had led Molly to behave monstrously towards her own daughter.

The truth? He probably knew it and certainly

could not face it. Yet Tom sensed that he and his wife were living on borrowed time. For Molly, some kind of deadline loomed, as if she had to deliver a story to a publisher any day now. But Molly was her own editor and, somewhere deep inside her complicated psyche, the truth was rising like dough in a pan. When it finally broke down all her defences, Tom would be here for her. He had always been here for her.

She was running. Based in Liverpool, she travelled to London, York, Chester – even to Scotland on occasion. The further she ran and the older she grew, the closer to the surface came her panic. Whatever lay at the seat of Molly's terror was huge. Behind the painted face and under the expensive clothing, a child fought for life. Maturation had not cured Molly's illness and it never would. Because the inner child seldom died – it simply rested beneath courses of bricks erected over a lifetime. And middle age marked the commencement of erosion. Would she be worn down, would she speak at last? There was no foundation to Molly. Molly was a condemned building in which her soul could not hide for ever.

Nothing had changed, Tom reminded himself as he made toast for his supper. Like his wife, he was developing a tendency to think about childhood – it was all a part of the process known as life and of the condition entitled human.

Yet he could not shake himself free of the suspicion that Molly's ride would end in a catastrophic crash. There was nothing he could do; there had never been anything for him to do. Tom Cornwell went to work, brought home the money, was fed and kept warm. His wife simply ran. And no one could catch her. Not yet, anyway.

FOURTEEN

The short, attractive girl arrived at Burbank
Hall a few days before Stuart was yet again
expecting to go into hospital after four post-
ponements. Because she had no idea about the
arrangements at the Hall, she presented herself
at the front of the main building. Isobel,
muttering darkly about rations, had gone off
into town with the intention of making the most
of her clothing coupons, and had left Molly
alone in the house.

'I'm looking for Captain Stuart Beddows,'
said the stranger.

Molly looked her up and down. She was smartly
dressed, pretty, and her manner was pleasant.
'Come in,' she said. 'I'll get the Burbank Wing
staff to buzz through to Chadwicke House for you.
Are you a relative?'

'Erm . . . no. I'm just an old friend.'

Molly sniffed quietly. This was more than a
friend – this might well be the answer to Molly's
prayers.

'They promised him that the operation would
be the Tuesday before last, then it was going to

391

be Friday . . . I've had to beg for a transfer from London, and Manchester was the nearest posting I could get. Oh, I'm Julia Watson, by the way, and I'm Red Cross.'

'Molly Cornwell – and I'm not cross at all. Sit yourself down while I send for somebody.'

'Thank you.' Julia perched among Buddhas, silk paintings, Chinese rugs and two very disdainful Pekingese dogs, one of which seemed to be having trouble with flatulence. They snuffled and shuffled, then, having decided that Julia was not worth their concern, fell asleep in an enormous padded basket.

Molly returned. 'Sorry about the perfume.' She waved a hand towards the dogs. 'Not exactly Chanel, is it? Mrs Burbank feeds them like kings – here we are, all on rations, while those two get a bit of black market steak and no questions asked. Still, they're all she has with her sons busy. The oldest one's Captain Beddows's doctor.'

'The psychologist?'

'And psychiatrist, yes. He helps them through the shock.' Molly's brain was galloping along in top gear. Dorothy was supposed to go to Chester Oakfields with Stuart. But this girl wore a proprietorial air when she spoke of Captain Beddows, so what was afoot? 'Known him long, have you?' she asked, excitement bubbling beneath a veneer of calm and face powder.

'Since school. We were engaged and then the war started. Stuart became a pilot and I joined the Red Cross in London.' She lowered her eyes. 'I'm ashamed to say that I couldn't cope with what had happened to him. Then I visited a hospital in Surrey and saw other badly burned airmen.' The chin raised itself. 'He's still going to be the boy I've always known, isn't he?'

'Of course he is.' And Dorothy would be free to pursue Molly's dream of a life of plenty. Dorothy looked the part, walked the part and almost spoke the part, while Molly had always been meant to belong somewhere decent. But she had to stay cool, had to contain herself. Determinedly she closed her mouth against a thousand questions.

'Is this your house?' Julia asked.

'No, it belongs to the Burbank family. I'm Mrs Burbank's companion and right-hand man, so to speak. She and her son handed over the house to the War Office for the duration.'

'Commendable.'

'Yes, indeed.' Molly fingered Florence's pearls. Very few women boasted the sort of complexion that could do justice to pearls; for a woman in her late forties to own such skin was virtually unheard of.

Ivy, flour-daubed and breathless, entered the room after a perfunctory knock. She eyed Dorothy's mother warily. No one liked her and no one, with the exception of Mrs Burbank, wanted anything to do with her. 'Did you ring? Only I'm up to my armpits in shortcrust and our Elsie's sat down with a cold, so she's in the kitchen doing nowt with Lois.'

Molly smiled broadly. 'This is Miss Julia Watson and she has come from Manchester to see Captain Beddows in Chadwicke House.'

'Oh. Right.' With a floury hand, Ivy pushed hair from her forehead and left a further legacy of white. 'Come on, then,' she said. 'I'll buzz and somebody will meet you at the gate. It's just along this corridor, Miss.' She led Julia towards Burbank Wing.

Molly sat in the dreary room when the two women had left. She would make so many changes here when she got the chance. All this Chinese rubbish wanted shifting to the local tip for a start – anyone with half an eye for antiques could see that it was virtually worthless. David – Donald – had never mentioned his wife and Molly could understand why he had sought company elsewhere. Isobel was dull and she lacked taste in all departments. Her expensive wardrobe was subdued to the point of boredom and her imagination was non-existent.

Oh, that ballroom. Molly inhaled deeply and sat on her excitement. Andrew Burbank loved Dorothy. Dorothy would marry Andrew Burbank very, very soon. The reception would be held in a room so large that it needed four fireplaces. Molly would wear blue to bring out the colour of her eyes and Isobel would wear something elegant and colourless.

Dorothy would do what Molly had never managed – she would walk up the aisle in white satin and Tom, who had always looked presentable in a suit, would give her away. Bugger the war, it would be done by fair means or foul – a three-tiered cake, unlimited meats, cream candles and lines of pale yellow roses set down the centres of three long tables. There would be the best linens and magnificent silver for place settings. Photographs would be in all the county magazines and Molly would get the chance to see herself as she should have been. She should have been Dorothy, beauty and opportunity combined in a perfect recipe. Julia Watson was going to make the dream come true. Thank God for Julia Watson.

A Pekingese broke wind again. Molly wondered, not for the first time, what on earth Isobel saw in these ugly, graceless creatures. They could scarcely breathe, possessed faces that looked like the result of a bad accident involving speed and walls, had no manners and ate very noisily because of their distorted noses. 'Why couldn't she have proper dogs?' she asked.

Ming eyed her balefully. He didn't like her and neither did Shang. Intelligent enough to act stupid, this pair of deliberately miniaturized guard dogs had the measure of Molly Cornwell. She was not unkind, because she dared not upset their mistress, but she was cold and distant. She never gave them scraps, never said a kind word and didn't approve of them. They, in their turn, awarded her a wide berth and no respect. With all the wisdom of ancient China etched deep in their bones, they chose not to recognize Molly as a person. Like the clock, the tables and the windows, she existed and was visible. Beyond that fact, she was of no consequence whatsoever.

Molly stood up and prepared to go on her rounds. She had already done most of the cleaning, but she still had to fulfil the other half of her bargain. There would be no need to worry about getting a doctored cake to Stuart Beddows – Michael Cooper was off the hook for a while. But the rapist still might prove useful at some stage and Molly intended to remind him of his debt. There would be no need for poison – Julia Watson would do the trick. It was time to sort out the land girls – one shotgun wedding, a lecture on drunkenness and a headcount – two girls and a pig had gone missing.

It was all part and parcel of life in the country, a life Molly intended to enjoy for the remainder of her days.

*   *   *

Tom and his daughter prepared for Christmas, each suspecting that Molly would be back, neither airing that opinion thus far. Molly was not a family woman, but she liked to organize her life into a shape she considered correct, and correctness dictated that families should be together for the holiday season. It was Christmas Eve, and the two residents of 33, View Street were preparing vegetables at the kitchen table. Tom, who was recovering from a slight accident in the pit, owned an eye that was blacker than usual and a bandaged left ankle, but he could peel spuds, so he set to while Dorothy dealt with carrots.

'Did she go peaceful, like?' Tom asked.

'Miss Isherwood? Yes, she did, but it was the only bit of peace she'd had in years.' Dorothy placed her peeler on the table. 'She left me some money. She gave it to me when I was five. I can't get it out of the bank for a few months yet, but it'll help when . . . It'll help.'

'When your mother gets home and you go off with young Steve.'

'Yes.' Steve's mother had suffered a slight setback, so marriage plans had been shelved yet again. One of the things Dorothy loved most about her young man was his devotion to his family.

Tom copied his favourite girl's temporary idleness. 'About your mam, love . . .'

'What?'

He swallowed. 'She weren't always like she is now.'

'Oh?'

Tom didn't know why he had suddenly started this conversation. Why now? Because he knew she'd be back any minute? 'Lived opposite us, the Bishops. Strict, they were. Kind, though. Her dad drank a bit, but he was all right at heart.' He nodded a few times. 'They let her feed me. Your mam kept me strong, Dorothy. We used to meet up the alley and she'd give me bread, cheese, meat, apples – all sorts. I looked after her at school and she looked after me at home. We got through together.'

'Did she play?'

'Aye, she played. She were on the quiet side, but she played. Till one particular day. I can remember the day, because we heard as Queen Victoria had passed. That were the day your mother changed.'

The speech thus far had been the most

complicated Tom had ever made within Dorothy's hearing. She held her tongue and waited for more.

'Something happened. I don't know what it were, but she went as quiet as the grave afterwards.' He knew what he thought it was, but he had never been sure. 'Molly didn't buck up again until she got to about thirteen. Then she started – well – she started being a bit like she is now. In all them years of quiet, she still fed me, though. When I got bigger, she even started giving me her dad's cast-off clothes and shoes. I were the best dressed and the best fed in our house.'

'So she was kind to you?'

'Yes.'

'Even when she began to be like she is now?'

'Yes.' He picked up a potato and dug to remove an eye from the flesh. 'I can still hear her laughing back then – when she were about seven and before the old queen died. She were a giggler.'

'Did she go into mourning for Victoria?'

'It were closer to home than that, petal. All I'm saying is that your mam were an ordinary child in an ordinary house with a life like everybody else's – except they were better off than most, because Mrs Bishop never had any more children. Then, at the end of January that year, Molly changed. She stopped laughing, stopped playing, but carried on feeding me.'

'Did her mam and dad lock her in?'

'No. She locked herself in. She locked herself inside her head and inside her house. I stopped asking questions after a while, because she went glassy-eyed when I tried to talk to her in the back street. It were a bit like she'd shut down and put the bolts on. At the finish, I gave up trying.'

'She's cruel, Dad.'

'I know that.'

'And she goes about with all kinds of men.'

'I know that and all. I can't fathom it any more than you can. All I'm saying is there's nowt can be done. More than anyone else in this world, I'm sure of that. But . . .' He lost his words.

'But what?'

The agony in his eyes blazed as he spoke. 'Summat's happening to Molly. She's simmering like a pan left on to keep a dinner warm. Sometimes, she nears the boil and she lashes out – breaks pots, chucks pans across the back kitchen, talks to the mirror. One day, it'll all come out.'

Dorothy swallowed painfully. 'How will it come out?'

'I don't know.'

'Will she kill somebody or hurt herself?'

'No, love. She'll fall apart like a vase that's been glued back together too many times. Every flaw in the glass'll give way and she'll pour out all over the bloody place. It's not going to be pretty to watch.'

Dorothy stared at the man who was her father. A watcher, a piece of flotsam bobbing on the waters of Molly Cornwell's life, he had taken in and contained all he knew about Molly. He understood people, was capable of predicting their behaviour, was a lot cleverer than his wife had allowed him to be. Tom was not a shadow – he was a willing slave.

'If owt happens to me—' he was saying now.

'No!' she shouted. 'Nothing's going to happen to you.'

He smiled reassuringly. 'I'm not intending to drop dead in the next five minutes, lass. All I'm saying is she'll need helping one day. She might even need hospital, doctors and medicines in a quiet room.'

'A padded room, Dad?'

He thought for a moment. 'Maybe. Whatever it is, it goes deep. I couldn't get to it with a miner's pick and shovel. She'll not let go. Her whole life's been about not thinking, not remembering. But she wakes in the night wet through with sweat and she says some funny things. Not laughing-at funny – I mean strange. It's in her. It's in her that far down that she can't fathom it while she's awake. In her sleep, it comes to her.'

'What does?'

He couldn't say it, couldn't tell Dorothy of his suspicions. There was nothing concrete, anyway, he reminded himself. 'If I knew, I'd mend it.'

Dorothy's eyes were wet. This lovely man adored Molly Cornwell right from the top of her head to the soles of her feet. She had fed him and clothed him all the way through an impoverished childhood and he had been paying her back ever since. And he didn't mind.

For a reason that was beyond Dorothy's ability to fathom, Tom Cornwell was anxious to protect his wife no matter what the cost to himself.

When the vegetables were finished, Dorothy went upstairs and lay on the bed. Sleeping Beauty? Were she capable of adding together all the hours she had spent in this very room, the resulting sum would represent a huge slice of her childhood. And now Dad was trying to explain Mam, needed to apologize for her, to account in some way for all the years of abuse endured by his daughter.

'He certainly loves her,' she told the ceiling. 'He chose her. I didn't.' Children did not get to select their parents. Had Dorothy been able to choose, she might well have picked someone like Beryl Isherwood to rear her. No, not someone *like* Miss Isherwood – that lady would have been the child's absolute favourite.

'She'll be back,' whispered the girl on the bed. Molly Cornwell would arrive in a cloud of perfume and temper, would complain about the chicken, the vegetables, the gravy, the decorations. Dad had bought a little tree and Mam would not like that. There were streamers in the kitchen. Even the back kitchen – as people hereabouts dubbed the scullery – boasted a couple of multi-coloured paper chains in its window. 'With red included,' said Dorothy, smiling.

She was shaken to wakefulness after a short sleep. 'I'm back,' Molly announced.

Dorothy yawned. 'So I see.' She sat up. 'Have you brought your little black book of poisons with you?' Immediately, she wished she could have bitten back the words. Usually the recipient of venom, she seldom invited the wrath of her mother.

'You're back, too,' said Molly, deliberately ignoring her daughter's jibe. 'Tom tells me Miss Isherwood died.'

'Yes, she did.'

'I'm sorry.'

Dorothy scarcely heard the automatic response. 'How long are you staying?' she asked.

'I don't know. I've been to Sotheby's.' She was clearly proud of this achievement. 'I've seen paintings worth more than all the houses in this street put together. And furniture – oh, my God, there are French armoires and Dutch tables – it's a different world. But . . .' She paused. 'I may not go back. I'll have to think about it.'

Dorothy groaned inwardly. Another lover had bitten the dust, of that she had no doubt. 'I'm getting married soon,' she said.

But Molly seemed not to be listening. She was waxing on about the landing shops in Chester, the Roman walls of York, Westminster Palace, auction houses in Liverpool and Manchester. 'I held in these very hands a Bible from Queen Victoria's house on the Isle of Wight. She might have touched it, might have used it. And I held it. Leather-bound, it was.'

Dorothy stood up. 'You'll remember the day she died, won't you?'

Molly blinked twice. 'What?'

'Everyone who was alive remembers the day

Queen Victoria died. I don't know why. From what I've read, she was too busy being miserable and poking about all over Scotland to be much loved here. Have you forgotten?'

Once again, Molly's eyelids were lowered. 'I was very young.'

'You were seven.'

'No, I can't remember.' She left the room in a hurry, bequeathing to her daughter the odour of expensive perfume and an atmosphere of discomfort.

Dorothy gazed at the window and its bars. No matter what Dad said, Dorothy could not live with this. Steve and his family had been fore-warned that she might arrive at any time on their doorstep. She could sleep on the sofa over Christmas, then would stay with an elderly neighbour until the wedding, which would take place as soon as Steve's mother started to mend again. There was a house to be found, there were preparations to be made. It would not be a fancy affair, just bride, groom and his family. Dad could not come without Mam, so Dorothy would make the journey into wedlock with no relatives at her side.

'I don't care,' she muttered under her breath. She did care, but could not afford to indulge her sadness. Mam might make a scene and scenes were items to be avoided. Dorothy walked to the chest of drawers and took a few items of underwear to hide in her bag. There was no point in making the grand exit with suitcase and parcels, because this was Molly Cornwell's house and nobody but Molly Cornwell was allowed an opinion within its walls. Also, she wanted nothing from here. She was eloping, was escaping to a new life and needed no reminders of the old one. As for the full-scale drama involving a carving knife and slashed arms – Dorothy was too tired for that.

She entered the kitchen just as her mother was carrying out the little tree that had been decorated earlier by Dorothy and Tom. The back door slammed and Tom looked up at his daughter. 'She's back,' he said, a half-smile doing battle with a frown.

'I'm going now,' she told him.

'Where?'

'To Steve's. I'm sorry, Dad, but I can't stay with her. She poisoned me for weeks on end before I went to Miss Isherwood's and I nearly lost my job. I've come to the end of my rope and I can't manage any more of this. I've tried for long enough.'

He scratched his head. 'There'll be a right kerfuffle when she finds out you've gone.'

'I know. I'm sorry to spoil your Christmas.' It could not have been a good Christmas, anyway, not with Mam in the house. She was already clearing out items she considered clutter and there would be no revelry on the following day. Gifts would be exchanged but, apart from that, it would be just like any other Sunday.

Molly returned. 'Going somewhere?' She pointed to the handbag on her daughter's arm.

'Yes, I am.'

Molly glanced at the watch that had been a gift from David Bradley. 'At this time? It's pitch black and freezing out there. This street is very slippery.'

View Street had been a slippery slope for most of Dorothy's life. For answer, Dorothy strode past her parents and out to the yard. She picked up the tiny tree, carried it back into the house and replaced it on a corner of the dresser. 'This is my father's tree,' she said, chin held high. 'He works hard. If he wants a Christmas tree, he can have one.'

'Never mind,' said Tom. 'It's all right, Dorothy.'

'No, it isn't all right at all,' the girl cried. 'How many hours a week do you crawl about in muck just to keep Madam happy? How many men has she brought here while you've been breathing in dust that'll kill you in the end? If you want a bloody tree, you have a bloody tree.' She glared at her mother. 'Give my dad some peace,' she screamed.

Molly patted her hair. Dorothy's dad did not crawl about in coal. He was at least three thousand miles away practising medicine in America. 'I don't like mess,' she said quietly.

'Then never look in my head,' replied her daughter, 'because the mess you've made of me is chaotic. I have to go through life knowing that the woman who birthed me is an evil, man-mad lunatic. I have to wake every day hoping that there's nothing of you in me and that I'll turn out decent like Dad. You have given me enough misery. Leave my dad in peace.'

Molly tapped a well-shod toe on the floor. 'Have you done?'

Dorothy snapped shut the clasp of her bag. 'Yes, I think I have done. I am done and dusted, thank you.'

In the hall, she took from the stand her heaviest coat, put her arms through the sleeves, fastened every button. The vestibule door reflected electric light from the hall, blues and reds glinting in their beds of lead. Mam never cleaned this door, because she couldn't touch the red bits. Dorothy remembered looking through that door and seeing the Town Hall clock in many different shades, remembered watching multi-coloured children at play in the huge, free world that had been denied to her.

Outside, Dorothy Cornwell breathed in cold air and liberty. The town below, lit by gas lamps, was covered in a fine layer of snow. She stood on the very spot where Steve Dyson had lost his balance and one wheel of a dilapidated scooter, smiled as she recalled the expression on his face. 'My mate's got a better one,' he had said. 'Would you like a go on it?'

At the bottom of View Street, Dorothy glanced to her right and looked at Sunning Hill school, the place where she had not been allowed clogs, where she had first heard the story of Sleeping Beauty. 'Thank you, Miss Isherwood,' she mouthed. The school was in darkness, as was Beryl Isherwood, whose bones rested in Heaton Cemetery.

On her way to Steve's house, she caught a glimpse of Pilkington Street. The Catholic school was up there. How hard Sister Agatha had tried to get Mam to allow Dorothy to sit her grammar school entrance. Twice, Molly Cornwell had been approached; twice, she had refused point blank to allow her daughter the chance of an education.

A little further down and out of sight was the spot where Bolton Fair was erected twice a year. What had the gypsy promised? Money, the love of three good men, some children and a great deal of happiness. Dorothy didn't need three men – Steve was enough and would always be enough. Mam was the one who used men like buses – catch this one, get off at a later stop, travel in a new direction on a different man's ticket.

She felt pity for Dad, who was to be left alone in the View Street house, often with a crossword and a wireless for company, sometimes with Molly Cornwell, the self-created princess who flitted about the country whenever she pleased. For a moment, Dorothy's skin crawled. Like her mother, she had been a young princess, a child lying on a bed and waiting for Prince Charming to hack his way through undergrowth. But Dorothy had grown out of all that – or so she hoped.

She raised a hand to knock on the Dysons' door, paused for a moment and smiled to herself. A princess? With some clean knickers and, apart from that smuggled bounty, just the clothes on her back? Nonsense. She had eloped all by herself and the marriage was some months ahead, but she had made the break.

Dorothy-soon-to-be-Dyson knocked four times on Steve's front door. This was a poor house that had contained several children, a hardworking father and a mother whose recovery from pulmonary TB had been slow, whose health remained uncertain. With all four children working, the light at the end of the tunnel was finally visible. It was a light in which Dorothy, too, would be able to bask. For her whole life, Dorothy Cornwell had been lost in a desert, with no map by which to calculate her eventual destination, no ability to plan. But all that was over and she was home at last.

In the end, everything seemed to dovetail perfectly and Dorothy knew that she had finally turned the corner. Steve's older brother was offered a good job in a Manchester factory. Recently married, he and his bride took Steve's parents to live with them in an almost-new semi-detached house in Fallowfield. The rest of the Dyson family members were established in relationships and, on the day after Dorothy and Steve were married, the door of the old family place was closed for the last time.

Mr and Mrs Stephen Dyson set up home at 34, Emblem Street and Dorothy became a person in her own right. She was manager of a small but happy household and she carried on working three days each week while her husband brought home the lion's share of their joint income. Their house, small and without a bathroom, was decently furnished and they began their new lives full of hope for the future.

Dorothy's nest egg, a legacy she supposed to have been bequeathed to her by Beryl Isherwood, remained virtually untouched. The couple hoped to have a family and left most of the money to gather interest so that they might buy a house with a garden in which their offspring would be able to play. Bent on owning a decent property, Steve and Dorothy ploughed every extra penny into the Bolton Savings Bank and the future seemed rosy.

At the weekends, when Steve was out watching Bolton Wanderers at Burnden Park, Dorothy began an acquaintanceship with two neighbours. Lois Melia, widow of a steeplejack, was now a cleaner in several houses at the better-off end of town. A large woman, she wheezed her way through other people's chores on weekdays, then tackled her own house on Saturdays. She lived at one side of Dorothy and Elsie Shipton, queen of the street, lived on the other.

At first, the newly-wed found herself reticent in the presence of the older women. Beryl Isherwood remained the only mother figure in her life and, now that her former teacher was dead, Dorothy experienced difficulty in relating to other senior females. Elsie Shipton was bossy, sharp and sometimes scathing, but Lois was easy. She laughed a lot, coughed a lot and seldom employed heavy criticism of her neighbours, so it was in Lois Melia's kitchen that Dorothy had her first close encounter with the awesome Mrs Shipton.

Elsie breezed in, a ship in full sail, no knock to announce herself before entering the house of one of her oldest friends. She looked Dorothy up and down, made a cursory greeting, then ploughed ahead. 'She's still not done that bloody step,' she announced. 'It looks like she's waiting for the next Preston Guild before pulling herself together.'

Lois made the introductions, but Elsie swept all niceties aside. 'I know. She were thirty-three View Street and he's one of them Dyson lads – decent family, mother had TB.' Without drawing breath, the woman motored onward. 'It's a disgrace, that bloody house. I don't know when she last dolly-blued them lace curtains. They are lace and all – they've got more holes than they started off with.'

'That'll be the cat,' said Lois, pouring tea for the invader. 'It's half Siamese, so it climbs everything. I've seen it swinging from her upstairs pelmet and all.'

Dorothy tried not to smile. There were rules in Bolton's terraced streets and she sometimes wondered whether laws concerning the dressing of windows and the cleaning of steps were on government statute books in some secret place at Westminster. All steps and 'first' flags had to be cleaned and donkey-stoned on a daily basis. The earlier they were done, the better regarded was the housewife who resided behind those well-scrubbed items.

Sash windows were also subject to regulations. The lower, movable halves were to be covered in lace. The lace should be white or cream and no other colours could ever be contemplated. The upper, fixed halves of the windows owned gathered valances, and pairs of curtains to match said valances should be pulled open no later than eight o'clock on weekdays and nine on Sundays. Exceptions were allowed in the event of illness, particularly when a child had measles, as light was rumoured to affect the eyesight when measles flourished.

A woman across the street was ignoring these requirements and was, therefore, a bad housekeeper who did not belong in Emblem Street.

'She wants telling.' Elsie took a slurp of tea. 'She wants telling and I'll have to be the one to do it – as always.' Her tone, supposedly mournful, wore an edge of self-importance. She awarded her attention to Dorothy. 'As the one who's lived longest in this street, I do the telling. It's quite a responsibility for a woman what's getting on in years.'

Dorothy could think of no reply.

'Her husband drinks,' offered Lois.

'Then she wants to be seeing to him and all. There's no excuse for any of it. He should come home to a rolling pin and a few choice words. And she should get her hands on some dolly blue and a donkey stone. Cleanliness costs nowt. I'll get across there now.' She marched out of the house.

Lois grinned. 'Take no notice. Her bark's worse than her bite, lass, I can promise you that.'

Ten minutes later, Elsie returned with tattered lace curtains and a face like thunder. 'He's buggered off with some bloody barmaid from the Wheatsheaf. Poor Sadie's in bed with flu or some such thing and the kids have just

411

left her there. There's nobody to see to her.' She eyed Dorothy. 'Nip up to the top, love. We want beef to make beef tea and knock at the doctor's – we'll pay him, me and my Pete. See if you can get some lemons and all, will you?'

'Yes. And I'll do her step for her, Mrs Shipton. I'll donkey it tomorrow when I do my own.'

Elsie smiled at Lois. 'Aye, this girl's all right. Dorothy, hurry up, because poor Sadie's badly.' She muttered on about men who didn't know which side their bread was buttered, about kids who showed no gratitude after a lifetime of care from a good mother. Then she stormed off to darn and wash poor Sadie's lace curtains.

So Dorothy gained two firm friends, women who would hold her in their hearts until they breathed their last. They were there when the telegram came; Elsie was there when Dorothy's tiny, lifeless son was delivered some weeks after the death of Steve. They force-fed her, chided her, watched over her, grieved with her. When circumstances dictated, they followed her up to Burbank Hall, where she gained yet another friend, Ivy Crumpsall, sister of Elsie. They supported her, laughed with her, cried with her and gave her love.

But most importantly, they were simply there.

*   *   *

Lois was reading one of her 'penny dreadfuls', which items had been christened by her good friend Elsie Shipton. 'Eh, that were lovely,' sighed Lois as she closed the slim volume and gazed into the fire. Ivy was kneading dough, while Elsie, nursing a cold in the chair opposite her friend's, was darning a sock. She shook her head and considered the prospect of an evening with Lois, who would, no doubt, render a blow-by-blow account of the fairy tale she had just finished.

Ivy placed the dough to rise in bowls, then occupied a third chair in the massive Burbank Wing kitchen. She had a secret and she wasn't saying anything. A young woman was visiting Captain Beddows and hope fluttered in the housekeeper's breast. It was probably the ex-fiancée, the one who had left him after the accident.

Lois, still lost in her tale of lurid romance, spoke again. 'I could have swore she were going to marry the wrong man.'

Elsie looked up. 'She is going to marry the wrong man.'

Lois clicked her tongue. 'No, that were up to about page ninety. Then she gets back with the handsome grocer and—'

'And parks herself behind a counter to sell butter for the rest of her life. Then they all lived happily ever after, once she'd learned to pat her butter into shape. I were talking about Dorothy, you clown, not some daft ha'p'orth in one of your comics. I wish you'd start reading summat gradely.'

Lizzie Murphy, cap askew and eyes blazing, entered the forum. She used a feather duster to emphasize her words as she let off her latest head of steam. She had been cleaning the corridor leading from Mrs Burbank's quarters to Clarence Wing and had been accosted by Molly Cornwell. 'She looked at me like I were sh— cow muck on a shoe, and said she couldn't account for all the table mats in the dresser. I told her to look under the bloody dog bowls, because them Pekes have two of the mats. Then she told me as I were cheeky.'

'Fancy that,' said Ivy, attempting to conceal a grin.

'She gives herself airs,' snapped Lizzie. 'Just because she wanders round with a case and a pen, she thinks she owns the whole bloody estate.' She poked her head into the corridor and shouted, 'Come in here, love. These ladies'll sort you out one road or another.' She waved her implement at the congregation, and disappeared.

Ivy, as chief supervisor of Burbank Wing, went to meet the recent arrival, that nice-looking girl in decent clothes and not too much make-up. 'Hello again, love. Welcome to the zoo. The apes are this way.' She led a bemused Julia into the kitchen. 'Now, settle yourself in yon chair and I'll make you a cuppa.' She glared at her sister. 'You're too tied up with your cold to make us a brew, aren't you? And Lois is trying to get over reading that book.' She turned back to Julia. 'Did you see him?'

'I did.'

Elsie chipped in. 'Did she see who?'

Ivy sniffed. 'How did you find him?'

'A nurse took me to his room.'

'No, I mean how was he? In himself, like?

Because he's come on in leaps and bounds since Dorothy started looking after him.'

Julia lowered her gaze and stared at her hands. It had all been terribly embarrassing, and she didn't want to discuss the situation with three strange women and three bowls of rising dough. It appeared that Stuart, heartbroken by Julia's desertion, had allied himself to a woman so beautiful that no one on God's earth could hold a candle to her.

'Are you all right?' asked Elsie, the level of her interest reflected in the movements of her head.

Ivy turned on her sister. 'Go home and take Lois with you. You're getting on me bloody nerves, both of you. Go on. I'll come and see you both later on, then I can have a look at my house and check you've not ruined it altogether.'

Twin pictures of disappointment struggled into coats and left the building. Julia Watson burst into tears.

'Don't take on,' chided Ivy gently.

'She's so beautiful,' sobbed the visitor. 'He didn't know I was coming today – I thought it would be a surprise, but it seemed more like a shock. I've lost him. I am useless and stupid and I've lost Stuart. And I've transferred my posting to Moss Side.'

Ivy muttered platitudes and wondered what the heck to do next. This was more trouble than profiteroles with no chocolate to be had and no cream in the dairy. 'And you've been posted to Manchester?'

'Yes.' The girl dabbed at her tears. 'He could have told me in a letter, couldn't he? All he needed to do was tell me he was engaged. I could have stayed in London with the people I'm used to. Getting a transfer in the middle of a war wasn't easy.'

'No, it won't have been.' Ivy wanted to throttle Stuart Beddows, burns or no burns. He should have used a bit of sense instead of putting this nice young woman through such unnecessary pain. There were footsteps in the corridor. Ivy walked to the door and stood, hands on hips, until Stuart Beddows reached her. She grabbed his decent arm and pulled him close to her. 'Ah, so you've escaped from Chadwicke, have you? Now, listen to me, you daft beggar. You want a bloody good hiding,' she whispered. 'And if it's owt to do with me, you'll be having one. Now get in that kitchen and sort the poor girl out.'

Stuart, who knew better than to argue with the fierce provider of meals, did as he was told. Ivy marched away. It was nothing to do with her and she feared that she might get involved if she lingered. 'Men,' she cursed quietly as she made her way to the linen store. They had no idea. If you told them to make pea soup, they'd use runner beans, the daft buggers.

Half an hour later, she returned to the kitchen to find Stuart, Julia, Andrew Burbank and Dorothy sitting at the table, all laughing and joking and carrying on as if nothing of moment had occurred. Ivy blinked. There was something very peculiar about young people these days. It was as if they'd been put together differently, perhaps with a few bits missing or with some extra ingredients in the mix. She had seen Sam, had chosen Sam, had married Sam. This crazy lot were playing musical chairs with one another's feelings and it wasn't right. And Julia Watson was suddenly hanging round Ivy's neck like a heavy St Christopher medal, thanking her and kissing her. 'Nay, I've done nowt,' protested the older woman, blushing.

So it was all settled. They'd done an about-turn and Andrew, who was grinning like a Cheshire cat, was to marry Dorothy. Julia had not wasted her time by transferring to the north and she was to spend the rest of her life with the captain.

'Oh, get out of me road, all of you,' Ivy snapped. 'I've bread on the rise and a stew to finish.' Inside, she glowed and found herself reminded of Lois Melia when she'd finished one of those daft books. They would all live happily ever after as long as they didn't get bombed and if they got out of Ivy's kitchen immediately. Even during war, some days were wonderful.

Isobel Burbank had still failed to return from town. She would be discussing alterations in Henry Barry's, was probably trying to make four coupons do the work of twelve. Influence was a wonderful thing and Molly intended to acquire it by any means at her disposal. Like Isobel, she would learn to play the game once Dorothy was established in her rightful place.

She mounted her bicycle and decided that her first port of call would be Michael Cooper's farm. His wife had been returned to the bosom of her family in Rochdale and Michael needed reminding of his debt to Molly – a half-pound of extra butter would not go amiss, along with a small joint of pork and anything else he had lying about the place.

She was leaning her bicycle against the farmhouse wall when she noticed an older man running away from the house, his gait made uneven by some ailment or other that forced him to depend on one leg more than the other. Andrew Burbank was lame, but he would probably use money to ensure that he never deteriorated to the point where movement became so difficult. The ill-clad man disappeared into a barn and Molly dismissed him from her mind.

When she received no response to her knocking at the rear door, she entered the kitchen with the intention of leaving a note. Farmers were often out when she called, as the nature of their work made their hours spent outside both variable and unpredictable. She placed her document case on the table and surveyed the cloth with its many stains, dirty dishes and cutlery scattered all over its surface. It was plain that Michael Cooper had made no attempt to improve himself since the removal of his sick wife, and this room would probably present a health hazard when summer arrived.

Suddenly, small hairs on the back of Molly's neck raised themselves, while a cold finger seemed to trace its way along the full stretch of her spine. There was a special silence in the room, an atmosphere that contained rather more than the mere lack of sound. She turned slowly from the table and looked towards the chair that had, until a few weeks earlier, been Barbara Cooper's favourite.

He would never improve his hygiene now, would he?

The back of his head had been taken away. Apart from that, Michael Cooper seemed perfectly normal, hands placed like large claws over the ends of the chair's arms, feet stretched towards the fire, boots fastened, thick socks folded over their leather tops.

A bell sounded. It was a funeral dirge, a knell, an echo. The queen was dead. Where was Mam? That knife was so heavy – where was it? He needed putting back together. The head. She didn't remember the head. What had happened to the head?

She crawled across the floor and picked up pieces of . . . pieces of him. He was sitting in a chair and he could be mended. Red. White bits, sharp bits, slivers of bone. Slime. She scraped it up and pushed it into the gaping hole. Where was his hair? There were splashes on the wall, red, with bits of bone, tiny, tiny crumbs, and sticky stuff, red, with slime in it. None of it fitted. It dropped off all over his pullover and she plucked at it, picked at it, pushed it into that red cavern where it belonged. The pullover had been grey. It had red all over it now.

Someone shouted, 'The queen is dead, long live the king!' There was blood on Molly's hands and there was blood all over the room. It had happened. Molly had made it happen and the queen, too, was dead.

Muffled bells bounced around in her mind and she covered her ears. There was red everywhere. Mam? Where was Mam and who would be king now? Edward? Victoria had ruled for over sixty years. Some had wanted a republic because she couldn't be bothered once Albert had died. Mill hooters wailed outside.

The man was dead, too. He had a great big, red hole in the back of his head and nothing fitted. He didn't look right. It was as if all the fat had drained away from him with the redness. Across the street, people were running to tell each other the news about Queen Victoria. Molly could smell potato pie from next door where Mam was doing her baking. The washing must be brought in. When a queen died, there should be no bright, white sheets hanging out in back alleys.

By Monday, she had to know her seven times table. 'Seven sevens are forty-nine, eight sevens are fifty-six . . .'

There was no more to be done.

Molly Bishop, aged seven and a half years, seated herself at the table and waited for Mam to come. Once Mam arrived, everything would be all right again. The queen was dead and the bells of Bolton sent the message to all residents of England's biggest town. Mam would take the red away. Molly had to wait. And the words would change to *God save our gracious king*.

*

Darkness had begun to fall when Sam Crumpsall found Molly Cornwell. After digging spuds all day, he was ready to go back to the Hall for a plate of stew and some vegetables cooked by his wife. He was calling at the farmhouse only to tell Michael Cooper he was leaving. But Molly Cornwell was not for moving. Like a statue, she sat at Michael Cooper's table, the only sign of life her quick, shallow breathing.

Sam lit a lamp and saw the horror. A scream, frozen in his throat, seemed to make the short journey up into his skull. Michael Cooper had drunk his last pint and had enjoyed his last woman; the back of his head had been blown away, probably with ammunition from a shortened shotgun. The weapon was nowhere to be seen, but Molly Cornwell was covered in blood and brains.

He spoke to her again, but she continued to gaze ahead and he could not shift her. Short of picking her up and carrying her, there was no way of getting her back to Burbank Hall. The police needed to come. Andrew Burbank must be made aware of what had happened on his land. Poor Barbara Cooper was not here to see what had happened to her husband, thank God.

After giving up on Molly, Sam left the kitchen and found himself retching in the yard. His stomach, which had not been occupied since lunchtime, sent bile into his mouth. Muscles worked in vain until Sam's middle section gave him pain. He needed to run and his legs were weak.

Some twenty minutes later, he entered Ivy's kitchen and collapsed into her rocking chair. 'Get Mr Andrew,' he said, his voice shaking. 'Now, Ivy. Don't say anything – just get him. Now.'

Ivy, terrified by her beloved Sam's pallor, ran off to do his bidding.

Alone, Sam sat and waited for the arrival of his employer. When he closed his eyes, he lived the horror all over again, felt the rigidity in the form of Molly Cornwell, saw walls reddened by blood, handprints punctuating the scarlet. What had she done and where was the weapon? Sam hadn't examined the room properly – that was a job for the police.

When Andrew Burbank arrived, Sam was weeping. The big, gentle farmhand who had endured his own world war, who had tended the land all his life, who was the rock on which his wife depended, simply sat and allowed tears to flow. He told Andrew what he had seen, then stared into the fire and waited for the police to come. Something terrible had happened, and Molly Cornwell had lost her mind.

It was soon obvious that Molly had done nothing wrong.

The body of an older man was found hanging in a barn, a recently discharged sawn-off shotgun on the floor below his suspended form. Within minutes, the hanged man was revealed as the father of Jean Sharp, a Land Army girl who had been impregnated by the deceased farmer. A scribbled note in capital letters told the tale, and the police were satisfied that no one else need be sought.

But none of this was any help when it came to Molly Cornwell. She looked at Andrew, asked for her mother, rattled on about her seven times table and the death of Queen Victoria. He held her hands and told her that he and Dorothy were engaged to be married, yet she continued to talk about the demise of an unhappy sovereign and the need to bring in washing from the back street. She spoke like a child. Andrew suspected that she *was* a child, that some buried business had crawled to the surface, its emergence triggered by the finding of Michael Cooper's corpse.

Andrew released the woman's hands and laid them gently on the dirty table. He informed the police sergeant of his qualifications and asked that Molly be forced out of the farmhouse and into a car. 'Drive her to Burbank Hall,' he said. 'I'll go with her.'

But the vehicle did not stop at the Hall. Andrew told the driver to take him and Molly up to Chadwicke House, because Molly was not fit to keep company with people who would not understand. In a private room at the back of the building, he placed the bloodstained woman on a chair and sent for her daughter. Whatever was about to transpire would not be pretty, but he wanted Dorothy to be here. Someone would have to be around to pick up the pieces, and Dorothy was one of the few people on earth with a chance of understanding this beautiful, fragmented and suddenly retarded woman.

For the first time in years, Andrew experienced fear. He was about to dig up a past that had been carefully interred by a clever, troubled child. And that child might not survive the experience.

FIFTEEN

January 1901 was a bitter month. People shivered their way into a new century, while in Osborne House on the Isle of Wight a remarkable woman lay dying. The whole country seemed to hold its breath as the old lady teetered on the brink of eternity. Even before her death, the populace was mourning the loss.

In the narrow streets of Bolton there was snow, just enough to decorate the houses and turn them into buildings far prettier than they actually were. Molly Bishop pressed her nose against glass and breathed, watching her exhalations misting the window before turning into shiny crystals. It was bitingly cold, but it was a beautiful late afternoon, with a setting sun casting its final rays across ice to make the world a wonderful, jewel-encrusted ornament.

Margaret Bishop entered the room and clicked her tongue. 'Put that curtain down, Molly. I did those windows yesterday and I want them clean. It won't be long now; the poor old lady's sinking fast.'

Molly knew that the 'poor old lady' was

Queen Victoria. Rumour had it that she had already passed, so no child was playing in the streets. On the Isle of Wight, vultures from the press had been poised for days, pens ready to glorify a woman who had ruled for some sixty-three years. It had been said that the queen had died at half past nine on the previous evening, at seven o'clock this morning, that there was a notice affixed to Bolton Town Hall and that flags had been lowered, but the townspeople awaited confirmation. When it came to information, the *Bolton Evening News* was the Bible for people hereabouts.

'Mr Bailey says he heard it off his daughter who works in town,' said Margaret. 'But I want to see it in black and white with my own eyes.' It was hard to envisage a world without the queen in it. Soon, there would be a king, and Margaret Bishop didn't particularly approve of Edward, Prince of Wales. It was something to do with a woman named Alice Keppel, who was 'no better than she might have been and a sight worse than she should have been', and Molly could make neither head nor tail of it.

'Go and ask Mr Bailey if he's heard anything else,' Margaret suggested. 'I don't trust all these rumours, but you never know.' Some believed that the queen had been seen walking in the grounds of Osborne House on Saturday, others were absolutely sure that she had breathed her last on Sunday – everyone awaited confirmation. There was even a Bolton physician in attendance at Osborne House, a Thomas Barlow who had been born and bred in this very town. It was now Tuesday 22 January and no one knew what the heck was going on. 'She can't carry on much longer,' mused Margaret Bishop. 'Go round and ask him, Molly.'

Molly stayed where she was. 'I'm hungry,' she lied.

Margaret tutted, then went about the business of furnishing her daughter with food. Molly toyed with her meal, trying her very hardest to make it last. 'I feel sick,' she said when half the food had been consumed. 'Don't send me next door.'

Margaret clicked her tongue again. 'It'll take you five minutes at the most. Go on.'

The child didn't move.

'Molly? Did you hear me?'

'Yes, Mother.'

'Well? What are you waiting for?'

Molly faced her mother squarely. 'I don't like Mr Bailey.' Mr Bailey lived in the next house. He was very fat, with two or three wobbly chins, and he was always sweaty. 'Please don't make me go,' begged the child.

Margaret, who was doing her baking, could not spare the time to pop round to question her neighbour. The man got few visitors and, because of that, he droned on endlessly about the cost of living, the ingratitude of his children and the general decline in moral standards. He shared Margaret's opinion that the Prince of Wales was a womanizer and had no right to follow such a wonderful woman to the throne. 'Just ask what he has heard from his daughter, Molly. Then come home.'

Molly lowered her gaze. She didn't know how to put into words her reason for not wanting to obey her mother's bidding. The things Mr Bailey did were not normal and they involved bodily functions and physical parts that could not be mentioned in the course of a conversation with Margaret Bishop. No one would believe her, anyway. And she didn't know the words to frame a picture of what happened in that smelly house.

'Go on, Molly. It's looking as if the queen is dead and I want to know.'

'The teacher said she's probably dead, so it must be true.'

'Go and make sure,' her mother insisted.

The child sighed. If Mam didn't believe the teacher, why should she believe Mr Bailey? But Molly pulled on a coat over her dress and white apron. A coat would make it more difficult for Mr Bailey to touch her. He was always touching her and he stank like an ash pit full of rotted vegetable matter. He also reeked of the thing he did all the time, the activity that made him sweat and drool like a baby.

'There's a good girl,' said Margaret as her daughter left the house.

The street was deserted. Most men were on their way home from work, women would be busy in their kitchens while children, now that school was over for the day, would be kept indoors until the death of Queen Victoria had been confirmed or denied. If the queen had died, there would be no playing outside until the good woman had been laid to rest.

She knocked at the door and waited until he wheezed, 'Come in, Molly. I know it's you. I know my special little girl's knock.' Then she entered a place she was beginning to liken to hell. Mr Bailey's slovenly daughter gave the house an occasional wipe when she brought the man's meals, but the house hadn't been given a good bottoming for years.

He looked at the beautiful girl and smiled, eyes disappearing into heavy pockets of fat when facial muscles expanded. No longer able to climb stairs, he lived in the front room and slept in the chair in which he currently sat. 'Hello, sweetheart,' he said. 'Have you come to see your Uncle Arnold?'

He wasn't her uncle. He was a nasty, dirty old man and he was playing with his thing again. His mouth slackened, while his head tilted to one side as he pulled and played with the ugly, purple-headed monster that poked out stupidly from beneath his pendulous belly. 'Come here, love,' he whispered huskily.

Molly knew what he wanted. He wanted her to touch the thing, had even asked her to kiss it, though she never had. But she wasn't going to let him put that smelly stuff on her hands again. Nor would she perch on his lap, an area made dangerously shallow by the swollen belly. He wasn't going to get his thick, dirty fingers between her legs today. 'My mother wants to know about the queen,' she said.

He groaned, panted, then shuddered when the slime came out.

Molly relaxed. He was usually all right for

half an hour after the appearance of the slime. 'Is the queen dead?' she asked.

He nodded. 'Aye, they're saying she's gone and it's being kept a secret because her eldest son's no good.'

Molly didn't need to know any more, so she turned to leave.

'See,' he said. 'Take that half-crown off the table and come here. I fancy having a proper look at you. Will you take your clothes off for half a crown? It's a long time since I saw a pretty little girl with no clothes on.'

But he had only just done the bad thing, hadn't he? Was he going to start all that grunting and groaning all over again? He was hideous, dirty and stupid. He was just as bad as the Prince of Wales. The thing he did was connected with females, Molly felt sure of that. The prince probably did it with Mrs Keppel, which was why he was a disgrace . . .

Molly stared at the money. The table was under the front window and it still held the remnants of today's lunch. 'I don't want the money,' she said. 'And I don't want to get undressed – it's too cold.'

'I'll warm you,' he promised her.

'No.'

'Has your mam never told you to be obedient? I just want a look at you. You should listen to your elders and betters. Now, get your clothes off, Molly.'

Mr Bailey had told Molly all about the purple-headed monster and where it wanted to be. He wanted her to help him put that terrible article inside her body. She was a small girl and he was a huge man, and she could not begin to imagine the pain that would result from such hideous behaviour. 'No,' she said again.

'For ten bob? Would you do it for ten bob? I only want a look and a little feel. I won't hurt you.'

She continued to stare at the filthy lace curtain. Like everything else in this hole, it stank. He stank. Everything he did stank. Everything he was stank. There was only one answer and that was to be rid of him. She took off her coat, removed her frilled apron and, with her back turned towards the man and his monster, picked up a knife from the table. There was no other way. If he carried on living here and if the Bishops continued to live next door, it would be only a matter of time before he pounced. He could stand up. She had seen him standing up and waddling about. Some day soon, he would be behind the door and would throw his great weight onto her and . . . and she didn't want to think about what would happen next.

It was easy. He sat in his chair, trousers open, the shrivelled thing trying to raise its ugly head again below rolls of lard, eyes narrowing when she began to unbutton her dress. The knife, folded into her apron, was a large one. It had been used to shave slices off a small joint of ham. This knife had cut a pig and it would shortly cut another pig.

Molly drove the weapon into him so fiercely that the handle stuck between his ribs. He looked surprised, but not at all hurt, so she heaved the thing out and slashed it into his belly. Although she suspected that the first strike had killed him, she continued to stab until she ran out of energy. Breathless, she stood and stared at him. There was blood everywhere. It was on her clothes, on her face and in her hair. For a reason she could not fathom, she scooped up a few rivulets of red and poured them back into his clothes. He was so untidy.

Molly was seven years old – seven and a half – and Mr Bailey lived at number seven. Well, he didn't live there any more . . . And she had to learn her seven times table by Monday. She had stabbed him seven times, she believed. Two sevens were fourteen, three were twenty-one, and the door opened.

A bell began to toll. It was just one bell with one note, and it rang slowly, its sound muffled, as if the clapper had been wrapped in wool. The queen was dead. Four sevens were twenty-eight. A boy ran past. 'Special edition *Bolton Evening News*. The queen is dead,' he shouted, 'long live the king.' More bells joined the knell. All the churches were mourning.

Margaret Bishop stood with her back against the closed door, a hand to her mouth. She seemed fastened to the spot. She took in the horror, saw her daughter's dishevelled clothing, noted that the man's trousers were open. Without a word, she picked up her child, grabbed the knife and carried both out to the back alley. Quickly, she entered her own yard by the tall gate, bolted it, took Molly inside the house.

White-faced with terror, Margaret Bishop locked all the doors and windows.

The clothes were stripped away and burnt. Wetness caused them to sizzle and Margaret poked hard at the fire to get rid of the sound and the smell of singed blood. Molly, wrapped in a blanket, waited for the copper to boil. Mother scrubbed her body hard, washed her hair, towelled her dry, dressed her in clean clothes. Then she sent the child up to her room. Not one single word had been uttered during the cleansing of Molly and the burning of her clothes. Alone, little Molly Bishop stood at her bedroom window and looked out upon the chilly realm of a deceased queen. Someone else had died today, but the little girl could not remember the identity of the second person. The world seemed to be bright red. She closed her eyes, shook her head, looked again and everything was back to normal. She was going to be all right.

A woman screamed. Dad arrived home from work. He had bought the special edition and Molly could hear him commenting on and bemoaning the queen's death. People ran about, police came, someone downstairs was talking to Molly's parents. A big, black horse pulled a cart along and stopped outside on the cobbles. Four men brought a huge box out of the house next door.

The changes in Molly were not particularly remarkable, except to a boy across the road, one who protected Molly at school in return for food. She never got to grips with her tables, ceased to try at school, didn't play in the street, started to call her mother 'Mam', became quieter and almost sulky. She made no friends, stayed away from the picture house on Derby Street, never went to the fair, the circus, the theatre.

When she was thirteen, she woke up. Like someone emerging from coma, Molly Bishop suddenly began to notice things. The first object she studied was herself and the way men looked at her. She learned how to walk, how to smile, how to tilt her head, how to lower lashes that were long, thick and several shades darker than her hair. She allowed men to kiss her and to fumble with her body. Gifts came her way – a hairbrush, some rouge, a pretty scarf. When she finally managed to bring full relief to a man, she received a bottle of expensive scent. She worked hard to learn her craft and made sure that her tutors were older, experienced males.

Until she was a married woman, Molly Bishop remained technically intact. Tom Cornwell, whom she married, loved her very bones, but was incapable of taking her virginity. He was safe. With him, she was safe. But when she finally allowed herself full rein, something approaching contempt for him was born. He could hold her and stroke her, but he could not make the earth spin. Sometimes, in the night, when the need burgeoned, she would roll against him and remain unfulfilled.

When she met Ian Clarke, she was ready for him. He was perfect, virile and imaginative. This was the man she wanted, the one for whom she would have given up anything and everything, though she never told him that. The games began. She had to be in charge, needed to stay one step ahead of all men. She had been like this for as long as she could remember. But she could not remember any of the reasons, so she never fully understood why.

Sometimes, she almost remembered. When she gave birth to Dorothy and all the blood came, she found herself skirting the edge of a darkened mass, a place in her mind where lay a particular event that had probably occurred some time during her eighth year. Early childhood was easy to recall. But there was a smudged blot on the page containing the eighth year of her life and she could not account for it.

She had been seven, then she had been thirteen and extraordinarily beautiful. Six years of nothingness hung between those two numbers. School? She had sat at the back and had learned virtually nothing, yet she seemed to know everything. Tom? She had continued to feed him, because he was a certainty, a fixed point, almost a habit. The death of her parents she scarcely noticed, then she married Tom.

Life came to her in the form of Dr Ian Clarke. He gave her pleasure and a daughter and, with the daughter, came the fear. That dark red mass – whatever it was – must never touch Dorothy, because Dorothy was the new Molly and all pages had to be clean. Dorothy needed to be kept away from . . . from whatever it was.

Had Dorothy been a son, the whatever would not have been a problem, but she was not a son. The child was a Molly-in-miniature and she had to be kept safe.

Molly had been hell bent on marrying Ian Clarke. Yet she had loved Florence, had discovered her very first female ally, and that friend had left her. The second baby had poured away and Ian, too, had abandoned her. Lovers had come and gone, none of them able to awaken in Molly the feelings she had experienced with Ian Clarke.

Dorothy. Dorothy had learned her mother's weakness. Red. Tom had prevented Molly from smashing the glass in the vestibule door, and she had come to tolerate the small, scarlet sections set into the lead. But she had been unable to bear those moments when Dorothy had cut herself. And the girl had gone, had left Molly all alone in a world she failed to understand, a world without Ian, without joy.

And now something else had happened, so the demons had to be faced and the price needed to be paid.

In a room that contained just herself, her daughter and a gentle doctor, Molly Bishop, now Cornwell, relived the horror. The tone she used was unvarying, but she answered every one of Andrew's questions until the full truth had been displayed. Yet even now, with the patient in a trance-like state, Andrew could not retrieve the missing years. Molly had glided from the age of seven to the age of thirteen without stopping, had deleted irretrievably half her childhood.

When she had finished, Molly leaned back in her chair and stared at the wall. Scarcely blinking, she fixed her eyes on one spot and remained motionless. Then she offered an after-thought. 'Donald said he was David. We had a flat in town. Antiques. He showed me how to buy, then he died. They all die or go.'

Andrew glanced at his white-faced fiancée. 'She was my father's mistress, Dorothy. She was my mother's unknown, unseen and greatest enemy. Your mother probably gave my father the happiest time of his life. This is a very small world.'

But Dorothy scarcely heard him. She was staring at her own monster, a mother who had been cruel and cold, who had contained Dorothy to the point of imprisonment. Molly had used every device at her disposal to narrow her child's life and that child had hated her for it. 'Mam?' she whispered.

There was no response.

Dorothy sobbed. 'Will she go to prison?'

'No. I shall check the records for the death of Arnold Bailey, but it can remain an unsolved murder as far as I am concerned. I think you will agree that your mother has suffered enough.'

'Yes. But will she come right, or will she stay in this state?'

Andrew, who had witnessed catatonia and other strange conditions of the human psyche, could provide no answer.

Dorothy tried again. 'Mam?'

Very slowly, the head turned. Molly, still covered in the dried blood of a murdered farmer, awarded her daughter a half-smile.

'Who's my father?' Dorothy asked. No matter what, Tom Cornwell would always be her dad, but, after Molly's disclosures, it was clear that some other male was responsible for the existence of Molly's only child.

'Dr Ian Clarke,' Molly answered. 'He was the love of my life, Dorothy. I would have followed him to the ends of the earth, but I wasn't sure of which end he had travelled to. Somewhere in America, you have a father, a half-sister and two half-brothers. Their mother was my friend and she respected me. The friendship wasn't meant to happen, but it did. Florence Clarke gave me pearls. I shall pass them on to you on your wedding day.'

Andrew, relieved beyond measure, closed his eyes for an instant. She was back. Molly Cornwell looked and sounded different from her old self, but she had returned to the here and now. 'Do you remember all that you have just told us?' he asked.

'Yes,' she said. 'It was always there, I expect. It's just that I must have tied a thick bandage round it.'

He could not have expressed it better himself. 'You're not going back to my mother,' he told her. 'You will stay in Burbank Wing and get to know your daughter.'

Tears welled in the older woman's eyes. 'I know why now, Dorothy. The bars and the straps and the trying to keep you away from other people. You were a piece of me. I didn't want it to happen all over again.'

Dorothy was still coming to terms with the concept of Dr Clarke's having fathered her. He had run away from Mam; that was the most likely reason for his exit from the scene. She looked at her weeping mother. Molly Cornwell never cried. She was harsh, cruel, terribly hurt and sobbing her heart out. Dorothy crossed the room and, for the first time within memory, embraced her mother. 'Don't cry, Mam. Nothing bad will happen now. It's all over. I promise you.'

Molly was rigid in her daughter's arms. She didn't understand this kind of physical contact, didn't think she'd been hugged by her own mother, but she'd forgotten so much, perhaps she was mistaken. 'I don't know how to talk to you,' she said.

Andrew joined the two women and placed a hand on Molly's shoulder. 'You fragmented,' he told her. 'You split up your life into boxes and put some of them into storage, far away. What has happened tonight is another trauma – facing forgotten shock is, in itself, a shock. Just don't blame yourself for everything that's wrong in the world.' He sniffed back a stream of emotion. 'And Molly – don't hate yourself.'

She didn't know whether or not she hated herself, because she scarcely understood who she was. The knowledge that she needed to begin again was tiring. 'Dorothy,' she said, 'I must get a bath.' It was time to come clean and to begin all over again.

*

The mending of Molly Cornwell was not going to happen overnight. Weeks passed by while she sat quietly and stared through windows at a world that sometimes seemed new, often felt frightening. She aged. Her beauty did not desert her completely, but the seemingly eternal youth she had enjoyed began to slip away from her. She had some aches and pains, a bad cold, migraines.

Molly took her mother into town with the intention of interesting her in something or other, and Molly, who had been quiet throughout the expedition, went into a shop, handed over money and coupons, came out with a red cardigan. She removed her grey jacket and put on the new garment, gaze fixed on her daughter. Then the left eyelid lowered itself into a wink. 'We can do this, girl,' she said. 'I might be sixty when we get there, but it's a journey that has to be made. No matter what, the sun will rise every morning and set every evening and we can't change that. But we can change us, Dorothy.'

Two women sat in the café into which Isobel Burbank had taken Molly a lifetime ago. They talked about the wedding, about Tom, about years to come, about a future that could begin only once this ghastly war had ended. It suddenly occurred to Dorothy that she was speaking without guarding her words, and she was reminded of Miss Isherwood, that grand lady who had been a mother to her two decades earlier. 'Mam?' she said.

'What?'

'That red cardy doesn't suit you at all.'

Molly's eyes twinkled over the thick white cup. She placed the latter in its saucer and looked down at her arms. 'It's horrible, isn't it?' A thought occurred. 'You're saying that because you want it. Right?'

Dorothy nodded.

'Well, you can walk up the aisle in Florence Clarke's pearls, but you'd look daft in a red cardigan.'

'I can wear it any time,' said Dorothy. 'It's always been my favourite colour, but it makes you look washed out.'

Molly Cornwell grinned from ear to ear. 'No. It's my statement and I'm keeping it.' She blushed, reached across the table and took her little girl's hand. 'I love you,' she said. 'I suppose I always did, even when I was different.'

Dorothy sighed. 'I know that now, Mam. It just took you a bit longer than normal to say it, that's all.' She squeezed her mother's fingers. 'What are we going to do about Dad?'

'Tom? Oh, that's going to get sorted out. He won't leave the pit of course. Says he's fighting for his country. But then we're having one of the cottages in the village. Plenty big enough for two and we're used to one another. He'll be all right, you'll see.' She pondered for a moment. 'You know, Dorothy, I reckon your dad always knew I'd killed Arnold Bailey. And never once did he go against me, even when I was crackers. He was a good lad and he's a good man. Stood by me through thick and thin.'

Dorothy frowned. 'Lower your voice, Mam. You don't want the world to know.' Andrew had checked, and the murder still lay on file as unsolved. 'That wasn't a man,' she whispered, 'it was a devil – and don't you ever forget that. You did the world a favour.'

'I couldn't have told my mother,' answered Molly. 'She wasn't easy to talk to.'

Dorothy almost choked on coffee that was mostly chicory essence. 'That must have been dreadful,' she said. 'A girl needs to be able to talk to her mother, doesn't she?'

'Oh, shut up. Shall we go and look at the market?'

They wandered past the stalls, daughter's hand through the mother's arm. It was never too late, Dorothy told herself. Red cardigan, jokes, secrets shared – life was improving all the time.

SIXTEEN

Everybody was at sixes and thirteens, as Ivy put it. She reckoned that sixes and sevens didn't go far enough, so she chose the bigger number. Her sister, Elsie, was getting on her nerves. 'Go and be confused on your own somewhere,' she snapped. 'I've a wedding cake to make out of three currants and a bowl of fresh air. I can't be doing with you having a brainstorm in my back kitchen.'

Elsie fiddled with a button on her cardigan. 'She changed overnight. I don't trust changes overnight – they never last.'

Lois put down her novel. She had progressed from thin, colourful booklets to Jane Austen and she was proud of herself. 'Nobody talks proper no more,' she complained. 'Mr Darcy talks proper, so does Elizabeth Bennet. It's a shame.'

Elsie sighed. 'And she's always with Dorothy. Dorothy couldn't stand sight nor sound of her till a few weeks back. Now it's all "Mam said this" and "Mam thinks that". World's gone crazy.'

Lois nodded. 'It has. But what I want to know is, where did they all go to the toilet?'

Ivy stopped weighing dried fruit, while Elsie simply shook her head. Lois was good at going off at tangents.

'That ball at Mr Bingley's house – when Elizabeth dances with Mr Darcy even though she doesn't like him – there must have been hundreds there. Where did they go? Did they have tipplers in the back yard or were there loads of buckets? I wonder who got rid of all that afterwards? Makes you think, doesn't it?'

Ivy looked at the ceiling as if seeking divine intervention. The conversations in her kitchen were getting out of hand, the master of the house was about to be married, while the mistress, mother of said master, was having fits on her own in twelve rooms with no help except for a slapdash female from the village. 'Who cares, Lois?' she asked.

'You'd care if you'd had to empty all the bloody buckets,' came the swift response. 'Then there were all them horses. What about that lot?'

'They'd grow lovely roses,' snapped Elsie. 'Look, Lois. We've had a murder, a suicide and a big family row. Mrs Burbank isn't talking to her son, Molly Cornwell's ready for being made into a saint, we've a wedding coming up, you're going for an operation and I want to know what Molly Cornwell's playing at.'

Ivy brandished her wooden spoon. 'Go home,' she ordered. 'There's neither of you any use or ornament. Jane bloody Austen, Molly and Dorothy, Mrs Burbank not coming to the wedding – I've had enough. Take your *Pride and Whatever* home and think about lavatories there.'

'*Pride and Prejudice*,' pronounced Lois, who now thought of herself as a woman of some education.

Lizzie Murphy dashed in. Her cap was askew and she panted like someone who had just run a mile. 'She's gone,' she gasped. 'Upped and left without a word till she were halfway to Bolton.'

The wooden spoon clattered to the table, while Ivy, at her wits' end, sank into a chair. Wedding cake? She had a better chance of producing an egg-free omelette in the middle of this pantomime.

'Who?' asked Lois. 'Who's gone, Lizzie?' The young orderly looked anything but orderly. She was crumpled, hot, and her colourful hair was clearly trying to escape from the confines of the white cap.

'The missus,' panted Lizzie. 'She's took them two daft dogs with her and most of her clothes. Amos drove her to the station in the old carriage. He were supposed to be sworn to secrecy, but he says she's gone to Harrogate. There's a ladies-only hotel and she's stopping there. I don't know whether it's just till after the wedding or until the war ends.'

'Good bloody riddance,' said Ivy.

Andrew wandered in. 'Oh,' exclaimed the harassed housekeeper, 'it's my lucky day – we nearly have a quorum.' She turned to Andrew. 'Your mother's buggered off to Harrogate. And you lot can follow her for all I care. I'm trying to make a cake here.'

Andrew Burbank frowned. 'Have any of you seen Molly?'

'No,' they chorused.

He turned on his heel and collided with Dorothy.

Ivy swore under her breath. It had now gone past quorum and was fast becoming an annual general meeting.

'She's gone to do it,' said Dorothy softly. Andrew grabbed her hand and they fled the scene.

Ivy's face was now a picture of desperation. She wanted her cake done, dusted and in a tin so that she could pour some precious brandy into holes that would be made by a fine knitting needle. She needed marzipan or almond paste, needed to start begging, stealing and borrowing sugar, wanted time off for a well-deserved nervous breakdown. She fixed her steely gaze on Lizzie. 'Out!' she roared.

Lizzie bolted. The other two women needed no further instruction. One glance at her sister's face was enough – Elsie grabbed her coat and Lois followed swiftly with Mr Fitzwilliam Darcy clutched to her bosom.

The silence was beautiful. Accompanied only by the movements of an old clock, Ivy got on with her cake. Mr Andrew was going to marry Dorothy, Julia Watson would be marrying Stuart Beddows in a few months and all would be well except for some folk. It appeared that the mothers of the Burbank groom and his bride had both gone missing, and it was safer to concentrate on flour, eggs, dried fruit and stolen sugar.

Lizzie crept back in.

'What the bloody hell do you want now?' Ivy asked.

'I were looking for Mrs Shipton and Mrs Melia.'

'They've gone. I threw them out. Make us a cup of tea, Lizzie. My throat's like the bottom of a parrot's cage.'

Lizzie did as she was told. When Mrs Crumpsall was in this kind of mood, it was best not to ask questions. Something odd was going on. Mrs Cornwell had become nearly nice, but now Mr Andrew and Dorothy had swished away in the car, gravel flying all over the place when the wheels moved faster than lightning, while the newly improved version of Mrs Cornwell was missing, Chadwicke House was lacking in supervision and Lizzie was slightly bewildered.

The two women sat at the table.

'Cake coming along all right?' asked the younger.

'Aye, but I got a bit distracted. Lois has gone all Jane Austen and our Elsie's gabbling on about Dorothy's mother all the while.'

'Well, she's buggered off and all. Dark suit, hair done, white blouse. Looked like she were ready for an interview. Mr Andrew was as white as a sheet when I followed them to the car, then Dorothy started crying. They shot off without a word to anybody. They both looked as if they were scared stiff.'

Ivy sipped at her tea. Living in this madhouse was becoming a sore trial. She grabbed at a ray of

447

hope. 'Never mind, eh, Lizzie? Little Matthew'll get adopted by Dorothy and Mr Andrew. That'll make for a happy ending, won't it?'

A happy ending was a long way from the minds of Andrew and Dorothy as they sped towards Bolton. Andrew was grasping at straws. 'I know people,' he said. 'I have some influence and they'll listen to me.'

'You'd probably have to get my mother certified as insane.' Dorothy clung to the leather strap as Andrew negotiated a corner at considerable speed. 'We'll be no use to her dead,' she told him.

'And we'll be no use late.' He stopped the car so suddenly that both occupants shot forward. 'Sorry,' he said. 'Stay there, I'll be back in a few minutes.'

Dorothy was staying nowhere. She jumped out of the car and followed him into the building. Molly was there. She was seated on a bench, hands folded in her lap, handbag at her side. 'Mam. You can't do this. Come on, get in the car and we'll take you home.'

Molly looked at her daughter. 'I can't,' she said.

'Have you spoken to anyone?' Andrew asked.

'Not yet. They seem to be very busy at the moment.' Molly found herself on her feet, Dorothy at one side, Andrew at the other. They dragged her outside and pushed her without ceremony into the rear seat of the car.

Dorothy placed herself next to her mother. 'If necessary, I shall sit on you,' she promised.

'Perhaps a lock on your door, bars at the window and straps on the bed might help? What the hell are you doing, Mam? You are forty-eight years of age – what happened to common sense?'

It had nothing to do with common sense.

Andrew, in the driver's seat, turned round and stared at his future mother-in-law. 'You were easier when you were nasty,' he informed her. 'Now, you seem to be reclaiming your mislaid childhood and that simply isn't appropriate.'

'I killed a man,' stated Molly baldly.

Andrew shook his head slowly. 'Now, listen, Mrs Cornwell. I am the expert here – agreed? I'm a fully trained psychologist, psychiatrist and now racing driver. Would you like me to steer you in the direction of a long journey lined by and paved with guilt? Would you?'

Molly offered no response.

'You killed a man. You were seven years old. Until you found Michael Cooper with his head blown off, you remembered nothing. Because you suffered. The suffering was so bad that you stuck it away under lock and key. He would have hurt you, might have raped you, might have raped and killed another child. You saved other children.'

Molly stared down at her folded hands. 'I just want it off my mind,' she whispered.

'Fine.' Andrew smiled. 'Wonderful idea. Go back into the police station and tell them everything. It'll be in all the newspapers and Arnold Bailey will still be dead. Dorothy will be pointed at and discussed, as will any children we might have. Now. That's the guilt trip. Do you want a first class ticket? Do you want Dorothy to travel behind you in the luggage van? Would you like your daughter's children to be related to a self-declared murderer? They'd never get a first class ticket with a label like that stuck to them, would they now?'

Molly sighed and gripped her daughter's hand. 'I'm being selfish again, aren't I?'

'Yes.' Andrew opened the door and stepped out of the car. He leaned forward, poking his head through the open window in the direction of his two passengers. 'I'll go in with you if you like. I'll tell them you're crazy – I'm qualified to do that. Well?'

Molly shrugged. 'I'd be achieving nothing?'

'That's right,' replied her daughter. 'No one else was arrested and hanged, so what's the point, Mam? Come home. We can't have both our mothers missing when we get married. Andrew's mother's run away to Yorkshire.'

Molly thought about that. 'Yorkshire? Who'd want to run away to Yorkshire? They're all tight-fisted and they talk like yokels.'

Dorothy grinned. If her mother ever became completely pleasant, the world would rock on its axis. 'Promise me you'll stay away from police stations, Mam?'

Molly shrugged. 'That was a very nice-looking desk sergeant,' she answered. 'Oh, come on. Take this silly old woman home and let's have a nice cup of tea.'

*

The visiting surgeon stripped layers of bandage and gauze from Stuart's face. Here, in Chadwicke House, the young man was enduring his second unveiling. 'Marvellous,' the doctor exclaimed. 'We'll get you over to Hollywood one of these days, young man. Now, ignore the bruises, narrow your eye and imagine your face without the black and blue bits.'

Stuart looked in the mirror. 'I look like a plate of corned beef hash with red cabbage.'

The man known as Emperor sighed. 'Thanks a lot. Use your imagination, sir. In six weeks, you'll be halfway there. I need to tidy up the eye socket, stick in a glass eye—'

'And Bob will be my uncle.'

'That's about right, yes. Now, where's this Dr Burbank of yours?'

Stuart lifted his chin and looked at his neck. 'That looks flatter,' he said. 'Ah – Andrew? He baled out at ten thousand feet about an hour ago. Rumour has it that his mother escaped.'

'Right. He seems satisfied with your progress, anyway. You'll be home in the bosom of your family in a couple of months. So, I'll be on my way. It's good to see Lancashire again after all these years, so I'll dally around the countryside for a while.'

Stuart was about to ask the American about his acquaintanceship with Lancashire, but the man had already left. With the mirror tilted first this way and then that, Stuart decided that an improvement had been made and carried on reading his newspaper.

The visitor stopped halfway down the corridor.

Andrew Burbank was walking towards him and on his arm was a woman so familiar that the surgeon rocked back on his heels. 'Molly?'

Dorothy looked at him. He was tall, grey-haired and elegant. 'I'm Dorothy,' she said. 'Molly is my mother and you . . .' She swallowed. 'You are Dr Clarke.' Her knees were weak and she clung to her fiancé's arm.

'This is the Emperor,' said Andrew. 'Have you two met before?'

'Yes,' answered Dorothy. 'He was our doctor when I was a child. Then he went to America.' She addressed her biological father. 'You trained as a plastic surgeon, I take it?'

Ian was lost for words. A man who had lectured from coast to coast in the USA was suddenly tongue-tied. How often had he dreamed of Molly? How long had it taken him to settle down, find a wife and begin again? He knew he had been taking a chance by coming back; he also knew that his country had needed him, that it still needed him, that pilots and crew were depending on his skills in order to have a chance of an almost normal life. At the end, there would be soldiers, too, who would need him. 'Yes,' he managed finally. 'I decided to specialize and . . . and here I am.'

Andrew was glancing from one to the other, his mind in overdrive as he remembered all that Molly had disclosed after the murder of Michael Cooper. This man, the famed and feted Emperor, was Dorothy's father. Andrew cleared his throat. 'We are about to have tea in my office – would you care to join us?'

They walked along, the surgeon behind, Dorothy still clinging for dear life to Andrew's arm. Andrew had given a key to Mam and Mam would be joining them in a few minutes. Was that wise? Molly had only just been prevented from blurting out her most dangerous secret to the police – how would she react when she saw Dr Clarke?

Dorothy made tea in a kitchen next door to the office, both doors left open so that she could hear the conversation. The two doctors concentrated on patients and procedures, and for that Dorothy was temporarily grateful. Should she waylay her mother? Should she find some excuse to prevent the encounter?

Tea was poured and passed round. Dorothy noticed that Ian Clarke's cup rattled slightly when he placed it on its saucer. Footsteps approached; Dorothy recognized them as her mother's. She stared at Andrew and he saw the panic in her face.

Andrew jumped up. 'If you'd care to step through into the records room, I have some notes that might interest you. That rear gunner – Jenkins – the one with the mangled left arm – I was wondering if he might fare better with an amputation at the elbow and a prosthesis? He's very adept with his right hand and the burns aren't too deep on that side, so . . .' The two men disappeared just as Molly arrived.

Dorothy jumped up. 'Here's your tea. Bring it with you – we'll visit Stuart. He had his bandages taken off today and I promised Julia I'd go to see him, because she's on duty.'

Molly followed her daughter out of the office and went to exclaim over the undoubted improvement in the pilot's appearance.

In the records room, Andrew brought his conversation with Ian Clarke to an abrupt halt. 'Right,' he said, 'back in the office.' He locked the door so that Molly could not return. 'Hell's bells,' he declared. 'What a bloody pickle. I knew you were Beauchamp-Clarke, but not for one moment did I suspect—'

'Beauchamp was my mother's maiden name,' said Ian. 'When I came over, I was based in Kent – I never suspected that I'd be sent up here. Of course, I wanted to look at Lancashire, because I thought I'd never see it again, but . . .' He ran a hand through thick, silver hair. 'I certainly didn't expect to find Dorothy here.'

'Molly's here, too,' said Andrew.

'What? Why? Is she ill?'

'She's always been ill,' replied Andrew tersely, 'as well you must have known. But I accidentally got to the bottom of her problem and there was a damned good reason for her condition. Suffice it to say that a trauma suffered in childhood left huge gaps in her memory and prevented her from getting close to anyone. Her ill-treatment of Dorothy was not her fault. That's all I am prepared to say about the matter. I suggest you leave as soon as Molly is out of Chadwicke House. I shall need to lock you in here while I arrange for her departure.' He stood up. 'You may be the best when it comes to your field, Dr Clarke, but you certainly shirked your responsibilities in the past. You abandoned my fiancée and her mother.'

Alone in a locked room, Dr Ian Beauchamp-Clarke closed his eyes and swallowed several sobs. He saw her in the firelight, arms raised, hair flowing down her back, the beautiful body toned and ready for anything. He saw her walking on the street, men's eyes riveted to her as she sashayed along in that deliberately casual way. But mostly, he saw and heard Florence. 'Where's Molly?' she had asked many times towards the end. 'Get Molly. Only Molly can make the bed right for me.'

He stared through the window. Trauma. Andrew Burbank was the expert when it came to trauma and subsequent fragmentation, but no expert had been needed when Molly's baby had come away. Ian had seen the resulting crisis, had watched Molly as she deteriorated before his eyes. Any normal human would have recognized the illness in her. And he had deposited her at the hospital, had packed up his life, had fled to the other side of the globe.

Sheets of tears, she had wept at Florence's bedside. They had flowed in a continuous stream, no accompanying sound, no dabbing with a handkerchief. 'I never cry.' How could he cleanse himself of his heinous sin? Yes, he had been desperate to save his children, but he should have done something for her, should have alerted a psychiatrist, a colleague in general practice, her husband.

'Tom already knew,' he advised the empty room. 'He lived with it constantly, yet could do nothing.' But Tom was a miner – Ian was a doctor.

Time crawled by on crippled knees. Gone was the desire to look at the moors, to visit Mansfield Avenue, to call on fellow doctors who continued to practise. All Ian wanted was to go away and think. Think? He had been thinking for twenty years.

Dorothy was a stunner, the image of her mother, but without that carefully constructed edge of hardness. She was his daughter. Florence's children were established abroad, one in law, two in medicine. They had good lives, a decent stepmother and admirable partners. Dorothy was an aunt twice over and she would probably never meet her American relatives. What a bloody mess.

Ian's shoulders sagged with relief when the door finally opened. He turned to look at his future son-in-law, swallowed hard when he saw Molly.

'She never could keep anything from me,' she said as she closed the door behind herself. 'I only needed to look at her to know something had upset her. So I tortured her with words until she told me you were here, and then I bullied Andrew into giving me the key. How are you, Ian?'

For the second time that day, Ian experienced verbal constipation. She was still beautiful, but older, gentler and softer. 'Molly?' he achieved at last.

She sat down. 'Ian, I nearly did a terrible thing today. I almost hurt my daughter again, because I wanted to clear my own conscience. Now here you are, the love of my crazy life and you can't even talk to me.'

'God, Molly. I was a pig.'

'Yes, you were. And I was a whore. We both improved. I am proud of you. We looked at Stuart's face and that's not far short of a miracle. Yes, you have made a difference in the world.' She told him about the upcoming wedding, about her plans to settle in the village, asked about Edward, Sarah and Daniel.

He finally opened up and described his life in Connecticut. She seemed to absorb every word, was clearly interested in all he had to say about his home life and his work.

After twenty or so minutes, she rose to her feet. 'If you are still up here, please come to the wedding. But her dad will be giving her away.' She crossed the room and kissed him on the cheek. 'It was love,' she whispered, 'but I was too sick to know that. Go now. All we have to do in this world is make a difference in a good way. You are doing that, and I am trying.'

Blinded by tears, the most famous surgeon in the sphere of reconstruction stumbled off down the corridor. Molly had come good. He wanted to run back to her, but that was not the right thing to do. He had to walk on, walk away, go home.

Molly sat at Dr Andrew Burbank's desk. For the second time, he had left her. She felt strangely fulfilled, as if she were a Catholic just emerging from the confessional. It was over. Her whole body was relaxed and her mind was finally at peace.

'Mam?'

'Hello, love.'

'Has he gone?'

'Has who gone?'

Both women grinned. Molly wiped a tear from her eye. 'Come on. Let's see how that wedding dress is coming along. If all else fails, we'll have a decent parachute.'

Arm in arm, mother and daughter walked back to Burbank Wing. The sun was shining, birds were singing and Molly Cornwell, no longer at odds with the world, had finally come home.

THE END

THE BELL HOUSE
by Ruth Hamilton

Madeleine Horrocks, pretty and outspoken despite her strict 1950s Catholic upbringing, doesn't understand why religion seemed to force people apart. Surely, she would argue to her friend Amy, believing in God should be all about love and forgiveness, not hatred? But Amy has been brought up to believe that mixing with other religions would result in eternal damnation, and when Maddy becomes friendly with George, the good-looking Jewish boy who lives nearby, Amy fears the worst. But as they grow up she, too, becomes friends with George, as well as with other young teenagers who are Catholic, Anglican – even Methodist. They would all meet secretly at the Bell House, an ancient place of burial, but when a body is found in the nearby reservoir they become threatened by tragedy and danger.

Father Sheahan, the whisky-soaked priest from the local church, has meanwhile discovered that his secret past is catching up with him. Bigotry, lust and hatred have been so much a part of this community that it takes the combined forces of young and old – and particularly George's formidable grandmother Yuspeh – to make everything right again.

'For those who like Catherine Cookson,
try Ruth Hamilton'
Daily Express

0 552 15167 X

CORGI BOOKS

CHANDLERS GREEN
by Ruth Hamilton

The Chandlers had been making candles in Bolton
for five hundred years, and had given their name to
the village of Chandlers Green. The dynasty, now in
decline and ruled by Richard Chandler, is reduced
to an unhappy household and a few tenanted
properties.

But Richard continues to behave as though he were
Lord of the manor. Jean, his wife, is terrified of
him; his aunt, Anna Chandler, has moved out of the
house and is writing a history of candlemaking; his
grown-up children despise him, but fear for their
mother if they should leave home. And now
Richard's arch-enemy, Alf Martindale, is planning
to move into *his* village, and Richard knows that the
past is catching up with him fast. A crisis forces
him to leave his manor for a while, and he has
no way of knowing that Jean is arming herself
against his return. The past and the present are
about to come together in a way that can
only end in tragedy . . .

0 552 14906 3

CORGI BOOKS

MATTHEW & SON
by Ruth Hamilton

When Matthew's beloved wife Molly died, long before
her time, her son Mark grieved as much as anyone.
He had always known that his parents were completely
devoted to each other, and sometimes he had felt
excluded from this close partnership. Since he was a
small boy his mother had been sickening with the
illness that eventually carried her off, and now at the
age of sixteen Mark longed to earn his father's respect
by assisting with the family business, a prosperous
antiques shop. But his father, in grief, seemed
beyond help.

Tilly Povey, famous for her whiplash tongue and her
copious ironing, watched the boy's lonely existence
with a heavy-heart. Stella, Molly's sister, had done well
for herself – now a doctor, she had always loved
Matthew, and wondered whether he might, perhaps,
turn to her in his hour of need. Matthew, obsessed
with his loss, was gradually falling apart and none of
those who were closest to him could, it seemed, do
anything to help. But Tilly, whose uncompromising
exterior hid a warm heart, was determined to
help this troubled family.

Matthew & Son is another masterly novel of power and
compassion from this exceptional writer.

0 552 14906 3

CORGI BOOKS

SATURDAY'S CHILD
by Ruth Hamilton

'Saturday's child works hard for a living . . .'

And so they did – three females, one born in the 19th century, two in the 20th, each a worker, each driven by that unseen hand which shapes destiny, every one of them born on a Saturday.

It was 1950. Magsy O'Gara, her husband killed in the war, plodded through her daily routine as a hospital cleaner, dedicating all her spare time to Beth, her genius daughter. Pursued by men who admired her great beauty, she was determined to remain a widow. Nothing was to divert her from her gruelling schedule. Her goal was simple: Beth would become a doctor.

Beth, however, wanted the normal life – a brother, a sister, a stepfather who might make her wonderful mother happy. This was, after all, the 20th century; gone were the days when a woman stayed at home to mind her family. So Beth was delighted when a personable man began to court Magsy.

Across the road at number 1, Nellie Hulme, trapped in a world of silence, watched the other two Saturday girls. Deaf since infancy, Nellie had a secret so huge that it amused her. What would folk round here have thought had they known her true position in life? And why, why did she 'hear' in her dreams?

In another of her wonderfully complex tales, Ruth Hamilton draws us into a web of passion, mystery and deceit.

'Very much the successor to Catherine Cookson'
BBC Radio 4

0 552 14771 0

CORGI BOOKS

MULLIGAN'S YARD
by Ruth Hamilton

It all began with the turn of a card in a seedy gambling den. In 1920 the Burton-Masseys lost their home, Pendleton Grange, their lands and several businesses in the heart of Bolton, including Massey's Yort. Reduced to a life of hardship, Alex Burton-Massey's widow and three daughters took refuge in Caldwell Farm, all that was left of their former wealth.

James Mulligan was the man who now owned their lands, and Massey's Yort quickly became known as Mulligan's Yard. He was a silent brooding character whose manners teetered on the brink of rudeness, but in spite of this many women found him attractive. Who was he? What was he? Did he hide a dark secret in the cellars of Pendleton Grange? And why did he involve himself so deeply in the lives of the Burton-Massey girls?

Mulligan's Yard is one of Ruth Hamilton's most powerful and impressive books, teeming with rich and colourful characters and evoking the mood of a bygone age.

'I believe that Ruth Hamilton is very much the successor to Catherine Cookson. Her books are plot driven, they just rip along: laughs, weeps, love, they've got the lot, and they're quality writing as well'
Sarah Broadhurst, Radio Four

0 552 14770 2

CORGI BOOKS

A SELECTED LIST OF FINE NOVELS
AVAILABLE FROM CORGI BOOKS

THE PRICES SHOWN BELOW WERE CORRECT AT THE TIME OF GOING TO
PRESS. HOWEVER TRANSWORLD PUBLISHERS RESERVE THE RIGHT TO
SHOW NEW RETAIL PRICES ON COVERS WHICH MAY DIFFER FROM THOSE
PREVIOUSLY ADVERTISED IN THE TEXT OR ELSEWHERE.

All Transworld titles are available by post from:
Bookpost, PO Box 29, Douglas, Isle of Man IM99 1BQ
Credit cards accepted. Please telephone +44(0)1624 677237, fax +44(0)1624 670923
Internet http://www.bookpost.co.uk or
e-mail: bookshop@enterprise.net for details.
Free postage and packing in the UK.
Overseas customers allow £2 per book (paperbacks) and £3 per book (hardbacks).